BEN-HUR

BEN-HUR

A TALE OF THE CHRIST

CAROL WALLACE

based on the bestselling novel by **LEW WALLACE**

Tyndale House Publishers, Inc.
Carol Stream, Illinois

Visit Tyndale online at www.tyndale.com.

Visit Carol Wallace's website at carolwallacebooks.com.

Visit the motion picture website at www.benhurmovie.com.

TYNDALE and Tyndale's quill logo are registered trademarks of Tyndale House Publishers, Inc.

METRO-GOLDWYN-MAYER is a trademark of Metro-Goldwyn-Mayer Lion Corp. © 2016 Metro-Goldwyn-Mayer Studios Inc. All Rights Reserved.

Ben-Hur: A Tale of the Christ

BEN-HUR © 2016 Metro-Goldwyn-Mayer Pictures Inc. and Paramount Pictures. All Rights Reserved.

Cover and insert photographs copyright © 2016 Metro-Goldwyn-Mayer Pictures Inc. and Paramount Pictures Corporation. All Rights Reserved.

Author photo taken by Jim Anness. Copyright © 2015. All Rights Reserved.

Cover photograph of travertine stone copyright © silverspiralarts/Adobe Stock. All rights reserved.
Cover photograph of metal plates copyright © Andrey Kuzmin/Adobe Stock. All rights reserved.
Cover photograph of golden background copyright © Hillman/Adobe Stock. All rights reserved.
Interior photograph of marble tile copyright © Gray wall studio/Adobe Stock. All rights reserved.

Book cover and interior design by Nicole Grimes

Edited by Erin E. Smith

Published in association with Dupree/Miller & Associates, Inc.

Scripture quotations are taken from *The Holy Bible*, English Standard Version® (ESV®), copyright © 2001 by Crossway, a publishing ministry of Good News Publishers. Used by permission. All Rights Reserved.

Ben-Hur is a work of fiction. Where real people, events, establishments, organizations, or locales appear, they are used fictitiously. All other elements of the novel are drawn from the author's imagination.

Library of Congress Cataloging-in-Publication Data

Names: Wallace, Carol, date. | Wallace, Lew, date. Ben-Hur.
Title: A tale of the Christ / Carol Wallace ; based on the novel by Lew
    Wallace.
Description: Carol Stream, Ill. : Tyndale House Publishers, Inc., 2016.
Identifiers: LCCN 2015033841| ISBN 9781496411051 (hc) | ISBN 9781496411068 (sc)
    | ISBN 978-1-4964-1107-5 Collector's Edition
Subjects: LCSH: Jesus Christ—Fiction. | Tiberius, Emperor of Rome 42 B.C.-37
    A.D.—Fiction. | Bible. New Testament—History of Biblical
    events—Fiction. | GSAFD: Christian fiction
Classification: LCC PS3573.A42563 T35 2016 | DDC 813/.54—dc23 LC record available at
http://lccn.loc.gov/2015033841

Printed in the United States of America

22   21   20   19   18   17   16
 7   6   5   4   3   2   1

In memory of my father, William Noble Wallace, the family historian

Acknowledgments

It was my nephew Tom Burns who prompted me to read *Ben-Hur* in the original form. John Kilcullen of LightWorkers Media then performed some magic and introduced me to Mark Burnett and Roma Downey, executive producers of the magnificent new film.

Thanks go to my agent Emma Sweeney for her clearheaded advice and to Jan Miller and Lacy Lynch of Dupree/Miller & Associates for finding the right home for the project.

I am deeply grateful to the team at Tyndale House: Karen Watson and Jan Stob on the acquisitions side; Nicole Grimes and Dean Renninger in the art department; Ruth Pizzi for the maps; Caleb Sjogren, Danika King, and Sarah Mason Rische, wizard copy editors; Midge Choate, who kept us on schedule; Cheryl Kerwin and Katie Dodillet for getting the word out. I especially loved working with editor Erin Smith, who has been meticulous, humorous, tenacious, and unbelievably fast.

The General Lew Wallace Study and Museum in Crawfordsville, Indiana, was a major resource for our book, so we are all grateful to director Larry Paarlberg and associate director Amanda McGuire.

Richard Bayles, with a casual suggestion, gave me the ending—just one more instance of his generosity.

My husband, Rick Hamlin, has, as always, been endlessly encouraging, supportive, and practical. I depend on his judgment in so many ways.

And my father, William Wallace, an author like his great-grandfather Lew, a devotee of American history, would have been tickled pink to see this book.

Foreword

Maybe you grew up with *Ben-Hur*. Maybe your family watched the movie every Easter. You've probably come across clips of the chariot race on TV award shows—they're certainly all over YouTube. Maybe there's an image in your head, right now, of the 1959 film's logo, those massive stone letters spelling out *Ben-Hur*.

I grew up with *Ben-Hur* too, but in a different way, because my great-great-grandfather wrote the original book. *Ben-Hur* was published in 1880 and, for over fifty years, was the bestselling novel in America. That meant there were copies of it everywhere in our house because people kept giving them to us.

It didn't mean we read the novel, though. We were a bookish family and happily devoured almost anything between covers, but *Ben-Hur* was too much of a challenge. It stood to reason that there was a story in there somewhere—why else would it have been adapted for the stage and the movies? We just couldn't find the excitement buried in Lew Wallace's old-fashioned prose.

But recently I picked up an old dark-blue hardcover (with an inscription dated 1892 on the inside cover) and sat down to read in earnest. It was work, I have to admit. The plot moves very slowly and the dialogue was obviously written to sound antique. Characters swear in Latin, for instance. What's more, the descriptions of settings and scenery last much longer than they need to. In 1880, before much of the Middle East had been photographed, those details were new and exotic. Now they just get in the way of the action.

All the same, I finally understood the durable appeal of *Ben-Hur*. It's both exciting and moving. Lew Wallace, an Indiana lawyer and author, was inspired to write the novel as an exploration of his Christian faith. The adventures of the heroic Judah Ben-Hur dramatize the moral and spiritual choices so urgently presented in the early days of Christianity. In the original novel, the famous chariot race is certainly the most iconic scene. But it lasts only eleven pages and occurs two-thirds of the way through the book, which means there's much more to our hero's story. Judah Ben-Hur's heart and soul are at stake.

As a writer, I could see the potential in my great-great-grandfather's much-loved book. It could be brought up to date with some cutting, some rearranging, more depth for the female characters, faster pacing, and contemporary language.

So here it is, a lively retelling of a story that has excited and enlightened millions of readers around the world for over 125 years.

Carol Wallace

When I sit down finally in the old man's gown and slippers,
helping the cat to keep the fireplace warm, I shall look
back upon Ben-Hur *as my best performance.*

LEW WALLACE, 1885

Extent of the Roman Empire
in AD 20

BRITANNIA

GERMANIA

GALLIA

R O M A N   E M P I R E

DACIA

Black Sea

DALMATIA

Tarraco

Valencia

Palma

SARDINIA

ITALIA

Rome

Misenum

MACEDONIA

Thessalonica

ACHAIA

Corinth

Athens

ASIA

Ephesus

GALATIA

Iconium

Antioch

SYRIA

CYPRUS

Sidon

Damascus

Carthage

AFRICA

Mediterranean Sea

CRETE

JUDEA

Cyrene

Alexandria

Jerusalem

EGYPT

0   500   1000 mi.

0   500   1000   1500 km

PART 1

CHAPTER 1

YOUTH

I t was early. The courtyard was still in shade and the cool air hadn't evaporated the water spilled by the gardeners. Judah Ben-Hur leapt over a puddle at the bottom of the massive staircase. At seventeen he was too old to be hopping around like a child, but he couldn't help his excitement: Messala was back! Judah would be far too early for their meeting, but it didn't matter. He wanted to leave the palace before one of the women saw him and asked where he was going.

But . . . "Judah," called Amrah, his former nursemaid, rounding the corner from the kitchens. "Where are you off to so early?"

"Nowhere," he said. "Out."

"Does your mother know? When will you be back?"

He looked down at her brown face, wrinkled beneath the veil. "No, she doesn't. I'll be out all day." He knew he sounded surly, so he leaned over and kissed her cheek. "Messala is back, Amrah. I'm going to meet him. I'll be home around sunset." And before she could say anything, he moved his arm from her grasp and slipped through the door cut in the massive gate, waving to Shadrach the gatekeeper on his way.

This had always been the plan. Messala was Roman, from a powerful and rich family. His father had been stationed in Jerusalem for years as a tax collector. Rome ruled its client states with the help of their strongest citizens, so Prince Ithamar of the house of Hur, a merchant and trader with fleets of ships and warehouses all over the East, had known Messala's father. Thus the boys became friends. They had spent days on end together, exploring Jerusalem, building slingshots, telling stories. At fourteen, Messala had been sent back to Rome to finish his education. Five years later, he had returned, and now Ben-Hur pelted through the narrow streets to meet him. He ran through blocks of shade and sun, feeling the difference in heat a few steps later. When he neared the palace gardens, he slowed down. He didn't want to meet Messala while he was gasping for breath.

A wagon rolled past, leaving billows of dust, and Ben-Hur stepped back into a doorway, brushing down his white linen tunic. He glanced at his sleeve, where Amrah had clasped his arm, but the creases were set in the fine fabric. He shrugged and told himself that Messala wouldn't notice.

Minutes later he reached the meeting place, a marble bench near a pool in the palace gardens. They were empty at this time of day as the sun poured over the marble terraces and the palm trees dropped long-stemmed shadows. No Messala. Ben-Hur sat on the bench. Was that a pebble in his sandal? He wriggled his toes. Maybe a thorn. He slipped off the strap and slid his foot out. But before he could find the thorn, he heard Messala's footsteps on the gravel and stood up to see his friend.

A man now! The distance in their ages had always been important. Two years is an eternity when one friend is twelve and the other fourteen. Ben-Hur knew he had changed. He had grown, developed; his voice had changed. The face he saw in the polished bronze mirror was no longer that of a child. But Messala! Urbane in his thin wool tunic edged with red. Taller, solid. Tanned by the sun, but elegantly groomed. As they embraced, Ben-Hur caught a whiff of some exotic pomade. Then Messala held his friend at arm's length to look at him. Ben-Hur suddenly felt gauche, standing on one foot with his sandal in his hand.

"So here we are again!" Messala said heartily and sat on the bench. "Come, sit. Get that pebble out of your shoe and make yourself comfortable."

Judah sat and pulled the long thorn from his sandal where it had become wedged between strap and sole. He held it up to Messala. "I suppose your paved Roman roads are always perfectly clean."

"Always." Messala nodded. "We have slaves sweep them. You could walk over them barefoot in comfort." Then his face changed. "I was sorry, Judah, to hear about your father's death. He was a good man."

"Thank you," Judah answered, looking at his hands in his lap. "He was. We miss him."

"I'm sure all of Judea misses him. How did it happen?"

"A storm at sea," Ben-Hur said. "There were no survivors, but some of the wreckage washed up on the coast of Cyrenaica. There were reports later of a sudden tempest. Some said a waterspout."

"How long ago?"

"Three years now," Ben-Hur replied.

"And your mother?"

"She grieves."

"And what about little Tirzah? How old is she now?"

"Fifteen."

"A young lady, then! She must be very pretty."

Ben-Hur nodded. "She is, but she doesn't know it. She is still almost a child."

"Time to be thinking of marriage, though," Messala said. "Has your mother chosen a husband for her?"

"Not yet. I think my mother would like her company for a while yet."

"Because you, my friend Judah—you will be going out into the world soon?"

"Oh, I don't know," Ben-Hur temporized. "It's not easy. My mother doesn't say anything, but I think she would like me to start thinking about my father's business. We have a manager, but my father worked so hard. Someone in the family should take an interest."

"And keep the shekels rolling in," Messala said sardonically. Judah looked at him in surprise. "Well," Messala went on, "everyone knows how much Jews care about money."

Judah felt himself blushing but managed to retort, "That's ridiculous! Especially coming from the son of a tax collector. Don't I remember your father with his strongboxes of coins and his ledgers?"

Messala was silent for a moment, then said, "You're right. I've been away too long. Such things can't be said in Jerusalem."

"Or thought, I hope," Judah added.

"Oh, certainly not," Messala said, standing. "Let's walk. I'd forgotten how hot the sun is here."

Judah hurriedly buckled his sandal and leapt to his feet. "What is Rome like?" he asked. "As a city, I mean."

"You'll have to go see for yourself sometime," Messala told him. "There's nothing like it in the world. Not just because it is beautiful—though it is. You never saw such magnificent buildings."

"More so than the Temple?"

"The Temple Herod started to build here is fine for a provincial capital with a primitive religion," Messala began.

"No," Judah said, standing still. "Remember? You can't say that."

"About the provincial capital?" Messala asked. "Or the primitive religion?" He clapped Judah on the shoulder and gave him a little push to get him walking again. "All right, I'm sorry. It's just the way everyone talks in Rome."

"That doesn't mean it's right or true," Judah argued. He thought he might sound sulky, so he added, "I'm your friend, so I know you don't mean it. But if you were overheard . . . There's strong feeling against Romans. You need to be more careful."

"Fine," Messala said breezily. "Where should we go? The bazaar?"

"Yes, of course," Judah answered, "though it won't be much cooler."

"At least there will be shade," Messala said.

They walked in silence for a few minutes. Judah eyed Messala, comparing his old friend to the man who strode along beside him. Finally he said, "I know what it is! You walk differently!"

Messala burst out laughing, and for the first time Judah recognized the young man he had known. "That's exactly what I remembered about you," he said. "You are so observant!"

Judah shrugged, but he liked knowing that Messala had an opinion about him. "Well . . . I hope you aren't offended."

"Not if you explain what you mean."

"Oh, nothing important. But you walk . . ." Judah drew himself up and pulled back his shoulders. "Like a soldier, I suppose."

"Well done! You guessed without my telling you!"

"What, that you've joined the army?"

"I have," Messala said. "Remember? I always wanted to."

"I do," Judah answered. "Everything we found we turned into weapons."

"Especially swords. You could make a sword out of anything. Do you remember those massive leaves? Huge leathery things from the roof of your palace?"

Judah laughed. "That we cut into sword shapes, yes. And then old Shadrach, the porter—he's still there, by the way—helped us stiffen them. With, what? Slivers of wood?"

"Yes, because the gate was being mended!" finished Messala. "They were lethal! Look, I still have a scar." He held out his arm, where a tiny line of paler skin ran from his shoulder halfway to his elbow.

"The one time I got lucky," Judah said. "Is it all you hoped, being a soldier?"

"It is," Messala said. "It's a glorious thing, the Roman army. Better even than I could have dreamed."

"Real weapons, anyway."

"Real weapons, real drilling, real officers. And real opportunities, Judah! You'll see—I'll explore; I'll conquer new lands for the empire. When I'm done, I will rule all of Syria! And you can sit at my right hand, my old friend." He linked his arm through Judah's as they left the palace garden and started in the direction of the bazaar. "That's what being in Rome really taught me—ambition. Ye gods, the world out there! Did you know that there are places in the north where it rains all the time and the natives paint themselves blue? There are Romans there, building roads and subduing those wild men. And in the sand hills south of Libya, they say there are cities built entirely out of gold. Why should they not be Roman too?"

Judah began to feel uneasy again. "And why *should* they be Roman?"

"The gold, for one thing. Which Rome can make better use of than a horde of barbarians. And Roman rule brings benefits: Law. Roads. Buildings. Water. Protection from warring tribes. You know about the Pax Romana."

"What if people don't want it, though?" Judah asked. "This Roman peace. Here, for instance. Jerusalem isn't populated by savages. There was a city here when Rome was still a swamp."

"Judah, you have no idea," Messala countered, shaking his head. "Jerusalem is just an outpost. Not even a very important one. What do you have here? The Temple. Your dry hills. Your quarreling tribes. The doctrine of this and the ordinance of that. Men bending over books, running their fingers down columns of your backward script, muttering about this prophet and that law, shaking their beards— that's what Jews produce. No art, no music, no dancing, no rhetoric, no athletic competitions, no great names of leaders or explorers. Just your nameless god and his lunatic prophets."

"Lunatic?" Ben-Hur protested.

"Oh, all that nonsense about burning bushes and parting seas . . ."

"This from a man whose people turn their own rulers into gods!"

"Ruling Rome and the empire is a task for gods," Messala answered coolly. "If you stay in Jerusalem, you'll end up as a nearsighted rabbi, hunchbacked from crouching over your books. I can see it now, Judah. There's nothing else here for a boy like you."

Judah slipped his arm away from Messala's and took a step back. The two were at the edge of a narrow street, with high walls on each side and a constant rumble of wagons passing.

"Why did you come back, then?" he asked Messala. "Why not just stay in Rome?"

To his surprise, Messala blushed. Judah wasn't sure at first; an ox cart rolled by and its shadow slid across Messala's face, but once it was past, Judah saw clearly the evidence of his old friend's embarrassment.

"My father wanted me here," Messala said curtly. "He sent for me. There are always new cohorts coming out here from Rome. He arranged it." Judah studied him. Messala went on, more fluently. "My mother was worried. She would like me to be nearby for some months. There's no telling where I'll be sent next. I'm sure your mother worries about you, too."

"No," Judah answered, "I don't think she does."

"You probably haven't given her any cause," Messala answered, and Judah was surprised by the bitter tone in his voice. "You were always a studious, rule-abiding boy. A typical Jew, in fact." He watched Judah as he said this, with frank malice in his eyes. He seemed to be waiting for a reaction.

But Judah was too stunned to answer. Was this even the same person who had been his friend? Messala had been constantly at the Hur palace. He had teased Tirzah; Judah's mother, Naomi, had sung for him. Even the servants had liked him, though Judah now remembered that Amrah had always held herself aloof. Had she sensed something about Messala's character that she disapproved of?

The silence between them lengthened; then Messala turned on his heel and began to walk away. But before he had taken three steps, he turned back. "I looked forward to seeing you today, but I see we can't be friends. My father warned me of that. He said it would be different now and he was right."

He paused. Judah waited for his friend to say something about regret, lost friendship . . . something kind. Instead, Messala went on. "The new procurator arrives today. Did you know? You must hate that. Hearing the troops marching around your old shambles of a house—seeing them fill the streets from gutter to gutter with their polished weapons. You must have to wait, sometimes for several minutes, as they march past the door, before you can even step outside. That's what life in Jerusalem is these days. And you know, Judah, you do not live in the glory days of Solomon and his Temple. You live *now*, under the reign of Caesar Augustus and his successors."

Judah stood still, willing his face into a mask. Messala was leaving. Let him go. Ignore him; make him vanish. Reacting would just keep him there. Messala stared for a few seconds longer, then spun around and walked away. The sun glinted on his black hair and his blue gauze mantle.

Messala turned a corner and was lost to view. Judah stood by the side of the road, leaning against the wall, looking at the ground, until a small boy came past with an unusually large flock of goats. The goats pushed him out of the way.

CHAPTER 2

DISASTER

Judah Ben-Hur did not go right home. In the Hur family palace there were too many sharp female eyes that would notice his mood. And he needed to think, so he walked.

Was Messala right? Was Jerusalem provincial? Or was it a stronghold for the chosen people? Could both things be true, perhaps? And what was wrong with being provincial, anyway? He, Judah, had not traveled. He had seen the sea once, before his father's death. They had gone together to Joppa to visit one of his father's ships, and Judah had been enchanted by the water extending beyond the horizon. But in Messala's view, Joppa barely mattered. Judah knew the maps. He knew that Rome sat at the center of the Inland Sea. Messala dreamed of fighting and exploring at the distant edges of the Roman Empire. Judah could almost imagine it: foreign men in startling climates, tamed by the Roman yoke. There had been some truth in what Messala said: Jerusalem raised men to study, not to fight. Was fighting always wrong?

Judah roamed around his city all afternoon, looking and thinking. His feet grew sore, so he stopped for a while and sat on a half-hewn building block watching the masons at the Temple. The air was filled with dust and the chorus of tapping hammers while the priests and worshipers picked their way along paths to and from the sanctuary. He grew hungry and bought some figs from a roadside stand. He wandered to the Damascus Gate to watch a camel train enter, followed by several herds of long-haired goats. A merchant near the gate had the skin of a lion hung over a wooden frame, and a scrawny dog barked at the pelt. Judah's hands felt sticky, and sweat prickled along his spine. He turned for home, thinking of the fountains in the courtyard and a cool beaker of fresh water, drunk in the shade.

Why was Messala so different? Had he always been that sure of himself? Had he always been so cruel? Judah felt so much smaller now than when he had left the Hur palace that morning. Jerusalem felt smaller too. He could almost feel it shrinking under his feet, reduced from the Holy City to a landlocked trading post—or a Roman toy! And the Romans were everywhere with their shiny helmets and short, swinging skirts of leather strips.

The closer he got to his home, the more Roman soldiers crowded the streets. Messala as a soldier—Ben-Hur could imagine it easily. Messala was tall and strong; he already had an air of command. An officer strode past Ben-Hur, shouldering him into the corner of a building, never even looking back. Dust clouded Ben-Hur's eyes for a second and all he could see were vague brown shapes punctuated by spots of Roman red. When his vision cleared, he saw that there were groups of soldiers converging on the Antonia Tower, the great imperial fortress. Messala had told him that the new procurator was adding another cohort to the legionaries already garrisoned there. Judah had heard that news days earlier without reacting. Now, though, it made him angry.

Twilight was settling into night by the time Judah finally returned to the family palace. He opened the wicket gate quietly, wishing he could enter unnoticed, but of course that was not possible. The old porter Shadrach bowed low and greeted him and had just latched the wicket closed when Amrah rounded a corner with a pitcher and a towel. She nodded toward the low bench near the porter's booth and Judah sat. First he held out his hands and Amrah poured the water over them. It had been sweetened with herbs and sharpened with lemon, Judah noticed. Then Amrah knelt and pulled over the basin that always stayed by the gate. Judah took off his sandals and let Amrah wash his feet, though the lemon stung on his various blisters.

"What's this?" she said, fingers running over the laceration from the thorn.

"Nothing. There was a thorn."

She looked up at him. If he had been watching, he would have noticed her face soften. She had been prepared to scold, but his far-away gaze stopped her. "Your mother is on the roof," she said instead. "Let me bring you some supper."

"No, thank you," he answered. "I will change my tunic and join my mother shortly, though."

"A man needs to eat," Amrah said, drying his feet. She clambered to her feet and bent down to empty the basin, but Ben-Hur forestalled her. He picked it up and tossed the water into the garden behind him. A chorus of indignant squawks told him he had disturbed the birds nesting there for the night. Amrah took the basin from his hands and said, "Go, Judah. She has been worried."

* * *

By the time Ben-Hur arrived at the summerhouse on the palace roof, his mother, Naomi, knew what there was to be known. Judah had left the palace early, had been gone all day, had returned exhausted and grim. She lay back on her cushioned divan, glad of the darkness. It might be easier for Judah to tell her his troubles if he could not see her face. For the thousandth time she wondered how her husband, Ithamar, would have handled Judah. He was a boy of such intensity and such potential! Surely it wasn't just a mother's love that made her believe Judah could be a great man. But could a Jew be great in Roman Jerusalem?

And perhaps that wasn't Judah's trouble at all. He was only seventeen. His tutors praised him; he was kind to his sister, attentive at the Temple. Maybe he was just getting feverish. But when Naomi heard her son's footsteps on the tiled floor of the rooftop, she knew there was more amiss than the physical.

She did not move but stayed in her shadowy corner, lit only by a small lantern on the low table nearby. She made her voice noncommittal. "Good evening, Judah. Can you sit with me for a while? I think this might be the coolest spot in Jerusalem."

He dragged a large cushion across the tiles and sat on the floor next to her divan. "You may be right, Mother," he answered. "I saw a great deal of our city today."

"And why is that?" she asked.

No answer but a long outgoing breath. She picked up a fan and unfurled it, then laid it beside her on the divan.

Judah reached up and touched the feathers with the tips of his fingers. "I saw Messala today," he told her.

"Your old friend? That Roman boy?"

"Not a boy anymore," he said.

"That's right. He is, what, three years older than you?"

"Two." He said no more but turned and faced away from her. They both looked out onto the rooftop garden, where the rising moon began to silver the clumps of small palms and the fountain burbled quietly. Tree frogs had launched into their rhythmic peeping, and a current of air brought a whiff of night-blooming jasmine into the summerhouse.

"He went back to Rome, didn't he?" Naomi finally said, to break the silence between them.

"For five years," Judah answered.

"And what did you think of him?"

"He is completely Roman now. Scornful. He believes nothing could be good that does not come from Rome."

"They are arrogant, those Romans," Naomi agreed. "And what will he do now that he is in Jerusalem?"

"He is a soldier."

Silence fell once more. Naomi waited for several minutes. She brought the fan up to move a current of air.

Judah sighed again. "Mother, what will *I* do?"

"What do you mean?"

"We Jewish men must have a profession. Should I become a scholar or a merchant or a farmer?"

"Do you want to do any of those things?"

"No." Another pause.

"And taking over your father's business? Is that something that beckons to you?"

"Is that what I should do, Mother? Would that be useful?"

Naomi folded the fan, lining up its plumes against each other. "Is that what matters to you?"

"Yes," Judah affirmed. "I want to be useful." But she heard something in his voice that contradicted his words.

"Nothing more?"

He leaned back against the divan, his head resting on his mother's knee. "There are so many limits to a Jew's life!" he exclaimed. "If I were a sculptor, I couldn't portray an athlete or a hero. If I were a philosopher, I could only think and write about our relationship to our God. Can't we be curious?"

"What do you want to know?"

"I want to know what I don't know!" he told her. "I want to be surprised! The world is large and Jerusalem is small. But I'm not allowed to look any further."

Naomi was sure she heard Messala's voice in her son's words. The friendship had always troubled her, but to some extent she had seen its value. Both she and her husband, while he lived, had understood the necessity of mixing with Romans and other Gentiles. Messala as a boy had been arrogant, but never less than respectful toward the faith of the fathers. Now, apparently, he had outgrown that basic courtesy. Worse, she had heard rumors about him. It was said that he'd been sent back to Jerusalem because he had fallen into bad ways in Rome. One source said gambling; another said women. Both could have been true, or neither; Naomi reserved judgment.

"Messala was always ambitious," she remarked, keeping her voice neutral. "What are his plans?"

"He wants to conquer new lands for Rome. He has it all planned. Exploration, conquest, promotion. He wants to rule all of Syria."

"Which means ruling Judea."

"That's his ambition," Judah said bitterly. "He said I could share his fortune and his glory."

"And how did you answer that suggestion?"

"I didn't know what to say." Judah stood and walked out of the summerhouse. His mother could see his silhouette moonlit near the fountain, where a nightingale had begun its song. She wanted to go to him and wrap her arms around him, but those days were long past.

He took another few steps and leaned over the tiled parapet, looking down into the street. Off to the left, the bulk of the Antonia Tower blocked out the stars. He lingered there for a few minutes, eyes on the fortress.

"They are busy tonight. Messala said the new procurator, Valerius Gratus, has moved another cohort of soldiers in there. For all I know, Messala is on duty tonight," he told his mother, returning to the enclosure of the summerhouse.

"Gratus is to make his ceremonial entry tomorrow," Naomi told him. "The parade will go right past our gate."

"The Romans in all their glory," he said. "With their drums and plumes and horses and swords and spears." He roamed around the summerhouse for a moment, fingering objects that were as familiar to him as his own hands—a bronze vase, the golden paterae on a marble-topped table, his mother's shawl.

Finally he came back to Naomi and sat, this time at her feet on the divan. "What is our glory?"

"The Lord's preference for us," she answered him instantly. "Think of it, Judah! Try to grasp the idea as if you'd never heard it before. As your friend has been telling you, the world is full of tribes and nations. But our God is the only true God, and we, the Jews, are the people he has saved and cherished. The *only* people. I can't help thinking that compared to God's favor, a sword is paltry."

Judah was silent as he tried to absorb this idea. "If he prefers the Jews, why does he let other people persecute us? Why is Jerusalem overrun with Romans?"

"Are you questioning the wisdom of the almighty God?" Naomi snapped.

"I suppose so, yes," he answered slowly. "I know that's wrong. But . . . aren't we allowed to wonder about these things? I'm not even thinking about myself. We, the family of Hur, have nothing to complain of. But Jews have suffered thousands of years of insults, domination—even slavery. It seems like a harsh way to show favor."

"Yes, I can see how you feel that way," Naomi conceded. "I suppose we all do from time to time. Maybe you should go to the Temple and ask Simeon to explain it. The point is that we, as a people, have endured for those thousands of years, retaining our Scriptures and our values. We've outlasted the Egyptians and the Babylonians, and we will certainly outlast the Romans. Other people worship many gods. Or they turn their rulers into divinities, the way the Romans do. We Jews have a covenant with the one and only God. Knowing that, there's nothing more to wish for." Naomi paused. A blade of moonlight lay on her son's hands, clasped on his raised knee. He still had the outsized knuckles of a boy whose muscles had not grown to match his bones. He tapped one finger against another, without thinking, and she knew he was trying to take in what she had said.

He was so young. Sometimes it was hard to remember.

"If you could do anything," she said, laying a gentle hand on his shoulder, "if you could have any occupation at all—what would it be?"

His rawboned boy's hand came up and covered hers, enveloping it completely. "I would be a soldier."

"Like your friend Messala," Naomi said flatly.

"No. I was thinking of it before. I didn't want to tell you."

"Why not?"

He twisted around to smile at her with the sweetness that had always pierced her heart. "Because no mother wants her son to take up arms. I understand that."

"But every mother wants her son to follow his ambitions," she answered, smiling back at him. "I would never want to hold you back from something you cared about. And God's chosen people need soldiers as well as scholars."

He squeezed her hand and let it go. "I would have liked to make my father proud," he said quietly.

In turn, she patted his shoulder before removing her hand. "I know. I think often how proud he would have been of you. Be sure of that." She swung her legs down from the divan and gathered up her fan and veil. "I think it is cool enough now that I will sleep in my bedroom. What about you?"

"I will stay here for now. Will you have Amrah waken me in the morning before the procession begins?"

"I doubt you'll be able to sleep through the commotion," Naomi said drily, "but I'll send Amrah just in case."

* * *

But the next morning it was neither of those women who wakened Judah. Instead he became aware that he was dreaming, and that in his dream, a harp was playing. At first it was the shepherd-king David; then somehow in his dream his father was listening to King David; but finally he knew, without opening his eyes, that he was awake and his sister, Tirzah, was the musician. He lay for a long moment, feeling a faint breeze circle around his toes. He tried to guess the time from the warmth on his knees; the sun slanted into the summerhouse and reached the divan only early in the morning.

"I can tell you're awake," Tirzah said, continuing to play. "You closed your mouth. It was a good thing. There was a fly buzzing around and you would have swallowed it."

"No. That's impossible," he answered.

"How do you know?"

"Because even asleep, I look like a handsome living statue and my mouth would never be open. I think that string is flat," he added. "With my eyes closed, I can hear so much more keenly . . . That one—no, that one."

Tirzah laid her palm against the strings and silenced them. "They are all in perfect tune. But you should get up. There is a huge crowd in the street."

In an instant Judah had rolled to his feet and padded over to the edge of the roof. He turned back to splash a handful of water from the fountain onto his face and onto his neck, leaving long wet streaks on his crumpled tunic.

He reached the parapet and looked down. Tirzah was right—the street was already crowded. He could see turbans and veils and fezzes, and every kind of headgear normal on the streets of Jerusalem, pinned against the sides of the buildings by gleaming Roman helmets.

Then a new sound cut through the low chatter of the crowd.

First came the rhythmic tramping of soldiers, followed by a trumpet fanfare, around the corner but not far away. Tirzah had joined her brother, still holding her harp. "So early in the morning for a parade!" she said.

"Probably to avoid trouble," Judah told her, craning over the tiled parapet. "They've moved more soldiers into the tower. Maybe they expect some kind of uprising."

"I'm going to get Mother." Tirzah turned away, leaving a faint, sweet residue of jasmine in the air beside him. Judah looked around to tease her about her new perfume, but she was already out of earshot, with the clamor from the street below. All he could see was her slight figure in a pale-green dress and a sheer striped veil floating behind her.

He turned back to the spectacle below. It was impossible not to admire the Roman troops. The guards lining the road stood exactly spaced, motionless despite the constantly increasing crowd. The rooftops all around were also teeming with an audience by now. Jerusalem's people were curious about their new procurator. The percussive beat of footsteps grew louder and the people's murmurs died away as the troops came into sight. First, the flag, scarlet and gold, attached to an extra-long spear tipped with an eagle. The flag bearer strode out alone, setting the pace for the procession. As he took his measured steps, the crowd grew silent.

Behind him came the men. Judah was so used to the Roman presence in Jerusalem that he had forgotten the message of might signaled on the street below. There were so many soldiers, marching shoulder to shoulder and in rows so close that if one man stumbled, the next would be on top of him in a flash. As one leg stepped forward, all legs stepped forward. They moved like one gigantic creature, and on every face the same blank expression of confidence and concentration gave them apparently similar features.

And how they glittered in that raking morning sun! Its rays struck glinting highlights from helmets and spear tips and breastplates and buckles. Judah looked from the strutting scarlet-and-gold cohort to the crowd of onlookers, mostly shabby, silent, and awestruck.

A break came in the stream of marching men. Strangely, the crowd remained silent as the footsteps grew more faint, so that the trumpet when it sounded had an impact like thunder. One, two, three trumpeters rounded the corner from the fortress, followed by another flag and a cavalry unit riding matching black horses. Judah looked back to the stairs leading up from the ground floor, hoping to see Tirzah and his mother. Tirzah loved horses.

Following the cavalry came a small guard of heavily armed soldiers, carrying not only spears and swords but also tall, curved shields. Judah eyed them with some envy. In battle they could move into a small, tight formation, covered entirely by their shields above and on every side, but bristling with the wicked spear tips. He wondered how much the shields weighed. How long could a man march while he carried one?

He was so absorbed that he didn't at first notice the sound of the crowd. From silence a murmur had grown, then a buzz, then jeers. The marching order left a gap between the guard and the man on horseback who now turned the corner. The ceremonial space made him easier to see, easier for his subjects to recognize. He sat astride an immense chestnut stallion, easily controlling the beast with one hand on the reins. His body armor was gilded, the saddlecloth purple, and he wore, instead of a helmet, a laurel wreath.

So this was Valerius Gratus, the new procurator, Judah realized. And at the same moment, a voice from the crowd shouted, "Romans, go home!" and was instantly answered with cheers.

The atmosphere changed in a flash. The space around Valerius Gratus closed as the guards surrounded him, lifting their shields to create a marching fence. The pace of the procession increased. More shouts came from the onlookers, followed by catcalls. "Tyrant!" one woman cried and flung her sandal. It missed the procurator but hit his horse squarely on the rump. The mount shied, leaping sideways and scattering the guardsmen before Valerius Gratus could get it under control. The crowd began howling with glee, and further missiles rained on them: half a dozen shoes, a rotten squash, the contents of a chamber pot. Gratus's face was set in a scowl as he came level with the Hur palace.

Judah leaned forward. As the guard passed, he might be able to see how the soldiers held the shields—were there two handles mounted on the inside? His outstretched hand landed on a tile on the parapet and he felt the tile move.

It hurtled downward. The angle of the parapet was ideal for launching it into space. As Judah stood openmouthed, the tile sliced through the air and exploded against Valerius Gratus's forehead.

Every head turned. Every man and woman with a clear view saw the young man on the roof of the palace with his arm still outstretched. Fingers pointed; shouts rang out. Gratus, streaming blood, crumpled and fell to the ground, his horse rearing up behind him with a desperate whinny. The guards formed their square, some standing and some crouching with their shields enclosing the procurator.

Judah could not move. He stood frozen. His hand finally fell to his side, but everyone had seen it. It must have looked as if he had thrown the tile. And the procurator on the ground! Was he dead?

The shell of shields fractured and the guard stepped back. Gratus sat up. Blood streaked his face, but he shouted a few orders and quickly remounted his horse. He seized a corner of his scarlet cloak to wipe his face. A soldier plucked his laurel wreath from the dust and shook it clean before handing it to the procurator.

As the procession moved forward, Judah saw ten soldiers detach themselves from the cohort. In the crowd behind where they had been, a familiar face looked up at him. For an instant, his eyes met Messala's; then he saw his old friend slip away and cross the road just in front of a unit of cavalry.

At the same moment, an immense crash shook the rooftop. All the birds took flight, squawking, and a shriek came from downstairs.

Judah pelted across the roof garden and down the stairs. "Tirzah! Mother!" he called, leaping down the steps two at a time. He heard another crash and a shout before he reached the courtyard. Dozens of Roman soldiers had broken down the gate. They were everywhere, shouting, swords unsheathed. The servants cowered in a corner, clutching each other and staring at the body of the old porter, who lay in a pool of blood. His severed hand, fingers curled around his palm, lay several feet away from his wrist until one of the soldiers impatiently picked it up and tossed it into the watering trough.

But Judah Ben-Hur didn't notice. His attention was fixed on the dreadful tableau of his mother and sister, gripped in the hands of Romans. His gaze met his mother's. She was pale as ash, her eyes immense. She seemed unaware of her lustrous hair loose around her shoulders or the trickle of blood marking her cheekbone. She did not speak, but a fierce message passed from her to her son: *"Be brave. Don't forget us. Remember your father; remember your God."*

✳ ✳ ✳

Naomi would have said those words aloud, but she knew the man holding her might cut her throat. A quick sideways glance at Tirzah by her side told her they were at some precipice of violence. The man holding her daughter fast had looped Tirzah's russet hair around his fist. The girl's bare arms were already showing bruises, and her gown was torn. Naomi looked back at her son.

"What is all this?" he called out. "Who is in command? Why have you broken in here?"

A tall soldier with a plumed crest on his helmet strode through the shattered gate, leading a black horse. "I am in command," he answered. "Who are you, boy? Someone in this house has assassinated the new procurator!"

"But I saw him remount and ride away!" Judah protested, and Naomi's heart sank. He had just given himself away.

"And I saw you throw a tile at him," came another voice. Messala stepped through the debris of the shattered gate. Naomi looked at him, appalled. The young Roman, friend of her son, was barely to be seen in this swaggering man.

"Messala," Judah exclaimed happily. "You can explain. I just leaned over—I wanted to see the shields. My hand knocked a tile loose. It was an accident."

Messala looked at the commanding officer. "You see?" he said. "He confesses."

"But this is just a boy," the officer remonstrated.

Messala stood a fraction taller. "Boy or man, he hates enough to kill. You have his mother and his sister, I see. That is the whole family."

"But, Messala!" Judah cried out. "You know I would never do such a thing!"

"Do I?" his old friend answered. He nodded to the commanding officer and retraced his steps. Naomi looked at Judah's face and watched, in that instant, her son's youth end. His eyes followed his former friend in disbelief. He straightened up, struggling against the hands of the soldiers who held him. He looked back at his mother. She tried to put all of her love and encouragement into her gaze, but she did not dare speak.

Judah turned to the commanding officer. "Spare my mother and sister, at least," he said. There was a note in his voice Naomi had never heard—he spoke as a man to men. "I know the Roman Empire rests on law. The law will show that I've done nothing wrong. It was an accident and the procurator will live."

Without responding to Judah, the officer said, "Chains for the boy." He crossed the courtyard to where Naomi and Tirzah stood, still in the grip of the soldiers. He examined them, then stepped back to look around what he could see of the palace. The servants and dependents huddled in a corner, wide-eyed and clutching each other. From the street beyond came another fanfare of trumpets and a series of shouted commands. "You," the officer ordered, pointing to the man who held Tirzah. "Let go her hair. We will take the women to the Antonia Tower." He looked at the servants and called out, "Someone give me a cloak for the girl." To Naomi he said, "Bind up your hair and cover it. We are going out in the street. You should not be seen like that."

Naomi pulled her arms loose from her captor and swiftly twisted her hair into a knot. She had been wearing a gold brooch to fasten her sash, so she unclasped it and thrust it into her hair. A length of coarse gray fabric was flung over her shoulders, and she pulled it over her head, never knowing where it had come from.

"Now," the officer called out, "six men to escort the women!"

In an instant they were surrounded, and Naomi turned around but saw only broad, armored shoulders and red cloaks. Judah—she had missed her last look at her son!

"Sir!" she cried out, reaching toward the officer. "Can't I say good-bye to my son?"

"No," he answered indifferently. "You would not want to see him in chains."

"What will you do with him?" she asked, almost screaming.

"The galleys," he said. "March!"

But Naomi could not march. She had fainted away.

CHAPTER 3

WATER

Two days later, around noon, a decurion with his command
of ten horsemen arrived at a small village, coming from the
direction of Jerusalem. A few flat-roofed houses straggled
along a narrow path where stones and the manure of sheep lay side
by side in the pocked dust. Far in the distance, across a valley ran-
domly quilted with fields and orchards, lay the hazy blue gleam of
the Mediterranean.

Nazareth was so insignificant that the appearance of any strangers
brought every inhabitant out to stare at the spectacle, even in the
heat of the day. Of course the Nazarenes feared and despised the red-
cloaked Roman soldiers, towering over them from the backs of their
massive horses, armor clanking, shouting in their incomprehensible
language, frightening the children. But curiosity is strong too. And
the Romans, it appeared, had a prisoner.

He was surrounded by the horses, choked by the cloud of ochre dust their hooves stirred up from the ground. He stumbled forward, unaware of the staring villagers. His hands were tied behind his back, the rope held carelessly by a mounted legionnaire. His bloodied knees showed how often he had fallen on the road, but he seemed indifferent to the pain, as he seemed indifferent to his sunburned back, the dust, the threatening proximity of the horses' hooves, the eyes of the Nazarenes.

The Romans were heading to the well, of course. The horses needed water. The villagers fell into a ragged group behind them, muttering to each other. Who could that prisoner be? What could he have done that warranted such a heavy guard? Where were they taking him? He was so young, said a mother. He was so handsome, said her daughter.

One of the legionnaires was ordered to draw water, and he obeyed quickly, passing a clay pitcher to his fellow soldiers and filling a trough for the horses. The prisoner, ignored, collapsed to the stony soil and lay in a heap, his face in the dirt. The villagers eyed each other with growing discomfort. Shouldn't they help him? Did they dare? Then one of them whispered, "Look! Here comes the carpenter. He will know what to do."

An old man had rounded the bend in the road. Below his full turban, his long white hair joined the beard flowing down his chest, half-covering his coarse gray gown. He carried a set of crude tools—an ax, a saw—that seemed almost too heavy for a man of his age. As he neared the well, he stopped, setting down his tools for a moment.

"Oh, Rabbi Joseph," a woman cried, running to him. "Here is a prisoner! Come ask the soldiers about him! We wonder who he is and what he has done and where they are going with him."

The rabbi's face was expressionless, but after a moment he stepped away from his tools and approached the officer. "The peace of the Lord be with you," he said calmly.

"And the peace of the gods with you," the decurion answered, nodding.

"Are you from Jerusalem?"

"Yes."

"Your prisoner is young," the rabbi commented.

"Only in years," the officer told him. "He is a hardened criminal."

"What did he do?"

"He is an assassin," the officer replied dispassionately, eyeing his prisoner. The youth still lay with his eyes closed, though all around him the villagers whispered to each other, eyes wide.

"Is he a son of Israel?" continued the rabbi.

"He is a Jew," said the Roman. "I don't understand all your tribes, but he comes from a good family. Perhaps you've heard of a prince of Jerusalem named Ithamar of the house of Hur? He lived in Herod's day and died a few years ago."

The rabbi nodded. "I saw him once."

"This is his son."

The eyes of the villagers grew even wider. How could this young man, little more than a boy, be an assassin? How could this bedraggled captive be the heir of a prince? The whispers grew to murmurs, and the decurion raised his voice.

"In the streets of Jerusalem, just two days ago, he nearly killed the noble procurator Valerius Gratus by hurling a tile at his head from the roof of his family's palace. He has been sentenced to the galleys."

For the first time the rabbi's composure was shaken. His eyes flew to the huddled figure and he said to the decurion, "Did he kill this Gratus?"

"No," the officer answered. "If he had, he would not be alive now." He stepped over and, with his sandaled foot, rolled the young man onto his back. One of his eyebrows had been split, and the blood crusted over the eye. His lips were parched, his mouth half-open, his breathing shallow. "A fine oarsman he will make," the Roman said, shrugging. He looked around at his men, who responded to his glance by moving their horses away from the trough and preparing to mount.

But suddenly there was one more man in their midst. He, too, was young, much the age of the prisoner, with long hair like the rabbi's and a remarkable air of dignity. He had quietly come around the corner behind Joseph, depositing his own ax with the other tools, and now he picked up the pitcher standing on the edge of the well. Without even glancing at the Romans, he dipped it full of water and knelt in the dust. He slid his arm beneath the prisoner's shoulders and held the pitcher to his lips. The officer took a breath as if to stop him, but somehow did not continue.

The prisoner's eyes opened. The young carpenter dipped a corner of his sleeve into the pitcher and gently wiped the blood from Ben-Hur's eye. The two youths exchanged a long glance; then the prisoner drank again. Revived, he sat up, and the carpenter's hand moved from his shoulder to his dusty hair. It rested there for a long moment—long enough to say, or hear, a blessing, though no word broke the silence. Ben-Hur glanced up again into the eyes of his helper and seemed to receive a message. He scrambled to his feet, restored.

The young carpenter replaced the pitcher on the lip of the well and picked up all of the tools, then went to stand next to the rabbi, apparently unaware that everyone watched his every movement. The decurion found himself taking the rope that bound Ben-Hur's wrists and leading him to the heaviest horse. With a gesture, he indicated that the prisoner should ride behind one of the soldiers. In silence the troop rode off, and in silence the Nazarenes scattered.

That was the first time Judah Ben-Hur met the son of Mary.

CHAPTER 4

SHUTTERED

Days passed. Back in Jerusalem, the populace settled down. After the parade of Valerius Gratus, enough men had been punished to reestablish calm. There was no more shouting, no more throwing things, just sullen silence when Roman troops marched through town. The cut on Gratus's head healed.

The Hur palace was sealed. Placards were nailed on both gates saying, *This is the property of the emperor.* The tenants and servants had been turned out of the house and everything valuable—livestock, stores of food, jewels—taken to the Antonia Tower to be sold or sent to the emperor.

But early one evening, when a sullen layer of cloud shrouded the sunset, Messala walked down an alley alongside the palace and put his hand on an unobtrusive door. It swung open silently and he went through.

He followed the passageway before him and came out into the

great central court, where he stood for a while, looking around. Dust had begun to gather. The leathery leaves from the palm trees lay where they had fallen. The fountains were dry, and every shrub or flower had turned yellow and dropped its blossoms.

He crossed the court to the front gate and paused where he'd stood on that day. He wasn't sure himself why he had come. Just to see it, he supposed. To see what had happened to the palace of the mighty Hur family. What happened to Jews who defied Rome.

The women had been dragged out mere steps away from him. Little Tirzah had been sobbing beneath her cloak, but Naomi had paused for a moment and looked at him. He felt it again, that shock when her eyes met his. What was it? Hatred? He wanted to believe that. Grief, maybe. Fear, of course. Fear would be normal. But sometimes he wondered if that look hadn't been one of contempt.

Remembering that look always made him want to move, so he crossed the courtyard and ran up the stairs. He roved through the rooms he'd known as a boy, rooms where the family ate and gathered and slept. The furniture was still there, though damaged. There were shards of things in some corners: bits of pottery, the leg from a table. He roamed farther, to the servants' quarters, where nothing had been worth appropriating for the emperor. Here, the soldiers had mostly smashed what was left. A stool, a box. Bedding was piled into corners, where it was already starting to smell. There would be mice. Rats.

Did he hear scurrying? It was darker in the stairwell heading up to the roof. Scuffling? A footstep?

Of course not. He emerged onto the rooftop. Any footstep would be his own. The gates were locked and sealed. Nobody besides himself would know of the little postern door. The servants had all been paid off and driven away from Jerusalem.

The garden on the rooftop looked worse than the courtyard. There had always been several gardeners puttering away up there, plucking browned flowers and weeds, trimming branches. Messala peered into the tiled pond, now filled with a brownish sludge and reeking. The fish, of course. Dead and rotting.

The trees were full of birds, and their droppings spattered in rings around the trunks. A flock of parrots had taken over one of the palms and flew in circles around it, creaking and cawing. Messala crossed the roof to look down into the street.

This was why he had come, he realized. He wanted to see where Judah had done it.

The light was fading and the street was empty except for a pair of Jews shuffling along, arm in arm, heads together, skullcaps bobbing in unison. Nothing like that morning with the gleaming sun and the ranks of soldiers strutting in straight lines of gold and red. Judah must have had a good view.

Where had he stood? Messala stepped up to the edge of the roof. Here? He leaned out to see the Antonia Tower. Maybe a little closer? He stepped sideways.

Behind him a flock of swifts rose into the sky and wheeled around, then settled again on the roof of the summerhouse.

He reached forward as Judah had. Braced himself on his hand. There was a tile missing in the row. He moved slightly, leaned farther. Felt the rough terra-cotta shift beneath his palm, and before he knew it, another tile clattered down the slope and flew off. Seconds later he heard it shatter.

No one turned around. He pressed down again, and another tile fell. And another.

Stupid, to let your house fall into disrepair, he thought. People could get hurt. He turned his back to the street and looked across the garden with its trees now silhouetted against the sky.

Had Judah thrown that tile? Probably not.

He crossed the rooftop toward the stairs, kicking over a stool as he went. Inside the summerhouse someone had cut open the pillows from the divans. Brown-and-white feathers had burst out and blown around. Below them, something gleamed, and Messala leaned down. He picked it up: a gold hairpin. He bit it: solid gold. Well—that was worth something. He owed someone a little bit of money. Such a pity that he understood how money worked, yet it didn't stick to him. Not like some. Not like the Hur family.

After a second he hurled the shining pin into the pond. Once again, he'd seen that look of contempt on Naomi's face.

He ran down the stairs sure-footed and slipped out the postern door.

PART 2

GERMANIA

SARMATIA

DACIA

DALMATIA

Adriatic Sea

Black Sea

ITALIA

Rome

Misenum Neopolis
Paestum

Tyrrhenian Sea

MACEDONIA

Thessalonica

Marmara Sea

ACHAIA

Aegean Sea

ASIA

GALATIA

Iconium

Ionian Sea

Corinth Athens

Ephesus

Antioch

NAXOS

CYPRUS

SYRIA

CRETE

Mediterranean Sea

Sidon
Damascus

JUDEA
Jerusalem

Cyrene

Alexandria

EGYPT

Red Sea

0   500 mi.

0   500   1000 km

CHAPTER 5

AFLOAT

Very early one September morning three years later, the Roman tribune Quintus Arrius walked with two friends down the broad breakwater at Misenum, on the Tyrrhenian Sea not far from Neapolis. The sun had not yet broken the horizon, but before him the sky glowed pink behind the silhouetted masts of the Roman fleet. The air swirled with the heavy scent of burning Egyptian nard from the escort of torchbearers. On Arrius's left, Lentulus staggered slightly and jostled the nearest torch. Arrius reached out and steadied Lentulus's elbow.

On his other side, his more sober friend Caius said, "You've barely had time to get used to being on land. You should at least stay in Misenum until you've won back what you lost last night."

"Obviously the goddess Fortuna only favors Quintus Arrius at sea," Lentulus muttered.

"Well, she is kind to me this morning, anyway," Arrius answered.

"Look, the west wind has brought in my ship." He dropped his companions' arms and stepped out of the circle of torches, deeply inhaling the sea air. A gust of breeze tugged at the myrtle wreath he wore, and he absently held it to his head as he gazed out into the harbor. Skimming across the blue water, its sail rosy in the dawn light, came a galley, gilded by the first angled rays. The two banks of oars dipped, rose, paused . . . then dipped again into the glittering water. "She moves like a bird," Arrius said softly.

"And where will you fly off to in your new command?" Caius asked, shading his eyes against the sudden brilliance as the massive golden sun slid clear of the bay.

"We head to the Aegean," Arrius answered, his eyes still on the ship.

Lentulus, who had been vomiting into the harbor, straightened up and wiped his mouth. "Why go so far for glory, Arrius? Why not stay here with us and take an easier command?"

Arrius turned to face his friends. "Because this is what the emperor needs. There's a fleet of Crimean pirates harassing the grain merchants in the eastern seas. They've actually broken out through the Sea of Marmara into the Aegean. A hundred galleys leave Ravenna today to bring them under control, and I will join them in the *Astraea*. As commander." He pointed to the ship still speeding toward them.

"Well, that *is* an honor!" Caius exclaimed. "Next thing we know you will be promoted to duumvir."

Arrius looked at his friend sharply, then pulled a scroll from his toga. He handed it over without a word, and Caius unrolled it, letting Lentulus read the words aloud:

"Sejanus to C. Caecilius Rufus, duumvir

"Caesar has heard good reports of the tribune Quintus Arrius, especially of his courage in the western seas. He

wishes Quintus to be transferred to the East, where he will command the fleet against the pirates who have appeared in the Aegean."

Arrius, meanwhile, watched the galley's approach. He tossed the broad, purple-banded end of his toga in the air, and seconds later, a scarlet flag unfurled at the vessel's stern. Several men swarmed up the rigging, and the vast sail was taken in while the ship's bow came around. The rhythm of the oars increased so that she bore down on the broad stone jetty, directly toward Arrius and his friends. He watched the maneuver with satisfaction—the ship's instant response to his signal, her speed and her efficiency, suggested she would perform well in battle.

Lentulus tapped him on the elbow with the rolled scroll. "We can no longer tease you about your future greatness, Arrius," he said. "Obviously you are already great. What other surprises do you have for us?"

Arrius slipped the scroll back into his toga and said, "None. My detailed orders are on board in a sealed packet. But if you plan to make offerings at any of the altars today, pray to the gods for a friend at sea somewhere near Sicily." He looked again toward the harbor and shaded his eyes.

As the galley raced toward the breakwater, its details became clearer. The prow sliced through the water so fast that it cast waves on each side rising almost to the deck, twice a man's height above the water's surface. The lines of the hull were long, low, and rakish, suggesting speed and menace. The three men watching all knew—as would any enemy—that speed and maneuverability were not the galley's only weapons: extending forward from the prow was the armored beak, a kind of underwater spear that would be used in battle to ram and pierce the hulls of enemy ships.

But of course it was the oars that defined the galley, as they continued to flash in the morning sun. One hundred twenty of them moved as one, cutting into the sea and propelling the ship recklessly forward. Soon more details were visible: the seams on the one great square sail, the shrouds and stays that held the single mast upright, the handful of sailors hanging on the yard to reef the sail, the solitary armed man in the prow. The regular splash as the oars cut the water was audible, along with the rhythmic thump that gave the rowers their pace. One of the torchbearers gasped as the galley came ever closer at breakneck speed.

Then, past the point when collision with the breakwater seemed inevitable, the man in the prow raised his hand. Suddenly all the oars flew to vertical, poised a moment in the air, and fell straight down. The water boiled around them, and the galley shook in every timber as its momentum was blocked. Another gesture of the hand, and again the oars arose, feathered, and fell. But this time those on the right, dropping toward the stern, pushed forward, while those on the left, dropping toward the bow, pulled backward. Three strokes, and the galley pivoted around, then settled gently broadside to the breakwater.

Lentulus, still somewhat drunk, began to applaud, but Caius shushed him as a trumpet blew on deck. Out from hatchways poured a troop of marine soldiers in brilliant bronze helmets and breastplates, armed with javelins and shields. More soldiers ran barefoot along the deck and scrambled onto the yardarms. Arrius's friends understood: this was the welcoming salute of his new crew. As he stood between them with the freshening breeze ruffling his hair, he was no longer their affable gambling companion. He plucked the wreath from his head and handed it to Caius. "If I come back, I'll look for revenge at the dice. But if I don't destroy the pirates, you won't see me again. Hang this in your atrium until you hear my fate."

A gangplank had appeared with the same silent efficiency that seemed to rule Arrius's new command, and his crew awaited him, prepared to salute.

"The gods go with you, Arrius," Lentulus said. The tribune nodded and turned to step onto the plank. As his foot touched the wood, more trumpets sounded, and at the stern of the vessel rose a purple flag, the pennant of a commander of the fleet.

Quintus Arrius had spent the entire night at the dice table, risking his gold with little success despite his frequent and generous offerings at the altars of the veiled goddess Fortuna. At sea, though, he placed less trust in her. He knew that his life now depended on his officers and crew, so as soon as he had read his orders and instructed the pilot to set his course, he inspected his command. He paced the deck from stem to stern, experienced eyes assessing every knot in the rigging and every gesture of the men who handled the sail.

Arrius spoke to the commander of the marines, the supply master, the master of the fighting machines, the chief of the rowers, the sailing master. Though he had not mentioned the fact to his friends, this command was more than an honor—it was also very dangerous. As Arrius had seen over and over again, the smallest error or flaw in equipment would sink a ship in battle. The pirate fleet terrorizing the shipping in the eastern seas was surely well equipped and well manned. Luck—dealt out by the veiled goddess—would certainly play a part. But Arrius was sure that Roman training and discipline, so evident on board the *Astraea*, would tip the scales toward victory.

By noon, the galley was skimming the sea off Paestum, with the wind still coming from the west. An altar had been set up on the foredeck, sprinkled with salt and barley. Arrius solemnly made offerings to Jove, Neptune, and all the deities of the ocean, praying for success and lighting incense to waft his prayers skyward. But even as he performed the ritual, he found his mind wandering below, to the banks of rowers.

Galleys were rowed by slaves. They were men who came from all over the Roman Empire. Maybe they had been taken captive in battle or tried to escape from a cruel master. Most of them had fallen

afoul of the law, and it was the Roman practice to put these criminals to use rather than simply executing them. Few men survived
the galleys longer than a year or two, but it was worth feeding them
for that long. The Roman navy was responsible for keeping peace in
the Inland Sea and beyond. The job could not be done without the
speed and reliability of galleys; winds might shift or dwindle, but
men with oars could always keep a ship on course. If they died, they
were replaced; there were plenty of slaves.

As the sun passed the zenith and the color of the sea became a
darker blue, Arrius mentally summed up what he had seen. His ship
was brand-new, well provisioned, and well equipped. His officers and
seamen seemed capable. The marines, as seagoing soldiers, could not
be assessed until they went into battle, but Arrius had spent enough
time among fighting men to know that these were seasoned warriors.
Yet none of this would matter if the galley could not move swiftly
and accurately under the worst conditions. So, after a glance at the
brilliant sky, Arrius stepped belowdecks, into the main cabin.

It was the heart of the ship, a compartment sixty-five feet long and
thirty feet across. Square shafts of sunlight from the gridded hatches
in the deck provided what light came below. Just aft of the center,
the immense mast pierced the space, surrounded by circular racks
bristling with axes, spears, and javelins.

But it was the smell that hit Arrius, who had been breathing the
fresh sea air on deck. He was startled for a moment—how could
he have forgotten? Sixty unwashed men sweating as they pulled on
the immense oars for six-hour shifts; no room, no time for bodily
needs; no water, no rest. The stench was overwhelming.

All the way aft, facing the slaves, sat the hortator, or chief of the
rowers, on a low platform, pounding the oars' pace on his table with
a large, square gavel. Arrius walked toward him, glancing from side to
side at the rowers' backs. The muscles shifted beneath the skin as each
man hauled his massive blade through the water, turned it horizontal,

and set it down again to slice into the next wave. It was a constant struggle between man and matter, wood and water, ship and sea.

Beyond the chief's platform, elevated by a set of steps, was the tribune's own quarters, separated from the oarsmen by a gilt railing and elegantly furnished with a couch, a table, and a cushioned chair. Turning to face the slaves, Arrius sat and leaned back, his legs stretched out before him.

The chief of rowers ignored his commander's presence and continued to beat the rhythm. As in other biremes, the rowers were on staggered banks, some sitting and some standing, to pack as many men—and oars—as possible into the hull. The arrangement was duplicated in the cabin below with another sixty men. They all moved together, reaching forward, pulling, feathering the blades, dipping them; relentless, automatic movements, forward and back, like an enormous loom.

The Roman Empire encompassed most of the known world, and every part of it was represented on the galley's benches: Briton and Crimean, Libyan and Scythian, Goth and Longobard. Skin colors ranged from inky to milky, though marked with scar tissue and whip wounds. Arrius saw hair pale as flax and dark as a crow's wing; long, tangled beards and cheeks barely marked with pale fuzz.

They had all learned different languages as children, and few could have spoken to each other in any setting, but conversation was no part of the galley slave's life. There was nothing for him beyond his oar and his bench. He rowed past exhaustion; the watches changed and he wolfed down his rations, then slept as long as he was allowed. He had no name; he was known by the number of his seat. A slave was brought to the galley as if to his grave; he left his identity behind him.

Yet as Arrius sat quietly, his eyes roving along the benches, he noted differences among the men. A few had begun to waste away from sickness or starvation, and they would die soon. Their bodies would be tossed overboard and other men would replace them as number 33 or number 8. If the upcoming battle went well, Arrius thought, the brawniest of the pirates taken captive could replace some of the feebler slaves.

There was a momentary check in the ship's motion, and Arrius's eye flew to the knot in the pattern, the unmanned oar where a small redheaded rower had suddenly crumpled to the deck. A loose oar could be a calamity, entangling the others, catching the sea, changing the ship's course—but Arrius saw that a dark-haired man caught the long shaft, while somehow maintaining the grip on his own oar. In an instant, the limp body of the fallen slave was hauled aside and a hatch opened from below. A wiry, golden-skinned man with a long black braid slipped onto the bench and seized the oar. Within seconds, the entire company was restored to unison.

Arrius continued to scan the company of slaves. His eyes flickering through the gloom were drawn here and there by a streak of light on a shoulder gleaming with sweat or teeth flashing in a grimace as a slave hauled his oar through yet another wave. The regular creak of the oars overlapped the rhythmic crack-crack as the chief of rowers kept hammering out the pace. The crew, for Arrius, was a unit—120 slaves formed into a tool that propelled his galley eastward to the battle waiting for them. And yet he found himself glancing again at one man, the slave who had rescued the stray oar. The fellow's bench was near Arrius's platform, and with each forward push of his oar handle, his face moved into a column of light striking down from the deck above. He lingered there for an instant, his wrists turning the massive wooden cylinder to position the blade and lower it exactly perpendicular to the water—then his weight shifted back, and as he pulled, the muscles in his arms and chest rippled.

He was very young, barely twenty, and tall. Dark curls were held out of his eyes and off his shoulders with a filthy rag while his cheeks and chin were obscured by a straggling growth of beard. He moved with a kind of economical grace, and Arrius noted the leanness that revealed every muscle on his torso.

He must have felt Arrius's gaze on him, for his dark eyes met the tribune's. With a start, Arrius realized the young man was a Jew, unusual in the galleys. For his part, the slave seemed equally startled, for he hesitated and his grace left him for an instant. He paused too long, dropped his oar half-feathered, and took only half a stroke, but recovered. He kept his eyes on his hands after that.

What was he doing in the galleys? Arrius wondered. Under Roman rule, the Jewish people were generally hardworking and law-abiding. Arrius's eye wandered once again along the packed banks of rowers. Not one seemed elevated much above the animals. But this man's momentary gaze revealed a lively spirit and . . . could that be a kind of judgment in his eyes?

A voice from the deck called out, and Arrius climbed the steps to respond. The salty air, whipped by the stiff breeze, had never smelled so good. In the distance, a dark plume from Mount Aetna streaked the vivid blue of the sky. Arrius answered the sailing master's question and set the new course, then stayed on deck for the next few hours as the galley slipped through the Strait of Messina and rounded the Calabrian coast. From time to time he wondered about the young Jewish slave, but when he returned to the cabin, the shift had changed and the youth was nowhere in sight.

CHAPTER 6

A SLAVE

Three days later the *Astraea* was speeding eastward on the waters of the Ionian Sea. Arrius wanted to catch up with the large Roman fleet before they reached the island of Cythera, so he had spent most of the intervening days on deck, helping the sailing master coax the most speed from the combination of sail and oar. Periodically he descended to the cabin to rest or consult with the chief of rowers. Sometimes the young Jew was at his oar, and sometimes not. Finally, unable to contain his curiosity, he asked, "What do you know about the slave who sits at bench 60?"

"Over the course of a day, Your Honor, that could be several men. Which one do you mean?"

"The young Jew," Arrius answered.

The hortator nodded. "I thought he might be the one who caught your eye. He is our best rower."

"Anything besides that?"

"Remember the ship is only a month old, and we are all new to her. The slave works hard; I can say that. And once he asked me to switch him daily from the right side to the left. He believes that men who row only on one side become misshapen. And that in a sudden storm or a battle, it might be important to shift men from one side to another. He thinks they should be equally strong rowing on either side of the ship."

Arrius nodded, struck by the idea. "He could be correct. Is there anything else?"

"He goes to great lengths to stay clean. Some of them . . ." The hortator shook his head. "They might as well be beasts."

Arrius ignored this. "Do you know anything about his past? Why he is here?"

The chief of rowers shrugged. "With all due respect, sir, you must remember: These are slaves. They row; they die; we throw them overboard. All I know about any of them is how well he pulls his oar."

"Well, I am curious about this one," Arrius insisted. "When his next rest comes, send him to me. Alone."

Two hours later, Arrius was on deck, standing astern. It was a quiet moment. One sailor stood watch on the yardarm but several more slept in the shade of the sail. The rower emerged from the hatchway and walked silently toward Arrius, but he paused for an instant to look around at the blue sky and the tautly curved sail. As he approached, he bowed his head and said, "I was told you wished to see me. Sir."

Before speaking, Arrius studied the young man, who, in the dazzling Mediterranean light, was even more remarkable. Arrius himself was not small, but the rower loomed over him. He wore nothing more than a ragged loincloth, and his tangled black curls flopped over his eyes. Yet he stood upright, swaying easily to the roll of the ship, with a self-possessed air that surprised the tribune. In his years of naval action, he had met with slaves who were angry, sullen, resentful, vicious, terrified, and so deeply distressed that barely a spark of humanity showed in their eyes. This man, in contrast, looked directly at him with wary curiosity. His body was young, but his face showed the marks of a long-held grief—or anger.

"The hortator says you are his best rower," Arrius began, surprised to feel somewhat at a disadvantage.

"He is kind," the slave answered flatly. Courteously, but only on the surface. Rage simmered not far below.

"Have you seen much service?" Arrius went on.

"About three years."

"All of them at the oars?"

"Every single day," the rower answered, stressing each word equally.

"Really?" Arrius exclaimed. "Few men survive beyond a year."

The oarsman paused and met Arrius's glance before answering. "Sir—the hortator told me you are a tribune, named Quintus Arrius, and that you have been a naval officer. So naturally, you have some idea of our lives." Arrius was surprised to be spoken to almost as an equal, but he nodded to encourage the rower. "Spirit can improve endurance," the younger man went on. "I have seen some weak men survive where men who were physically stronger weakened and died." He said no more, but the implication was clear enough: he had chosen to live.

"Am I right in thinking that you are a Jew?" asked Arrius.

"I am," the young man said. "My ancestors were Hebrew before Rome ever existed."

"And you exhibit their pride," Arrius answered, taken aback.

"Pride is always loudest in chains."

"And what cause do you have for pride?"

"That I am a Jew," the rower answered simply.

Arrius smiled. "I've never been to Jerusalem, but I have heard of its princes. I even knew one. He was a seagoing trader. He was rich and cultured and as proud as any king." Arrius looked away for a moment, at the whitecaps racing toward the bow, regularly spaced across the sparkling water. "What is your position in life?"

"My position," the young man said, with a biting tone to his voice, "is the position of a galley slave. I am a galley slave," he repeated. He glanced into the distance, as Arrius had, and his voice was almost whipped away by the strong, steady wind. "My father was a sea-going trader and was rich and cultured. He probably came through the Strait of Messina dozens of times. I often think of him, on his deck, with his precious cargo, navigating these seas where I pull an oar. My mother always said that he was a frequent guest of Augustus in Rome." The breeze flung his curls back from his face, and for an instant he closed his eyes tight.

"What was his name?"

"Ithamar, of the house of Hur."

"You are a son of Hur?" Arrius exclaimed. "How is that possible? How did you become a slave?"

There was no answer for a long moment. Arrius watched as Ben-Hur took one deep breath, then another in the effort to master himself. Those large hands curled into fists but his voice was even when he turned to Arrius and said quietly, "I was accused of trying to assassinate the procurator Valerius Gratus in Jerusalem."

"That was you?" Arrius realized he had taken a step backward, away from the rower, and stood straighter to compensate. "Rome spoke of nothing else for days. I heard the news myself on shipboard, in the Iberian Sea."

The two men, elder and younger, tribune and slave, stood silent, each reconsidering the other. For Arrius, the tumbled hair and shaggy beard, the prominent muscles and the bare feet now seemed to disguise a different man, the son of the princely merchant he had once known. He noted the fine features and told himself he could see the father in the son, while Judah for his part found himself talking not to a commander, but to a man who had known of his family in another life entirely. In a real life.

Arrius spoke first: "I thought the Hur family had vanished from the earth."

Ben-Hur's eyes flew to his face. "But you have never heard anything about my mother and my sister? They were taken away because of what I did. . . ."

"Nothing," Arrius answered. Ben-Hur had moved closer, his immense callused hands touching Arrius's cloak where it had fallen from the tribune's shoulder. That momentary sense of menace was gone and the Roman felt a pulse of sympathy. Ben-Hur must have been little more than a gangling teenage boy when he came to the galleys. Roman justice was harsh and swift—as it had to be, Arrius knew, to control the vast empire around the Inland Sea. He had not considered it, though, from the viewpoint of those who were not Roman.

The young man glanced down at his hands and dropped the fine purple fabric, taking a half step backward. But he kept talking, as if he couldn't stop, with a new tone of desperation. "It has been three years, and every hour a lifetime of misery—a lifetime in a bottomless pit where the only relief is to be stunned by labor. All that time, I've never heard a word about my family. Not a whisper." He shook his head. "I know that I have been forgotten by the world, and sometimes it seems I have deserved it. Wiped away as if the family of Hur, the princes of Israel, had never existed. All through my action! But . . ." He looked away from Arrius, squinting into the sun to try to master his emotion. "I may be forgotten, but I can't forget," he went on more softly. "My father was dead, I was the head of the family, and my mother and sister were dragged away, looking back, pleading, waiting for me to help them."

He faced Arrius with a bleak expression. "I don't have to tell you about the many ways death arrives in the galleys. You can die from battle, starvation, exhaustion, plague, fire. I've seen men fall from their oars and drown in a few inches of bilgewater. I've seen them flayed to death by a wicked hortator, and I have envied them." He looked down at his palms and rubbed them together. "We do become like animals, you know. But these years would have been more tolerable if I really were the brute beast the hortator sees. Then I wouldn't remember my sister's eyes on mine as two Roman soldiers lifted her off the ground and dragged her away to a fate I . . ." He stopped speaking, then added in a near whisper, "I would be glad to know that my mother and Tirzah were dead. Two sheltered women at the mercy of . . . And all my doing."

"Do you admit you were guilty? That was a capital crime," Arrius pointed out sharply.

Ben-Hur's face hardened. "No, I don't. By the God of my fathers, I swear that I am innocent."

Arrius turned away from him and took a few steps toward the bow, then looked back. "You pleaded innocence at the trial?"

"There was no trial."

"What? Roman law . . . ," Arrius began. "No charges? No witnesses? Who passed judgment?"

Ben-Hur shrugged. "They chained my hands behind me and hauled me to a cell in the Antonia Tower. I saw no one. No one spoke to me. Next day soldiers took me to the port, and I have pulled an oar ever since."

"Could you have proven innocence?"

"It was an accident! I was on the roof, looking down at the procession as Gratus entered the city. I leaned over and dislodged a tile. It fell—Gratus fell. What a ridiculous way to try to kill someone, though! In broad daylight, surrounded by his soldiers, all fully armed. And I had so much to lose! Tribune, you understand these things. Rome rules with the cooperation of people like my father. We had a great estate. I was just a boy. Why would I ruin a good life?"

"But is there any proof? Who was with you?"

"No one. My sister, Tirzah, had just left me," Ben-Hur answered, looking down at the deck. "She was fifteen. Very sweet. Pretty. Innocent. She knew nothing outside our world; she never left the palace without my mother or a servant. I can't imagine her surviving imprisonment." He looked directly at Arrius. "Sir, since you are a tribune, could you find out?" But he had said too much; he knew right away. He had gone too far. "No," he said. "Of course not. I'm sorry."

Arrius was still looking at him soberly. He was shaken by Ben-Hur's story. He had spent his life in the service of Rome, and he believed in the empire. He knew that its laws were strict, but he also knew that Roman rule brought order and prosperity to the lands it subdued. If the Jew was telling the truth—and it was well-known that slaves lied—an entire family had been destroyed to atone for what might have been an accident.

"That's enough," he said. "Go back below."

Ben-Hur bowed his head to the tribune and turned away. After a few silent steps he spun around and said, "But I beg you to remember that I only asked you for news of my family. I requested nothing for myself."

Arrius watched him cross the deck, moving with the ease of a natural athlete. What a competitor he would make in the arena! He had the balance, the stamina, the mental fortitude, and the physical strength to make an invincible gladiator. "Wait!" Arrius called and followed him. "What would you do if you were free?"

Ben-Hur's eyes narrowed. "Don't mock me, tribune. I know I will die a slave."

"No, it's a serious question."

"Then I would never rest until my mother and Tirzah were brought back to the life they knew. I owe them everything they lost; I would recover it, somehow. Our palace, our ships, our trading partners, our warehouses, our bales of silk and barrels of spices, down to the last golden pin for my mother's hair—I would get them back. And I would wait on those women day and night, more faithfully than any slave."

"And what if you were to find out they were dead?"

There was no answer for a moment as Ben-Hur contemplated the clean white boards of the deck. Then he sighed and said, "The night before the accident, I had made a decision, and it would be the same today. I would train as a soldier. And in all the world, there is only one place to learn that profession, even for a Jew."

"In a Roman palaestra!" exclaimed Arrius.

Ben-Hur shook his head. "In a Roman military camp."

"You would need to learn the use of arms," Arrius commented, then caught sight of a sailor within earshot. He had been carried away. As commander of the ship he had no business discussing a future with even this remarkable galley slave. The man was his best rower. The ship must reach Cythera and join the fleet as fast as possible, and no man could be treated as anything other than an element of a fighting machine.

Yet he could not resist adding, "Just think of this. There can be no glory for a soldier who isn't a Roman citizen, and that's impossible for a Jew. But a gladiator, of any origin at all, can earn honor and wealth and recognition from the emperor. Go back to your bench now and take up your oar. Don't dwell on this conversation. It's the fruit of an idle moment."

But Judah Ben-Hur went below the deck with a tiny jet of hope in his heart.

CHAPTER 7

CHAINS

The sun raked across the lapis surface of the Aegean, striking glittering bands where the wind fractured the waves. In the distance, veils of haze hung over one island or another, but the people of Naxos, from their hilltop, directed their eyes southward to where the Roman fleet was gathered. There had never been such a sight in all the years of the boat-owning, seagoing, island-dwelling observers. The galleys sailed in precise formation, four abreast, heading eastward, then wheeling north like so many lines of cavalry, each row of galleys coming about at the same point. Flags and pennants streamed from the masts, but even more remarkable was the relentless precision of the oars that drove each ship forward.

"So many!" a shepherd cried, gasping for breath as he crested the hill. He shaded his eyes against the setting sun and counted the columns still gliding toward him. "Are they going to kill the pirates?"

"Or be killed," his neighbor answered.

"There must be scores of them," the first man continued, adding on his fingers as he turned to estimate the ships that he now saw stern-on.

"A hundred. And the pirate fleet, they say, is sixty strong. Biremes and triremes—two and three banks of rowers."

"So then, the Romans will win."

"The pirates are real desperadoes; you know that. They eat men up there beyond the Bosporus. They eat babies to help their beards grow."

"Every enemy eats babies, they say. And the Romans won't let a bunch of thieving corsairs get near them. They'll use those galleys to ram and sink the pirate ships; then they'll pour oil onto the water and set it on fire."

"I forgot about the oil. Have you ever seen it?"

"No. Just heard of it. Like eating babies. It probably isn't true. Look, the sun is setting."

The light was turning redder and redder, the span of the rays diminishing. There were only three more columns of sail left to round the invisible mark and turn northward.

"Let's go. I hate this hillside after dark."

"But I just got here," the shepherd protested.

"What more will you see once the sun's gone down?" his friend asked, setting off.

"I would like to see the battle, wouldn't you?" the shepherd asked as they filed down the narrow path.

"Yes, but I heard the pirates headed north. If I were the pirate chief, I would slip into the channel between Euboea and Hellas. There are lots of rich towns there; the fleet can move from one to the next, raiding as it goes."

"What do you know about rich towns and Hellas and raiding?" the shepherd scoffed.

"At least I've been off this island," his friend retorted. "And once we were blown all that way north in a storm. Right through the

Cyclades, all the way to Athens. The bay there, they told me, narrows and goes all the way up the coast, just like a finger of water. The raiding fleet can hide from the Romans."

The shepherd didn't answer for a moment as he crossed a steeply tilted boulder. "The problem with shelter is it can also be a trap," he said. "It happens all the time with sheep. They wander into a gully, feel sheltered and safe; then they can't get out. Maybe that will happen to the pirates, too."

"What a piece of luck for the Romans if it did," agreed his neighbor.

* * *

When the news reached Arrius that the pirate fleet had indeed slipped into the channel between Euboea and Hellas, he was sure that the goddess Fortuna was smiling on him. He could split his fleet, stationing half of them at the southern end and sending the other half north toward Thermopylae, snaring the pirates as the shepherd on Naxos had described.

Once the fleet had rounded Naxos, the order went out to make all possible speed to the northwest, threading through the islands clustering in the Aegean until Mount Ocha reared up black against the twilit sky. At a signal, the fleet rested on its oars while small boats went from ship to ship, making sure that every single captain understood his orders. Arrius was to lead one group into the mouth of the channel, while the rest of the squadron would sweep northward along the coast of Euboea, then turn south into the channel to pin the marauders between the two Roman forces. There would be no escape for the pirates.

* * *

Meanwhile Ben-Hur and the other slaves remained at their benches, pulling their oars. No one spoke to them. No one explained where they were going or why. No one mentioned the vast, orderly fleet in formation behind them, each galley powered by its scores of slaves. Night fell and the pace set by the hortator did not slacken, but a new scent drifted down the gangway from the deck: incense. Ben-Hur closed his eyes for a moment, shutting out the gloom of the cabin and the impassive face of the hortator. Incense! That meant the altar had been erected in the bow and the tribune had made a sacrifice. On every ship where Ben-Hur had pulled his oar, this had been the first step in the preparation for battle.

On the benches all around him, he sensed a new alertness. The perpetual struggle with the oar kept every part of the body busy; there was no way even to turn and catch a fellow rower's eye. But as he pulled the blade of his oar through the dark water outside the hull, he heard single whispered words hissed along the benches as rowers understood the prospect before them. For a sailor, or for one of the marines on board, battle meant struggle, danger, excitement, glory, wounds, or death. For the galley slave, there was even more at stake. If the ship were captured, the slaves also changed hands. They might have a new master, for better or worse. They might even be freed. On the other hand, during a battle every slave was chained to his bench. If the ship sank or caught fire, the men who had pulled the oars suffered the same fate as the planks of the hull. It was what everyone dreaded most, that helpless plunge into the sea, shackled to the timbers. Down and down, struggling for air, into ever-darker water . . . Ben-Hur shivered and tried to redirect his thoughts. Had he not told Arrius that he longed for death? Then why did he flinch from its potential approach?

Soon a sailor brought lanterns into the cabin and hung them on the stanchions supporting the deck. The marines trotted down the stairs silently and began assembling the battle machines, light catapults, and a boarding bridge. Spears and javelins as well as sheaves of arrows were handed out, breastplates and helmets secured. Finally great jars of oil were carried up from the hold along with baskets of cotton wads that would be soaked in it, set alight, and hurled at the enemy.

But the worst moment for the slaves was still to come. Ben-Hur's eyes followed the tribune as he retreated to his platform, where his helmet and armor lay ready. A soldier came to the steps below and held out a large key; Arrius saw the key and nodded. The soldier walked forward between the ranks of slaves behind Ben-Hur and began shackling them. The chains clanked and the key made a distinctive click as each heavy circle of iron was made fast around an ankle. Ben-Hur tried not to count as the soldier came nearer and nearer: two clicks for each oarsman, three on each side of the aisle, ten rows from bow to stern. He stared at Arrius, buckling on his sword belt, loosening the sword in its sheath.

In that moment Ben-Hur was glad of his oar. He felt the grain of the oak, worn smooth by his hands in the short month since the ship had been launched. As he pulled the long shaft of wood through the water, pressed the handle down, and lifted it free, he thought about the lead weight in its core and how it offset the length of the shaft. There was a moment in each cycle of movements when the long cylinder was perfectly balanced. Ben-Hur focused on this, trying to see, in his mind's eye, the instant when the oar hung weightless in the oarlock, blade parallel to the water, before he turned his wrists and dipped it and pulled. It was a movement he had made so often that he was rarely conscious of it, but on that night, with the incense of the altar swirling through the cabin, the clatter of weapons being carried to the deck, the ever-nearing clank of the fetters, he tried to think only about his oar.

He tried not to hope. Arrius had been careless, talking to him. As a commander he should not have singled out a mere slave. As a human he should not have mentioned the future to a man who could be chained to a bench, with no hope of escape. Ben-Hur felt the anger surging in him and a bitterness that was familiar from his first days as a galley slave. He thought he had mastered them.

Against his will, he glanced again at the tribune, who lay now on his couch with his eyes closed. The soldier with the key was beside Ben-Hur when Arrius rolled upright and made a sign. The soldier moved away, leaving the chains and fetters lying on the boards next to the bench.

Nothing had changed. Yet he was not chained. Ben-Hur rowed on, wrestling his long spar of oak through the dark, salty sea and trying not to feel hope. He was still one of 120 slaves laboring to propel a fragile ship into battle against a foe he couldn't identify or imagine. On deck men were sharpening their daggers and the barbed heads of spears. One shouted as a jar of oil tilted, threatening to spill. Arrius huddled into his cloak a few feet away, resting while he could, but every other man was alert and apprehensive. All the same, Ben-Hur felt himself a new man. The Roman tribune had singled him out and acknowledged him as an individual. Surely the God of his fathers was smiling on him now.

But as the hours passed, Ben-Hur's sense of good fortune diminished. The galley slaves were never more of an asset to the Romans than in battle, when the ability to maneuver a ship with precision and speed could turn the tide of the fighting. Yet at those moments, they had more incentive than ever to try to escape. The long months of routine labor might crush all initiative in them, but when they were exposed to mortal danger, animal instinct took over and they would take any risk to survive. Enslaved by Rome, they were Rome's enemies as surely as the antagonists bearing down on them—who might even be their compatriots. For slaves and masters alike, battle threatened the balance of power. Thus the chains. And as the preparations continued, every man's sense of danger grew. The bull-hide armor was hung over the side of the ship, but what protection would it offer if the hull was rammed? Buckets of water were stationed near oil tanks and fireballs; netting was stretched over the deck. The marines had their shields and breastplates and helmets. Yet the enemy was similarly prepared. And the greatest danger—one never faced by soldiers on land—lay in the water all around them, the enemy of pirates and Romans alike.

The slaves, both the rowers and the relief crew, were crowded below deck, surrounded by guards, wearing only their tattered loincloths and their chains. The ship suddenly rolled, and there was shouting on deck that quickly died away. Ben-Hur thought he heard a new, faint sound—maybe the rigging of another galley or the splash of its oars nearby. The *Astraea* had been the only ship on the sea when Arrius called him on deck, but now it seemed she had joined a fleet. As tribune, Arrius would be the commander in chief, Ben-Hur knew, and the ship would fly the purple pennant of his command. That made it a prominent target.

At a signal from the deck, the rowers halted the galley, then resumed rowing slowly. The slow pace and the silence from above seemed like a warning; every man tensed his muscles. Even the ship seemed to hold its breath.

Suddenly trumpets rang out above with a bold, commanding chord. The hortator responded by hammering on his sounding board, and the rowers reached forward. They dipped their oars deeply and pulled with all their force. The galley leapt forward so fast that everyone standing staggered. Before they had regained their balance, a chorus of trumpets sounded from behind the rowers, but it was muffled and mixed with what might be a clamor of voices.

One more stroke; then a mighty blow hit the ship. Men fell, scrabbling over each other to rise, but the slaves on the benches gripped their oars and strained to keep moving the ship forward. There was a tremendous groan, scraping, an infinitely long moment when every man heaved on his oar till it bent; finally the galley shot forward again faster than ever, leaving behind it an inhuman chorus of screams.

Terror, agony, wood grinding on wood, metal meeting flesh, limbs torn apart, a hellish confusion of sound and image beyond the hull of the ship—but inside it, nothing to see besides the orderly ranks of slaves pulling their oars and their replacements standing at the ready. Yet the men were aghast. Eyes rolled; brows furrowed. The death and destruction just dealt by *Astraea* might be invisible to them, but it was still very real. Worse, at any moment, they might suffer likewise. Outside more shouting, more trumpets; Ben-Hur felt pounding and rumbling beneath the keel. Something broke. Something jagged scraped the whole length of the hull. A long, bubbling howl rose and rose, then stopped abruptly with a thump. Every man aboard envisioned a skull meeting the ship's rudder.

In that instant the galley was free, moving swiftly again, and joyful shouts rose from the deck. *Astraea* with her lethal beak had sunk an enemy ship. But there was no time to spare; soldiers ran down the gangway and began plunging cotton wads into the jugs of oil, then passing them, dripping, back up to the deck. Clamor from above and a word of warning, followed by cheers: the catapult had found its enemy.

Ben-Hur heaved steadily on his oar, listening to the tumult. He could make out the twang of bowstrings, the creak of the siege machines, and he thought, not far away, the hortator of another ship, shouting as he set the rowers' pace. The *Astraea* suddenly heeled over so sharply that the starboard oars no longer reached the water. The timbers groaned and on deck the soldiers cheered, but shrieks could also be heard more faintly, along with the whine of a winch. An enemy galley had come within range of *Astraea*'s grappling hooks and was now being lifted by its prow, shedding men and weapons into the water as it rose. Higher, higher—Ben-Hur had seen the seagoing crane in action on another ship. The arm of the crane would extend its full length, dangling the enemy craft over the surface of the sea like a fish on a hook, and finally release its hold and drop the galley vertically into the water, which would rush into its hull and sink it. Every man aboard would die.

The noise was all around them now, noise and worse. Injured soldiers were carried down the gangway, out of the way of the fighting. Their groans and howls so near at hand, the blood running beneath the benches and the torn flesh of their wounds went unattended as the slaves kept rowing and the battle above continued. Other galleys had launched fireballs, and a yellowish smoke came billowing into the rowers' cabin. It bore the unsettling scent of roasting flesh, and more than one man turned pale. They had rowed through the remains of a burning galley, where slaves died chained to their benches.

"Oh, gods, let me drown instead," muttered a man behind Ben-Hur.

"Silence!" the nearest soldier shouted.

With a crash, the ship stopped. Oars were jerked from the rowers' hands as they tumbled off the benches, and a trampling sound from the deck was quickly drowned out by a long, deep grinding against the hull that could be felt as much as heard. The galley had run afoul of another ship and the two vessels were locked in a violent embrace. The hortator's gavel paused, and when it resumed, it could barely be heard through the din as clashing and roaring erupted above.

But the regular blows of the mallet on the wooden table could not restore order. Some slaves were staring upward as if they could see the battle through the wooden planking of the deck; others darted their eyes around, searching for escape as they forgot the shackles on their legs. Another soldier dashed down the hatch, but this time, Ben-Hur saw, he was not Roman. A thick black beard and pale skin divided his face in half while his shield was made of bull hide and wicker. Where had he come from?

Suddenly Ben-Hur understood: they had been boarded. The hull pressed against *Astraea* belonged to pirates. From the uproar on deck, the fighting was vicious. Now a sequence of loud, howling cries was heard and a rush of feet. Three Roman soldiers were driven partway down into the cabin, then rallied and pushed back upward while all the time the hortator continued to hammer out the beat for the rowers.

But not a slave touched his oar. Panic had overcome discipline. Ben-Hur looked around the cabin and saw that each man was thinking only of himself and how he might escape or survive. And upstairs—what was becoming of Arrius? An icy needle of fear sliced through Ben-Hur's mind. Arrius had seen him as a man, not a slave. What if the tribune was dead or wounded? What if the barbarian pirates had taken him captive?

Ben-Hur was moving before he finished his thought. Arrius had kept him unchained, an act that could save his life. But he was still a slave. If Arrius died, he would never be anything else. If Arrius lived, he might have a future. As he leapt up the stairs, he saw once again the image that had haunted him for so long: his mother and sister dragged off by soldiers as he cried out. His mother in a dead faint, his sister shrieking, their captors expressionless—he could never erase that sight without help from the Roman commander.

He caught a glimpse of a red and murky sky. His hand touched the deck and slid in the dreadful glaze of oil and blood. The air was thick with ash, stinging his eyes and throat. With another step upward he saw ships on every side, shattered or burning. Close at hand, men struggled in a meaningless melee, forward and backward with roars and wails, too close to use their weapons.

Then his foothold was abruptly knocked away. The deck seemed to be lifting itself and breaking into pieces. In a shocking instant the hull split in two, and as if it had been lying in wait, the sea hissed and foamed over the shattered boards. It leapt over men and weapons, mast and sail, swallowing everything, and Ben-Hur knew only darkness.

CHAPTER 8

FLAMING SEA

The water sucked him downward in a relentless whirl, slamming him against spars and debris. His lungs burned and burned worse. A freak current hurled his heels above his head. He was about to give in to the pressure, open his mouth to the searing liquid, when his head broke the surface and he gasped air instead.

His eyes smarted, clouded with salt and the oil floating on the surface. He could make no sense of what he saw. Brilliance flashed on blackness. A huge patch of dark loomed above him, blotting out the erratic light, then struck him so hard on the head that he saw stars and sank for an instant. But in a gesture faster than thought, his long rower's arms reached up to the edge of the floating mass. His hand tore on a nail, found a better grip. After a pair of ragged breaths, he lifted his torso onto the wreckage and lay with his face on the wet wood, retching. All around he heard shouting, explosions, crackling and hissing, a bellow of agony, and the constant little lap of water against the spar he clung to.

A hand reached up and seized his wrist, followed by a pallid, bearded face. The man shouted something at him and brandished a crescent-shaped dagger. Judah saw his own hand reach forward, tear the dagger from the man's hand, and thrust it at his face. Before he knew it, the man had sunk in a flurry of red-tinged bubbles, and Ben-Hur looked at his own hand, still holding the dagger. Had he just killed a man? So quickly, without thought? There was blood on his hand. He had broken one of the commandments. But what else could he have done?

He rolled onto his side and looked at the sky, gasping. To his right, not far away, a ship was burning and the black shadows of soldiers fell writhing from the deck to the sea while the galley slaves bawled below. A hand tugged his ankle and another face looked up at him with one blue eye, the other dangling from a shiny red concavity on the cheek-bone. Ben-Hur lifted the curved dagger and the hand let go. A bank of smoke descended, so acrid that he coughed convulsively. Isolated for a few seconds, he emerged into the midst of a pitched battle on the surface of the sea. Romans with their daggers hacked furiously at pirates with wicker shields, clinging to a length of mast and most of a sail. Both sets of men saw him, turned, and tried to grasp his bit of planking, momentarily distracted from their struggle.

In that instant Ben-Hur understood his position. He was every-one's enemy. Luck, on his side for once, had provided him with a piece of wood that could keep him alive in the stinking melee of the sea battle—but only if he clung to it and beat back all others. He drew his legs out of the water and tucked them beneath him. A glance over his shoulder showed him a massive swell coming. The mountain of water was studded with debris. Ben-Hur spotted a smooth cylinder skimming the forefront of the wave and like lightning secured his dagger between his teeth.

The years at the bench had sharpened his reflexes. His eyes and his body had recognized a fragment of an oar and prepared themselves for its weight so that when his hands closed around the oak shaft, his legs and trunk accepted the heft provided by the lead at the core. One of the Romans had an arm halfway across the planking, and Ben-Hur rotated to bring down the oar on it. The arm broke and the man roared as he slid back into the sea. The roar stopped short when he sank.

But there was no respite. A new sound of rushing water and a telltale regular thump came from the right. A veil of smoke tore and a two-deck galley appeared, headed in Judah's direction. He threw himself down to try to paddle his plank. The fragment of oar had no blade, so he tucked it beneath his belly and used his hands, cupping them to move the water. The galley came on, throwing a tall bow wave. On deck, Roman armor glittered, reflecting light from patches of burning oil on the water. The hortator's rhythm quickened, and Ben-Hur found himself obeying it, paddling at the beat to escape the rushing menace. The iron beak made the water boil in advance of the bow, and Ben-Hur dug his hands as deep in the water as he could, pulling with the same effort he had used on the rower's bench just minutes earlier.

The beak passed beneath him and his luck held: the bow nudged the end of the plank, sending him alongside so that, in the strangest moment of that grim night, he lay on his plank, gliding next to the ship, between the towering hull and the blades of the oars. Above him the loom of oars swung back and forth as the slaves pulled; to his side the blades dipped and turned, one stroke, two, three . . . And the galley was gone, leaving a glossy wake on the black water.

Ben-Hur crumpled to the surface of his plank, gasping for air. He lay shuddering for a long minute. Near and far, he heard the din of battle: thuds and crashes, cries, wails, splashing. He hardly noticed the muffled clang as his plank hit another floating object, but a moan followed and he lifted his head. He had to be vigilant. His precious plank might keep him alive through the night, but every man in the sea who could still think would have the same idea. Men outnumbered planks—he could be knocked into the sea at any time. He glanced into the water.

There was a Roman sinking beside him, red cloak billowing around his face. The helmet dipped beneath the surface. An elaborate patterned breastplate swam upward, drifted downward. The face broke the surface and the mouth gaped. Judah felt his mind moving slowly as the face fell away from him through the water again. Wait . . . He reached out a hand. That face . . . His hands stretched forward and met the cloak. He hauled. The body turned over. The cloak tore away from the breastplate. His fingertips caught the back of the helmet, and leaning off the plank, he managed to flip the body over and bring the face back to the air.

It was Arrius. Ben-Hur's fingers were more clever than his brain, feeling for the clasp of the helmet's strap. He unhooked it and pulled it off, letting the polished bronze sink to the depths. Then he leaned out farther, trying to get a purchase on the buckles of the cuirass. One buckle, two; he wrestled with the sodden leather to pull off the hammered metal. All that carving, all that gilding, the grandeur of the empire, nothing more than a faint gleam as it followed the helmet into the murk. Now Arrius was just a man, just flesh and blood like Ben-Hur. Easy enough to grasp beneath his armpits. He dragged the Roman tribune's head out of the sea. One more heave and his shoulders lay on Ben-Hur's plank.

It had all taken less than a minute, and the two men lay half-submerged on the plank, riding lower in the water. Ben-Hur allowed himself a few deep breaths to recover, then pulled Arrius a little bit closer. Arrius! The one man on the *Astraea* who had seen him as a human being! The one man worth saving, among the hundreds floating nearby in agony! Ben-Hur looked down at the Roman's pale face, put his ear to Arrius's chest. The heart was fluttering; the man was breathing. What luck that quirks of the current had delivered Arrius to Ben-Hur's improvised raft! Or was his God looking after him still?

Off to the right the galley that had nearly run over Ben-Hur impaled a pirate ship, and the sounds of battle rang out over the water: clanging and crashing, shrieking and moaning. The pirates uttered a high, rhythmic war cry that pierced the night. Arrius coughed and gasped at Ben-Hur's elbow, then vomited seawater. Ben-Hur turned him on his side so the vomit ran into the sea and looked back at the fighting ships just in time to see the flames leap up the sail and rigging of the pirate ship.

In an instant, the Roman ship was on fire. Marines stationed on the rigging frantically beat at the flames licking the sail. On deck, soldiers paired up to heave barrels of oil overboard. The hortator howled loudly enough that Ben-Hur could almost make out the words—he was ordering the slaves to back their oars and pull away from the enemy. The ships were fastened by grapples and the iron beak, but now they must be pried apart or sink, locked together. Ben-Hur could not tear his eyes away. If the flame reached the oil, it was all over. Both ships would burn, perhaps even explode. He realized the plank was drifting too close to the battle and lay back down to try to maneuver it away.

The warning came as a flash of light and a sound like rushing wind, then the earsplitting boom of the explosion. Ben-Hur flung himself over Arrius's chest to shield him from flying debris. He spread out his arms and gripped the edges of the plank as hard as he could, waiting for whatever the water would do. Down they went, covered once more by a wave.

Yet the wave receded with a long, sucking tug, leaving Ben-Hur and Arrius in place. Where the ships had been was now a floating bonfire, lighting the night around in a vast, glittering orange circle.

Ben-Hur felt movement beneath him and glanced down. Arrius's eyes were opening.

He rolled off the Roman's chest but kept a grip on his arm; another explosion might come. Arrius shook his head slightly and muttered something. In the light from the burning ships, Ben-Hur now saw that Arrius's silver hair was darkening in one spot above his ear. Darkening fast, as a wound reopened. Ben-Hur felt gently and found the gaping edges of the skin. The bone beneath seemed unharmed, but it was a long gash and bleeding fast.

Ben-Hur glanced around him in a circle. Mayhem ruled. The surface of the water was dotted with black shapes, rising and sinking. Here and there he could make out an arm, a foot, a random chunk of muscle, but they did not stay afloat. The fire crackled and hissed while all around, wounded men wailed and shrieked. The acrid scent of the fire gave way to drifts of the smell of cooking flesh. In the farther distance, Judah thought he saw other flashes. The scene of death and destruction before him must be repeating itself all across the narrow stretch of sea.

And what next? He looked down at Arrius, unconscious again. Would he live through the night? What about the next day? What if the pirates won and captured him? Arrius would probably be ransomed. He, Ben-Hur, would remain a slave. What if the Romans won, though? Arrius would go back to Rome. . . . Ben-Hur stopped himself. What if they were not discovered? That was far more likely. The victors of a sea battle tried to pick up survivors, but that could take days. Arrius would not survive for days.

It was warm, though, Judah told himself. He had heard of men cast into a sea so cold that within hours they simply fell asleep and sank. He would not do that. His fortune—his God—had put him on this piece of wood and sent him the one man who could change his life. There must be some reason for that!

CHAPTER 9

ADRIFT

In the next hours the ships burned to the waterline and the fires went out. The cries of the dying slaves stopped, though a charred stench hung in the air. The wind died and the water stilled. Smoke evaporated into the sky and the stars appeared. Once or twice a distant flash pricked the horizon, then faded as the battle continued far away.

Ben-Hur knew the night was almost over when the seabirds returned. One by one, then in groups, they soared around the floating wreckage as the sky lightened. By the time the horizon was pale, they bobbed on the surface, peering and pecking at whatever might float. Judah tried to tell himself they were finding remnants of the sailors' rations, but that was harder to believe after a hand floated past only to be scooped up by a pelican that hurtled out of the sky, then surfaced with a pair of fingers sticking out of its beak. After fixing its beady yellow eye on Ben-Hur, the bird gave a mighty flap, heaving itself skyward. It left a powerful fishy odor behind. Seconds later, the hand dropped back to the water, rejected by the bird.

When the sun was well above the horizon, Arrius spoke. He muttered at first, waking Judah from a doze. He rolled his head from side to side and flinched.

"Wait; be careful. You were wounded," Ben-Hur said, putting his hand against Arrius's brow. The tribune frowned at him, closed his eyes, and lapsed back into unconsciousness.

But some time later, Ben-Hur looked down to see that Arrius was studying him silently. When Judah met his gaze, the tribune smiled wryly. "My luck as a commander seems to have run out. So much for my offerings at Fortuna's altar. What happened?"

"The pirates sank *Astraea*," answered Ben-Hur. "I went up on deck just as the ship broke apart and everything fell into the water. This plank was nearby, so I seized it and shortly afterward found you. That's all. Except that if I had been chained to the bench, like the other slaves, I would have died. So I owe you my life."

"And I owe you mine for picking me up, so we are even." Arrius drew his elbows in and tried to raise his head but closed his eyes and lay back. "Did my head get hit?"

"It must have. There's a big gash there above your ear."

"They always say salt water is good for wounds," Arrius answered. "Did you see any more of the battle?"

"A Roman galley went down along with a pirate ship not far away from *Astraea*, but you must have seen that. It was before we sank. Late last night there was still fighting in the distance, but I couldn't make it out. The wreckage doesn't tell me much."

"No ships visible nearby?"

"Not a sail."

Arrius was silent for a long moment. "I think we will be rescued," he said. "The strait is narrow. It's easy for a ship to sweep from shore to shore." His voice sounded thin and he had to stop often for breath.

"Maybe you should not be talking," Ben-Hur said.

"No, I need to . . ." His voice trailed off. He lay still, then visibly mustered his strength. "Broken ribs, I think." His hand crept along his side. "Yes—here and here. Feel."

Judah hesitated. It was one thing to handle the unconscious Arrius, to haul him from the water and examine his wounds. But the man speaking . . . Three years in the galleys did not fall away that quickly. Arrius was still the tribune, the Latin speaker, the wearer of red, the one who gave commands.

Also the one who understood. "I say that not as master to slave," Arrius added. "I think the night we just endured wiped all that away."

Ben-Hur nodded and stretched his big hands out over Arrius's chest. He tried to be gentle, but even so, Arrius stiffened as Ben-Hur touched his sternum. "Can you breathe?" Ben-Hur asked.

"Not as well as usual," Arrius admitted.

"Then we must hope for rescue," Ben-Hur said. In truth, Arrius's injuries didn't matter. They would die of thirst or starvation in a few days anyway. Arrius spoke lightly of ships coming to rescue them, but Ben-Hur knew that was unlikely. This was the difference between a tribune and a slave: a tribune could still expect that luck would go his way.

Arrius lay back, but his hands moved at his side. He seemed to be measuring the edges of the wood that he and Ben-Hur lay on. A smile curled his lip. "You really are the son of Prince Ithamar of the house of Hur, aren't you?" he asked.

"Of course I am. Why would I lie about that?" Judah answered.

"I knew your father well, you know," Arrius said. "We were good friends. He would have been quick to see the joke here."

"What joke could that possibly be?" Ben-Hur asked.

"Do you know what we're lying on? It's part of a rower's bench. Sometimes the gods mock us this way."

"Your gods, not mine," Ben-Hur said. "Don't forget I am a Jew."

"Of course," Arrius said. "I should have remembered."

"And my God does not mock."

"No," Arrius agreed. "But mine have been known to."

Silence fell between the men for a while. The sun rose further. The heat increased. Ben-Hur felt his skin drying out and the thirst beginning. He had been thirsty and hungry before, but he wondered how Arrius would tolerate the discomfort. Like a Roman soldier, no doubt.

"I am grateful for what you did," Arrius said suddenly. "I know that your saving me puts your own life in jeopardy. There's not much room on this bench, and our combined weight may sink it."

"I could not leave you . . . ," Ben-Hur began.

Arrius lifted a hand. "No. Let me finish. Take the ring off my finger." He held out his right hand to Judah. The ring was a massive gold signet with a carved stone at its center. "Here—put it on. If I don't survive, you can take it to my villa at Misenum. The overseer will give you anything you ask for when you tell him how you got this."

Ben-Hur drew a breath to speak but Arrius kept on talking. "If I live, of course, I can do more for you. I'll free you. And send you back to Jerusalem if you want. I can help you find your family, or at least find what happened to them."

Again Judah began to answer, but Arrius shook his head. "This is the least I could do. I am of some value to the empire, and I haven't asked much for my services over the years. I have no children and no wife. It will give me pleasure to serve the son of my old friend Prince Hur."

Ben-Hur watched Arrius, who lay back now with his eyes closed. The hand with the gleaming gold ring rested on his chest. The sun caught the rich, reflective yellow of the metal as Arrius breathed. "Take the ring," Arrius said. He lifted his hand, and Ben-Hur slid the ring off and onto his own forefinger.

"But I have one request," Arrius said. He took another pair of breaths. "Maybe you know that we Romans must not outlive our successes. Do you see any sails yet?"

Ben-Hur shaded his eyes and scanned the horizon all around. "There may be a sail to the north, but it could be a cloud."

"We will know soon enough. And if it is a sail, we will have to wait to see whether it's Roman. If it's not, I am a dead man."

"You have value as a hostage, don't you?"

"That will not happen," Arrius said, and his voice sounded clearer and more confident. "This is the promise I want from you. Swear by the gods—"

"By God," Ben-Hur interrupted. "My God, not your gods."

"By your God," Arrius continued, "that if a pirate ship reaches us before a Roman one, you will push me off this raft and let me drown."

"No," Ben-Hur said instantly and began to tug the ring off his finger. "The gift of life is God's. It's not for us to take it away."

"Have you never killed a man? Maybe last night, in the dark and the fire, as you tried to save your own life?"

Ben-Hur did not answer right away, but he remembered the red cloud of blood in the sea as he watched the man he'd killed sink. "I did," Ben-Hur finally said. "It will be counted against me, I know. But I won't help you do this."

Arrius sighed. "You remind me of your father. He was stubborn too. Don't you see the shame for me, as a Roman, to submit to captivity? Success and honor are everything for us!"

"But not for us, tribune. We have laws. I saved your life, so I am responsible for it. Take back the ring."

"And if I were to command you?"

"You can't. Just for now, I'm not a slave. I may become one again. I think that is a sail off to the north. I know the pirates will put me back on the bench. But at this moment I don't have to obey your command and I choose not to honor your request. Just now I am a Jewish man obeying my laws. So I give you back your ring." He pulled it off and held it out.

Arrius shook his head and Judah opened his hand. No response from Arrius. So Ben-Hur tilted his flat palm and the ring dropped into the cloudy water. It glittered for a second, then was gone.

"That was a mistake," Arrius said. "I can do nothing for you now, if I die."

"Tribune, you have already shown me more kindness than you could know. For three years I have been nothing more than an animal to every single person I met." He paused. "No, there was one other: a man my age gave me water in Nazareth, two days after it all happened. But since that moment, nothing, until you spoke to me of my family. How could I kill you after that?"

"I don't need your help to die, you know," said Arrius. "I could just slip from the bench. It will get easier as the day goes by."

"Then why ask me?"

"It's the Roman way," Arrius said with a shrug. "And the Greek. When Socrates wanted to die, someone gave him the hemlock."

Ben-Hur shook his head. "That has nothing to do with me. And I think we will know, long before the end of the day, what our fate is going to be. There *is* a sail, and it is coming our way."

The previous night had seemed long, but it was nothing compared to that morning. Arrius was too severely injured to do more than lie supine, fretting. Pride kept him from peppering Ben-Hur with questions, but he was restless and agitated. Ben-Hur was desperate for a better view of the distant craft, but the waterlogged bench was too narrow and unstable to allow him to lift his head much above the waterline. Which raised another problem: if the ship did approach, how could Ben-Hur and Arrius ensure they were seen? Ben-Hur was regretting that he'd let Arrius's cuirass and helmet sink when he rescued the man; the sun flashing off their beaten metal could have attracted eyes to them.

But what if the wrong ship came? Ben-Hur glanced at Arrius, lying with his eyes closed now. Was he paler than he had been? Would he even live through the day?

"Tribune, how can I tell a Roman ship from the corsairs?"

Arrius looked startled. "You don't know?"

"The only time I ever went on deck was to transfer from one ship to another," Ben-Hur reminded him. "All I know is inside the hull. And every ship I have seen was Roman."

"Roman ships always carry a helmet at the peak of the mast," Arrius answered. "And . . . do you see any flags?"

"She is still too far away."

"Flags would mean a Roman ship celebrating victory."

"I will hope that's what appears, then." Ben-Hur looked down at the tribune. "But it will take some time. Can we tear your tunic to cover your face from the sun? It's going to be merciless. And the thirst will be easier to bear if you're covered."

Arrius lifted the hem of his tunic and tried to tear it. "You're stronger than I am. See what you can do."

"Since I've refused to take your life, I still feel responsible for you," Judah said with a tiny smile. He leaned over to tug at the hem. It was finely woven, seamless, and refused to give way. Ben-Hur tried to tear it with his teeth but the fine edge held.

"Roman weaving," Arrius said. "Meant to last forever. Like the empire."

"It would be a pity if the garment outlasted its wearer," Ben-Hur said.

"That's in the hands of the gods now," Arrius retorted and closed his eyes.

He might have slept. He might just have wanted to retreat. Ben-Hur couldn't blame him. Their chances of survival looked poor. In the water all around, he saw only wreckage. Destruction ruled: charred planking, frayed ropes, shattered spars. Much of the material floating could not be identified, though some of it had to be human. Eventually it would all rot and sink. Or the scavengers of the sea would swallow it, from above or below the surface. At that thought, Judah had to prevent himself from pulling his trailing feet out of the water. That would upset the precarious balance of the plank and give Arrius the end he seemed to want.

Ben-Hur wondered if he wanted to die. Not yet, of course. He had not survived three years as a galley slave to allow this opportunity to slip away. But there was something impressive about Arrius's resolution all the same. Ben-Hur admired the notion that a man might control his own destiny. The choice between success and nonexistence seemed reasonable. Even attractive. But not the way of the chosen people.

He lifted his head as high as he dared. The galley in the distance was still heading toward them, but he could make out no special features. What did the barbarian galleys look like? It would have been useful if they had distinguishing features, like striped sails or brightly colored hulls. Useful in battle, too, Ben-Hur thought, to tell an enemy from an ally in the chaos of a fleet action.

He turned, scanning the horizon again. A breeze had picked up, ruffling the water's surface and producing small swells, and as the plank reached the top of one, he glimpsed a sail coming from the other direction. Much closer than the galley he and Arrius had been watching, and coming toward them with some speed.

He touched the tribune's shoulder. "Tribune, there is a sail closer to us. It may be Roman, but I can't quite see."

Arrius lifted his head. "Where?"

"There . . . right behind you."

"I don't dare move," the tribune answered. "I'm feeling weak. I need not have asked you to push me from our bench," he added. "I think I can achieve death on my own."

The mast was just visible at the crest of each wave. It kept coming closer, and more of the sail was visible each time the bench was lifted on a swell. But there was nothing to tell Judah any more. If the galley kept to its course, it would pass well to their right, and he and Arrius might not be seen. It would be worth making the effort if there was a chance of rescue near at hand. But what if the ship belonged to the pirates? Ben-Hur glanced down at his huge, callused hands. He looked like a galley slave, and he would go back to being one. Arrius . . . The tribune lay with his eyes closed and his mouth open, rolling slightly as the bench glided over each small swell. His skin was already reddened by the sun and the wound over his ear gleamed. He might still be bleeding.

Take the chance? Make the effort to greet the nearer ship or wait for the farther one? That one might belong to the pirates too. The issue, Ben-Hur realized, was whether he tried to reach a ship sooner or later, and sooner was the obvious choice. He began kicking, gently at first, to see how the bench responded. It was a steady movement, so Arrius lay still. He slipped down into the water to see if that helped; the bench seemed to rise slightly, but he could see less. Could he maintain his course? Could he steer at all?

He kicked more. Part of his mind noticed that he was not as strong as usual. Or maybe it was that his legs weren't as strong as his arms. But pulling an oar, you had to brace yourself with your legs. When the hortator beat the rhythm for a charge, men rose off the bench with each stroke, leaning the entire weight of their bodies against the oars. He should have been stronger. They were going nowhere. He slithered carefully back onto the bench to gain the few inches of height that would let him see a little bit more of the sail. Were they closer? Were they in the galley's course?

A bigger swell headed their way. Arrius was in a deep sleep or maybe unconscious; his head rolled from side to side as the bench moved. Ben-Hur seized Arrius's shoulder as the bench crested the swell—it would be too easy for the tribune to drown now, when rescue might be at hand. The swell lifted them high enough to relieve Ben-Hur: the galley was still heading toward them. But there was something disturbing about the sight. Was the sail full enough? Ben-Hur knew nothing about the mechanics of sailing. That was left to the men on deck. Maybe it was normal.

There was something missing, too—the steady thump of the hortator's block. Shouldn't that have been audible?

The next swell lifted them higher yet and brought more of the galley's sail into view. It was Roman, Ben-Hur decided. He could not say why he thought so—maybe something about the clean white sail and the . . . Was that a helmet on top of the mast? Ben-Hur squinted, willing his eyes to tell him. There was something, certainly, a rounded shape that didn't seem to belong there.

Each swell brought the ship closer, but Ben-Hur grew more puzzled as more of the sail came into view. Was it slack? Could expert Roman sailors be letting it spill the wind? He looked back over his shoulder to check on the course of the original galley they had spotted. He didn't see it, but another swell showed the sheet of the nearer ship, hanging in a loose curve . . . Unmanned.

The galley must be empty of men! How could that be? Was it a trap? Ben-Hur rejected the thought. Trap for whom? Still, there was something uncanny about the ship floating without direction. Soon the empty deck came into view, then the bank of oars, abandoned like a handful of straws at crazy angles.

"No flags," came Arrius's voice.

"No," Ben-Hur agreed. "And no crew. Why?"

"Lots of reasons," Arrius said. "Injuries, deaths, most of the men taken off to man another ship. There may be a skeleton crew on board."

"They'd never leave the sails up and the oars out," Ben-Hur objected.

"Unless it's part of a ruse." Arrius sighed. "And the other galley? The first one?"

"Still there. Still far away."

"Could a lookout from that ship see this one?"

Ben-Hur shook his head. "I don't know. I don't know how far you can see from the top of a mast."

"No, of course not." After a pause, Arrius added, "Quite a distance."

What next, then? Ben-Hur wondered. Try to reach the empty galley? Was there any advantage in that? He eyed the ship, imagined himself somehow scaling the hull . . . but Arrius was too weak. That was out of the question.

The galley that was farther away might come to investigate this one. If that was a Roman ship, all would be well. If not, they would have put themselves into danger. He craned his neck again. Was the farther ship . . . ? Yes. As a rower, he knew. The pace of the oars had picked up. He watched them, just distant sparks in the sun as the blades turned over the waves. Fast. Someone had ordered speed.

It was probably not an hour. Probably less than half of that before the distant galley had overtaken the near one. And had, on the way, answered Ben-Hur's hail. Both ships, it turned out, were Roman. The distant ship had come to investigate the unmanned one—and found the two men drifting on the sea.

CHAPTER 10

ROMAN

It was difficult to transfer Arrius into the boat. One of the oars-men recognized him as the tribune and commander of the fleet, and out of respect, the sailors were all too timid to grasp and haul him off the waterlogged bench. Judah had to take charge, reaching out from the gunwales with his long arms and using his enormous strength to lift the Roman into the bottom of the boat.

"And who are you?" the boat's captain said. "You look like a galley slave."

"He saved my life," Arrius whispered. "Show him every respect." He spoke no more, and the men rowed in silence back to the galley.

It was a strange moment for Ben-Hur when he mounted the deck of the ship. Within moments a steward had approached him with a robe. Soon there was a meal, and water was heated so that he and Arrius could wash off the salt water. A healer was summoned to look at Arrius's wound and insisted on rubbing a salve on the cuts on Ben-Hur's hands. The healer looked at his calluses and glanced at Judah's face but asked no questions. By then everyone knew that Ben-Hur was to be treated as Arrius's protégé. Belowdecks he could hear the hortator. Sometimes at night, he listened, twitching to the beat, to the creaking of the oars. It was strangely difficult to sleep on a couch, and he often rolled himself in a blanket and fell asleep on the floor.

Arrius recovered quickly from his wound and took command of the ship. When they rejoined the fleet, he and Judah transferred into the biggest galley, a trireme, and hoisted his flag. From the new ship he directed the action that captured the entire pirate fleet. Ben-Hur was fascinated to see how he managed both men and ships. By the time the entire Roman fleet and its captured ships returned to Misenum, the two men had spent hours discussing philosophies of war and leadership. When they walked down the gangplank onto the shore at Misenum, there was an obvious ease and affection between them. After the official greeting, the trumpets, the trophies, the speeches, the introductions, two men lingered to greet Arrius with warm embraces and laughter. One of them carried a laurel wreath that he tried to put on Arrius's head.

"No, Caius," Arrius said, laughing. "The man who deserves the laurels is this one—you'll know him from now on as young Arrius, because I am going to adopt him as my son. He fished me up after *Astraea* sank and held me on a piece of planking until we were rescued."

"Well, then, here you are," Caius said, turning to Ben-Hur. "Maybe you could bend your head. I can't quite reach it. Only Arrius would have the luck to be rescued from a burning ship."

Ben-Hur smiled and settled the laurel wreath onto his head with one hand. But when they walked past an altar to Fortuna, he caught

Arrius's eye and twitched it off his head. Arrius nodded and watched as Ben-Hur laid the tribute on the altar.

* * *

That gesture, it turned out, was typical of the young man. Arrius had known from their first meeting that he was intelligent, but his young protégé had an uncanny sense of what was expected of him. He watched and listened and acted with a perfect sense of tact. He spoke little until he had mastered the style of Latin spoken in Arrius's household. He resumed his education, studying mostly in Greek like other men of learning. He dressed like a Roman. He followed Arrius's style of worship. In time, Arrius adopted him and he was known throughout Rome as young Arrius.

Arrius wasn't given to examining men's motives, but he did wonder from time to time why the former slave stayed on with him. Gratitude? Obligation? Ambition? Or simply because there was nowhere else to go? When they'd first returned to Rome, Arrius had naturally inquired about the fate of the Hur family, but no information returned from Jerusalem, and even a private investigation found only dead ends. So perhaps to this late-come son of his, Roman life was as good a choice as any.

He certainly made good use of his opportunities. Mutual gratitude, both men found, could be a foundation for a friendship. Arrius spoke often of his position in the Roman government, and Ben-Hur paid attention. Before long, he was spending many hours each day in the famous Roman palaestra, which trained soldiers for battle or athletic competition. Which was just ritualized battle anyway.

To Arrius's pride and pleasure, Ben-Hur became known as a fierce competitor and skilled fighter. He had a hunger for knowledge. To his hours in the palaestra, he added weeks in military camps, observing and eventually joining the ranks of the young officers. He was admired but not especially liked. He smiled very little and rarely laughed.

If it hadn't been for the horses, Arrius thought, Ben-Hur would have become a hard man at a young age. Jerusalem was not an equestrian city—too dry, too congested—and Jews were more at home with donkeys. But the Roman army depended on its cavalry, and Ben-Hur turned out to be a natural horseman. He had a calm demeanor and met each new horse with an air of respectful curiosity. He learned to ride and drive and soon acquired the level of skill he expected of himself—which was complete mastery. And that did not surprise Arrius. But he also believed that Ben-Hur's care for his animals fed something essential in the young man. Other drivers stepped out of their chariots and tossed the reins to a groom, but Ben-Hur always walked his horses until they were cool, leading them on foot to watch their gait, their breathing, their communication with each other. He sometimes took the brushes and groomed them himself. The quiet of the stables, the simple tactile pleasure of leaning against the warm bulk of a horse gave him a comforting sense of a benign universe. He never connected it with the comfort and routine he had known in the Hur palace in Jerusalem.

For the rest, he watched and learned. He acquired deadly skills. He kept his ears open for mention of Messala, whose military career seemed to stall as he was transferred to one remote outpost after another. Five years passed this way, and when Arrius died, he left all of his immense property to Ben-Hur. It took several months to settle the estate, and during that time Ben-Hur made his preparations. He put an overseer in Arrius's villa in Misenum. He politely declined suggestions that he run for political office; people had evidently forgotten that he was a Jew and could never be a Roman citizen. And one day he simply vanished from Rome. He had spent five years making the most of Roman military training. Now, for the first time since Valerius Gratus crumpled to the ground outside the

Hur palace, he was free. So he took ship and headed east. His father had a business manager in Antioch, a port where the silk and spice roads from the East met the shores of the Inland Sea. This Simonides might have news of Naomi and Tirzah. It was a long way to go for a very slight hope.

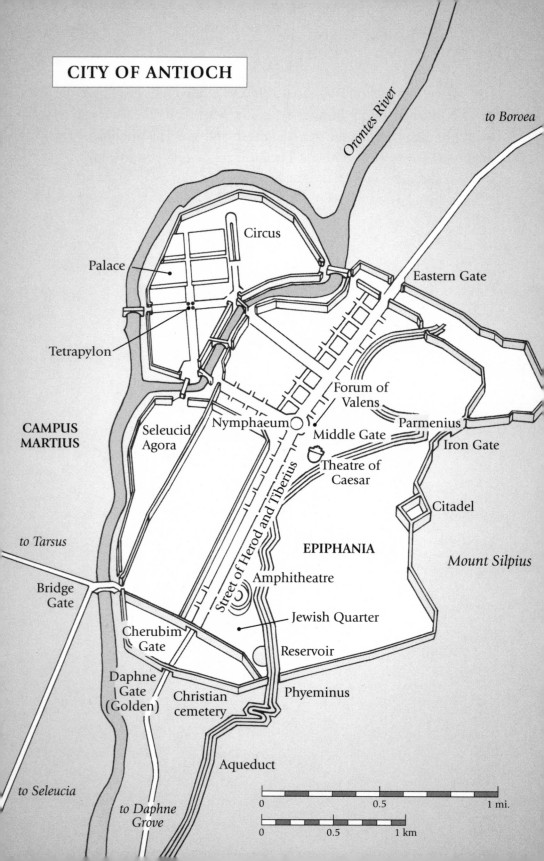

CITY OF ANTIOCH

Orontes River

to Boroea

Circus

Palace

Eastern Gate

Tetrapylon

CAMPUS MARTIUS

Forum of Valens

Parmenius

Seleucid Agora

Nymphaeum

Middle Gate

Iron Gate

Theatre of Caesar

Citadel

to Tarsus

Street of Herod and Tiberius

EPIPHANIA

Mount Silpius

Bridge Gate

Amphitheatre

Jewish Quarter

Cherubim Gate

Reservoir

Daphne Gate (Golden)

Christian cemetery

Phyeminus

to Seleucia

Aqueduct

to Daphne Grove

| 0 | | 0.5 | | 1 mi. |

| 0 | | 0.5 | | 1 km |

PART 3

CHAPTER 11

BROKEN

Esther could tell it was going to be a good day for her father. He never complained, but he couldn't control the gray tinge his skin took on when his injuries bothered him. He would not admit pain, of course, and once he had fully recovered from the second beating, he never allowed her to nurse him. But she knew it all. He had been unconscious when they brought him back the second time and for days had lingered near death while she and the servants and the healers did what they could to repair his broken body. It seemed to her at the time that he was making up his mind whether to live or not. Or possibly waiting to see what force might emerge that would allow him to live. Most of the time, she thought that force was anger, burning like a tiny, fierce flame somewhere at his core.

So on days when the servant wheeled him into the atrium and his dark eyes gleamed, she was glad. On a day like that he would eat a little bit more. He might let her wheel him out onto the balcony overlooking the River Orontes, to survey the ships of his fleet that lay moored below. To please her, he might even close his eyes and rest in the middle of the afternoon, during the sultry hours when nobody else in all of Antioch was doing anything more strenuous than slowly plying a fan. He might even tease her a little bit, gently.

On this day one of his ships had returned from the far side of the world with an impressive cargo of spices. When Esther pushed her father's special wheeled chair into his office, his assistant Malluch was already there, arranging a series of small ivory boxes on the big worktable. There was much sniffing of various brown and tawny powders, along with exclamations about purity and freshness. The scents of cinnamon and turmeric began to cover the familiar odor of seaweed and mud wafting up from the riverbank below.

The business was not Esther's primary focus. As her father and Malluch worked their way through a bundle of papers, she moved around the house, from rooftop to cellar. Her concern was simple: her father's comfort and health. Housekeeping was not easy when you lived over a warehouse next to a wharf. But Simonides could sit on a balcony and watch the crates and bales and barrels travel from the hold of a just-arrived ship into the vast warehouse and watch them leave again on wagons or camels or smaller ships for ports on the Inland Sea. On an especially good day he even consented to be carried down the stairs and gently lowered into a small skiff so that Malluch might row him around the ships swinging at anchor in the river. He claimed he could learn a great deal about his captains by the state of their ships' hulls.

So Esther battled the dust and the disorder, the noise and the smells. Her father's satisfaction each time one of his ships arrived was her reward. They flew small canary-yellow flags at their mastheads on the return from a trading voyage to indicate success from far away. Esther could not remember the last time one of her father's ships returned without the yellow flag. She had heard a competitor joke about this once in the market: "His camels only die of old age; his ships never sink; his slaves never cheat him."

That was true. But he would never walk again, nor live a day without pain. Esther thought his trading triumphs were poor consolation. Yet she admired her father immensely. He had kept his secret through the first beating, though the Romans had left him bleeding and unconscious. Months later they had come back. Esther's mother had pleaded with her husband, begging him to give up the secret. Esther did not hear the reply—she was only a teenager at the time, lurking outside her parents' bedroom door—but she knew what it was. Her father had been entrusted with his owner's estate. He would yield it to the heir and no one else.

As she trotted down the stairs to the courtyard, where the slaves were beating the carpets, Esther liked to think she would do the same thing as her father. But who could say where their own courage ended? And who would wish for that trial?

From the courtyard to the kitchen she bustled, from the kitchen back up to the rooftop, where her father worked in a small house surrounded by a garden, invisible from the hurly-burly of the docks. She squeezed a few oranges and poured the juice for her father and Malluch, serving it along with a dish of dates and another of blanched almonds. She and Malluch had an understanding: Malluch would eat, hoping that Simonides would absentmindedly do the same. So far it was only the assistant who got fat, but Esther did not give up easily.

She ran back down the stairs and into the warehouse, where rats had been spotted in a dark corner. She threaded her way without thinking through the aisles of barrels and shelving, bolts of fabric and sacks of grain. In one corner a slave was sweeping a pile of peppercorns onto a paper, turning away to sneeze so as not to lose a single precious one.

She almost ran into the man. He was wandering slowly, looking everywhere with visible fascination, as she came around a tall stack of carpets. She jumped back, startled, and instantly felt two large hands on her shoulders, steadying her.

"Forgive me!" a deep voice said. "No one seems to be here to ask . . ."

Esther moved out of his grasp and answered, "How can I help you?"

"I was told I might find Simonides here," the stranger answered. She looked past him, to where the watchman should have been standing at the warehouse entrance.

"There was no one at the gate?" she said. "No one at the door?"

"No, but many men gathered at the dock. Something seems to have gone wrong with the unloading. There was a donkey in the water."

Just then the watchman came into sight, followed by half a dozen other workmen, and Esther nodded. She took another half step away from the stranger and looked at him properly for the first time. "This is the house of Simonides. May I know who is seeking him?" He was tall, this man, and strikingly handsome. His dark hair and eyes suggested he was Jewish; his finely woven linen robe and soft leather sandals indicated wealth.

"Forgive me," the man said, "but I would rather save my tale for Simonides. It is complicated."

Esther hesitated. Her father hated to have strangers in his office. He claimed the Romans were still trying to spy on him to find his master's fortune. But the man before her didn't look Roman.

"Come with me, then," she said and led him to the stairs. As they climbed, Malluch came down and stopped on the landing so that they might pass. He raised his eyebrows at Esther, who simply kept climbing. She noticed that the man behind her was not breathing hard, though most newcomers found the stairs steep and long.

Her father must have heard two sets of footsteps, one of which was new to him. When Esther and the stranger entered the rooftop office, Simonides's chair was in the center of the room, below the wide purple-mica skylight. Esther happened to be watching as her father caught sight of the man's face behind her, and for a moment he turned paler than usual, while his hand clenched a fold of his heavy silk robe. But he recovered instantly.

"Who is this?" he asked mildly.

Having brought the stranger upstairs, Esther went to stand behind her father's chair and put a hand on his crooked shoulder. There was a tension in the room she did not understand. The tall man was staring at her father with a kind of hunger. "I am the son of Ithamar of the house of Hur, a prince of Jerusalem," he said, and Esther felt a shock go through her father. "The peace of our God be upon you and yours."

"And peace be with you," Simonides responded with a calm voice. "Esther, a seat for the young man?"

She picked up a sandalwood stool inlaid with mother-of-pearl and moved to set it next to the man, but he took it from her hands and placed it himself, at a respectful distance from her father. He did not sit.

"I apologize for coming here unexpectedly," he said. "I arrived in Antioch last night. As we came up the river, we passed one of your ships, and a fellow passenger told me a great deal about you. So of course since you knew my father . . ." His voice faltered.

"Certainly I knew Prince Hur," Simonides said. "Please, won't you sit down? And, Esther, would you pour a glass of wine for our visitor?"

She moved to a nearby table and filled a silver cup with wine, which she gave to the young man. But he still stood, and he didn't drink. "Am I right in understanding that you managed my father's businesses?"

Simonides paused before answering. Esther had gone back to

stand beside him, facing the visitor. She saw that the man was studying her father's face as if it might provide the answer to a puzzle.
"I did manage Prince Hur's business," Simonides said.

"And do you still?"

"Why do you want to know this?"

The visitor looked puzzled. "Because I am the son of Ithamar. If
you were in charge of my father's affairs . . ."

"Then they are yours now?" Simonides broke in. "You don't
imagine you're the first person to make this claim, do you?" Esther
moved closer to her father's chair. His voice—normally so clear, so
measured—had gone up a notch. "The prince left substantial assets
when he died," Simonides went on. "And when misfortune came to
the family, the Romans wanted to seize them. They . . ." Simonides
broke off but gestured with a hand to his chair and his crooked
body. "They tried to make me tell them where everything was," he
continued. "Twice."

The visitor looked at the cup in his hand and took two long steps
to return it to the table with the pitcher. "Forgive me," he said. "Of
course I didn't know. I have been in Rome for many years. I've made
a mistake. I realize it looks as if I came to claim my father's money,
but I did not. I was adopted by a Roman tribune who made me his
heir. I am already rich. I only came to see if you knew anything about
my family."

"What family?" Simonides asked, casually curious.

"When the Romans came and took me away, they took my
mother and my sister, Tirzah, too. But I went to the galleys. And my
family seems to have vanished completely."

"The galleys?"

"That day, the day of our misfortune . . ." He paused. "I should
explain. I was on the roof of our palace in Jerusalem, watching the
new procurator's entry. I knocked loose a tile and it hit the procurator. He was just slightly injured, but his guards broke into the palace

and took us all into custody. I was hauled off to sea. I don't know what's become of my mother and sister."

"What about the palace?" Simonides asked. "Who owns it now?"

"The emperor took it over. I was able to find that out. It apparently stands empty." The stranger paused and looked around the room for a moment as if he had forgotten why he was there. "Forgive me," he said. "I don't understand. If you are Simonides, and if you served Prince Ithamar of Hur . . . why don't you . . . ? I am his son," the man said, clasping his hands at his chest.

Esther was moved. He seemed so puzzled, even hurt. But she did not speak. In matters of business, her father always took the lead. "Do you have any proof?" Simonides asked mildly.

The man dropped his hands to his sides and stared. It was obvious that he had not thought of this. "No," he said, shaking his head slightly. Esther could almost see him running through the possibilities. "Arrius . . . He met me as a galley slave. I had already served for three years. I had nothing. Not even clothes. And before that, they took me away. . . ."

"No one can vouch for you?" Simonides's voice was still emotionless, and Esther began to feel impatience with him. Couldn't he see that this man was in distress?

"No," he answered. "No. I have no one from that life. If I could find my family, of course . . . Maybe the servants from our palace in Jerusalem, but they will have scattered, I'm sure. Those who weren't killed by the Romans."

"Well," Simonides said drily, "it is unfortunate. And I am sympathetic. But you see, I can't take any chances. Ithamar of the house of Hur left an immense estate. The Romans took what they could— ships, trading stock, warehouses. But they could not locate the gold. A business of that kind must possess a great deal of various currencies, in various locations. If I knew where they were—and I do not say that I do know—I would only transfer them to a true heir of the house of Hur. The Romans," he added, "are still looking for the gold. I know this for a fact."

The big man finally sat, suddenly, on the little stool. "Of course," he said. "I understand that."

"And there's something else as well," Simonides added. "You may not have thought of this either." He took a deep breath and straightened his spine to the extent that he could. "Prince Ithamar owned me. I was his slave. My daughter, Esther, is also a slave. Since you have served in the galleys, you may understand this better than most men who come here from Rome. But think about this: if a true heir of the house of Hur did survive, he would own me. He would own my daughter, who is all that is left of my family. He would own my house, my warehouse, every one of my ships, and everything they contain down to the last nail. Not to mention every single one of *my* slaves. So, you see, it is not very simple. You are asking me to give you everything. And I don't know who you are."

The stranger sat there for a long moment. Then he nodded and slowly stood. "Yes. I had not thought of that." There was a baffled look on his face. He bowed politely and said, "Forgive me. I will have to think . . ." He seemed to lose his train of thought, and his voice trailed off. Then he resumed, "I will have to think of something. May I call on you again if I do?"

"Of course," Simonides said, and this time Esther thought she heard a note of sympathy in his voice. "I am always here."

The younger man stood still for a few seconds, lost in thought. Esther felt she could almost see him recovering from the shock of his reception. Then he straightened up and turned to go.

After a few steps, he turned back. "Peace be with you and yours," he said to Simonides and bowed his head. "Thank you for talking to me."

"And peace be with you," Simonides answered.

As the man's footsteps receded down the stairs, Esther moved around to face her father. "Why were you so cruel to him?" she asked. "And so harsh?"

To her stupefaction, her father's face was aglow. "Dear Esther, only because I had to be. I must be absolutely certain. If that young man is who I think he is, he will find a way to prove his identity. But he gave me a terrible shock when he came in. He is the very image of his father."

"Couldn't you have been more sympathetic?"

"Come here," he said. "To my side. Sit." She pulled over the stool that the stranger had used and sat at her father's knees. He took both of her hands in his and she felt the crookedness of his fingers. "I have been waiting for this day. I never thought it would really come, but everything I have done for the last eight years was in hope of the moment that just passed. Everything!" He dropped her hands and clasped his own. Esther was alarmed to see a pair of tears trickling down his cheeks, but he wiped them away. "It's hard to grasp," he said. "I never really thought young Judah could have survived. What that man must have been through!"

"Young Judah?" Esther repeated. "He didn't tell you his name."

"His father spoke of him often. He was very proud of the boy."

Esther began to protest again. "But—"

"No." Her father cut her off, shaking his head. "Think, Esther. If that man is who I think he is, he owns you. And me and everything we see here and downstairs and out on the dock and in the harbor and as far away as the western seas. *He owns you.* For myself, I don't mind. If he is truly Judah Ben-Hur, my work is done. But for your sake I must assure myself that he is his father's son in character as well as looks. Ring for Malluch. I will send him after young Judah. He is new to Antioch. I expect he will visit the Grove of Daphne. There could hardly be a better test of a man's moral fiber."

CHAPTER 12
MANY GODS

Ben-Hur ran down the steep stairs as quickly as he could and threaded his way through the warehouse out to the docks. Without thought, he cut through the crowded narrow streets, heading away from the waterfront. Away from the smells, from the creak of the hulls against the docks, from the clatter of rigging and constant chorus of shouts and the half-naked bodies of the slaves loading and unloading the cargoes. From anything that reminded him of his own years of slavery. When his only escape had been thoughts of his family.

He kept going, walking aimlessly but quickly. Walking so as not to think. Scanning the streets, taking note of the crowds. Antioch was the trading center of this end of the Inland Sea. The silk roads from the East ended here, at the port on the Orontes River. Ben-Hur was used to the bustle and crowds of Rome, but Antioch had a different flavor, a richer palette. Fur-trimmed hats passed him, along with turbans and headscarves and skullcaps. Here a magenta sleeve, there a voluminous black robe. Every man absorbed, pursuing his own business.

And what should *his* business be? Ben-Hur wondered. What could he do next? How could he prove who he was?

He could not blame Simonides, he told himself, but a pulse of anger raced through him all the same. Was his word not good enough? Was this the end of his hope?

Then the image of the daughter came to him. The daughter, also a slave. *His* slave, if he could prove his identity. Modest, soft-spoken, competent. She had a beautiful voice. And green eyes. Her father had been crippled to protect the Hur property. Crippled by the Romans.

Unaware, Ben-Hur lengthened his stride. More than once he jostled someone in the crowd, but one look at his forbidding face stifled any protest. He found himself clenching his fists and forced himself to relax them. He and Simonides had so much in common! Why would the man not acknowledge it?

He walked on, more slowly now. The streets had opened up, and he was on a straight paved highway worthy of Rome itself, with balustraded lanes marked out for pedestrians, chariots, and men on horseback. The roadways themselves were punctuated with marble statuary, and in the distance rose a green hill crowned by a temple.

The crowd around him had changed too. These were not individuals intent on business, but groups on holiday. There was singing. Some danced. Pipes and drums and bells competed with each other. A pair of young girls slipped past him, wearing nothing but a layer or two of rosy gauze and leading two snowy goats. Of course—he had found his way to the famous Grove of Daphne.

He'd heard about it in Rome. Sometimes young men in the palaestra would brag about days on end spent there, singing and drinking and consorting with the servants of the temples. There were no limits to the pleasures, it seemed. Tales were told of those who never returned, choosing to spend their lives in the service of this god or that. The grove was dedicated to Apollo, but the entire Roman pantheon was worshiped, as well as some of the earlier deities, spirits of wood and water. Pan was said to roam the grounds with his satyrs. Bacchus was celebrated.

Bacchus, god of wine. Pan, who led his followers into wild adventures, running free to satisfy all desires. What would that be like?

Not like the galleys, Ben-Hur thought savagely. Not like the dark, brutal, hopeless years at the oar. His eye fell on a white bull ahead of him, laden with wicker baskets of grapes. A pudgy blond boy rode easily on its back, squeezing the grapes into a golden goblet and offering the goblet to all who passed.

Even in Rome, Ben-Hur had led a measured life. A manly life, with hours of military drill, increasing skill with weapons, constant striving toward greater strength. Conversation at Arrius's table had been serious. Rome's domination of the Inland Sea, the governance of the colonies, naval tactics, the problems of supplying troops, financing exploration—these were the subjects Arrius had enjoyed. Some people felt Rome was creeping toward decadence, but Arrius's Rome was stern and upright. Antioch appeared to be its opposite.

The road to the grove ended at a lush meadow furred over with grass of an eye-searing green. Ben-Hur lifted his eyes to the tall trees and saw dozens he could not name. Some bloomed vivid pink or white. A cool breeze carried an intensely sweet odor, almost too heavy to be pleasant. Streams meandered among the trees, pausing to gather into ponds or rushing downward over artful waterfalls. A young man wearing only a loincloth dashed from a glade, followed by three long-haired girls carrying garlands of flowers. They shrieked; he laughed. They captured him and toppled into a pile of gleaming limbs. The young man looked up and caught Ben-Hur's eye. "Come join us!" he called.

And why not? What else was there? Ben-Hur walked on but

kept wondering. Who would know if he did? What if he spent an afternoon lolling on that soft grass? What if some golden-haired girl played the lyre for him and fed him grapes? What if he slept on moss, woke at twilight, followed Pan? Who would care?

No one. He knew no one in Antioch—and apparently no one knew him. Simonides had been the last link to his family. Simonides refused to acknowledge him as Judah Ben-Hur. Enough, then! Enough of the Roman rectitude, the Jewish patience and faith in a future. All around, the crowds were dissolving along the winding paths, vanishing among the trees, joining dances. If he was not recognized as Judah Ben-Hur, just who was he? And why stay true to the faith of his fathers? Ten commandments! How many of them had he broken, anyway, while living as a Roman? Worshiping multiple gods, ignoring the Sabbath . . . and killing. He'd killed without hesitation, floating on that slippery plank in the burning sea.

So why not enjoy what was so plainly offered here? Why hold back from these pleasures so freely displayed and so apparently natural?

He stepped off the path. The grass was soft beneath his sandals, springy as a cushion but cool. A citron tree rose ahead of him, its smooth bark wrapping around a trunk naturally shaped into the form of a chair. Suddenly Ben-Hur was tired. The tension of his voyage from Rome, his anxiety to find Simonides, his disappointment all washed over him. The grass all around was dappled with sun and shade, the air moving just enough to create a soft current against the skin. He sat beneath the tree, stretching out his long legs before him. A glance upward showed blossoms, fruit, and tiny fragments of blue sky through the foliage. He leaned back and within moments was asleep.

✳ ✳ ✳

Malluch had watched it all. The young man might or might not be young Prince Hur—either way he was conspicuous and unaware of it. Walking a few paces behind, Malluch had seen the passersby eyeing the young man with curiosity, admiration, and more. The women in particular could not tear their eyes away.

Not only that—Malluch could also read the man's emotions from his very walk. First angry, unfocused, desperate to put distance behind him, heading anywhere. Then settling down, resigned, more curious about his surroundings. And now, in the Grove of Daphne . . . Well, the young man was succumbing, wasn't he? It was almost funny how openly he stared. You might think he had never seen a naked woman. And he'd turned away from the couple on the tiger-skin rug with what seemed like shock.

It took some people that way, the grove. Any pleasure available, under the guise of worship. No wonder the young man had fallen asleep. It was one way to shut out the temptations. And not a bad idea in the heat of the day. So Malluch followed suit, lying in the grass a few yards away.

The trumpets woke them both. Malluch sat up slowly, clasping his skullcap to his head and pulling his robe down over his knees. The young man was staring at him, startled.

"Forgive me," Malluch said. "I saw a man of my faith dozing beneath a tree and thought it was a wise idea. Peace be with you."

"And with you also," the man answered. "Did you hear trumpets? Or was I dreaming?" As he spoke, they sounded again, a sharp fanfare.

"As you hear," Malluch said. "They'll sound once more."

"What for? That's a military noise for a place like this."

"It's a summons to the stadium." Malluch got to his feet and brushed off his robe. "We've slept through the heat of the day. Now that it's cooler, they'll start the contest."

"What contest is that?"

Malluch was impressed to see how lightly the man stood up, almost leaping to his feet.

"The chariots. Is this your first visit to the grove?"

"It is. Do you know the way to the stadium?"

"Oh, of course. I live here in Antioch. My name is Malluch, and I am a merchant. I would be happy to have your company."

"I am Judah," the tall man said. "For the last five years I have lived in Rome, where I learned to drive, so of course I am curious about your Eastern horses."

They made their way to the stadium through a belt of cypress trees in an open area between two hillsides. The sun of late afternoon gilded half of the dirt track, while the two pavilions for spectators nestled in shade.

"It's laid out on Roman lines," Judah said, sounding surprised.

"Oh yes. I believe the measurements were taken from the Circus Maximus. We are far from the empire's center here, but Roman ways dominate."

"So I see," Judah commented as a chariot drawn by four horses abreast entered the circuit of the track. "They drive four horses? The drivers must be skillful," he added.

"Roman sport, Roman standards," Malluch said with a shrug. "Look, here come the other teams. Let's sit."

So the two men found a pair of seats high up in one of the stands, where the entire circuit of the track was visible. Malluch watched Judah, who was focused wholly on the teams, eyes ranging from one to another, comparing, admiring, doubting. Some trotted; some walked. One driver leapt down to adjust the simple harness, then walked slowly in front of his team, tweaking a rein here and a halter there, pulling a handful of mane from beneath a horse's collar. "Those grays are too calm," said Judah. "And too big. Military horses, maybe, trained for the field. Strong enough to carry an armed man, steady enough to tolerate battle. But they won't be fast or nimble."

As he finished speaking, a new team entered the stadium and began trotting along the outside of the track. "Now those horses!"

Judah said. "Will you look at them? Those are the true Arabs. I doubt the emperor himself has anything finer." Even Malluch, who often went for days without seeing a horse, could appreciate how splendid they were. Perfectly matched bays, with dark-brown coats shading to black at the legs and muzzle, they seemed almost too small for their task. But what they lacked in height, they made up for in curved muscle: the lavishly arched necks, the deep chests, the rounded quarters—all spoke of power compressed, while their gleaming coats and long, untrimmed manes signaled perfect condition.

Indeed, they were hard to hold back. The driver stood braced on the chariot's floor, the reins stretched tight in his hand with the ends wrapped around his body, but despite his hold on them, the two inner horses began cantering. One on the outside joined in; one still trotted, then gave in. In a flash all four were galloping, but their strides did not match. The driver leaned back farther, hauling on the reins with all his weight. Even so, he could not control the speed. Down the track, the slower chariots scattered. Judah left Malluch and ran down the bank of seats to the rope slung between upright javelins that marked the edge of the stands. Around the curve they came, the runaway bays, now matching strides, eating up the ground, but the driver was utterly helpless.

"Aiiiieeee!" came a voice from the other end of the stand. "Stop them!"

Judah glanced over to see a small figure, a white-bearded Arab in black robes. "Go! Go to their heads," he shouted to the group of men around him. "They won't make the next turn!" In an instant half a dozen tall young men had run onto the track, fanning out across its width.

"They'll be killed!" Malluch exclaimed, arriving at Judah's elbow.

"No, look," the taller man answered. "They know him." The heaviest of the men—a sturdy, short-haired fellow in white—had caught the bridle of the bay on the outside. Running alongside for just a few seconds, he had broken the momentum of its flight. In an instant, each of the horses had a man at its side, running along, then trotting, speaking soothing words.

By the time the chariot drew level with where the old man had sat, he was down on the track. He stood before the team, and the other men all drew back. One by one the horses came to him, completely calm now, rubbing his chest with their heads, nuzzling his shoulders. He spoke to each of them quietly and ran his hand down their slender legs. Then he stood back. The horses did not move but watched him attentively.

Then their owner walked back to the chariot, where the driver stood panting in the dirt. His left arm, which had held the reins, hung loose as if damaged. He dug a toe into a print left by a hoof.

Nobody could hear what the Arab said to him, but Malluch and Judah were close enough to see the driver's face redden. He nodded, then handed the whip to the Arab and walked away. The Arab snapped his fingers, and one of his men leapt into the chariot, moving the horses off at a decorous walk.

"Who is he?" Judah asked. "Some desert chieftain?"

"Exactly," Malluch answered. "Sheik Ilderim. He controls a huge territory beyond Moab, along with immense herds of camels and access to the important oases. As you can imagine, he's rich . . . oh, vastly rich. His horses are legendary. Their lineage goes back to the stable of the first pharaoh. The horses live in the same tent as the sheik, and he treats them almost like his own children."

"And do you know the unfortunate driver?"

"No. Roman horsemen sometimes end up here, hoping to make a living by racing. Army veterans, most of them. And speaking of Romans, here is another."

Even at a distance, you could tell. Was it the gilding of the chariot? Certainly these were the only horses with cropped tails and manes, giving them a severe, almost-artificial appearance, like prancing sculptures on a frieze. The center two were black, the outer pair snow-white, and all wore red-and-yellow ribbons knotted into the short bristles of their manes. Applause had begun in the stands as the chariot came closer. Bronze flashed on the wheel hubs while each spoke was formed of an elephant's tusk. The chariot's basket was woven of gilded willow twigs, which Judah was admiring when something about the driver caught his gaze. His posture? The set of his shoulders? He rode easily, balancing with the movement of the light carriage, his fine red wool tunic fluttering around his knees. With a flick of his long whip, he urged the horses into a trot and then a canter.

It was as the chariot rounded the curve and headed directly toward him that Judah saw the driver's face. It was Messala.

CHAPTER 13

A DAMSEL

Messala! Judah couldn't take his eyes off the man. Dark-haired, handsome, slender, he steered his horses with what looked almost like carelessness. Yet he also had an air of command, as if he wore an invisible wreath of laurels. The crowd continued to applaud, and now, as his team passed the stands at a slow canter, many of them stood and cried his name: "Mess-a-la! Mess-a-la!"

"This man is quite a favorite here," Judah remarked, pleased that his voice sounded casual.

"So it would seem," Malluch answered. "Another wealthy Roman. What do you think of his horses?"

"They're impressive. I see he has Arabians as well, though it's a pity he crops their manes and tails. He's a good driver. The chariot is somewhat showy."

"Showy. A good way to put it! Worthy of Apollo himself," Malluch muttered.

But at that moment one of Sheik Ilderim's men stepped onto the empty track and called up to the stands. "Men of the East and West, I have a message from Sheik Ilderim! You have just seen his beautiful bays. You have seen that the driver could not control them. The sheik seeks a new driver for the race six days hence. As a prize he offers untold riches. Tell this news to men all over Antioch: The man who believes he can control the Sons of the Wind should make himself known to Sheik Ilderim the Generous."

The crowd buzzed in reaction, but Malluch noticed that his new friend Judah went still instead. As if he were thinking. As if the message were meant for him.

But Judah turned to Malluch and said, "Is there something more I should see? What else is the grove famous for?"

"There's a tradition that the first-time visitor should not leave without having his fortune told," Malluch answered.

"My fortune!" Judah answered. "What, should I go consult some ancient sibyl in a temple and receive an answer I can't understand?"

"No, no, there's nothing so ordinary here at the grove. Here we have the Fountain of Castalia. You buy a fresh piece of papyrus from a priest and dip it into the spring. Immediately writing appears on it, telling you your future. In verse."

"Well, I've heard of the spring. And I suppose the verse is worth a few pennies. Though I wonder if I believe such things. This is not a case where one can put a question to a deity?"

"No," Malluch conceded. "That's not the way it works."

"All right," Judah said, beginning to descend the grandstand steps. "I might as well see the famous fountain."

But he was silent as they walked. The way took them past a steep hillside, where a series of fountains spilled water from the highest level to end in a small lake, where tiny boats could be paddled with immense palm leaves. Judah did not seem to notice. Nor did he notice the band of priestesses walking in procession behind a pair of tambourines played by little girls. His open interest and enjoyment in the sights of the grove had vanished, and Malluch was concerned. In the brief time they'd been together, he had warmed to this stranger. Simonides had wanted to know what the man did in the grove, whether he met anyone, how he reacted. It was the horses, Malluch decided, that had turned his mood of enjoyment. Was he considering taking up Sheik Ilderim's challenge? Malluch's heart sank a little bit. From what he could tell, those bays could not be driven, least of all in a race. The competition in chariot racing was vicious, injuries frequent. Deaths, even, were not uncommon. Was it the money this young man sought?

✳ ✳ ✳

Judah would have laughed if he'd known Malluch's thoughts. Money! What use was that to him? As Arrius's adopted son, he possessed lands and gold in Rome, and Arrius's villa in Misenum waited ready for him, with servants prepared to welcome him at any moment. He would spend any amount to find his mother and sister. That was his only goal.

And now he had seen Messala! So his mind, as he and Malluch navigated the lovely trails through the Grove of Daphne, was focused entirely on his Roman enemy.

His enemy who thrived. The years had obviously been kind to Messala. Judah knew what horses like those cost and knew also that for the four on the track there were many more in training or recovering from injuries. The gilded wicker basket of Messala's chariot was light, but flimsy—he must need a new one almost every time the horses were exercised. The stables, the grooms, the trainers, the harnesses were all inordinately costly. And Messala enjoyed them; that was clear. He enjoyed the public's admiration. He looked like a man who had never known doubt.

Or pain. Or danger he hadn't chosen.

Let alone slavery.

Let alone terrible loneliness.

The guilt of having brought catastrophe on his mother and sister.

Except that it was Messala who had done that! Messala had stood in the courtyard of the Hur palace in Jerusalem and accused his friend Judah of murder, allowed him to be chained. Messala—who alone might know the fate of his mother and sister.

And as Judah Ben-Hur paced through the Grove of Daphne at Malluch's side, he barely saw the trees, the fountains, the lawns, the temples, the beauty and seduction. His mind was wholly set on vengeance.

Finally the two reached the Fountain of Castalia and Judah's interest in his surroundings revived. He joined the crowd around the fountain, examining the steep granite face from which flowed a jet of water. Below it stood a shell-shaped basin of black marble, where the water whirled and bubbled before draining away, and at its side, an old man who was accepting coins and plucking leaves of papyrus, which he would hand to the buyer. Apparently fortunes did appear, because time after time, a man would dip a leaf into the water and read, then exclaim and share his fortune with a friend.

Judah and Malluch had edged close to the priest, and Judah handed him a few small coins. He accepted the papyrus leaf and dipped it in the clear water of the fountain. But just at that moment, a distraction appeared. At the crest of the road leading down to the spring, a haughty, black-eyed face approached at a languid pace. Instants later, a long neck, a massive chest, and a gorgeous howdah followed—it was the largest white camel anyone had ever seen.

Tall, silky, dignified, the camel trod silently down to the fountain, and the people fell back. Camels were nasty; everyone knew that—and this camel, superlative in every other sense, was probably nastier as well. It was led by an enormous Nubian on horseback, who kept well out of range of that mobile mouth. And as the group came closer, it was possible to see the occupants of the howdah. Even Judah stared.

The man was old. That was the first thing you would say about him. You could barely add anything else, he was so tiny and wrinkled and frail-looking. He wore an immense green silk turban that looked as if it would crush his head. But his eyes, Judah noticed, were bright, as dark as the camel's and far livelier.

Judah's eyes lingered on the old man, but no one else paid attention, for the other passenger was a woman. And even in Daphne, where female charms were casually displayed, she was remarkable. Women of her rank were not as a rule seen in public. Their beauties were saved for their families. Judah's mother had never left the palace of Hur without covering her hair and drawing her veil across her face. But this woman was bold. She sat tall in the howdah, looking out with careless interest at the crowd, her eyes passing from face to face, noting the fountain and the priest, apparently unconscious of the stares. Straight blue-black hair framed her face, then poured over her back and shoulders. Her skin was pale yet still somehow warm, her eyes dark, her features fine, emphasized by kohl around her eyes and cochineal on her lips and cheeks. Gold armlets shaped like asps clasped their tails in their mouths high above her elbows, and tiny golden coins woven into a glittering web draped over her hair in what could have been called a veil. But it displayed rather than hid her beauty.

She spoke a few words to the Nubian, who reined in his horse and dismounted. The camel halted, then collapsed to its knees with indolent grace. The woman reached out, holding a golden chalice to the slave. Someone was thirsty.

The crowd around the spring had fallen silent to enjoy this

unusual spectacle. They parted to let the Nubian approach the fountain. Even the priest watched him fill the chalice. But as the Nubian turned back to the camel and its riders, his horse whinnied and shifted its weight.

Ben-Hur turned quickly, frowning, and the crowd followed suit. They all heard the same sound, then saw its source: a chariot racing toward them, drawn by four horses at a gallop. Two white, two black, and the driver cracking his whip over their heads.

The masses scattered in a flash, but no camel reacts that quickly. The Nubian dropped the chalice in the fountain, but before he could reach his master, Ben-Hur stepped forward. In two long strides he had reached the oncoming four-horse team and grasped the harness of the horse nearest him. He braced his legs and held firm while the horse reared, pulling its nearest fellow up with him.

The chariot's yoke rose, upsetting the basket. In a flash, the driver cut the reins wrapped around his chest and leapt free of the wreckage. He glanced at Ben-Hur and walked boldly to the camel.

"Apologies!" he cried as he approached. "I did not see you in the crowd. I planned to pull up in time." He smiled at the how-dah's occupants. "I admit I was hoping to have a joke on these good people. By frightening them a little, you know. Making them run like chickens. The joke is on me instead." He looked at Ben-Hur and added, "Thank you, my man, for your quick action."

Then he turned back to the howdah and said, "I am Messala, and I sincerely beg your pardon. Sir, I regret having disturbed you. And you, my fair lady, all the more for your beauty. Do tell me you forgive me!" Ben-Hur could see how the Roman's eyes ran over the woman's face and lingered on her bare arms, but she seemed unperturbed. Instead of answering him, she spoke to Ben-Hur, still standing at the horses' heads.

"Sir," she said, "my father is thirsty." She produced another golden goblet, the twin of the one dropped in the fountain. "Could you fill this for him? We would both be grateful."

Messala laughed. "I see I'm to be ignored. All right, my fair one. But I will seek you out and know more of you. There's no lovelier woman in Antioch; I swear it." He moved over to take the bridle of his horse from Ben-Hur. The two men were face-to-face, hands almost touching on the harness for an instant. Malluch was close enough to see that Ben-Hur stiffened as if holding himself back, and his face as he turned to the howdah was stony and pale. For a few seconds, he looked like a much older man. Then Ben-Hur relinquished the bridle and stepped over toward the camel.

"I'm happy to serve you," he said to the woman and took the chalice. Malluch noticed that as Ben-Hur walked to the fountain, the woman watched Messala, now busy with his team's harness. She did not seem the least bit embarrassed by his flirtatious manner. Malluch thought for a moment of Simonides's daughter, Esther, who would never act so boldly, and wondered what country this beauty had come from.

When Ben-Hur returned to the camel with the full goblet, he handed it to the woman. She passed it to her father, steadying it as he drank with shaky hands. When he had finished, she held it out to Ben-Hur, saying, "Thank you. The chalice is yours, full of our blessings." At a signal from the Nubian, the camel unfolded its legs and stood, impassive as ever, then began to move away.

"Halt," the old man said in a quiet but steely voice. He peered out of the howdah to address Ben-Hur. "I am grateful for your intervention today and I thank you in the name of the one God. I am Balthasar the Egyptian. Not far from here lies the Great Orchard of the Palms. My daughter and I are the guests there of Sheik Ilderim. I hope you will come to see us so that I can express my gratitude more fully."

Then the camel moved off silently, following the Nubian slave on his horse. Ben-Hur noticed for the first time that the horse was another beautiful Arabian. He turned to Malluch.

"I think I will have to go to this Orchard of the Palms, don't you? For Balthasar the Egyptian, if not for the sake of the sheik's horses."

Malluch smiled. But he thought the woman might have her own attractions for his new friend.

CHAPTER 14

DARKNESS

When one sense is useless, the others become stronger. Hearing, for instance. You would not think that bare skin on bare stone would make a noise. But it does.

Breathing. If you share a small space with another human, you know that person's breath. In, out. Quiet. You can hear when they're sleeping.

You can hear when they aren't.

Hair has its own sound. Tirzah could not be sure, but she thought her mother's hair might have gone white. How could she know that? It might sound heavier? Coarser?

Hair was important. They tried to keep it controlled. They had no combs, of course. But they spent some time each day grooming each other. It was something to do. It was some comfort. Each woman took her turn leaning back against the other woman's knees. They curled up their fingers and ran their hands through the tangled locks, working patiently to unravel knots and snarls.

Patiently, my God! Patience! There was no hurry in here.

Wherever *here* was.

They had talked about it at first. How far they'd been taken. How big it seemed. The thickness of the walls. They'd been blindfolded as they were taken from the Hur palace, but Tirzah almost laughed to think how much she and her mother could have learned, if only they'd understood how. They could have counted the steps. They could have listened for echoes. They could have taken notice of the commands.

They hadn't been put on horseback. Naomi thought she'd heard hooves on the street, but Tirzah wasn't sure. After all, they hadn't been listening carefully. Had someone mentioned the Antonia Tower? Shouldn't they remember? It didn't feel like a tower, where they were. But every memory of that violent moment was confused.

It had all been so sudden, a sunny morning in Jerusalem shattered. Lives upended. Blood on the tiles. Just as well to be blindfolded. After all, it didn't matter where they were. Because wherever it was, they were not getting out.

Steps coming. Tirzah heard her mother wake up.

Maybe you didn't hear things as much as you felt them: the door of the next cell opening sent a tiny current of air through the sliding hatch between them. Tirzah heard Naomi pad, skin on stone, to the hatch and put down the wooden plate. And the pitcher.

The hatch slid open. The plate skidded through. The smell changed with the air from the next cell. And the food. On the wooden plate pushed through in exchange. Fish, possibly.

Tirzah felt saliva come into her mouth. It was amazing, really. After all this time. Years at least—they had calculated that much. All this time, and her body still wanted to survive.

For herself, Tirzah was not at all sure.

But she had not yet worked out a way to kill herself in the dark.

CHAPTER 15
SECRET

Where there is a port, there are taverns. Some are cheerful, bright, clean. Aboveboard. Others are not. Because where there is a port, there is money changing hands in an incessant stream. It takes many forms, only one of which is coin. It could be cargo ending up in the wrong place. It could be humans—their bodies or their minds—sold or selling themselves. It could be information. Taverns provide a marketplace free of scrutiny. Any man can go to one and meet any other man. By chance, as it were.

Any man could sit down at a splintered table with a rough pottery cup before him. He could lean into a corner, see and not be seen. Watch.

Only a Roman, though, would stride into such a place as if he owned it. Only a Roman would carelessly throw a cloak over a fine woolen tunic to visit the seedy side of town. In a port, where everyone knew how to judge fabric at a glance. Or the outline of a dagger making angles beneath the cloak. Or a gold ring. Real gold—nothing shines like it.

The Roman spotted his man and threaded through the tables to him. Sat down, his back to the room. The man suppressed a sigh and hoped he got paid before the Roman got knifed.

He was agitated. That wasn't good either. Spying is a job best done without emotion, for people who are similarly controlled. This Roman, Messala, had already shown himself to be vain and heedless. The spy was wondering if he wasn't also stupid.

"Simonides had a visitor," the spy announced.

"Is that all? From what you've told me, he has visitors all the time," Messala answered testily.

"True, but I've figured out who they all are by now. This one was unusual."

"And?"

"And you have no idea how hard this job is. I've told you over and over, Simonides is cautious. Most of the time I'm in a room in the warehouse with my slate, counting things. What is it exactly you're looking for, anyway? I could do the job better if I knew."

Without looking up, the Roman signaled to a serving man. Two fingers: two cups of wine. They arrived, slopping onto the table. The serving man hovered, waiting for payment. Messala looked up. The man was tall, with deep-set eyes and a broken nose. Messala found a few coins and slapped them down on the table. He pushed a cup toward the spy, then took a deep swallow from his own. From the face he made, the spy thought it wasn't the kind of wine he was used to.

"All right. So who was this visitor you're so excited about?"

"A tall Jew, possibly new to Antioch. He had to ask the way. He went down to the dock first. Then to the warehouse. The watchman wasn't at the gate—and he heard about that later from that dog Malluch. So the man went right in."

"Did you watch him? Follow him?"

"Of course I did. What are you paying me for?"

"And?"

"He just looked around. Like he'd never seen a warehouse before. Didn't touch anything. Then the daughter found him. He asked for her father by name. And she took him right upstairs."

"What's upstairs?"

"The rooftop, where Simonides mostly stays. Hardly anyone gets up there. He's no fool, the old man."

"Did you follow them? Hear anything?" Messala had drained his cup and was looking around to find the server.

"No, that's what I'm telling you! There's no way to get close to him!"

Messala turned back and looked directly at the spy. "Well, what good are you, anyway?"

"Do you want to wait and let me tell you what I did find out?" the spy asked. "Or maybe you should pay me first." He finished his first cup of wine and took a swallow from the second.

Messala moved. Perhaps he was going to stand up and leave. The spy sat still, considering. Now he had some new information. Messala was a nervy, difficult client. The spy was tired of him. And what Messala was looking for didn't seem to be there anyway. Gold that didn't belong to the shipping business? Records relating to an enterprise in Jerusalem? The spy was good at his job, and those things did not exist in the house on the river.

So what did it mean that this Roman soldier was so . . . ? What was he? the spy wondered, watching Messala toss back his second cup of wine. Tense? Excited, really. Excited about this tall Jew who had visited Simonides. Jew. Jerusalem. Hmm.

He just sat still while all these thoughts ran swiftly through his head. Really it didn't matter whether Messala listened to him or not; he would get paid for what he had learned. "You're not the only person looking for him," he improvised. A lie, but one that might squeeze more money out of Messala. "And he stands out." Not that it mattered, but Messala didn't know that.

"All right." Messala slapped a coin on the table. The spy picked it up and held it in a shaft of light. Caesar's face on it. Always good to be paid in Roman coin, he thought. Say what you would about them, their money held its value.

"Your fellow just arrived in Antioch today. So that was the first thing he did, right? Go to see the Jewish merchant. I happened to be outside when he left. Whatever he came for, he didn't get it. He stormed out of there." He stopped and drank more wine.

"That's all?" Messala asked, pushing back the bench to leave.

"No," the spy answered tranquilly. "Because I waited around for a little while. Counting barrels outside. Looking busy. So when Malluch left five minutes later, he didn't even see me. But he took off after the tall Jewish man."

"Describe him."

"Malluch? He doesn't look like anything. Honestly that fellow disappears—"

"No, you fool, the Jew. What did he look like?"

A repeated question. Interesting. "I wasn't close to him, you know, but in general—very tall. Dark hair. Young—maybe about your age. Simple clothes, linen robe and sandals, but high quality. Looks rich, but doesn't care about it, I would guess. Moves well. Strong."

"Looks rich?" Messala asked. "What do you mean by that?"

"Well, like you. Clean, strong. Stands up straight, steps out like he owns the road."

Messala stood. "Not possible. No Jew could own the road," he snarled. He looked down at the spy. "All right. Let me know if anything else happens."

The spy nodded and leaned back, then watched his client leave. He watched the faces of the men who looked after Messala. A few of them narrowed their eyes, and one of them spat. It was not a tavern where Romans were welcome. The spy wondered if, as a Roman, you just got used to being hated.

CHAPTER 16
OASIS

The Orchard of the Palms lay east of the Grove of Daphne. As Malluch explained it to Ben-Hur, the distance could be covered in two hours on horseback or one hour on camelback.

Ben-Hur looked up at the sky. "Faster is better, I would say, wouldn't you? Do we risk being benighted?"

"Oh no," Malluch said. "I will go back to Antioch afterward and I'll get there before it's truly dark."

"But you can't—why would you go all the way to the oasis, just to leave again?"

"Because I've never seen it," Malluch said. "Not everyone gets invited to visit the sheik. And besides, Jews help each other."

Ben-Hur slapped him on the back, and Malluch stumbled a little. The man didn't know his own strength, apparently. And when it came time to haggle with the man who hired out camels, Ben-Hur expertly brought the price down to what Malluch knew was appropriate. Useful skills, Malluch thought.

The two beasts available were undistinguished, resembling the tall white camel from the grove only in the basic features: large eyes, a haughty expression, and a plunging, uncomfortable gait. Ben-Hur sat uneasily in the saddle at first. Malluch watched as he concentrated, shifting his weight, resisting or accommodating the long, lurching strides. Ben-Hur caught his eye. "Not much like riding a horse, is it?"

"You never rode a camel in Rome?"

"Why bother, when you can sit comfortably on the fastest horses in the world? The emperor's stables are famous, and what he cares for, all Romans care for." Ben-Hur adjusted his position on the wooden saddle, then said, "And speaking of horses, what more can you tell me about Sheik Ilderim?"

Malluch nodded. He had been anticipating the question. "As you may expect, his people are nomads. They control huge tracts of land. They don't own it as we do. In fact, the land is valuable only because it provides grazing for their herds and because people have to pay him to cross it."

"Why would Ilderim be entering his horses in this race if he doesn't have a driver for them?"

"You ask good questions," Malluch said with a sideways glance. "We all have our weaknesses. By reputation Ilderim is canny, making only the decisions that will benefit his tribe. But when it comes to Rome, he is different."

"I wonder if that isn't true of everyone in this part of the world," Ben-Hur suggested.

"Of course it's not," Malluch answered. "Many people do very well under Roman rule. The roads are magnificent; the taxes are collected; the little wars among neighboring peoples are suppressed. Trade flourishes. You can get anything, anywhere." He did not continue, and Ben-Hur now looked curiously at him.

"But?" he asked. "Many people do well, but what?" Malluch didn't answer, and Ben-Hur went on. "Oh, I understand. I have been living as a Roman! So you believe I think like one?" He laughed, but there was a bitter tone to it. "No, Malluch. I assure you, I love the Romans even less than your sheik. Finish his story. And then, if we still have time, I will tell you mine. But if Rome is your villain, I will not be dismayed. Or surprised."

"All right. When I say that Ilderim controls territory, part of that control means that he guarantees the safety of people passing through. At his oases, in the passes between his hills, in the long, flat stretches of desert, travelers need not fear brigands if they are under the sheik's protection. For a price, of course. So of course the Roman tax collectors voyage through his lands if possible. You can imagine the temptation they present: trains of camels laden with boxes of gold. It takes the strength of a Sheik Ilderim to keep them safe."

"What would happen if, for example, a group of Parthians happened to capture such a camel train?"

"Ilderim has his . . . You cannot call it an army, because to me that means lines of Romans marching behind their flags. Ilderim arms and trains and maintains these groups of—well, to be honest, they are brigands themselves. Only they are Ilderim's brigands, fierce and disciplined. Usually the consequence of a raid within Ilderim's land would be an answering raid inside the territory of the raider."

"That could become a kind of border war."

"It could. Sometimes it does. Believe me, this sheik is ruthless, as was his father and his father before him. You will see him with his horses, and he seems almost foolish about them. You will not see the armory that travels with the tribe, even to the Orchard of the Palms. There are a great number of very sharp weapons that can be snatched up in an instant by people who know exactly what to do with them."

"So then, the Romans?"

"As you might expect. A train of tax collectors was raided on Ilderim's land and the Romans held him responsible."

"Which is only justice, in some sense," Ben-Hur said reluctantly.

"In some sense," Malluch agreed. "Ilderim repaid every sestertium. Even using the Romans' estimate of what they lost, which was certainly exaggerated. But they also claimed his horses. All of the foals of that year, they took back to Rome."

"What?" Ben-Hur was startled. "How? On shipboard?"

"I don't know the details. I have heard they sent some by land. Many of those sent by sea died. But enough reached Rome to satisfy the emperor."

Ben-Hur sat up. "Oh! I remember! I remember when they came! It was a scandal. I didn't quite understand. I was new to Rome. Some had been ill-treated. But others recovered and were raced. And bred. They were magnificent."

"And the offspring return here from time to time. That Roman driver today, who tried to run down the crowd at the fountain? Those were probably the offspring of Ilderim's horses."

"And that dog Messala wants to run them against the beautiful bays!" Ben-Hur broke out.

Malluch was startled. "That dog? Do you know him? Or are you just, because he is a Roman . . . ?"

"I know him, Malluch," Ben-Hur said. "I'll tell you in a moment."

"But he saw you! Face-to-face, you were closer to him than I am! How could he not recognize you?"

"I have changed," Ben-Hur said bitterly. "He last saw me as a boy. He probably believes I am dead."

Malluch twisted around on the saddle to look Ben-Hur full in the face. The camels were crossing a vast field of tall green grass. On the road ahead, beyond a range of hills, the broken canopy of palms announced they were nearing their destination. "Look—the Orchard of the Palms. See how the road winds? It will be well guarded. Ilderim keeps his people safe."

"And his herds, I suppose. After the Romans humiliated him."

"Yes," Malluch said. "I think that was the worst part of that episode. To be Sheik Ilderim is to protect what is yours. And Rome made him a liar. Now tell me your story, quickly, before we arrive."

Briefly and without emotion, Ben-Hur ran through his tale: the parade, the tile, the capture, the parting from his sister and mother. The galleys, the sea battle, the years in Rome as Arrius's adopted son. The sentry had stepped forward to block the road when he finished.

"And Messala?" Malluch asked. "What is his role in all of this?"

"He was my best friend," Ben-Hur said. "And he betrayed me to the Romans."

The men had only time to share a long glance before the sentry challenged them. Ben-Hur did not bother to answer the challenge; he merely lifted the gold chalice so that the sentry could see it. Malluch was amused: his new friend might hate Rome, but he had acquired some of a Roman's lordly ways.

CHAPTER 17

IN THE TENTS

Even the fiercest nomadic desert chieftain may have a favored oasis. He would not, of course, admit such a weakness; as a nomad, all places, whether parched or lush, windblown or sheltered, must be alike to him. But when the long train of Ilderim's camels and herds and humans wound its way into the Orchard of the Palms, there was always an air of merriment about. And even the sheik himself, when he thrust his sword into the soft green grass to show where his tent pole should be planted, smiled broadly at the men and women who surrounded him. At the orchard they could let down their guard. Encircled by hills, with one easily watched entrance, lying next to the lake, it provided safety, water, and endless forage for the beasts. Life was easy at the orchard.

And this year it was also proving interesting. There was the usual business to be transacted in Antioch; even a desert chieftain may have to handle money and supplies and commercial agreements. While he was there, Ilderim would pass many an hour with Simonides, working out the canniest way to move goods from the East through the wild areas under Ilderim's control. The two men would bicker and bargain with gusto.

Then there was the unexpected pleasure, this year, of Balthasar's presence—though Balthasar's daughter, Ilderim thought, was creating some tension among the people. If only she would *truly* veil herself like the other women! And stop walking by the lakeside all alone. With her arms uncovered. As he stood at the opening to his tent, Ilderim wondered if a word to her father might help. He began to formulate what he would say, but no useful phrases came to mind.

A warm breath blew in his ear, and one of the horses dropped its head onto his shoulder. That was the best thing about the orchard, thought Ilderim: the horses loved it. Every year when they arrived, they dropped to the grass and rolled and rolled.

But the race! He took a deep breath, remembering the earlier incident on the track. The horses were unharmed. There was that. He felt a nudge from behind—another of the horses, curious, not wanting to miss anything. But who would drive them now? He'd been a fool to trust that Roman. But when his own driver had broken a leg, what could he do? And he so deeply desired to win the race! He had never had a better team. There would never be a bigger crowd, not outside of Rome. And none of his own men . . . He squinted, trying to decide how to put it. None of his own men had earned the respect of the horses, he decided. He squinted again. Visitors? His long sight was fading. Another thing to worry about.

Yes, visitors. Two scruffy camels, animals he'd be embarrassed to ride. And on one of them, Simonides's man Malluch. The other man was a stranger. The sentry had let them pass without a challenge or a message. Interesting.

So Ilderim left the door of his tent, followed by two of the bay horses, picking their way gracefully over the grass.

Malluch's camel knelt, but the stranger's camel refused to. The man laughed and swung his leg over the saddle, then vaulted lightly to the ground. "Never again, Malluch, I swear it. I will not ride another camel," Ilderim heard the man say.

"Peace be with you," Ilderim called out. "You are welcome among us."

"And peace to you also," both men answered.

Then, to Ilderim's surprise, the horses ambled forward. The tall man held out his hands and let the velvety muzzles run over them. One of the bays took another half step and rubbed his head against the stranger's chest.

"Ho, Aldebaran," called Ilderim. "No need to startle our guests."

"I'm grateful," responded the man. "I admired these fellows at the grove today." He ran a hand down Aldebaran's neck, smoothing the satin coat and murmuring under his breath. The horse's ears flickered—they understood each other.

"Your Honor," Malluch said, drawing the sheik aside, "forgive me, but I came here only to show the way. We met Balthasar today at the Grove of Daphne, and my friend was able to perform a service for him. Balthasar summoned him here."

"All the better," Ilderim answered. "Of course a service done to a guest of mine is also a service to me. But you can't do me the honor of entering my tent?"

"Alas, no. I am expected back in Antioch. But I will return to the orchard tomorrow."

"Thank you, Malluch," Ben-Hur said. "I am so grateful that our ways crossed today. May I rely a little further on your kindness?"

"Of course," Malluch answered.

"Would you take that beast back to Antioch with you?" Ben-Hur pointed to the camel. "And perhaps send a saddle horse to replace him?"

"You don't care for our ships of the desert?" Ilderim asked.

"I think perhaps my ship was closer to a raft," Ben-Hur answered. "I've never met an animal I disliked more, and I'd rather walk back to Antioch barefoot than ride it again."

"I feel sure that won't be necessary," Ilderim said. "Now, please, come into my tent. Aldebaran, Rigel, show him." He clucked with his tongue and gestured. Nudging the newcomer with their noses, the bays urged him toward the wide door of the tent, where a serving man waited at the edge of a vast, magnificent carpet.

The horses pushed their way through a curtain that divided the tent, while the two men let the servant take off their shoes and outer robes. A young woman appeared with fresh white linen robes, and another with a bowl of water. The men sat on the wide divan that ran around three sides of the tent, piled with cushions and bolsters, while the woman washed their feet. Ilderim noticed his guest's eye roving around the tent.

"Have you ever been in a nomad's dwelling?" he asked.

"No," his guest answered. "I admire the arrangements very much." He looked up at the tent pole and the tightly stretched roof. "How long does it take to dismantle?"

"In case of a raid, you mean? That depends on how many men I have," Ilderim answered. "But if we need to be swift, we can be."

"And the fabric—is it woven from your sheep?"

"From the goats. It's more durable. But these—" his hand rubbed the yellow cover of the divan—"need not be so sturdy. They come from our sheep. Which of course are not yellow. I believe they use turmeric for the dye."

"And forgive me the curiosity," Ben-Hur went on, "but is it common to share a tent with horses?"

"No," Ilderim answered. "But as you seem to have understood, these particular horses are more to me than animals." He turned to the servant and said, "Go to the tent where the Egyptian is staying and tell him that a guest has come. We hope he will join us." And to Ben-Hur, he continued, "I would be more than honored if you would stay the night with us. Or indeed as long as you can honor us. But certainly you will dine. And if you must return to Antioch after nightfall, I will send you with an escort. On a horse."

"Thank you," Ben-Hur answered. "Your kindness makes me understand why the hospitality of the desert is famous."

"And now, if you will forgive *my* curiosity, may I know something more about you? We learn to judge people quickly in the desert, but I admit I am puzzled. Malluch did not introduce you."

Ben-Hur paused. "I am called Judah," he said after a moment.

Sheik Ilderim might have expected more than simply a first name, but he smoothly said, "A Jew, then. I have never known one who could make friends with a horse so quickly."

"I am a Jew," Ben-Hur answered. "But I have spent the last years in Rome—a good portion of that," he added with a smile, "around stables. The emperor's stables, in fact."

"Ah," Ilderim answered. "In what capacity?"

"I would say, as a competitor."

Now Ilderim looked at his guest more carefully. It made sense, of course: he was built like an athlete, tall and loose-limbed, with long arms and huge hands. The better to hold a handful of reins, Ilderim thought.

As if reading the sheik's mind, Ben-Hur held out his hands, palms up. "Yes," he said. "You see the calluses. I have raced a chariot in the circus in Rome."

Ilderim frowned. "But I don't remember a Jewish driver," he said.

"No," Ben-Hur answered. "While in Rome I was known as Arrius, after my adoptive father. But he died recently, and I have reclaimed my original name."

"And what brings you to Antioch?" Ilderim asked.

But at that moment, Balthasar appeared at the door of the tent, followed by his daughter. Ilderim felt a spurt of annoyance; surely the women of Egypt did not go everywhere the men did? But he rose to his feet at once, as did Ben-Hur. And by the time they were all settled again with a special cushion for Iras's bare feet, Ilderim saw with surprise that Ben-Hur held a golden chalice in his hand.

He crossed the carpet and held it out to Iras. "When I saw you at the Grove of Daphne," he said, "I was startled by your kindness and did not think to refuse this. But of course I cannot accept such a gift. It was my privilege to be of help to you."

"What I give, I do not take back," Iras said, looking up at him. "Whether you choose to keep it is not my affair."

"Your thanks are all I could possibly value." He set the chalice next to her on the divan. Then, with considerable dignity, he resumed his seat near Ilderim.

"And who will explain this to me?" the sheik asked.

"Today at the grove," Balthasar spoke in his reedy voice, "we were nearly run down by some boor of a Roman. We had stopped at the Fountain of Castalia for a drink, and this fellow whipped his horses into a gallop just to have the pleasure of frightening the crowd. The camel, of course, could not be budged. But this man—" he gestured to Ben-Hur—"caught the harness of the leader and brought the team to a halt. Not many men would have had the strength or courage to do that," he said directly to Ben-Hur. "Perhaps I will find another way to convey my thanks."

"Truly, sir," Ben-Hur said, "you make too much of a moment's impulse."

"But what boor of a Roman?" Ilderim asked, eyes narrowed. "I saw only one Roman at the track today. Driving the black-and-white team. In fact I wondered if they had not been horses from my bloodlines."

"I wondered that too," Ben-Hur said quickly. "They looked similar to the bays. Not as fine, to be sure. But the way they carried their heads and the strength of the hindquarters . . ."

"And how would the Roman come to have horses from the desert?" Balthasar asked.

"Oh, my friend, Roman spoils," Ilderim answered. "You know all too well how it is."

"I do," Balthasar answered, nodding. He turned to Ben-Hur. "Although I am Egyptian, I spent a year living with the sheik in the farthest corners of the desert. The Romans leave their traces even there."

"I understood that you were Egyptian," Ben-Hur said. "You are a long way from home."

"True." Balthasar glanced at Ilderim and smiled. "Shall I tell him the story?"

✳ ✳ ✳

Ilderim looked at his young guest, and Ben-Hur felt for a moment that he was being judged, though he could not have said why. "Yes, I think you should," Ilderim answered with a little smile. "I think this is a man who would like to hear your tale."

"Many years ago . . . ," Balthasar began. "But perhaps I should go back further. I will tell you only that I had for some time been seeking wisdom. Reading, studying. Searching the writings of Greeks and Egyptians and other wise men for the truth, which I felt I had not yet encountered. Is there one god? Are there many? What should men do while they are on earth? Will they live beyond death? The Romans worship their great men as gods; can man be divine or become so? All of these questions were a torment to me.

"Then at a certain point, I knew. Not what the truth was—far from that. But I knew that I had to go out and find it." He looked down at his hands, lightly clasped in his lap. "I was already old, you know. Far too old to go out searching like that. But I had spent so much time wondering, and this intention was so clear. So I went." He shook his head. "It was the oddest thing. I knew what I was to take, and how. Just one camel—the camel you met this afternoon, in fact. Not even my favorite beast—an unpleasant creature even for a camel. But that was the one. And certain supplies. And I was to follow a certain path. I had no sense of where I was going—east, of course, then north, I could tell from the sun, but I never knew from one day to the next where the path would lead. The camel seemed to have understood. I let it find the way. And one day, I met two other men. Do you know how we say, 'in the middle of nowhere'? It truly was the middle of nowhere. But there they were, each of them on a camel that could have been the brother of mine."

Balthasar paused and Ben-Hur noticed that his daughter had left without anyone's noticing. She had probably heard the story before.

"One of them was Greek, and one a man from India. None of us spoke another's language, *but we all understood each other.*" Balthasar lifted his hands and let them drop into his lap. "We did not know how. And all three of us were on the same mission. We were all seeking the truth. The way to be good men, I suppose. And to make the most of our lives. And whether there is any hope of a life beyond this one." He nodded, and the peacock plume on his turban dipped.

"It is a long story," he said to Ben-Hur. "And my daughter, Iras, has heard it too often. She does not like to think about her father's folly because by the ways of the world, this was madness. Though as you see, I survived."

Balthasar was silent for a moment and did not notice when a servant entered the tent silently. Ben-Hur saw that outside the door of the tent, the sunlight on the lake was turning golden and the palms cast dark stripes of shadow on the grass. Ilderim whispered to the servant, and Balthasar looked around as if he had forgotten where he was.

"We traveled together, the three of us," he resumed the story. "Eventually a star came to guide us. It sounds like nonsense, but I will just tell you this part of the tale as it happened. A star came and guided us, and we knew, somehow, that we were going to find a savior. Do you understand what I mean?" he asked, looking at each of them. In the telling of the story he had somehow gained stature and authority. "A savior who would be our Redeemer."

"But you mean . . ." Ben-Hur paused. "Could you mean the Messiah?"

Balthasar nodded soberly. "We in Egypt do not have that belief. Nor do the Greeks, nor the Hindus. The three of us, we all came from lands where many gods are worshiped. We had all come to believe, though, in one God. Like the God of the Jews," he added, gesturing toward Ben-Hur. "One God, a great and all-powerful God. Who was grieved by his people and wanted to lead them out of their evil ways. And we had, all three, been sent to find the new leader he had given us.

"Which we did. I believe this most firmly. The Savior was an infant who had just been born to a Jewish couple in a khan in Bethlehem. We saw the baby. They were in a stable. We worshiped the baby. I cannot describe it. But I would give my life to be in his presence again."

There was another long silence. Neither Ilderim nor Ben-Hur moved. Then Balthasar drew a breath and said, "Instead, here I am. In a dream we had received a message while we were still in Jerusalem. We were to see Herod and inquire, 'Where is he who has been born king of the Jews?'"

"Wait," Ben-Hur broke in. "Could you say that again? It was 'he who is king of the Jews'?"

"No." Balthasar shook his head. "'He who has been *born* king of the Jews.'"

"And Herod, who was king of the Jews, was appointed by Rome. You said this in front of him?"

Balthasar shrugged. "We were told to. What could we do? And after we worshiped the baby, we left."

"When was this?" Ben-Hur asked.

"How old are you?" asked Balthasar.

"Twenty-five," Ben-Hur answered.

Balthasar nodded. "He should be just about your age, this king of the Jews. If he is going to lead us, now is the time, don't you think? He is a mature man, but young enough to establish a lengthy reign. I believe he must declare himself soon, and I could not stay in Egypt while he might be coming. Iras is furious. She believes I am a senile old man, going mad before I die. She came with me to be sure I didn't do anything foolish. But of course the whole venture is foolish," he added with a creaky laugh. "I believe his time is coming, the time when he will make himself known. And it will not happen in Egypt. It will be somewhere in Judea. I want to be there. I want to see him again before I die."

CHAPTER 18

DUST

As dusk unfurled across the Orchard of the Palms, it caught up with Malluch on the outskirts of Antioch with the two scruffy camels. At Simonides's house the doors were all locked against the night, but the owner himself still sat on the rooftop, watching the last shards of sun glitter on the surface of the river. Quiet settled on the Grove of Daphne, broken by snatches of song and muffled laughter.

※ ※ ※

Miles away in Jerusalem, the courtyard of the Hur palace was nearly silent. Birds were settling into their nests on the rooftop, but it was a windless evening. Not even a palm frond moved—until a regular scratching sounded on the stairs.

It had become routine for Amrah by now. Every evening, brush the stairs. Just enough to keep the cobwebs away so that she could pass up and down without leaving a trace. From time to time a Roman detachment would come from the fortress to look through the rooms. They broke the seals on the front gate, posted guards, tramped around shouting at each other, and sealed the gate again when they left.

They never took anything or broke anything. There was always an officer in charge to see to that. The orders on that count must have been very strict. Aside from the wreckage of that first day, the palace lay as it had for years, undisturbed. Almost as if it were ready for someone to move into it.

Only it wasn't really undisturbed. The soldiers didn't know that. There were attics and storage rooms they'd never found that showed what an empty house really looked like after years of abandonment. They had that dead smell. The floors would crunch if you walked on them. And the cobwebs would veil your face so that you spent long minutes trying to brush away something that almost wasn't there.

Amrah wasn't keeping the house clean for the family. She knew it would take a miracle to bring them back. Judah was dead for sure. Nobody survived the galleys. The mistress and Tirzah—dead too. Or so she hoped.

But the Romans hadn't claimed the palace completely. Had they planned to sell it? If so, no buyer had stepped forward. So the house remained empty except for Amrah. And just in case, she told herself, just in case something changed, she stayed. To tell the story, maybe. Tell someone about the family who had lived there, prospered, taken care of their people, loved each other, and been torn apart by the harsh hand of Rome. She didn't often allow herself to think about it, but the vision crept into her head from time to time. Someone would knock on the door. Not just wrench off the seal and enter, but knock politely. Someone would call out—"Hello?" So as not to disturb whoever might live there. Someone would walk around openly, looking but not touching, continually calling.

Not like Messala. How he had frightened her those years ago, creeping in like that! For weeks afterward her heart pounded whenever she approached the postern door, to enter or to leave. She had almost given herself away, nearly stumbling over him as he climbed the stairs to the roof.

But he had not expected to see her, so he had not seen her.

Just as, on that terrible day when it happened, a careless soldier had overlooked her crouching behind a row of barrels in a storeroom. He had been bored by then, she could tell—how many storerooms had he looked into? There would be no plunder for him, no hidden swallows of wine or silver coins to sweep up. Just a tramp along endless corridors of stout wooden doors and a cursory glance inside to make sure all the occupants of the palace had been driven out.

She had stayed in that storeroom for several days. Or maybe not. The waiting had felt long, but it was dark. All the time. And after that, it was definitely another day before she crept up the stairs. She only took the chance because she needed to eat.

She needed to eat because she needed to stay alive. That was clear. Eat and drink and remain hidden. Just in case. Fortunately she didn't need much. The mistress had always laughed at how little she ate: "Amrah, you are like a bird!" she would say. That turned out to be a good thing. For a long time she lived on what was left in the kitchen, grains and dried fruits and nuts. There was water—the Romans had not poisoned the cistern. She roamed around the palace in those days. Just looking at what the Romans had done. What they'd broken, what they'd taken. Things, really. None of it mattered, compared to the family.

But one day she saw a footprint in a dusty corner and was terrified until she realized that it was her own. After that, her routine changed. She roamed with a purpose. She swept, roughly, so that she could pass without a trace. She let the spiders have their way but kept the centers of doorways clear. She let the mice burrow into cushions but tidied away most of their skeletons.

Eventually she had to leave the palace. She had eaten most of the supplies that were left, and her robe was tattered. She crept out just before dawn, startled by the openness, the enormous sky, the sounds, the pure rush of air around her. She visited a modest market, bought what she needed with some of the coins she'd found in hidden corners of the palace, then returned home.

In, out, drifting as quietly as a breeze, Amrah grew used to her invisible life. Sometimes she felt despair, but there was always something to do. She tried not to look forward or to look back. She simply needed to be there. Just in case.

CHAPTER 19

LUCK

On Simonides's side of the broad Orontes River, trade dominated, with its wharves and warehouses and constant traffic
of boats. But on the opposite side stood a massive palace, as
imposing as any in the East. It was there, naturally, that the Romans
in Antioch made their headquarters. It held stables and armories, a
vast hall for official ceremonies, courtyards and sleeping rooms, storage and kitchens. There were timbers and tile, marble and bronze,
sawdust on the surface of the indoor training ground for the horses.

And in one large room on an upper floor, there were five bronze
chandeliers shedding a hot glow from a high vaulted ceiling. Tall
windows would have let in a breeze, if there had been one. Slave boys
carried fans, but the men in the room wouldn't stay still to be fanned.
Soldiers need to move.

They were a handsome group—young, healthy, prosperous.
They had spent the day marching or drilling or riding or driving or

throwing javelins or shouting at recruits or battling each other with their swords. It was fashionable to ignore wounds or injuries, but some of the tanned limbs and faces bore scars or bandages.

They were noisy, too: the hard surfaces in the room threw back the sound of their voices, and these were voices trained to be heard across a parade ground. There was some singing, though it was early for that. Beneath the voices the sharp clack of dice came from the tables around the room. Servants circulated with pitchers of wine and platters of fruit, but the fruit was largely ignored.

Messala stood at a table near the window, tossing a pair of dice from hand to hand. "No takers?" he said. "Come on, that's why they call it gambling! Flavius?"

The man next to him said, "I could manage a denarius, but I know you won't bother to shake the dice for that."

"Of course not; where is your courage? Myrtilus, bring me some more wine for Flavius. I'm determined to separate this man from his caution tonight."

"Separate me from my paltry soldier's pay is what you mean," Flavius answered.

"I'd take that sword belt with the handsome clasp," Messala offered.

"Have to get it back from the moneylender first," Flavius told him.

"I know; you don't trust your hand with the dice. Let's bet on what time Consul Maxentius arrives tomorrow. I'm saying high noon, so those fops in his guard keel over in the heat while they wait for the ship to dock."

A cheer rose from the men who heard him. The newly arrived Roman troops had not made friends with the men stationed on the Orontes.

"Let's bet on how many of them faint before the consul disembarks!" cried a voice. There was laughter, but it died away as a new group of men joined those at the table.

They looked subtly different. Less browned, less knotty with muscle. Messala and his friends all wore the lightest of tunics with sleeves and skirts as short as was decent. The newcomers were hot; it was obvious. They had not anticipated the humidity of Antioch, and their tunics clung to them. They were older, on the whole, and watchful. They smiled, but not with merriment.

"I was hoping we'd find some wagering here," said the tallest, a man whose hair was already thinning. "I am Cecilius, with the consul's staff. We could bet that I will be the first to keel over in tomorrow's sun." His smile turned into a grin, but his teeth were bared.

"Not I," said Flavius. "You long, stringy men can stand anything. You'll be standing there upright till the sun sets."

The group around Cecilius laughed. Flavius had evidently hit on the truth.

"Dice, then?" Cecilius suggested. "I don't want to bet on the race until I've seen some of the competition."

Messala straightened. "You drive?" he asked.

Cecilius nodded. "Yes, but I don't expect to win."

Laughter erupted all around. "He certainly does expect to win," a quiet voice said.

"I don't recognize you," Messala said. "I know most of the Roman drivers."

"Ah! You must be Messala, then!" Cecilius said. "I bring you greetings from all of the horsemen in Rome. They said you were the man to beat here. I arrived in Rome just after you left."

"And where did you drive before?"

"In Thessalonica, in Greece. I had a lot to learn when I came home." The smile flashed again. Definitely not friendly, but Messala did not seem to notice.

"Is your team here?" he asked.

Cecilius nodded. "I sent them around by land. That's the best thing about being on the consul's staff. Anything that adds to his consequence—done! Yes, sir! Extra horses? A chariot? Fodder? To join the wagon train to Antioch? Yes, sir!"

"Cecilius likes to be *sir*," added the quiet voice. That got a real smile.

Messala looked around the room, suddenly restless. "Well, we will meet on the track, then. Maybe have a friendly gallop or two before the race next week."

Cecilius nodded. "Friendly. Good. I may need pointers."

Messala tried his own mirthless grin. "I don't give pointers. I race to win."

His friends laughed in their turn.

"Too bad Arrius isn't here," said one of the newcomers. "That would have been something to see."

"A race worthy of the consul," agreed another. "Three of the best drivers in the empire!"

Messala frowned. "Who is this Arrius? There was no driver by that name when I was in Rome."

"How long have you been in Antioch?" Cecilius asked politely.

"Four years," Messala answered. "Much too long. I'm just waiting for a transfer."

"That's a long time to be so far from Rome," Cecilius said with apparent sympathy. "They must need you here, then. And before that?"

"In Tarraco," said Messala, tossing his dice from hand to hand.

"Brave man! They'll certainly bring you back to the capital now. They need men who've seen what it's really like to administer an empire. But that explains why you don't know Arrius. You two would have a lot in common, I think."

"They even look alike," said one of the men from Rome. "Dark hair, strong build, about the same age . . ."

"Like most of the men in this room," Messala said. "Still, I'm surprised. I had been racing for several years when I left. I thought I knew all the drivers, even the young ones just starting to train."

"The strange thing about this Arrius," said Cecilius, "was that he just appeared. He'd been rescued off some ship by the duumvir Quintus Arrius. You must remember him."

Myrtilus nodded. "Something about a sea battle . . . I don't recall exactly—the younger man saved Arrius's life and the duumvir adopted him, though he was obviously a Jew. Not that he ever made an attempt to hide that. But he learned our language and our ways. Won all the races in the circus for several years and then devoted himself to the palaestra. I lost track of him after that."

"He learned to fight like the gladiators," said a willowy youth in a tunic with a broad purple border at the hem.

"And how would you know that?" Cecilius asked, laughing.

The youth blushed. "My father said. The gladiators all liked him because he was so brave. They said they wished he could fight a lion."

"Who is this paragon you're talking about?" asked Flavius, who had drifted away in search of more wine. "Who should fight a lion? Aside from Messala here, of course."

"Did you ever hear of young Arrius in Rome?" Messala asked his friend.

"Of course," Flavius answered. "He really was a paragon. What's more, he's here in Antioch." He went on, pleased by everyone's surprise. "You see, I'm not the best driver or the best swordsman, but I do always have the best gossip."

"Well, it hardly matters," Messala said restlessly. He looked around the room. "We're here to gamble, not to gossip! If I can't persuade any of you to bet against me, I'll have to find someone else."

"Oh, I'll happily play," Cecilius said. "But tell me—" he turned to Flavius—"what else do you know about young Arrius? Is he here for the race?"

"This was the interesting part," Flavius answered. "He arrived very quietly on a cargo ship, dressed in Jewish robes. If he'd come with the consul, that would not have been surprising. But he's not staying here at the palace."

"Well, didn't the duumvir die?" Messala asked. "So maybe this fellow he adopted has gone back to his people. Quite a comedown, though. I don't even know why we're talking about him; none of us has met him."

"The thing is," said Cecilius, "he was the duumvir's heir. He could buy and sell all of us together. I have to say, I envy the man."

Messala looked at him. "But why? He's just another rich Jew."

"Maybe," Cecilius replied with raised eyebrows. "But he drives like a demon. I admire his courage."

Messala shook the dice again. "All right. The game is calling. What will we play for? A sestertium?"

Cecilius looked coolly at him. "They said the stakes were high here in Antioch, but I had no idea how high. You're a brave man to risk so much on the fall of the dice."

Messala met Cecilius's gaze. "It's my motto: no one dares what I dare." And he threw the dice.

CHAPTER 20
HORSES

There were no dice in Ilderim's tent. No dice, no noise, no wine, no shouting, no drunkenness, no songs, no vomiting, no blood on the floor after someone hit his head when falling, no slender serving boys, no men turning pale as their bets went bad. The tent flap stayed open and the moon rose over the lake, spilling a gleaming white ribbon on the black water. Dinner was served, eaten, cleared. Balthasar went off to his tent on the arm of the tall Nubian, who could more easily have simply carried him.

Ilderim glanced at his guest. "I usually take the horses down to the lake for a last drink," he said. "Would you like to accompany us?"

Ben-Hur's face lit up. "More than anything," he said. "Our conversation tonight was absorbing, but I confess I was aware of our tentmates as well."

"Yes, they are sociable. Did you see their outlines when they pressed against the dividing curtain?" the sheik asked as he gathered up his robe to stand.

"I did. And the muzzles where the curtain meets the ground. Do you ever let them in here?"

Ilderim looked at him with a rueful smile. "I know I should not. And I never do when I have guests. But I admit that sometimes when I am alone, they join me for dinner." He shook his head. "I have always been far more severe with my children than with these horses." He clucked his tongue and untied the thong that enclosed the bays. One of them nickered in answer, and they swarmed out of the tent onto the grass, surrounding the sheik.

"This one, whom you have met, with the star—he is Aldebaran. He is the youngest of the four. They all have the names of stars. Here with the blaze is Antares. Rigel is unmarked. And Atair—it's hard to see by moonlight, but his dark points are very pronounced."

"But aside from the markings they are almost identical," Ben-Hur said, walking around them. "Do they all have the same sire?"

"No, the same dam. She is Mira. My forefathers have always had a dam named Mira, the fastest and bravest and most beautiful of the herd."

"Have you raced them before?"

"No," Ilderim answered. He turned and started walking toward the lake. "Not publicly. This, I admit, was vanity. I wanted to train them in the desert, then appear in Antioch in the most public way and trounce those thieving dogs of Romans."

"Who drove them in the training?"

"One of my sons. A good boy, very brave. But I wonder now if he was strong enough. Anyway, he had an accident. He wasn't terribly injured, but he is still recovering. His mother is furious with me." Ilderim's smile gleamed in the moonlight.

"How did you choose that driver I saw today?"

Ilderim shook his head and Rigel pawed the ground in response. "Oh, look, now you know the worst: I teach them silly tricks." He shook his head again and Rigel pawed. "Not very dignified."

Ben-Hur laughed. "No. But they are obviously clever."

"You have no idea. We have to change the knot on the tent fastening every week or so because they learn to untie it."

"And yet they run."

"Yes. They are true Sons of the Wind. Tame as a child's plaything with me, but they love to gallop." He sighed. "It would break their hearts to lose this race. And much as I want to win, it would break my heart to break theirs."

"Malluch told me the rules follow Rome's."

They had reached the lakefront and the horses fanned out in the shallows along the shoreline to drink their fill. The ripples from their movement broke up the silver satin of the moonlit water. "Yes. In fact, everything must be exactly as it is in Rome. You know this race is in honor of Consul Maxentius, who arrives tomorrow. He is mounting a campaign against the Parthians. There will be a parade and other competitors, wrestling and footraces and the javelin toss . . . Oh, but you have just come from Rome. You know all this."

Ben-Hur nodded. "Yes. Some of his staff were on my ship—the ship I took from Rome. But then I realized I was tired of Romans, so I went ashore in Ravenna and waited for a Syrian vessel."

"You have no love for the Romans?"

"For one Roman, yes," Ben-Hur said. "But only one, and he died."

"Forgive my curiosity," Ilderim said, "but could you tell me your story? I have never met a Jew who could so easily pass for a Roman. Oh, look, there goes Atair. The only horse I've ever had who likes to swim." The bay's head and neck went arrowing through the moonlit water for a moment; then he turned around. When he stepped out of the lake, the other three horses shuffled away from him as he shook water from his head, tossing the drops from his mane high in the air. From nowhere a servant appeared with a long, tasseled blanket and began drying Atair's coat.

Ben-Hur told his story briefly, watching the grooming as he shared the bare facts—the friendship with Messala, the tile, the betrayal, the galley, Arrius. "I arrived in Antioch today," he said. "I went right away to visit my father's man of business, Simonides. I never met him when I was young, but I had someone find him." He looked up at the stars. "I had hoped he might know me. Or at least acknowledge me. But . . ." He swallowed hard and met Ilderim's gaze. "He has a daughter, Esther. He reminded me that they are slaves. My father owned them. So if I am who I say I am . . ."

"You own him. And Esther," Ilderim completed the sentence. There was a pause while he thought. "I know Simonides quite well," he finally said. "And Esther, of course. There was also the death of his wife, after the second beating. They were vicious, those men. And perhaps it is just habit with Simonides. He has for so long guarded the Hur fortune that he can't begin to think of another way to live."

"Possibly," Ben-Hur answered.

"And you know, young man . . ." Ilderim looked sidelong at him. "For some people who have suffered greatly, hope is a terrible thing. They can endure. That requires a . . . what? A kind of clamping down." Ilderim drew his arms close in to his sides and made his body narrow beneath his robes. "So then to hope, to draw a deep breath and look ahead and think about a change that might come . . . that is very difficult. Maybe Simonides is not brave enough for that risk."

"Maybe," Ben-Hur answered bleakly.

"And that could change," Ilderim continued. He turned to face the tent and snapped his fingers. The horses splashed their way out of the lake and came to him. Ben-Hur was touched to feel the warm bulk of one of them at his side—Antares, the stallion with the blaze. He reached up and rested his hand on the horse's withers, feeling the muscles move beneath the coat as they strolled toward the tent.

"You saw them today at the track," Ilderim said casually. "What did you think of the way they ran?"

Ben-Hur took a few steps before he answered. "It was hard to tell because the driver was so inept. But now that I know them a little bit, I think the problem is that they don't run together. As a unit. Didn't he have Aldebaran and Atair as the outside horses?"

"Yes," Ilderim said. "That was how we ran them at home."

"I would need to see them in action, of course—see their pace. But I wonder if Rigel should not be changed with Atair." He looked over at Ilderim. "There is so much to consider, you know. The length of the stride, of course, but we see right now, when they are half-asleep and half-playing with us, that they have different characters. Think how it is in battle, when you align your warriors so that one shares his calm and one his daring, one his experience and one his fierce joy."

Ilderim nodded. "You know, because you heard it, that I need a driver. I can see how much the horses like you. Perhaps you would do me the honor of harnessing them together tomorrow. Back that way—" he pointed toward the hills—"we have a track. You could show me what you mean. And perhaps we could trounce those Romans after all."

Ben-Hur grinned at him, a smile that lit his face and made him look, for an instant, young. Ilderim grinned back. In the velvet sky above them a spark of white streaked to the horizon. "Look," Ilderim said, pointing upward. "An omen!"

"If you say so," Ben-Hur responded. But he was still smiling.

CHAPTER 21
UNVEILED

Iras woke early. There was no reason not to. In Ilderim's encampment the men might chatter in their tents until the moon set, but the women slept early and woke before the sun heaved itself over the eastern hills that cupped the oasis. They had fires to start, children to tend to. Wheat to grind, flat bread to pat onto griddles over the open flame. They must all have hands as tough as leather. Without thinking, she rubbed her palms together.

She slept, as always, in a gown of white cotton spun so fine that the fabric was almost sheer. At home she might wear something similar all day and no one would be shocked. But here she must be covered. So her father had told her before they set out.

She had thought he was talking about the sun. But it turned out he was talking about the people. Not only the men—she was accustomed to men who stared at her. She was a beauty; it was normal. But the women here were worse. She could see the shock on their faces if an inch of her skin showed. Only at the Grove of Daphne could she uncover. And down at the side of the lake, if she went out early enough.

There was a long gray garment with a hood draped over the divan in her tent. The Arabs called it a burnoose. It covered everything. She flung it over her head and slipped past the tent flap.

There was still dew on the grass. That was something she liked. She never woke to see the dew in Alexandria. In any event, she was always indoors. With a cool marble floor beneath her feet.

The air was pleasant; there was that, too. And Iras had to grudgingly admit to herself that the lake was beautiful. She liked the stillness and the great pearly sky above. The burnoose dragging against the wet grass made the only sound.

But as she approached the lake, she heard something else and frowned. Splashing. Not an animal, she hoped. She would not be able to complain—her father did not know she left her tent alone. But she could not bathe where an animal had churned up the ground and possibly soiled the water.

No, not an animal. She spotted a head out in the middle of the water. Human. Male, of course. On a rock lay a creased robe, woven in stripes. For a moment she felt fury. She could *feel* the water, soft on her skin, lifting her heavy hair away from her neck. Sometimes she would wade out and lie down so that the water held her up. Women did not swim, of course, but she had seen drawings of young men playing in waves. She envied them.

And there was that handsome Jew, out there in the center of the lake, but coming toward her smoothly. She hesitated. Pull up the hood to cover her hair? No. He might as well be shocked. He was swimming in her lake. She turned and began walking back to her tent. Her footprints left a blurred dark trail in the wet grass.

She walked slowly. Just to see what would happen.

In a moment she had her answer.

Steps sounded behind her and he caught up. He had thrown the robe on, and water still streamed from his hair. "No need to leave. Were you going to bathe? I have finished."

She stopped and faced him. "I was. But I won't. The sun is rising. People will be awake. Look." She pointed toward the tops of the palms by the lake, where coral sun etched the fronds in sharp angles.

"Forgive me," he said. "Don't you have a handmaid who could go with you, somewhere further along the shore?"

"It's not the same," she said.

"No," he answered, meeting her glance. "I understand."

"But I will go back to the water's edge," she said. "Just for a few minutes."

He hesitated as she took a few steps; then she said to him, over her shoulder, "You may come with me. Or not. I don't need protection at this hour. But company is always welcome."

She almost heard him make up his mind, and in two long strides he was at her side. "Does . . . ? Do you and . . . ?" He paused and started again. "What did you make of the Grove of Daphne?"

She looked fully at him for the first time. The sun shone on his face now. Was that what made him look like he was blushing? Perhaps not. Sometimes it happened with military men: they spent so much time fighting each other that they never spoke to women. Probably never even saw women, except the ones paid to service them.

"Remarkable," she said. "Didn't you think so? We have gone several times, and I am always amazed."

They had reached the lake now. Iras walked into the shallow water at the very edge and felt the fabric of her burnoose pull at her shoulders as it began to absorb water. She looked at Ben-Hur, a step or two behind her. Even blushing, even dressed in a crumpled robe with huge damp patches where it had met his wet skin, he was strikingly handsome, she thought.

"And aside from that? How do you pass your days?" he asked.

"I just ask because I have never met an Egyptian princess, and this seems like a strange setting for you."

She nodded. "It is. I am . . . more content at home in Alexandria. I study; I make music; I see people. Women have more freedom there." She glanced at him. "But my father is so old. He was determined to come here. I felt I should be with him."

Without realizing it, he had closed the distance between them. "And your husband was willing to see you leave?"

She laughed. "There is no husband! No. We are not . . . With my father's ideas . . ." She glanced at him. He was frowning into the distance. "This idea that my father has, about one god . . . Even in Alexandria, which is tolerant, he is seen as peculiar. And as he grows more old, he grows more insistent. I am his daughter, so I am also seen as peculiar. Thus, no husband." It was true, somewhat. There was no husband, at any rate.

"But that seems impossible," he exclaimed with an energy she enjoyed. "A woman of your charms!" He was definitely blushing now. Iras thought back to the other young man, the one who had almost run them down, and his smooth, outrageous compliments. There was something endearing about this man's awkwardness. It would be almost cruel to flirt with him. Almost. "I always thought the Egyptians were connoisseurs of women," he went on. "How could . . . ?" He made a gesture and shook his head.

Iras shrugged. She bent down and cupped her hands in the water, then lifted her hair and rubbed the water on the back of her neck. "Each of us has his fate. This is mine," she said. "It has consolations. I have seen more of the world than some women. I have more freedom than these Arab women who are little more than beasts of burden for their husbands. I am here, talking to you. Not one of them could do that. But I hear the camp waking, don't you? I should go back."

She lifted the hem of her burnoose clear of the water and stepped onto the grass. After two steps, she stopped. "Wait a moment," she said. She bent down to pick up the hem and wring the water out of it, making sure that her ankles and calves were visible. She spent a moment twisting each side, squeezing as much fabric as she could. Now it would cling. They set off again. She tripped and reached out to steady herself on his arm. "I'm so sorry," she said, looking him in the eye. "I'm not usually so clumsy."

He seemed to be the one man in a hundred who would believe her. "Not at all. Can I help you?"

"No, it's just that the wretched thing got wet, and that drags it down. Don't look," she instructed him and leaned over to grasp the hem. Carefully and slowly, knowing that the neckline of the burnoose would fall open and reveal her skin to the waist. She straightened up and caught him whisking his eyes away.

"Permit me," he said and put a hand to her elbow.

She let it stay there for a moment, then said, "Better not. You are kind, but among these people, it would be misunderstood."

So they returned silently to her tent, and she thanked him and watched him go. It was amazing how simple a man could be.

CHAPTER 22

SON OF HUR

I t was also amazing how patient a man could be, but Iras didn't see that. Ben-Hur had to forge the sheik's horses into a victorious team in less than a week. He knew that as individual equine athletes, they were unsurpassed. But they were not yet a team. So Ben-Hur spent much of that day simply getting acquainted with the bays. Far at the back of the encampment, right against the hill, the rest of the sheik's animals were held in enormous enclosures. A dusty track had been laid out sometime in the past; one of the sheik's grooms assured Ben-Hur that the track exactly replicated the shape and distance of the track in the stadium. Throughout that long, hot day, the man and the four horses could be seen on or near the track. Ben-Hur harnessed them to a practice chariot singly and in pairs. He switched the pairs. He put them on long reins and cantered them around him in tight circles. They rested when it got hot, the horses dozing near Ben-Hur, who lay on a pile of clean straw. To his own surprise, he fell deeply asleep, waking suddenly when a blade of straw tickled his nose.

By the time the sun dropped behind the hill, he was satisfied with the day's work. He knew how he would harness the horses. The next step would be to get them pulling as one. As they walked together back through the encampment, the tall, agile man with the four bays ambling behind him, people smiled and greeted him or the horses. The sheik's people were proud of the Sons of the Wind, and word traveled fast. This new man would make them all proud.

Ben-Hur looked around appreciatively. It was an orderly camp and a prosperous one. The children were plump, the tents tightly woven, and good smells came from the cooking fires. As the sky turned darker blue, groups were gathering around the fires for the evening meal. Ben-Hur wondered if Ilderim would have returned from his business in Antioch in time for dinner.

But to his surprise, it was Malluch who greeted him at the sheik's tent, with a summons. "Sheik Ilderim sends his greetings," Malluch said, "and would be grateful if you could meet him in the city at the house of the merchant Simonides."

Simonides! Ben-Hur was startled. He had almost managed to forget! In his complete concentration on the upcoming race, he had pushed Simonides to the back of his mind. Well, and why not? The man had wanted nothing to do with him. Far better to spend his time with the horses.

Malluch must have taken his silence for reluctance, for he apologized. "The sheik said he was sorry to summon you after what he was sure has been a long day with the horses. But there is some strategy regarding the race . . ." When Ben-Hur still didn't answer, Malluch added, "We are to borrow Balthasar's camel."

The two men's eyes met and Ben-Hur smiled. "Oh, Malluch, not another camel!"

"I was instructed to add," Malluch said formally, "that Balthasar's howdah is also at your service. And that we will dine on the road." At that he smiled as well. "We'll get better food from the sheik's kitchen than from Simonides's, anyway. And I have to admit, I've been wanting to see the inside of that howdah."

Ben-Hur laughed. "All right, Malluch. I can tell when I am outmaneuvered. I will come with you. But pride requires that I wash off the dust of the stables—"

"And the straw from your hair," Malluch added helpfully.

"And the straw. I was getting to that. I will be with you, and clean, by the time the camel is ready."

He wasn't, but the camel had not been waiting long. The two men clambered into the howdah, and the Nubian driver led the beast out the winding path through the date orchard, lifting a hand as they passed the sentry at the entrance to the oasis. Ben-Hur was busy investigating a basket that held warm bread, dates, hummus, and a clay pot full of spicy meat patties. The two men focused on eating and did not speak until the camel had reached the outskirts of the city and begun threading its conspicuous way along the wharves. Ben-Hur gazed across the river at the vast Roman palace, wondering where Messala's horses were stabled. Then the camel suddenly halted and folded its legs so they could dismount from the howdah. Malluch said something to the Nubian that Ben-Hur didn't catch, and the Nubian turned away.

"We'll go on foot from here," Malluch said blandly.

"Malluch," Ben-Hur said, following him, "I find myself somewhat confused."

"Oh?"

"What language was that you just spoke with Balthasar's servant?"

"I suppose you would call it a kind of gutter Greek."

"Much spoken in Antioch?"

"Well, you know," Malluch answered. "In a town like this, most people speak a little bit of many languages."

"And why did you tell him to go back to the oasis?"

"Ah," Malluch said with a nod as he skirted a barrel broken open on the street. "You speak some Greek too."

"In Rome, too, people speak many languages."

"Of course."

Malluch had been leading the way, but Ben-Hur reached out and hooked a finger into the neck of his robe. "Am I being captured, Malluch? You wouldn't have whisked me away from the oasis for some purpose I don't understand?"

Malluch stopped and faced Ben-Hur. "Yes. I have. But it's nothing that will hurt you or interfere with the chariot race." The light was fading and they stood in a narrow alley, but even so he could see anger on Ben-Hur's face. "I apologize. I am under orders. You will understand very soon. That's all I can say."

"We are truly going to Simonides?"

"Yes. But it was thought better that the camel not be seen," Malluch answered and moved forward to lead the way again. "Or you, for that matter."

"By whom?"

"The Romans," Malluch answered. "Or those in their pay."

"But . . ."

Malluch turned back to him and said, suddenly serious, "Not here."

After that Ben-Hur could only follow him meekly until they rounded a corner and he recognized Simonides's tall house on the riverfront.

It was a hot, humid night with a feeble breeze that did little more than carry heavy, dank odors through the air. Ben-Hur couldn't help glancing at the ships swaying gently on their moorings, each with its sails tightly furled and a riding light amidships: a well-managed fleet.

To his surprise, Malluch did not go around to the main warehouse entrance but unlocked a narrow side door and beckoned. Without a word he led Ben-Hur up a steep, winding staircase. At the top, he knocked on another narrow door and entered without waiting for a response.

* * *

They were in Simonides's airy workroom. Tall lamps burned in each corner and the long windows stood open to the river. Sheik Ilderim rose from the divan where he had been sitting, cross-legged, and Esther rolled Simonides's chair around to face the two men. She had protested: it was late; her father needed sleep. But his old friend Ilderim was adamant that the meeting be held that very night. "There is no time to lose, Esther," he had told her privately. "And think of this: what we plan matters deeply to your father. You will see."

It was Ilderim who greeted the two men emerging from the private stair, and Ilderim who asked about the training of the horses. Courtesy required that the younger man reply politely, but he shot a glance at Malluch that made Esther uncomfortable.

Her father touched her hand. "Wheel me closer," he whispered. So she moved his rolling chair forward. He tapped her wrist again, urging her closer still, enough that everyone fell silent. "Son of Hur," he said, looking steadily into Ben-Hur's eyes. He waited for a moment and repeated, "Judah, son of my old friend Ithamar, of the house of Hur, I give you the peace of the Lord God of our fathers."

* * *

After his long day with the horses, and in his confusion, it took Ben-Hur a moment to take in Simonides's words, and when he did, he felt his face freeze. His eyes locked on Simonides's and he saw the older man smiling.

"Simonides," he answered solemnly, "God's holy peace be with you and yours." He struggled for a moment, rubbing a hand over his face. Then he knelt next to Simonides's chair and held out his hands to clasp, very gently, the broken and crooked hands in the older man's lap. "With you and yours forever. While it is in my power, I will do anything I can to preserve this household, in thanks for the sacrifices you made in my father's name."

Simonides lifted a hand and laid it briefly on Ben-Hur's shoulder. "Ah," he said in his surprisingly deep voice, "we have much greater projects in mind for you. Esther, would you get the papers?"

✳ ✳ ✳

Esther crossed to the worktable to fetch the papyrus rolls her father had been toiling away on all day. When she put them into his hands, she saw that he was smiling. "Thank you, dear girl," he said. "Would you get a stool for young Judah? Put it next to me."

As she moved the stool, she caught Ilderim watching her. He nodded slightly. Did he look smug? Perhaps. It didn't matter. If her father was happy, she was pleased. She set down the stool and stepped back next to Malluch.

"First let me explain why I didn't acknowledge you at once," Simonides began.

"No explanation is necessary," Ben-Hur said. "I can understand now how careful you must be."

"No, you cannot," Simonides said sharply. "You have known the harsh side of Roman power, but you are a young man still and physically whole. I did not suffer at their hands to give your father's fortune away by a careless mistake to the first man who appears to claim it. Though Esther protested, and though you are the very image of your father, I needed to know more about you. So I sent Malluch to follow you."

"Malluch was your spy?" Ben-Hur asked, turning around to glare at him.

"I apologize, son of Hur," said Malluch. "But I serve my master. So indirectly, I serve you. As I hope to do to the end of my days."

"Think of Malluch as my eyes and ears in Antioch," Simonides said. "I asked him to follow you because I needed to know if you were indeed who you said. And if so, what kind of man might you be? You must know that I have been searching all over the empire to find you ever since I got word that the Romans had taken your family. I had long since given up when you arrived at my door looking for all the world like a Roman!"

"Yes, of course," Ben-Hur said. "But what could Malluch have learned about me?"

"Many a young man has lost his way in the Grove of Daphne," Simonides said. "What with the women and the music and the pagan worship, there are many paths to destruction. A man who merely falls asleep under a tree is a man with a steady temperament."

"Or a man with other concerns," Ben-Hur added.

"Indeed," agreed Simonides. "And I ask your forgiveness. Again, it was Esther who pointed out to me how cruel it was to rob you of your last hope."

She felt herself blush as the young man lifted his dark eyes to hers. "How could I *not* forgive you?" he asked, turning back to her father.

"Ah, you say this even before you know!" Simonides almost crowed, tapping the roll of papyrus in his lap. "Here, son of Hur, is the accounting of your father's property. That is to say, not the property itself, which was appropriated by the Romans. The palace, as you know, and all the goods and warehouses and animals and ships your family possessed are gone. I suspect that Gratus did very well out of the fall of the house of Hur. But the money was held in bills of exchange, which they couldn't find. When I liquidated all of them, from Rome to Damascus to Valencia, the amount was 120 talents." He held up a sheet of papyrus, which Esther took from his hand.

"And it has been my care ever since to put this money to use and make it grow. So the assets you now possess are as follows." He gave a new page to Ben-Hur, who read aloud.

"'Ships, 160 talents. Goods in storage, 110 talents. Cargo in transit, 75 talents. Livestock, 23 talents. Warehouses, 17 talents. Money on hand, 224 talents. Bills due to be paid, 53 talents. For a total of 556 talents.'"

Judah looked blank. It was an enormous sum.

"And we add to this the 120 talents I had from your father to begin: the total is 676 talents!"

There was a hush in the room. Even Esther knew that a talent was the amount of gold that weighed as much as a man. The sum Ben-Hur now possessed would have filled the room, the warehouse—would have sunk all the ships floating in the river below.

"I think you must be the richest man in the world," Ilderim said from across the room.

"Yes," Simonides agreed simply. "He is. But the important thing is, *there is nothing now that you cannot do.*"

* * *

Ben-Hur laid the papyrus very carefully back on Simonides's lap and got up from the stool. With everyone's eyes upon him, he crossed the room to the little balcony and went out. He stood there for a long minute, silhouetted against the moonlit sky, facing the river, his mind completely blank. Then he turned and reentered the room.

He knelt at Simonides's feet. "Friend of my father, I will never be able to repay you for your stewardship of my father's property. The loyalty you have just demonstrated brightens my opinion of my fellow man. And I would like to mark my gratitude." He glanced over to the sheik. "Will you serve as a witness to my decision?"

"Happily," Ilderim said.

"Then let us make this official. Perhaps Malluch could write . . ."

"Not I," he said cheerfully. "I can't read or write. Esther often serves as her father's scribe, though." He bustled across the room and opened a cupboard, bringing out papyrus and ink.

Calmly Esther sat at a table and looked at Ben-Hur, ready with her brush.

"Everything you have just accounted for, warehouses and ships and livestock and goods . . . all 556 talents' worth of property and money that you have made over the years, I am returning to you, Simonides. I will retain the 120 talents that were originally my father's. The rest is yours."

Esther's hand faltered, but Ben-Hur continued.

"However, I add one condition. No, two. First, that you will continue to help manage this fortune. The mind that made it grow is worth more than any capital sum."

Simonides inclined his head to accept the compliment. In this realm, he knew his own worth.

"And the second condition is that you will join your efforts to mine to help me find my mother and sister. With eyes and ears like those of Malluch, in Rome or Jerusalem, surely we can find a trace of my family. What you have shown me today—" he laid a hand on the accounting—"is remarkable. But I can't rest until I know where my mother and Tirzah are, dead or alive."

"You must know that we have tried without ceasing to trace them," Simonides said gravely. "We will increase our efforts. If there is any trace of them anywhere in the empire, we will find it." He took another slip of papyrus from his lap. "The accounting is not quite complete. You have seen records of most of your father's assets, but here are three more. I will read the list." He held it up close to his eyes. "The slaves of Hur: One—Amrah the Egyptian, resident in Jerusalem. Two—Simonides, steward, resident in Antioch. Three—Esther, daughter of Simonides."

Ben-Hur stood still and gazed from Simonides to Esther. "You are slaves? Well, no longer. I will free you. Is there a legal process, or can I just declare you free?"

"No. In fact, Judah, you can't free me. I willingly became your father's slave in order to marry Esther's mother, Rachel. It is a permanent state and I have never regretted it. Esther, however, you may free, if she chooses."

"But I don't," she said calmly. "I prefer to stay just as I am. And as my father is."

Ben-Hur sighed. "It seems wrong. To think that I have power over your very lives . . ."

Simonides broke in. "You possess that power in any case, Judah. We are bound together for your father's sake if nothing else. You can do something for me, though."

"Whatever you ask is yours," Ben-Hur replied.

"Make me your steward as I was your father's."

"Of course! We will put it into writing . . ."

"No need," Simonides broke in. "Your word is enough."

"Thank you," Ben-Hur said simply. He turned and walked the length of the room and back. "But now . . ." He looked in turn at everyone—Esther, Malluch, Ilderim, and Simonides. "I inherited a fortune from Arrius. Suddenly I possess another one. I don't care about gambling or building a palace or any of the ways men use vast wealth. What should I do with all this money?"

Ilderim and Simonides exchanged glances.

"Well," said the sheik, "we have a notion."

CHAPTER 23

WHO?

That night the spy met Messala at the stable. He felt very clever about it. Until that point the meetings had all been Messala's idea, at places and times Messala named. On this occasion, though, the spy had information. Useful, important information that he thought Messala should pay a lot for. But it was information that would lose value if he didn't sell it soon enough.

He liked horses. Years earlier, in another life, he'd grown up in a country where wild horses roamed salty, marshy grassland. The skills you learn young are the ones you never forget—so it was easy for him to find a job at the Roman stables. There were never enough hands to carry water and manure and straw, let alone groom skittish high-bred animals. Besides, the surroundings were good for passing secrets: dark, busy, full of movement. Torches burned outside the stalls, but a man could hide behind a pile of straw, vanish into a storeroom, bend over to mend a bit of harness, and never be seen.

Better yet, people talked in stables. The spy knew lots of languages, being something of a mongrel himself. He smiled; he worked; he listened. And he assembled bits of information. It was a lot easier than keeping track of barrels in Simonides's warehouse, and he learned more.

Like the story of the duumvir Arrius, who survived a shipwreck and returned to Rome with the galley slave who had saved him. A Jew, whom Arrius adopted.

And word of a stranger staying at the Orchard of the Palms. Anything that happened in Sheik Ilderim's camp was usually a secret, and men who told Sheik Ilderim's secrets rarely prospered. So the spy cherished this bit of knowledge.

Along with the rumor circulating that very night that the sheik had found a new driver for his bays—a Roman named Arrius.

He thought about it as he cleaned the hoof of one of Messala's black horses. They were difficult. Quick to startle and quick with a flying hoof or a nip. He moved slowly and gently around them. Maybe that would be the way to handle Messala as well. It seemed possible to the spy that this new driver of Ilderim's was the duumvir Arrius's Jewish adopted son. Was it the same man as the Jew he had seen at Simonides's warehouse? And would it matter to his client?

The horse let him know his client had arrived. Its head flew up, and it yanked its hoof from the spy's hand.

The spy stood upright, with the horse's back between him and the Roman.

"You!" Messala exclaimed. "What are you doing grooming my horse?"

"Grooming your horse, naturally. What does it look like?" he answered. "I have news."

"Get away from him! This is a racehorse!"

"That's all right. I'm good with horses. And you want to hear what I have to say."

Messala looked around, frowning, trying to find something amiss in the stall or with the horse.

"It's a better meeting place than the inn," said the spy. "You and I both have reasons to be here. And nobody can overhear us."

"All right, quickly then." Messala pulled his cloak up around his neck as if to hide his face. Which was silly, when you thought about it.

"Is it possible that the man I saw at Simonides's warehouse spent some years in Rome?"

"In Rome! I don't know who that man was, let alone whether or not he'd been in Rome."

"Well, there's a story going around about the adopted Jewish son of the duumvir Quintus Arrius. I just wondered if they were connected."

"This is what you call news? Just because there are two Jews in Antioch?"

"Well, it's news if they are the same man. And the fellow I saw could have pulled a mighty oar."

"Why on earth would that matter?"

"Oh, I forgot to mention. Because Arrius's adopted son rescued him from a shipwreck. So he might have been a galley slave."

"Galley slaves are chained," Messala growled.

"All right," the spy said, raising his hands. "They are. Usually. I'm just telling you what I've heard. That's what you pay me for. And two more things." He clicked his tongue to the horse and walked around its head, scratching the forelock as he went. Now he was very close to Messala. Less than a step between them.

"Well?" Messala said, aggressively.

The spy put his hand out. "Money first."

"No. Tell me."

The spy put a hand back on the horse's neck. "I'm taking care of your horses. Money first."

"Are you threatening me?"

"No. I just don't trust you," the spy explained. "Am I wrong? I hear you're in debt."

The horse, feeling the tension, shifted its hindquarters and swished its tail.

"Everyone knows you gamble too much," the spy went on. "You should hear my news, but you have to pay my price."

"All right," Messala said, fishing for a coin. He held it up.

The spy shook his head. "Two. It's important."

"I think I decide that," Messala growled but gave him another coin.

"Right," said the spy. "The son of Arrius was a champion driver in Rome. Sheik Ilderim has a new driver staying with him at the Orchard of the Palms. Simonides and Sheik Ilderim are friends. Your tall Jew went to the Grove of Daphne yesterday, where . . ." He left off with a leading tone.

"Where Ilderim's horses ran away with that idiot Lucius! Yes, and I even saw a tall Jew at the Fountain of Castalia . . ." Messala's eyes widened. "Ye gods! It's hardly possible!" he muttered. "I'm sure he didn't know me." He took a step back and the horse moved away from him. "He would have had to survive the galleys. Impossible!" He spun around and left the stall, closing the door behind him. He strode away, then came back. "Find someone else's horses to groom, would you?"

The spy just raised his eyebrows. Now that Messala was gone, the horse relaxed. The spy bent down, nudged the horse's shoulder, and gently picked up another hoof.

CHAPTER 24

THE KING WHO WILL COME

Back in Simonides's house on the Orontes, Esther crossed the room and spoke to the servant who stood outside. When men began talking about plans, conversations extended and throats grew dry. She gave the order for refreshments to be brought: arrack—the soured milk she knew the sheik favored—wine, honey, and soft wheat cakes.

Reentering the big room, she went to an ivory-inlaid table and lifted it to place among the men. She was surprised when Ben-Hur crossed the floor in two long strides and took it from her hands. The older men watched silently as he set the table down between them. "Thank you," Esther said. "The servant will be up shortly with drinks. I will leave you now."

"But wait," Ben-Hur said. "Simonides, does this plan involve you and the mechanisms of your trading business?"

"It certainly does."

"And does Esther not assist you closely?"

"She does indeed," Simonides said proudly.

"Then should she not stay with us to hear more of this plan? Surely her help will be needed in some way."

The two older men exchanged a glance. Esther saw her father's minute nod and the sheik's answering smile. "In the tents of my people," Ilderim said, "such a thing would not be thought of. But—" he raised his palms from his lap—"what we have to discuss is perhaps a new world entirely. She should stay."

"Esther, my dear," Simonides added, "you will hear, and if you dislike our plan, you need be no part of it. What we contemplate, I must warn you, is without precedent, but not without great danger. Those who join us must do so with open eyes and whole hearts."

"I understand, Father," she answered. She heard the servant scratch at the door and opened it. There was a moment's bustle as the table was covered with a linen cloth, a stool brought for her, another cushion for her father, a lamp moved away to reduce the glare.

Simonides began. "Son of Hur," he said, "I wonder if you saw anything remarkable about the accounting I gave you earlier of the money I conserved for your father."

"Yes, I did," Ben-Hur answered. "I was amazed. In Rome, Arrius taught me how to understand the workings of his estates, and although he was very successful, there were always difficulties: failures, rents unpaid, a landslide that ruined a vineyard—that kind of thing. It is the way of life. Not every project succeeds."

"Exactly. Yet these setbacks have not happened to me. If there was a tempest, it passed over my ship. If there was a fire, my warehouse did not burn."

"I can attest to this," added Ilderim. "When Simonides's goods traveled through my lands, the guards we provided were unnecessary. The Parthians did not raid; the oases did not dry up."

"And strangest of all, not one individual who works for me

betrayed or cheated me. I rely more than most men on hirelings," Simonides went on, gesturing briefly at his broken body. "But no servant, no agent, no sea captain, no camel driver ever strayed from my commands."

"It seems uncanny," Ben-Hur commented.

"It is exactly that!" exclaimed Simonides. "This rate of success goes beyond what is reasonable. I thought for a while that, perhaps, after my misfortunes my luck had changed, but we Jews don't think much of luck. No. Eventually I concluded that this was God's doing."

Esther felt a little chill. Her father had never shared this with her. Of course he was devout, and so was she. Of course she saw the hand of God everywhere. But . . . in the warehouse? On the decks of a ship?

"And if it was God's purpose," Simonides was saying, "what for?" He paused and looked at his daughter. "I have believed this for years," he said to her as if he had heard her thoughts. "But I did not tell you, lest you think my wits were going astray. Hard enough to care for a father with a broken body. A broken body and a broken mind— that is too much even for a woman as capable as you." There was great sweetness in his smile. "So I just wondered in silence. And now I think I know." Esther, watching closely, saw him glance at Sheik Ilderim, who took up the narrative as if on cue.

"Son of Hur," the sheik began, "you heard the tale Balthasar told us in the tent, of following a star across the desert in search of a King."

"I did," he affirmed. "And it has been on my mind. I don't know what to make of it."

"No," Ilderim agreed. "Nor do I. Yet in spite of myself, I find that I believe it. After the three wise men worshiped the infant in Bethlehem, they had a dream. Each of them, the same dream."

Simonides interrupted. "You'll understand," he said to Ben-Hur, "that for practical men like the sheik and me, these mysterious happenings are very disturbing. How do three men have the same dream?"

Ilderim nodded. "But they did. In the dream an angel came to them and told them to flee Judea by a new route. The camels brought them to us, and indeed, we heard later that Herod sought for them everywhere. They were right to hide."

"And the babies, don't forget," Simonides said.

"Herod also slaughtered all the male Jewish babies in and around Bethlehem," Ilderim said, nodding grimly. "Evidently he had his own dream. Which makes me wonder a little bit about this business of dreaming. Nevertheless, the three wise men found us in the desert and stayed for a year, until they knew it was safe to leave."

"They were informed of that in another dream," Simonides added with a sigh.

"So they left. But during that year we spoke often of their vision of the infant," Ilderim went on. "Each of them believed he had seen the same thing: the birth of the one God. The true God."

"'He who was born king of the Jews,'" Simonides added. "Born, not made. Not appointed by Rome."

"No wonder Herod was frightened," Ben-Hur said. "If this is true, the entire world will change."

Again Esther saw the two older men exchange a glance, and she noticed that her father's eyes grew brighter, despite the late hour. "Exactly," he said. "The world will change. Now Balthasar interprets this as a new kingdom, not just of men, but of souls. A kingdom of wider bounds than the earth. He is not especially attached to the concerns of the world we live in. Perhaps because he is so old."

"Or because he lives in Egypt, where the Roman yoke lies easier on his shoulders than on yours or mine," added Ilderim. "Nevertheless, I was convinced by this story the three wise men told. Strange and wonderful things happened that night. So let us think of what that means. If on that night an infant was born to be king of the Jews, he would now be twenty-eight."

"In full manhood," added Simonides. "Young, strong, but mature enough to lead. To claim his kingdom."

"But Simonides and I have been considering," said Ilderim, "how this will all happen." Esther could tell, by the way the two men spoke, that they had been over this subject again and again. "How does someone become king of the Jews?"

"What does it take to be a successor to Herod? we asked ourselves," Simonides went on. "The answer is, of course, to follow the Roman way. With weapons. With armies and laws. With force, in fact. So if this new king of the Jews is to rule, naturally he will also need armies and laws. He will need to wield a force. But this is precisely what we Jews do not possess."

"It takes time to build an army," Ilderim took up the story. "You know this better than either of us. If the King will come to rule, he must start building his force soon."

"Very soon!" added Simonides. "And you . . ." The conversation had finally reached its point. "You have everything that is needed."

There was a long pause. Esther could tell that her father had not finished speaking, and that Ilderim knew it. They were simply letting the idea sink in. She glanced at Ben-Hur. His face gave nothing away. Did he understand what they were proposing?

"You know the Romans and their ways of warfare," Simonides continued. "The immense fortune you have just given back to me—I dedicate it to this cause. To building an army for he who was born king of the Jews."

"Of course an army cannot be assembled, armed, and trained under the eyes of its enemy," Ilderim added. "But the desert is mine. My lands can absorb any number of legions and keep them safe from spying eyes. So I offer the territory I control."

"That is the plan," Simonides concluded. "Together Sheik Ilderim and I can offer part of what is needful so that when the King appears to deliver us from the oppression that is Rome, an army fit to fight that oppression is ready on hand. What we did not have, until you arrived, was a leader. If you will indeed be that man."

Both of them looked eagerly at Ben-Hur. He stood and walked to the end of the room.

Then he turned back and looked at the two men. He was silent for a moment, holding them with his eyes. In that moment the power in the room palpably shifted. Esther thought later that she could almost see it, some kind of transparent glowing cloud, migrating from the older men to the young one. He was physically the same: still tall, still handsome, still graceful. But now he had authority as well.

"This has been a night of surprises," he said. He rubbed his hands over his face and added, "Actually, a day full of them. Two days ago I woke as no one, a man with a broken past. Today I am once again the son of my father, with riches piled upon riches." He paused, then went on. "Money to me is useful only for what it will do. What I want is to find my family. Or perhaps I should say, what I *wanted*. Because I know that you, Simonides, have already done everything in your power to find them, and I know also how broad the scope of your power is. There may be other . . ." He came to a halt and took a deep breath. "Forgive me. The hope is hard to give up."

"Nor should you abandon your hope," Simonides interrupted. "I have heard rumors of a new procurator for Jerusalem, a man called Pontius Pilate. A new leader, new rules, sometimes information escapes. I have people in Jerusalem. I don't offer much hope, but you most certainly should not give up."

"Still," Ben-Hur went on, "a man must do something besides wait for news." He fell silent again and returned to his chair. There he sat close between the two older men but looked only at the floor.

They waited. They were old men. They were used to waiting. Esther watched Ben-Hur's hands, fingers interwoven, lock and unlock. Finally he spoke, after a deep sigh. "My friends, I am honored. And at the same time, overwhelmed."

They waited more, so long that Esther wondered if he would

speak again. Simonides stirred and took a breath, but Ben-Hur finally went on.

"Friend Simonides, you mentioned your improbable good fortune with my father's money and how you wondered what it was for." He looked around the group and caught everyone's eye, each in turn. "You believed that there was a purpose, before the purpose became clear to you."

He stood and walked away a few steps. Almost, Esther thought, as if he were going to address a crowd. "My fate has been different. I had improbable bad fortune. I did not wonder what it was for. I assumed that there was no reason. That life was not a matter of reasons or consequences. Or even the concern of God or gods. I believed that life was a matter of accidents, good or bad. For men as for animals.

"And when I rescued Arrius from the burning sea and returned to Rome with him, that change of circumstance also seemed meaningless. Except in that it gave me, I eventually realized, the only opportunity I wanted. The opportunity to seek vengeance.

"I wanted vengeance against Rome and against one Roman. I thought the best way to punish Rome would be to use its own methods against it, and that is why I spent my time as I did, in the palaestra to train my body, in the camps to train my mind. I turned myself into a weapon.

"Now you have shown me the way that weapon can be used. If the King who will come is the king of the Jews, he must throw off Rome. Jews will never thrive until Judea is our own again.

"So perhaps this is the answer to my own question. Why did I suffer so? If the result was to help the King to his throne, I can only be glad."

"It is a harsh enough fate," Simonides spoke up. "You will have understood this: it is back to the parade ground and sword drill and long hours marching in the desert sun."

"More than that, I think," added Sheik Ilderim. "We should be sure Judah understands not just what he is taking on, but what he is giving up. You live here with your loving daughter and Malluch and your staff who care for you. I go nowhere without my wives and children and servants and followers. If Judah is to be a military leader, he will lead alone. That is the nature of it. And if he leads this army for the King who will come, he becomes an outlaw." He turned to Simonides. "For a young man with his life before him, this is a grave choice. We should give him time to think about it."

"I would have asked for that in any case," Ben-Hur said. "You have not mentioned the most important element." He smiled slightly. "Where are the men to come from?"

"You will raise them," Simonides answered calmly.

"How can you be so sure?" Ben-Hur asked.

"You have the gift. Men will follow you," Simonides replied. "Did you never talk about such matters with Arrius? He was an important figure among the Romans."

"But to discuss is not to do," Ben-Hur said.

"Like Simonides," Ilderim said, "I believe you will be able to raise the forces you need. And like you, I think the hardships you have been through will prove valuable. But it is late and we old men need our rest. I think we should leave Judah with these thoughts and talk again in the morning."

"Yes, I would be happy with that," said Ben-Hur. "But one more point. I said I wanted vengeance against Rome, and you have offered me the means to secure it. But I also want vengeance against one Roman, Messala. What's more, thanks to the sheik, I believe I can achieve it. Let us resume this discussion after the race. In the meanwhile I will think about what you have suggested."

CHAPTER 25
A JEW

Was it Ben-Hur? Messala kept wondering. Wouldn't he have known? He'd practically touched the fellow. How could he not have recognized him? Could he look that different, just eight years later? Messala kept remembering the chaos in the Hur palace: the women screaming, the blood pooling from the porter's hand, the servants scurrying around, and surely there had been goats? He remembered goats anyway. And in the middle of it all, Judah, his eyes huge with alarm in a pale face. Tall, dark-haired. Not memorable. Not really.

And besides, he should be dead. He'd gone to the galleys. The galleys killed slaves; it was known.

But that son of Arrius. He'd survived the galleys.

Once again Messala went back to that moment by the Fountain of Castalia, where he'd gone to meet Iras. Whom he still had not seen, except for a brief glimpse. So much for that assignation!

Instead there'd been a tall, dark-haired man in a Jewish robe. It had all happened so fast! The idiots clustered around the spring like sheep, the impulse to disperse them—like sheep. The man moving fast, trapping the harness in a huge hand.

A huge hand. So, yes, that was most likely the son of Arrius with the strength and limbs of a galley slave. Though why wearing the robe of a Jew? That was strange. He would be driving Sheik Ilderim's horses. He was well-known in Rome as a driver. Messala tried to tell himself that was all that mattered. Competition! A challenge! There was an Athenian driver too, and one from Corinth. The son of Arrius would have his hands full with those horses of Ilderim's, barely broken to the chariot as they were. He knew how hard his own team was to handle, and he'd been driving them for a full year.

He could beat Arrius. He could beat anyone. Especially a Jew. Especially Judah, the son of the house of Hur.

✳　✳　✳

A day went by and another one. He trained; he idled away his evenings with the other Roman soldiers, each night drinking more than he intended. He was exempted from guard duty. All his fellow officers were betting on him, especially since the newcomer Cecilius had withdrawn his team. He claimed one of his horses was lame, but Messala was sure he had simply realized he couldn't win.

Then three days before the race, a grubby youth sidled up to him as he left the stable. He was so busy thinking about the tension of the reins—Was he holding them too tight? Did his outside horse need a touch more slack?—that he didn't notice the boy or hear him until he felt the touch on his elbow.

"I'm to tell you," the boy said, "it's Ben-Hur. Definitely."

Messala whirled around. "How dare you! How dare you touch me!"

"Couldn't get your attention, Your Honor. To deliver the message. I was supposed to tell you, 'It's Ben-Hur. No doubt about it.'"

Evening was falling and the street outside the stable was busy. Nobody paid any attention to them. "Who sent you?" Messala hissed, hauling the boy around the corner into an alley.

"You know. He said you'd pay."

"This is ridiculous. Why should I trust him? Or you?"

"He said you would ask that. He said to tell you, the Jew at Simonides's house is Judah Ben-Hur. He came here to see if he would know what happened to the women." The boy pulled his arm out of Messala's grasp.

"Wait. Repeat that?"

"He said you'd need to hear it twice. If not three times. The Jew at Simonides's is called Ben-Hur, and he came to Antioch to see if Simonides knew where the women were. He didn't say what women. If you need me to say it again, you need to pay more."

"What! You dare . . ." Messala fumbled for a coin and threw it on the ground. The boy put his foot on it.

"Two," he said. "And also, he's done with you."

"One, and I'm done with him!"

"No," the youth said. "He told me to remind you he's good with horses. And he's taking care of yours. Two. In my hand."

Messala knew he was bested. He put the second coin in the boy's hand and turned away even before he'd picked up the first from the filthy dust in the alley.

But then . . . As his footsteps led him away from the stable, his mind was working furiously. Never mind the why, never mind the how. Ben-Hur, little Judah, *was* in Antioch. Had shamed him at the Fountain of Castalia. (And where was that Egyptian princess on the camel? Somehow she figured into Judah's situation. Another thing to hold against him.) And planned to race against him, Messala. A Jew, driving a team of four horses? The prospect was laughable!

Yet the horses, Messala knew, were a threat. If Judah could manage them . . . He almost laughed. It didn't matter what anyone said about the "son of Arrius" and his time in Rome. Judah would not have the courage or the cunning to win the race. Well, he might have the cunning. But he would certainly not have the cruelty, Messala thought. Horse racing sometimes got rough. For the men as well as the horses. Crashes were common, often causing injuries. Even deaths. There were all kinds of useful possibilities.

In fact, this was good news. Any advantage was useful in a horse race, and as a Roman, Messala was in a position to increase it.

He glanced at the sky and made his plan. First he visited the stadium at the Grove of Daphne, where the race officials were about to create the official notice of the entrants: their names, their colors, their nationalities, the owners of their horses. Wait, Messala said, new information! Sheik Ilderim's driver was not a Roman but Ben-Hur, a Jew!

Imagine, a Jew driving against the best teams in the East! The temerity, the folly! The program was changed amid laughter and jokes about Jewish dogs driving horses. They were all grateful to Messala for the correction. How shaming if a Jew had successfully masqueraded as a Roman! This would certainly change the betting odds!

Messala nodded. The fact had not escaped him. And what about the post positions? The race managers exchanged a glance. Normally, there would be a lottery. Each driver's name on an ivory plaque, the plaques mixed together and drawn one by one at random from a box . . . as was usual wherever Romans raced. Oh, the rules were very strict, very. There was so much advantage to the man on the inside of the track, whose horses traveled the shortest distance. Oh no, bribery? What a question! No one ever attempted to bribe the officials at an imperial stadium. Why, the games were put on in honor of the consul! What kind of honor would that be, if the results were not scrupulously fair? Of course it would be a wonderful thing if a serving officer in the imperial army should win. Naturally.

True, if the Roman driver had the inside position, that would be an advantage. A way to show the superiority of Rome, especially in the East. Oh, really? There were to be special rewards for officials if the race was satisfying? No, they had not heard. Unofficial, naturally. Understood. Everyone nodded. Some gold was found on a table after Messala left, in coins that divided nicely among the men.

His next errand was to the stabling in the stadium. To examine the stalls for his horses, he told the head groom. No detail too small, for a race as important as this.

The groom was flattered and perhaps influenced by the clatter of silver that drifted into his palm. Yes, the stadium was magnificent. Yes, plenty of room for all the teams. Yes, they would all spend the night before the race at the stadium. With their own grooms, that went without saying. A request? To have Sheik Ilderim's horses stabled next to his own? It could be managed. As the officer wished.

Messala was pleased.

He was even more pleased the next day when the official race lineup was released to the public. A Jew, a Jew! Driving the horses of that desert chieftain Ilderim! Gossip flew. Ilderim and his Sons of the Wind were well-known in Antioch. Swift and unmanageable, even by a Roman. What a joke, that a Jew should make the attempt! And he would line up by Messala's side at the start! Oh, how perfect.

Shoulder to shoulder. Eyes level. Braced on the light chariots, arms straining to hold the teams, Messala would meet Ben-Hur. After all those years. As boys they had fought with toy swords, raced each other through Jerusalem's streets on foot. Messala, the older, always won. The older and a Roman.

No reason why he would not win the chariot race.

CHAPTER 26

SONS OF THE WIND

Meanwhile Ben-Hur stayed at the Orchard of the Palms. He told himself he was not thinking about the proposition from Ilderim and Simonides. He was sure he had given up all hope of finding his mother and his sister. He was focused on one thing: beating Messala in this race. He was training the horses. He was single-minded. There was room for nothing else.

Iras actually helped with that. She was so often where he was! He would hear the chimes of her jewelry; then she would appear— always with a servant, always nominally veiled, so there was nothing improper about their meeting. Nothing anyone could precisely criticize. If she frequently leaned very close to him, what did that mean? He couldn't move away; she would laugh at him. She often teased him about being prudish. Shy, awkward, unused to women: those were some of the terms she used. And she was right, of course. He *was* unused to women. Aside from servants, he had barely spoken to one since the days in Jerusalem. Iras knew about that time. She had asked him about his boyhood. She wanted him to describe Tirzah and Naomi, curious, she said, about Jewish women. Though her questions made him uncomfortable, he did not know how to deflect her curiosity. Somehow, he did not like sharing his precious few memories with her, yet she kept asking: How did they dress? How did they do their hair? How did they pass their days? Could they go out unveiled? Could they meet men who were not their relatives? Ben-Hur was surprised at how little he knew of their lives. How had his mother managed the family palace, with all of its tenants, its storage rooms, and the animals and the staff? Had she had an office somewhere or a manager? Was she like Simonides's daughter, Esther, modest yet competent? Probably, but he had not paid attention. He had just been an oblivious boy. That was the phrase Iras had used.

Oblivious no more. He thought of her far too much. His eyes would catch on her wrist, her hair, the contour of her waist all too visible beneath the sheer gowns she affected. The damp heat, she said. It made her feel unwell. She would lift the glossy black river of her hair off her neck to let the air reach back there. Ben-Hur thought she might know how alluring the gesture was, with her round arms uplifted, showing the soft skin . . .

What was it she wanted, anyway? Was she just bored? He thought back to Tirzah and his mother. They had always been busy. Reading, making music, organizing, learning. There seemed to be little to interest Iras at the Orchard of the Palms. She did not seem to read or play an instrument or do much besides fan herself and linger by the lakeside. Balthasar rested a great deal. The sheik's women regarded Iras with wild eyes, as if she were an alien creature. As indeed she was.

The horses, unlike Iras, Ben-Hur understood. He spent as much time as possible with them. It was too hot to train in the middle of the day, so he would wake in the darkness and pad barefoot through the encampment to the stabling near the hills. The stars would fade to pinpricks as the sky became gray, then violet. By the time the first fingers of sunlight skimmed the hilltops, he would have the horses harnessed.

In the stable and on the track, there were no questions. No women, no enemies, no King who might be coming but might not. The horses liked him. He never found them asleep—they were always awake, ears cocked forward, eyes bright when he reached their enclosure. He supposed they heard his step. Or perhaps they knew his smell, as distinctive to them as Iras's to him. Sometimes as he led them outdoors, he would pause for a moment in the cool dawn and close his eyes and just feel them, breathing around him, glossy hides warm, velvet muzzles bumping him gently to keep him moving forward.

They loved to run. Much as they seemed to enjoy his presence, he knew they loved running more. He was almost certain that they liked him because he helped them to run better. And then he would decide he was foolish. They were horses, not men.

But the fact remained that they trusted him. They backed readily into their places, Aldebaran and Rigel, Antares and Atair, and stood still as the various leather straps and buckles were fastened. At first grooms had come out to help him, but now they knew better: it was faster to let him harness the four alone.

When he leapt lightly into the chariot, they picked up their heads, but they didn't step forward until he gathered the reins. Gathered the eight strips of leather, wrapped them up his arm, and then loosed them slightly. They understood.

Oh, it felt good! The damp air that Iras disliked so much often lay in a thin mist on the ground, and the smell was wonderful. Grass, herbs, horse—nothing finer. They would walk around the track at first. He let the horses play, snorting and snuffling, one breaking into a trot for a few steps, one tossing its head at a swallow winging its way to its nest. Then they would trot in earnest, around and around, faster each time. The breeze against Ben-Hur's face grew stronger.

Then with a shake of the reins, he would urge them into a gallop. They ran as one now, legs moving in the same rhythm. Aldebaran on the outside might set the pace, but Atair was the one with the stamina. He could go on forever.

They did sprints, galloping all out one length of the track. They ran around the curves over and over again, on the outside and on the inside. Sometimes Ben-Hur was almost alarmed to see Atair's hindquarters skim the track's fencing, but he knew he might have to cut that close to the edge of the track in the race. If there was going to be a disaster, better here, without teams piling up behind him. Better here than in the public eye.

And as much as he was training the horses, Ben-Hur was also training himself. The balance required was stupendous. Chariots had rails to grasp, of course. Some men wrapped the reins around their bodies to leave a hand free for the rail and one for a whip. But Ben-Hur needed to feel the horses' mouths—and they needed the contact with him. How else would they communicate?

So his legs had to be strong. And his back, to brace himself against the horses. His hands grew callused again, as they had been in the galley, and his face grew brown, and twice a day he swam in the lake to remove the dust from circling the dirt track behind four galloping horses.

It was all very satisfying.

Ilderim had left the training entirely to Ben-Hur. They met in the evening for dinner, but conversation was general and, Ben-Hur often felt, quite dull. Only Iras's presence gave the meals any interest. Ilderim asked, every evening, about the horses' progress, and Ben-Hur knew he visited them daily in the stables near the track. Then, two nights before the race, Ilderim invited Ben-Hur to walk with him by the lake after dinner.

"I have news," he said in a low voice as soon as they were out of hearing of the tent. "You are listed in the program under your own name. We had entered you as the son of Arrius. Is there anyone else in Antioch who could know you?"

"No," Ben-Hur said, startled. "It must be Messala's doing, then! I suppose he did recognize me at the Grove of Daphne."

"Perhaps," Ilderim answered. "I also assume he has been spying on us. As we have on him. And by the way, if there is any special information you would like that I might not think of, you must let me know."

"Truly? Then would you find out for me the measurements of Messala's chariot? Every single measurement: the size of the wheels, the height of the floor, of the axle, the length of the pole, any details of the harness . . . Can that be done?"

"Certainly," Ilderim assured him.

"Because one never knows when opportunity might appear," Ben-Hur added quietly. "In the heat of the race. Contact between the chariots is not unknown."

"No. It is well to know as much as possible. I will add that the starting positions have been published as well, and you are to line up next to Messala."

Ben-Hur stopped walking and caught Ilderim's arm. "I am? Do you think he made this happen?"

"Possibly," Ilderim replied. "But be sure that if he can make an advantage out of it, he will."

"Yes," Ben-Hur agreed, nodding. The two men resumed their slow stroll across the grass to the lakeshore. "I wonder if there is a way this news could bring us an advantage."

"Well, I think there is," Ilderim responded. "If you don't object. Apparently there is much laughter in Antioch that I am allowing a Jew to drive my bays. I am seen widely as an old fool. This, of course, is good news. The weaker and more foolish we look, the less careful Messala will be."

"True," Ben-Hur said. "We can surprise him."

"On the track, naturally," Ilderim said. "But we may also be able to extend our advantage with the betting. Knowing you to be a Jew, people will be all the more eager to bet on Messala."

"Of course," Ben-Hur answered. "The odds against my winning will be immense!"

"Yes. A fortune could be made or lost. And better yet, this could be done very publicly. Now Messala is known to have debts," Ilderim went on. "Do you think he will bet on himself?"

"Oh, certainly. And if he lost enough money, and publicly enough, that would be a source of great shame."

"Yes. He could be ruined, in such a way that half the empire knows the story. With the new consul here, all eyes are on Antioch. I can manipulate the betting, but you must promise me to win the race."

"Oh, never fear," Ben-Hur told him. "I will win the race. Or I will die trying."

"Then Simonides and I will do the rest," the sheik said.

CHAPTER 27
ODDS

One day more remained before the race. Out in the streets of Antioch, the excitement built. The entire day would be a holiday. At noon the procession to the stadium would take place, winding through the broad colonnaded streets: horses, soldiers, effigies of the various gods, musicians, banners, dancers, everything bold and shiny and noisy and brilliant would pass through Antioch on the way to the stadium. Once there, offerings to the gods would follow, then the usual sports: running, wrestling, leaping, boxing, javelin throwing, all the elements of battle that could be reduced to individual skills. The prizes, in honor of the new consul, were magnificent sums. Competitors had arrived from all over the empire.

But these would not be the most important events. Citizens who had no interest in men running over hurdles were clustered on street corners arguing instead about the chariot race. Boys roamed the streets selling knots of ribbon or scarves with the colors of the competitors. Bawdy songs from the taverns were adapted with new words supporting Cleanthes the Athenian or Messala. Though Ben-Hur's white colors could be seen along with Cleanthes's green in some neighborhoods, the Roman red and gold predominated.

Inside the great saloon of the government palace on the river, no other colors were seen at all, and if a man let a scrap of his white toga show, he was tossed a length of scarlet to cloak the white. Of course Messala would win—that was taken for granted. The only question was why Ilderim, who was known to be shrewd, had allowed that Jew to take the reins of his much-loved bays.

Not that it mattered. The victory was assured, and the room hissed with Messala's name. Bets passed back and forth on the other athletic contests, with Roman competitors favored, naturally. But there was little betting on the chariot race. On the margin of victory, of course, men would wager a few sestertii. One length? Six? Could Messala finish first by a whole lap? One could bet against the Jew finishing, but the odds weren't satisfying. And no one would take a bet against Messala's winning. It would have been like wagering that the sun would not rise the next day.

In fact, the men were soon restless. So early in the evening and so little excitement to be had! There were some yawns, some murmuring. More wine was brought and the dice came out, but they seemed banal. Messala himself lounged on a divan, ostentatiously bored.

"What it is to be so favored that no one will bet against you," teased Flavius. "I could solve all of my money problems by offering immense odds against you—oh, but then you would have to lose. No, not a good plan."

"It's no wonder you're always in debt," Messala commented, shaking a dice cup. "I wish something would happen. It's going to be a long night without any entertainment."

"I'm sure we could find some dancing boys or girls."

"Yes, but that's no fun if you have to stay sober."

"You could drive drunk. Now there's an idea," Flavius went on brightly. "Get publicly drunk. Spectacularly, loathsomely drunk. Insist on driving anyway. Then, at last, people would bet against you."

"Or simply bet with me," said a deep voice.

The two Romans, lolling side by side, sat up to examine the tall stranger. Unlike every other man in the vast saloon, he wore white—the long white robe of a Jew, made of heavy linen, closely tucked so that it swirled around him. Unlike the bareheaded Romans, he wore a pleated turban, and on one long finger gleamed a massive opal set in gold. But most importantly, he held a pair of ivory tablets. Tablets for keeping memoranda, perhaps. Records of bets?

"And who are you?" Flavius thought Messala's tone insolent, but it hardly mattered. A Jew, as this man obviously was, never took offense. Especially a Jew surrounded by Romans.

"I am Sanballat. Some of you may know me as a supplier for the Roman army." He looked around the room, scanning for familiar faces. "No, I see no acquaintances here, aside from the hero of the hour, Messala."

"And why have you come to disturb our festivities?" Messala asked.

"Is that what they are? How disappointing. I had heard so much about Roman orgies, but you are as solemn as the Sanhedrin."

Someone in the gathering crowd snickered, against a background of murmurs. Had this man just compared them all to the Jewish council?

"Still," he went on, "I understand that I am more tolerated than welcomed here. So let me get to business. There is a similar lack of excitement on the streets outside. On this night before Antioch's great festivities, the streets should be full of people shouting and wagering and arguing. Instead, there is agreement: Messala will win the race. It is known."

Looking around, Flavius saw the general nods of agreement. This Sanballat was clever, no question.

"So I offer my services to you," Sanballat went on. "As a man of business, that is my calling. I see a need and I fill it. The need here, as I understand it, is to accept bets that Messala will win. Since, clearly, no one else is taking these wagers." He unfolded his tablets and took out a stylus, looking around brightly. "Gentlemen? I am ready. First name your odds, then your amount."

More murmuring. Was there a catch? Did this Sanballat not understand he would be giving money away?

"I don't have forever," he said. "I'm on my way to the consul. I only stopped here as a matter of convenience to you all." He looked around, waggling the stylus. "No? No takers?"

"Two to one!" said a voice.

"You are only offering two to one? And your driver a Roman? No," he said, folding the tablets. "It's not worth writing down."

"Four to one," a very young man said, then blushed.

"Do I have to remind you that my driver—? You do understand this? I am backing Ben-Hur. A Jew. Who ever heard of a Jew winning a chariot race?"

"Why are you doing this?" Flavius asked. "You're bound to lose it all."

"Consider it a sacrifice to the gods," Sanballat said easily. "Not my God, of course, but . . ." He waved his hand toward the windows. "There are many gods out there. Some of them will be delighted. But not at four to one! I have heard nothing but Messala's name all day, seen nothing but red and gold throughout the city! Where is the nobility in betting only four to one on him? Where is the honor to Rome?"

Messala sat taller, looking from face to face. "Look at you all!" he finally said, springing to his feet. "I never thought you were cowards! I will bet on myself, at odds of six to one! You all make me ashamed!"

"Except me," drawled Flavius. "Everyone knows I never have any money."

Sanballat, ignoring this, was writing. "Listen, then: Messala of Rome bets Sanballat of Antioch that he will beat the Jew Ben-Hur in the chariot race. Odds, six to one. Amount, twenty talents."

"Twenty talents!" Messala exclaimed. "But . . ."

✳ ✳ ✳

Silence fell and lasted. Messala was a leader, admired for his courage and skills. But his arrogance had also made him enemies. From the back of the crowd, a voice called out, challenging Messala's motto: "Who dares what I dare?" followed by laughter.

His head whipped around as he looked for the speaker while scrambling for a response to Sanballat.

He would win the race, he knew. But if, gods forbid, he should lose, he would owe Sanballat 120 talents. He didn't possess five talents at that moment and had no way of finding 115 more. Yet he could not back down. He would never survive the shame. How had he let himself be maneuvered like this?

"No," he answered Sanballat firmly. "Not twenty. You set the odds; it's for me to set the amount. And I do not choose to set a bad example for the younger men here." There was a roar of laughter, but it was good-natured. "Some of them have been known to live beyond their means," he added, poking Flavius. "So I will bet five talents."

Sanballat looked at him without expression, then nodded. "I trust that you have the sum?"

Messala would have given anything not to feel the blood come to his face. "I do," he said. "Shall I send someone for the receipts to show it? Or will you accept my word of honor?"

"Oh, by all means, the word of honor, since you are a Roman," Sanballat said, writing the terms of the bet. "And as to the rest of you," he said in a louder voice, "I am backing the Jew, Ben-Hur.

I offer you a collective bet against him, at odds of two to one. Five of my talents say he will win."

There was another roar and a tumult as men waved their red and gold colors in the air, but no one stepped up to offer his money.

Flavius said to Sanballat, "Write the offer and sign it and leave it here. I am sure we will all agree to take your wager."

Sanballat stood and nodded, leaning over to sign the document. "That will do. I will be in the stadium tomorrow, sitting with the consul. If you get this to me before the race begins, the bet is good."

He folded up his tablets and bowed to Flavius and Messala. "Peace to you, and peace to everyone here. I must not keep the consul waiting."

The crowd parted as Sanballat left the room, his white robe billowing behind him.

CHAPTER 28

CROWDS

E sther had never regretted the pattern of her life. She knew she was indispensable to her father. She was always busy, and every day she saw how important her efforts were to the business that supported them all. Until Ben-Hur had arrived, she had thought little about the future. She never remembered she was a slave.

But now, lurching along on Balthasar's camel in the green silk howdah, with Iras by her side, Esther felt ill at ease. She was pleased that they were going to the chariot race and grateful to be moving through the streets of Antioch at a speed (and a height) apart from the enormous crowd. Balthasar had been very courteous to her, but now he seemed to be asleep, despite the camel's gait. Iras had greeted her with a smile but said nothing else, merely fanning herself and gazing around with calm effrontery. The farther Iras's spangled veil slipped down her shoulders, the more tightly Esther wanted to clutch her gray linen veil across her face. Though it really didn't matter.

Men in the crowd below looked at Iras, glanced at Esther, looked back at Iras.

Which was as it should be. There was only one man whose attention Esther wanted. And to him, she was invisible.

She sighed. Invisible. It was right. It was proper. He owned her. She was his property as clearly as the chairs he sat on and the ships at anchor outside her father's warehouse.

And besides, he was going to be a soldier. If he survived this race, he would vanish into the desert and dedicate himself to violence on behalf of the King who would come.

"Are you excited, little Esther?" Iras's voice broke into her thoughts.

"I suppose I will be," Esther answered. "I have never seen a chariot race."

"Do you know anything about the rules?"

"No. Are they complicated?"

Iras laughed. "No, no. But the races can be brutal, you know. They are quite dangerous."

"Yes, I can imagine," Esther said gravely. "Crashes and so on."

"Yes." Iras smothered a yawn with pink-tipped fingers. "I saw a race once in Alexandria where the yoke of the chariot splintered and impaled . . . Oh, I'm sorry. You would probably prefer not to know."

"Yes, you are right. Don't you find the heat oppressive? I think I will follow your father's example and rest until we reach the stadium." Esther pulled her veil down over her face and leaned back onto one of the down-filled cushions. It was a pity everything smelled so strongly of sandalwood, she thought. A lighter scent might have been more alluring on Iras. She entertained herself for the rest of the voyage by mentally creating a perfume for the Egyptian out of the spices and aromatic woods in her father's warehouse.

But the noise coming from the stadium, once they arrived, was so loud that she was spared conversation with Iras. The athletic contests had just finished as they negotiated the steps toward their seats. The tall Nubian held a parasol over Iras, and Esther was aware that, following behind, she must look like a maidservant. She would have liked to pretend, coolly, that she had seen everything before, but curiosity got the better of her.

The stadium itself was immense. Built of stone, rising sharply from the level ground, it held more human beings than she had ever imagined existed. The faces in the distance were nothing but thousands of pinpricks. Beneath a broad purple awning just above the porta pompae lay the seats for the consul and the high-ranking Romans. There the benches were covered with cushions and shawls, and palm fans moved over the toga-clad viewers, all of whom wore bits of scarlet and gold to announce their allegiance to Messala.

The porta pompae lay on the curve of the stadium, with a fine view of the track's two straightaway sections. Esther found, as she followed the Nubian down a steep aisle, that the spot chosen by Simonides and Ilderim was close to the front row. The Roman consul might see the whole of the stadium from a distance, but she would see a portion of it very clearly. As she sat next to her father, whose wheeled chair had somehow been brought into the stadium, the parade of victors passed below, so close that she could see the straw-colored hair and round blue eyes of the Saxon wrestler, followed by the stocky, dark Damascene whom he had beaten.

"That was a very pretty fight," her father said as she settled next to him. "The Saxon has the advantage of height and reach, but the Damascene knew some very interesting throws."

Esther looked at him with surprise, and he laughed, an unfamiliar rasping sound. "Long ago, I was quite devoted to the sport. I find it has not changed very much. I suppose there are not so many ways for one man to topple another to the ground. Did you enjoy your camel ride?"

"Moderately," Esther said, aware she sounded prim.

Her father reached out his hand and patted her on the arm. "You'll come back with me on the boat. I'd forgotten you would have to ride with Iras. I don't like that woman, and I think she has designs on Judah."

Esther glanced around, startled by her father's frankness, but in the noise surrounding them, Iras was out of earshot. "Well, that would never do," she answered, still somewhat sour.

"Esther," he said. "Look at me." She turned reluctantly, aware that she was blushing. He put a hand to her cheek. "Oh, my girl, I am sorry. I never thought . . ."

She thumbed away a tear and muttered, "It's nothing."

"No," he said, facing the stadium again, but this time with her hand in his. "It's not nothing. He is a good man. Perhaps a great one. But he has no time now for thoughts of women."

"Iras seems to think . . ."

"Iras is playing with him. Like a cat with a lizard. Sheik Ilderim tells me Balthasar is appalled, but there is nothing he can do. Anyway, after today, Iras won't see him anymore."

"And neither will I," she said, but it was a question.

"That I cannot say." He looked out at the noisy, sunlit, brilliant spectacle before him and went on. "We cannot know, Esther. What we have in mind is too great to understand. I believe in it, yet it terrifies me. Balthasar's faith is founded on a kingdom of souls; he doesn't dream of war. But Ilderim and I believe blood will run before the King comes. The Romans will not give way for anything less."

"And Judah has agreed? To form an army for the King?"

"He will give us his final answer afterward." He waved his hand toward the track before them. "He wanted first to win the race. I think for him this may be the first battle."

"I am not sure I am ready to watch a battle," Esther murmured.

"I think you will find it difficult to look away," said her father. "Do you see the striped pole directly below us? That is the finish line. The race will end here."

CHAPTER 29

SPEED

The horses were jittery. Naturally. The noise alone—as Ben-Hur checked the harness, he wished he had thought of it. They had never run before an audience of this size. He should have done something to prepare them, maybe arranged for some of the sheik's people to come out to the practice track and shout and wave things. He stepped back from Rigel, the steadiest of the four, and looked the bay in the eyes. Rigel tossed his head, his black mane lashing the air, then shook it as he settled back into place. Next to him Antares whinnied, and an answering whinny came from another horse down the line of enclosures. Ben-Hur thought maybe from the Corinthian's team, three chestnuts and one dappled gray. Taller than the bays. Heavier. Would that matter?

It was a long race—seven laps. Maybe he should have run the bays against other horses. Pure speed would not win this race; stamina counted too. But so did strategy. Anything could happen in seven laps. He had seen it so often in Rome: the best horses, the most careful training, the sturdiest chariot, the wiliest tactics could all be undone by a stroke of bad luck. And sometimes the opposite occurred: from time to time four horses and a man rose to a level they had never reached before and won when they should not have. The Romans would say that was in the laps of the gods. It was hard to imagine the Jewish Yahweh, with his stone tablets and his harsh pronouncements, concerning himself with the outcome of a horse race.

The warning call sounded down the broad passageway, and from outside, trumpets blared. The time had come.

The teams were in pens according to their starting positions, with the outside team closest to the entrance. Each driver led his team out into the aisle and, while grooms held the horses, mounted his chariot. Ben-Hur could hear the cheering as the driver from Sidon entered the stadium, the first competitor to appear. Silence and gloom in the long tunnel beneath the seats; glare and clamor outside. He felt a jolt of excitement.

Next the Corinthian with his three chestnuts and the gray. Then the Athenian, who had driven often in Antioch and whose green-clad supporters raised a mighty shout when his team broke into the sunlight. The driver from Byzantium was next, bursting out of the tunnel nearly out of control. Ben-Hur mounted his chariot.

He moved smoothly. He noticed everything and nothing. The graceful inward curve of Atair's ears, the encouraging smiles of Ilderim's grooms, the everlasting moment when his magnificent horses—harnessed, eager, ready—waited for his signal to move forward. Waited though they wanted nothing more than to run. Waited though they could see the sunlight, could *feel* the noise from their heads to their feet. They waited because he was the master. They waited for his signal.

He relaxed his arm a fraction. They felt it and moved smoothly forward, walking, walking, walking, breaking into a trot and sweeping out into the immense, beautiful bowl of humankind, all waiting for them.

There was an explosion of sound. Astounding that human voices could create such a tumult! Ben-Hur understood something of what the horses probably felt—the sound vibrating through his whole body. He lifted his face to the sun for an instant, then drew to a smooth halt before the porta pompae, where, like all the other drivers, he saluted the consul. Then he moved on.

There were tall cypress trees behind the stadium, casting pointed, graceful shadows over the top rows of seats and patterning the glare of the late-afternoon sun. The track was in perfect condition, soft and even. On his left an entire broad section of the people shouted and waved, every one of them in white.

Behind he heard another roar—Messala, the last driver to enter the stadium. Across the track he could see masses of red and gold flickering in the shaded seats. As Ben-Hur's team reached the curve of the track, he let them out into a canter. The whole stadium was visible to him now. How many dozens of thousands? All intent, all watching and hoping. Some green clothes were visible. Some everyday Antioch drab. More of the Roman scarlet and gold. Messala's supporters outnumbered his. But there were enough. Enough to see Messala's defeat.

Hoofbeats behind him, coming too fast. On his left, the inside. A shout: "Give way, Jew!" Ben-Hur's team pulled against him, but he did not let them speed up. Messala's black and white pairs pulled level, then passed him, galloping all out. Ben-Hur eyed Messala's chariot, glinting with its brass fittings, almost flying behind the horses. It was held down, Ben-Hur thought, only by the bronze lion masks protruding from the wheels. All that weight, for decoration alone—Messala in a nutshell.

The starters, halfway along the straightaway, were in place. The crowd settled, then hushed. The teams took their places, each in his marked lane, nearly wheel to wheel. On Ben-Hur's right the Byzantine caught his eye and nodded. They could have reached out to clasp hands. On his left was Messala.

The floor of his chariot was higher than Ben-Hur's, the wheels slightly taller, so Messala looked down to meet Ben-Hur's eyes. "I thought you were dead, Judah," he said, raising a hand to wave at the crowd. "But it doesn't matter. You're as good as dead now."

Ben-Hur did not react. It was not a time to think about Messala the man, his old friend who had betrayed him. Not a time to wonder about what Messala felt or thought. It was time, finally, to defeat him. Everything had been done to prepare for this moment. The horses, the training, the betting that would focus everyone's attention on their duel—everyone in the stadium knew that for the Roman and the Jew, this was mortal combat. Only one would survive. Why waste so much as a breath on Messala now?

A brass fanfare sounded and the horses took off. The starters began counting. It was the first test of skill for the drivers: the starters held a chalked rope at the height of a horse's chest and dropped it on an agreed count. To hit the rope too early was disaster—sometimes fatal. But to reach it too late was to yield advantage. Messala's team galloped ahead barely under control, and Ben-Hur understood in a flash that the Roman had fixed the start. The starters would drop the rope for him, even if he was there before the count was completed. Ben-Hur relaxed the reins and the bays sped up, but chaos had already developed ahead of him.

Each driver had to cross the rope in his own lane but was free thereafter to change lanes. Messala, on the inside, knowing he was safe, had let his horses reach their full speed before the starting post and flashed past it. But the Byzantine had taken a chance, cutting sharply toward the rail as he reached the starting line, crossing Ben-Hur's lane mere seconds behind Messala. He had tried too hard. His horses were out of control. He hauled on the reins, throwing his weight against the thousands of pounds of galloping horseflesh, unable to slow them, unable to steer them, aware of the pack behind him.

Ben-Hur didn't see the impact. He had time only to glimpse something wrong in front of him, a pattern going astray, and without thinking steered the bays to the right. On his left, howling. A man in pain? A horse? Gone. Done.

* * *

Esther hid her face in her hands. On the track, men jumped the rails to clear the wreckage. Tangled harness, shattered chariot, mangled flesh.

"How can they?" Esther whispered, horrified. "Tell me when it is finished."

"Watch them when they come around again, and you will understand," Simonides said. "There's glory in it. Shall I tell you what I see? Messala is in front, holding the inside. Judah is on the outside. They are running away from us now. I can't see . . . Yes, it looks as if he is last."

"Last!" Esther dropped her hands. She shaded her eyes and looked down the track. "No, he is not last. He is . . . Well, no, I believe the Athenian . . ."

"They will run seven times around, Esther. Judah has time," her father told her.

* * *

In the consul's box, Sanballat watched placidly. "I thought you had money on the Jew," the consul said.

"I do," Sanballat agreed. "Not enough, though."

"You think he will win?"

"Oh yes," Sanballat answered. "And if he doesn't, I will make money from Messala's men."

"What if someone else wins? I see five teams in this race."

"I see two, Your Honor. And three extras."

✳ ✳ ✳

That was not Ben-Hur's view of the matter. He saw four teams to beat, and they were all in front of him. Just where he wanted them. How like Messala to take the lead: showy, excitable, shortsighted. From the front, Messala couldn't see that one of the Athenian's wheels seemed to be wobbling slightly. Or that the Corinthian's horses looked as if they could run forever at this pace. Messala, out in front, could only know about his own team. He could be surprised.

But perhaps it was time to provide Messala with more information, Ben-Hur thought. More than he would get from his spies or the gossip of Antioch. Time to let Messala have a good look at the Sons of the Wind. Now, early in the race. Give him a chance to worry.

They didn't like running behind anyway.

He loosened the reins minutely and shifted his weight to the outside. As one, the bays picked up the pace. They veered slightly to the right. They started to gain on the Sidonian.

✳ ✳ ✳

"Look, Esther, he moves ahead," said Simonides. "Can you see?"

"Yes!" she said. "On the outside!"

"On the outside," Iras's voice came down to her, along with a length of sheer golden gauze. "May I sit here?"

"Of course," Esther said and pulled her robe closer.

"It's a foolish move," Iras said. "The horses will have more distance to cover. Of course when he was training out at the sheik's encampment, he spent many hours of each day running the horses. He was always exhausted. But I wonder if this is the right strategy."

"You are well versed in chariot racing?" Simonides asked politely.

"In Alexandria we go often to the races. The stadium is much more beautiful than this one. And the audience . . . well, naturally it is more sophisticated. Connoisseurs of fine horses."

"Like you," Esther said.

"Oh, I don't make that claim," Iras answered. "Look, Ben-Hur has actually passed someone."

∗ ∗ ∗

It had taken very little. The Sidonian, Ben-Hur thought, had never belonged in this race. He saw the line in the surface ahead where the track fell into shadow and sped through it, almost flinching in the faintly cooler air. The Athenian team was running strongly. He cast an eye on them, watching how easily they carried their heads. A team with stamina, he thought. But maybe not much speed.

∗ ∗ ∗

Where the race had started, the spy was on the dirt, weeping. The chariots were thundering down the track and the wreckage of the Byzantine's chariot had been cleared away, along with the glazed-red tangle of the driver's body. Three of the horses, plunging and rearing, had been mastered and taken back to the stable, but the spy crouched next to the remaining horse, whose right leg lay in a crazy zigzag on the ground.

"Do it! They're coming!" screamed a race official next to him. "We don't have time!"

So much to regret, thought the spy. Why had he become a groom? Why was it better than spying? Why had he bragged about his experiences? Whom had he told about his stint in the slaughterhouse? Where had this knife come from, and was it sharp enough for the job? He reached out with his left hand, located the spot, closed his eyes, and found himself . . . wishing? Praying? Thinking of the brave horse and sending it on its way as his hands were bathed in the hot, iron-scented stream of its blood.

"Quick, quick!" shouted everyone. The body was dragged away, dirt thrown on the wet patch, then more dirt, and scuffed into the earth so that the horses pounding down the track toward him would not smell the death of one of their own.

* * *

In the center of the track stood two sets of three columns, tall and massive, each set topped with an ornate horizontal entablature. On the end of the stadium closer to Esther and Simonides, the entablature was topped with seven enormous carved balls. On the opposite end, seven carved dolphins. Now, as the chariots rounded the curve and hit the straightaway, a man clambered up to the top of the entablature. "Look, Esther," Simonides said. "They will take down a ball each time the chariots pass. And the same on the other end, with the dolphins. This is how we know how much of the race remains. See, here it goes!"

But Esther had no interest in a ball crashing to the ground. She was completely absorbed in Ben-Hur. She understood now how good their seats were—she could see clearly the expression on his face: watchful, intent, eyes flickering from his team to Messala's to the wheel of Messala's chariot as he drew ever nearer to it. The noise was tremendous! The horses' hooves, even muffled in the dirt of the track, thundered along, and the chariots set up a rattle and clang as loud as a caravan compressed into a tiny space. But then came a small sound, a strange and unwelcome noise—it was the hiss and crack of a whip. Messala's whip, brought down on the backs of Sheik Ilderim's bays. Then again, and this time Esther gasped. Messala's lash had caught Ben-Hur's face.

* * *

Ben-Hur hardly felt it. A sting, a faint burn, what could that matter with every muscle in his body already screaming to keep him upright, to hold the horses . . . and to hold the horses after Messala's whip-ping? They were momentarily mad. They had never felt the touch of a whip before, and the instinct of each of them was simply to escape. Their unison wavered as each ran as fast as he could. Rigel, the slow-est, could barely keep up while Antares, the strongest, was pulling the chariot toward the center of the track. Ben-Hur gripped the reins with all of his strength and leaned against their force. For an instant he remembered the galleys, struggling with the oar. Fighting nothing less than the entire ocean. Back, chest, legs, arms all pulling—he had done it over and over again for years. He could do it again. But then something blurred in his eye. Worse. Darkening, smudging, burning with sweat, it must have been blood from the wound Messala had dealt him.

He dared not shift the reins from his left hand while the horses still galloped in terror. He dared not even lift his left arm to wipe his brow; who knew what signal the horses would take from the move-ment of the reins? So he dropped the whip from his right hand, hoping it would be removed from the track before the next lap so it wouldn't get tangled in his horses' feet. He pushed his right wrist up over his eyebrow, wiped the blood on the tunic at his chest, repeated the gesture. He was bleeding fast.

And they were coming into the curve with too much speed.

He noticed Messala check his team and had to grudgingly admire the skill. The four horses slowed a touch, shortening their uniform stride, then moments later stretched it out again, speeding up, appearing to sink slightly toward the earth as their bodies flattened. Ben-Hur knew how it felt, that smooth increase of speed.

But the bays were under control now. The curve got their atten-tion, and he was grateful for their hours of training together. It was as if they threw off the distraction of the whiplash to focus on the task at hand. He wiped his forehead again. Was it stickier? Was the wind on his face drying the blood?

* * *

Sheik Ilderim sat still as a stone. His hands gripped the bench on each side of his haunches, and he leaned forward as if trying to close the distance between himself and the bays. Whipped! That dog of a Roman had dared to whip the Sons of the Wind! The beautiful creatures who were dearer to him than his children, who knew his voice, his touch, his scent, who came to his call and read his moods—whipped!

And yet disaster held off. There had been a bad moment. From behind, as the chariots shot up the track toward the curve, it had looked as if Ben-Hur would lose control. Now they turned into the straightaway and the bays were running as one.

But they had lost ground. They were running last again. Still running strongly, Ilderim told himself. Smoothly. There was plenty of time.

The second dolphin fell to the ground.

* * *

The noise in the consul's box was deafening. "Mess-a-la! Mess-a-la!" the young men shouted, leaping in the air and waving scarlet-and-gold banners as the chariots passed. The entire section of seats nearby was equally noisy, but so were other parts of the stadium. There were not many rules in chariot racing. Like the other sports, it was akin to combat. What succeeded on the field of battle succeeded on the field of competition. Yet striking another man's horses was going too far. That, at least, was the opinion in boxes full of Phrygians and Cilicians and Syrians and Cypriots and all the cultural miscellany of Antioch. They might not have begun as supporters of the Jew. They might have been hesitant to claim allegiance. Most of them had to do business with Rome, and to do business with Rome meant visibly to conform to Roman habits. To do as Rome wished. But on this day, in this place, to see the Jewish man driving those Arabian horses—and Sheik Ilderim's horses were famous all over the eastern half of the empire—was not just a novelty. It was a new idea. Could Rome, in fact, be defeated? If on the track, then in battle? In the marketplace?

Maybe Rome itself thought so. Maybe that was why the Roman driver had whipped the Arabians.

Could the audience with white banners have increased? Weren't there more of them than before? Sanballat thought so. He did sums in his head at lightning speed. If this, then that. If Ben-Hur won, so much money. If Messala, a different sum. *Could* Ben-Hur win? Sanballat's losses were guaranteed by Simonides, so for the sake of his purse alone, the winner didn't matter. But he began to think about that possibility: a Jewish victory. A Roman defeat.

✳ ✳ ✳

The second ball fell. As the chariots hurtled past, Esther tracked Ben-Hur's face again. He was last except for the Sidonian, whose horses were already beginning to droop. In front of Ben-Hur ran the Athenian and the Corinthian, their teams galloping stride for stride, and out in front was Messala, handsome and proud and alone.

"He is magnificent, isn't he?" Iras breathed in Esther's ear. Esther turned and was surprised to understand: Iras was talking about Messala, not Ben-Hur. Iras caught Esther's eye and shrugged. "They are both handsome men," she explained. "But I prefer a hero."

So do I, Esther thought but kept silent. Ben-Hur's was a different kind of heroism; that was all. Easy enough to be a conqueror if other people had done the conquering for you. Harder if you were running near last, with blood in your eye and dust all over your face. Looking calm. Looking—could it be? Happy?

✳ ✳ ✳

Strangely, he *was* happy.

It always came in a race, this moment of well-being, unless it was one of those races where nothing at all went right. This was not one of those races. Despite the loss of the whip, despite Messala, despite the blood dripping into his eye. The blood had slowed down. It stung less. And the Sons of the Wind galloped along like music. Two laps finished, five to go. Plenty of time. The bays could run and run. The air rushed past and every sound faded but the constant rhythmic thud of their hooves. He anticipated the transition into shadow, when vision for a moment was confused. Past the dolphins. Now the curve: a hint of pressure on the reins. The bays collected themselves. In front of them the Athenian and the Corinthian ran neck and neck. Was this the moment? Should he pull out beyond them? Put an end to this phase of the race?

The horses read his thoughts. They made the decision for him. At the top of the curve as they dropped into their fastest pace, they shifted outward. Oh, it was splendid to feel that power and that union. Their wills and his traveled up and down the leather strips of reins, shifting and speaking through touch alone. Here on the curve, shadows flickered now from the tips of the cypresses at the top of the stadium. Each time around, the shade was slightly deeper. Something to think about for the next lap.

※ ※ ※

On they galloped, past the consul's box again. As they passed the purple awning and the highborn Romans, Flavius wondered if Sanballat would take a bet on Ben-Hur. A big bet. If the Jew won, Flavius thought, his money problems would be solved for a while. He stood and cheered with everyone else, shouting, "Mess-a-la" while watching the team of Arabians driven by the Jew. They ran smoothly, eagerly still. Flavius cast a sidelong look at Sanballat. No, he decided; a highborn Roman could not bet on a Jew in full view of Rome's consul.

Third ball down.

* * *

Cleanthes the Athenian pulled in front of the Corinthian. They were all strung out now, each chariot running along the inside, with space between them. The spy stood on the inside of the track watching them approach. Messala's team—were they straining a little? He watched as their feet met the ground, turned and watched their hind-quarters, caught a glimpse of Messala's face. How he hated that man.

He had been dispatched to pick up Ben-Hur's dropped whip from the track, and it lay on the ground beside him. Could he use it? As Messala had used it? A stinging blow across Messala's face? A satisfying thought, but a stupid one. He'd be caught, overpowered, and killed before the horses ran another lap.

And an intervention like that might not be necessary. The Arabians looked like they could run all day.

* * *

But Cleanthes felt a tremor. Or was it something else? Friction? Something had stopped moving smoothly, and at his elbow, with horror, he saw what it was—the wheel. It no longer ran straight. He glanced ahead, glanced down again. Was it real?

It was. The wheel was wavering. And as he watched, wavering more widely. He tried to pull to the outside, tried to haul on the reins to slow his horses and drag them out of the way of the other chariots. He could hear the Corinthian on his heels, shouting, then saw the noses of the Corinthian's three chestnuts and one gray. They were at his elbow. At his wheel. His horses knew they were coming and leaned against the reins, stubborn and fierce.

The Corinthian driver was level with him, pointing at the wheel. Cleanthes hauled harder on the harness, but the wheel was slewing back and forth and would come off any—

A gasp came from one hundred thousand throats, followed by

cries of horror. The wheel came free, rolling wildly across the track. The body of the chariot hit the ground hard and fell apart, strewing shards of wood and metal into the air. Cleanthes was tossed clear and lay, stunned, on the dirt of the track while the team dragged the shattered remains of the chariot along the rail. The horses were terrified, desperate to escape the lumpy, broken, noisy thing behind them.

The Corinthian had managed to run clear, but just yards away, Ben-Hur and the Sidonian pelted toward the wreckage. Cleanthes rolled over, sat up, and leapt for the rail, where the hands of the spy and other officials hauled him out of the way.

✳ ✳ ✳

Ben-Hur barely noticed. His field of vision had narrowed. He was aware only of his horses and the track in front of them. Off to the right somewhere the Athenian's team had come to a halt, shuddering and rearing, their coats flecked with foam. But the track was littered with debris. How to get the Arabians through it?

He looked ahead. There was a path, almost clear. Coming up fast. The horses' feet must not get entangled. At this speed a false step would break a leg. But there was a way . . . As they galloped together, for instants they were free of the ground. Perhaps they could leap; it was only a board, almost flat, wouldn't reach the chariot floor, if they met it right . . . No time . . . The wheels . . .

The wheels hit the board. The chariot flew. He grasped the rail, leapt with the chariot. Landed as lightly as he could.

The Arabians galloped onward.

✳ ✳ ✳

Esther buried her head in her father's shoulder, forgetting for once in her life his physical fragility. He managed to reach his arm up to her shoulder and said, in her ear, "It's all right. Judah is all right. The only damage was to the Athenian's chariot. The driver got free."

"I hate this!" Esther whispered to her father. "Why do people come and watch it?"

"They crave the excitement, I suppose," he said. "And it distracts them from their quarrels and discontents."

Esther sat up and pulled her veil more tightly around her shoulders. "People are horrible."

"Yes," Simonides answered, "quite often they are."

* * *

The fourth dolphin fell. Of the original six teams, only four were left. As Messala, the Corinthian, Ben-Hur, and—far behind—the Sidonian rounded the curve, every fragment of the Athenian's chariot was plucked from the dirt. The spy was sent out to help calm the Greek horses, which he did so effectively that they were soon unharnessed and walked into the tunnel to be examined for injuries. By the time the competitors came back around the consul's box, the track was clear.

"Only four chariots now," the consul said to Sanballat.

"Two—and two extras," Sanballat answered. "But surely you agree with me that the Sidonian is out of the race."

In fact, he was half the length of the track behind. "I agree that without another disaster, he cannot win," said the consul.

"And another disaster would be remarkably unfortunate," Sanballat commented.

"Luck plays its part in the races," the consul countered. "Just as in war. The goddess Fortuna is known to be fickle."

Sanballat only inclined his head. One must be polite to one's customers, but one need not agree with them.

Another ball fell.

* * *

As the Arabians rounded the curve, Ben-Hur's mind was also on luck. Two of the chariots were out of the race. The Sidonian was hardly a threat. The Corinthian, though . . . he had spent the race in front of Ben-Hur. There was nothing apparently remarkable about him, his team, his chariot. The race was more than halfway over. It was time to start winning.

* * *

Messala's team galloped on in front. They preferred to run in the lead. Some people thought he didn't understand his horses, but he did; he was an excellent horseman. These creatures didn't like to have dirt flung in their faces from other horses' hooves. And they pulled against the driver. It had to be said, they were a man's team—not everyone could control them. But set them going on the rail, get them out before the pack, and all would be well. He would make money from that grotesque bet with Sanballat. What an unfortunate wager for the Jew!

The curve came. He steadied the horses, then released the reins a fraction to let them speed up as they ran around it. Were they a little bit less responsive? Tiring, perhaps. Though they shouldn't be. They were as fit as any team on the track, he knew.

Still, there were just over two laps to go. He cracked the whip near the ear of the white horse next to the yoke. Just a reminder of that source of pain. There—they all picked up the pace.

But did he feel something new? Or hear it? Another team. Well, the Corinthian had stayed close. Maybe this was his final push. Messala leaned forward slightly and cracked the whip again. No reason to make winning easy for anyone else.

Five dolphins down.

✳ ✳ ✳

As the teams approached the porta pompae, a very young Roman in a spotless tunic approached Sanballat. "Is it too late to bet against the Jew?" he asked. "A hundred sestertii?"

Flavius stood and put a hand on the young man's shoulder. "Forgive me, Sanballat, for intervening. I am young Tertius's commanding officer and I feel I need to offer him a lesson here. Is this your first chariot race?" he asked.

"Yes," the youth answered, blushing.

"And since I know what your pay is, and I know your father's circumstances, I think someone has persuaded you this is a good idea? That the Jew is sure to lose?"

The young man nodded. "They all said so."

"And they may be right," Flavius answered. "But look now, as they approach. Tell me what you see. Do Messala's horses look fresh? Is he holding them back?"

"No, he has used the whip. Twice."

"And this Ben-Hur. Here he comes. What do you see there?"

Everyone in earshot looked down, as Flavius suggested, and they all noticed the same thing: the bay Arabians running smoothly, eagerly, and Ben-Hur in his bloodstained tunic, leaning back, still holding them in.

"I understand," the young man answered, crestfallen. "The Jew's horses look almost fresh."

Flavius nodded. "He will pass the Corinthian. There is only the Roman left. And I will tell you, as part of your military education, what lesson you should learn here. A good soldier never underestimates the enemy."

"But you don't think the Jew could win, do you?"

"I think two laps remain and it is a close race. If you are overspending your allowance, consider betting less at dice tonight."

As Flavius sat down again, Sanballat nodded to him. "That was well done. I did not need his sestertii."

Flavius smiled. "I'm just warning him away from my own bad habits."

✳ ✳ ✳

The drivers were all tiring now. Blisters were forming on their hands, filling, breaking, bleeding. Their backs and shoulders screamed with the effort of holding the reins against their teams. The Corinthian had avoided the litter from Cleanthes's crash, he thought, but somehow a splinter of wood had worked its way beneath his left foot and deep, deep into his heel. The Sidonian, Ben-Hur, and the Corinthian were all covered with dust: dust in their eyes, their hair, their mouths, gritty between their teeth. Sweat ran down their chests and backs, sliding down their legs. Even the muscles on their faces were tired from the natural grimace: eyes squinted against the sun and dust, foreheads furrowed in concentration.

On they went. Five balls down. Six dolphins. Six balls.

Now? Always the question in a race. Is this the moment to go all out? What if the leader pulls away, out of reach? What if you make the effort and have nothing left? What if you sprint too soon? Ben-Hur watched the bays, absorbing information. Ears pricked forward. They were sweating. Not bobbing their heads. Running evenly—not one was favoring a leg. And they were still eager. From their mouths to his hand he sensed . . . appetite. The Sons of the Wind were competitors. All the training at the Orchard of the Palms had not tested that quality.

But now they wanted to pass the Corinthian. He hesitated to let them. They had already had to run more on the outside than he would have wished. Once more, they'd have to move to an outside lane. But there was no other way. The Corinthian must be eliminated. Ultimately the race was going to come down to a duel between him and Messala.

And wasn't that what he'd wanted all along?

So he lowered the hand gripping the reins. *Now,* he thought, leaning forward, as if he could speak to the horses aloud. *You were born to run. Go. Run as fast as your Creator intended. Show these people what it is to be the Sons of the Wind.*

They heard him, somehow. Pulling out to the right, they passed the Corinthian's chestnuts and gray. The driver saluted as Ben-Hur glanced at him. His horses were finished. The remaining laps would be a match between the Roman and the Jew, which seemed right. His task now was to get his horses safely back to the stable. And if the opportunity came, to lend the Jew a helping hand. He had no love for Romans.

Seven dolphins down. Half a lap. No time. An eternity.

✳   ✳   ✳

Everyone in the stadium was standing, even Simonides, held up between Ilderim and Balthasar's Nubian slave. The noise was tremendous, hanging almost solidly in the air. Esther clambered onto a bench and craned her neck. In the consul's box, protocol had dissolved completely. The most junior soldiers and officials elbowed their superiors aside and leaned over the railing. A scarlet cushion and an eagle-feather fan fell to the dirt, where they lay unnoticed. No horse would come near them, so far from the contested inside of the course.

The race officials, grooms, and track workers—including the spy—spread themselves out along the inner rail, craning their heads to see the oncoming chariots.

Ben-Hur was safely past the Corinthian. Messala's chariot was just two lengths in front of his. But two lengths that shortened too slowly! He was gaining, gaining, but Messala had begun using the lash again. His tired team responded each time the whip touched them. Their strides lengthened, the pace quickened—then slowed again.

Now the curve.

✳ ✳ ✳

There was an art to it. A living art. The touch on the reins, the slackening speed, the renewed momentum.

Messala had no time for art. Judah was on his heels. He twisted around for the first time in the race. So close! And the Arabians still powerful! He lashed his team again. They leapt ahead.

But it was the wrong place. As you rounded the curve, a force pulled you outward. Messala could feel the drift of the chariot. He hauled hard to the left, but the team was galloping flat out.

And on the right, Judah. He turned again. Judah, his double. As a boy, he'd been spoiled, fussed over, treated as a prince. Unable to see the basic fact: Jews were rabble. All the same, there he was, so close. Messala spat.

Then turned forward again. But in that split second he saw his mistake. The rail was a horse's width away from him—too far. Judah was coming up on his right with smooth, amazing speed. A black nose—four black noses were at his elbow. Manes flowing behind them. Somewhere within, the best part of the man found the Arabians beautiful. They ran with joy.

They were almost around the curve. The purple awning over the consular box cast a sliver of shade onto the track now. The slanting sun caught every bit of metal on the horses' harnesses and the golden clasp on Messala's tunic.

✳ ✳ ✳

The iron tips of the axle on Ben-Hur's chariot did not flame up in the sun. Dark metal, absorbing light, meant for strength alone, heavy, durable—used for reinforcement.

Ben-Hur knew the iron was there but had forgotten. Days earlier he had taken the chariot apart with a wheelwright in Ilderim's camp. Every joint, every piece of wood was inspected, strengthened, or replaced. His chariot would not betray him.

Into the straightaway. This was the moment. The two chariots were almost even. Messala slackened his reins and whipped his team again. They leapt ahead with a jerk.

So did the Sons of the Wind. The mere sound of the whip, so new to them, so frightening, gave their feet wings.

And out of sight, between the two hurtling chariots, iron met ivory.

Did Messala's chariot swing outward, into Ben-Hur's?

Did Ben-Hur steer his chariot to strike his enemy's?

The effect was the same, either way. The iron tip of the axle met the polished elephant-tusk spokes of Messala's outside wheel and broke them . . . one . . . by . . . one.

Messala's wheel collapsed.

He was there—and then he wasn't. Ben-Hur looked to his left in confusion. Where? He looked back and saw mayhem. The team running wild. The Corinthian, too close to avoid the wreck. He heard the gasp from thousands of throats, then the horrible high scream of a horse in agony. Or was it a man?

The Arabians ran onward. He closed his ears. It was their race now. Let them run home.

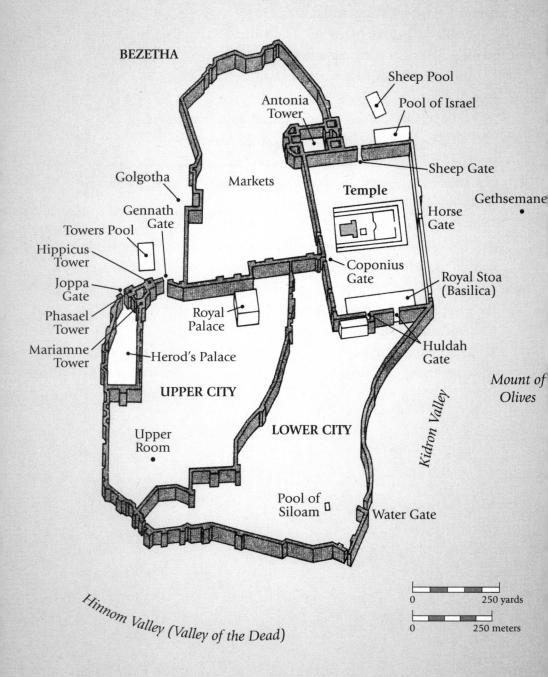

CITY OF JERUSALEM

BEZETHA

Antonia
Tower

Sheep Pool

Pool of Israel

Golgotha

Markets

Temple

Sheep Gate

Gennath
Gate

Horse
Gate

Gethsemane

Towers Pool

Hippicus
Tower

Coponius
Gate

Joppa
Gate

Royal
Palace

Royal Stoa
(Basilica)

Phasael
Tower

Mariamne
Tower

Herod's Palace

Huldah
Gate

UPPER CITY

LOWER CITY

Mount of
Olives

Upper
Room

Kidron Valley

Pool of
Siloam

Water Gate

Hinnom Valley (Valley of the Dead)

0   250 yards

0   250 meters

FIRST TO FINISH. LAST TO DIE.

BEN-HUR

Film stills from the motion picture *Ben-Hur* released by Metro-Goldwyn-Mayer and Paramount Pictures

Tirzah (Sofia Black-D'Elia, far left), Naomi (Ayelet Zurer), and Judah Ben-Hur (Jack Huston) look on in horror as the new Roman ruler parading past their home is attacked. ▶

TROUBLE BEGINS

▲Soldiers swarm the Hur palace to arrest Judah and his family, accusing them of attempting to assassinate the Roman governor.

Judah pleads with his childhood friend Messala (Toby Kebbell),
begging him to show mercy to him and his mother and sister.

A BLESSED ENCOUNTER

When Judah collapses and the Romans prevent
the Hur family servant Esther (Nazanin
Boniadi) from offering him a drink, a carpenter
named Jesus (Rodrigo Santoro) steps in.

Judah spends several years as a galley slave,
rowing to the beat of the hortator's drum.

PUNISHED AND SPARED

After Judah's galley is attacked
and capsizes, he survives by
clinging to the wreckage.

When Judah reaches land, he finds refuge in a wealthy man's encampment. Ilderim (Morgan Freeman) is training his horses for a chariot race and needs a new driver.

A SAFE HAVEN

Judah leaps onto an overturned chariot to stop Ilderim's prized team of horses from running away.

Judah races off after learning more about his mother and sister's whereabouts.

HOME AGAIN

Esther hardly dared to hope that Judah might still be alive and is overjoyed at his return.

Judah and Messala line up at the starting gates.

Messala takes an early lead in the race.

AN EPIC RACE

Racers round the corner of the first lap around the arena.

After multiple laps, Messala's and Judah's chariots collide, the wheels tangling and locking together.

FINAL LAP

Messala fights to push Judah out of the race.

Judah defeats Messala and claims victory, avenging his honor.

Judah offers Jesus a drink on the way to his crucifixion, just as Jesus had given water to him.

CRUCIFIED

Esther and Judah comfort each other at the foot of the cross.

PART 4

CHAPTER 30

A MESSAGE

There was a ceremony, of course. And it was too long—what ceremony isn't?

But all the winners must be given their crowns of laurel, their heavy purses of gold coins. They must all parade around the track, waving and calling out to friends.

Ben-Hur stood in his chariot, aware for the first time of his fatigue, and scanned the crowd. The blood on his tunic had stiffened and he could see, glancing downward, that his cheek, also cut, was swollen and crusted. The horses, though, pranced. They held their heads as high as if they wore laurel wreaths of their own.

The consul stood at the front of the box and bowed to the competitors. Some of the winners were Romans. Scarlet cloaks were thrown down to them from the consul's guests.

There were horns playing somewhere, and drums, but they were just a layer in the hubbub. Ben-Hur wished he were in the stable.

Or back at the Orchard of the Palms, walking the track to cool the Arabians down. Swimming with them in the lake.

On the left, by the finish line, he saw Sheik Ilderim. What a strange group: the tiny Balthasar, visible only as a blue silk turban with a huge jewel. Iras, a shimmering figure, and Esther, whose face looked as if she had been crying. Simonides was smiling and Sheik Ilderim waved both of his arms.

Then a section of Jews, waving kerchiefs, shouting and jumping, calling out to him. He caught the word *hero*.

But that wasn't right. He'd won a race. Nothing more.

He tried not to think about Messala, kept pushing away the sounds he'd heard as the chariot splintered to the earth. Had that been the Corinthian's cry? Who had sobbed as he was carried forward by the bays? Could that sound have come from him? Were tears mixing with blood and sweat on his face?

He raised an arm and waved to the thousands of tiny shimmering dots, each of which was a face in the crowd. What had he done? Those poor horses. How could anyone cheer after such a race? A flower hit his face and he flinched, then waved again. Trumpets played somewhere, cutting through the voices.

The mood in the stable was more muted. Two of the Corinthian's horses had died, as well as the one belonging to the Byzantine. Half of the chariots in the race had been destroyed. The Corinthian had died. Messala might die also. He would certainly never walk again. Even for this most dangerous of sports, it was a terrible toll.

Ben-Hur set to work with the grooms to cool the horses, to brush out their manes, to scrape the sweat from their coats and rub them with braided straw until they gleamed again. He was feeling one of Aldebaran's legs for swelling when the horse flung up its head and nickered, followed by his teammates. The sheik had come to share their triumph.

Ilderim gripped Ben-Hur's shoulders and embraced him wordlessly. Then he leaned back and touched Ben-Hur's bloody tunic. "You should be grooming yourself, not my horses!" he exclaimed.

"No," Ben-Hur answered. "The horses did all the work."

"Not all of it. By no means all of it," the sheik answered. Antares stuck his nose beneath Ben-Hur's hand and snorted.

For the first time since the race, Ben-Hur smiled. "To tell the truth, Sheik, I don't share everyone's joy. It was an ugly race. But the Sons of the Wind ran as befitting their name. Don't you think they know what they've done?"

"Most certainly they do. Look how proudly Aldebaran holds his head. I tell you, Judah, there will be joy in the black tents tonight and for many nights to come." There was a pause. "You won't come with us? You know the caravan is halfway to Moab. No point in staying around to reap the Romans' anger. The bays and I will be far from Antioch before anyone realizes we've left, and you might be wise to join us."

"I understand that. But one man is easier to hide than the caravan of a sheik. I will be with you soon."

Ilderim held Ben-Hur's gaze. "Men often feel dejected after battle, I'm told. What happened on that track today was battle of a sort."

Ben-Hur nodded. "Yes. I understand that. Thank you."

Ilderim paused before saying, "All right. And would you like to take your horse with you, or will he stay with his brothers for now?"

Ben-Hur frowned. "What horse?"

"Whichever one you want," Ilderim said with a broad smile. "They will never race again. My point is made, and my pride, more importantly, is satisfied. My reputation is safe for years now, as far south as Aqaba and as far east as the sea of the Scythians. Every ally who was thinking of leaving me will stay, and many more will join them. I can truly boast that I control the desert, and everyone who wants to cross it will have to pay me for the privilege."

"All because of a race," Ben-Hur commented.

"We people of harsh places require strong leaders," the sheik answered. "There are many ways to show strength. Contests like this are one of them. You know that I would not have this victory without you. I would give you gold, but you have that already and seem to care little for it. So one of my horses is to be yours. You will need a fine mount if you choose to build this new force for the mysterious King. You need not choose your horse now."

But Aldebaran, as if he understood, had draped his head over Ben-Hur's shoulder and was snuffling the wounded cheek. Ilderim nodded. "On the other hand, the horse may have chosen you." He was glad to hear Ben-Hur laugh.

"Then I can only thank you, Sheik."

"Good. Will he stay with me for now, until you join me?"

"Yes, please. I am not sure what the next few days will hold."

After the sheik left, Ben-Hur stayed in the stable. He finished grooming Aldebaran and visited each of the other three horses, all of them calmly resting now and showing no signs of their great effort. The stable was quiet. Voices murmured; strong teeth crunched grain; water ran into a trough. Outside, he knew, the streets of Antioch would be thronged with excited crowds. There would be music. Dancing. Fights, probably.

He went back to Aldebaran's stall once more and leaned against a bale of hay, suddenly exhausted. Too tired to think.

✳ ✳ ✳

The spy, turning a corner, stopped. Was this victory? This forlorn figure, drooping, still bloodstained? The horse behind him had been groomed, watered, fed, and now stood glowing with satisfaction and dreaming with one hoof cocked and his eyes half-closed. The spy thought the man could have used a groom himself. He coughed.

Ben-Hur looked up and straightened. "Yes?"

"I have a message for you," said the spy. He looked again at the horse. "But may I say first what a great victory that was?"

"Thank you," Ben-Hur answered gravely.

"And the Arabians are magnificent."

Ben-Hur turned to look at Aldebaran and his forbidding expression softened. "They are. And your message?"

The spy coughed again. He didn't like it. He hated the Roman. It had been a shock to get the new order. But with the order had come a reminder: the Roman could expose him. Once this last ugly errand was run, he would make sure he vanished. Perhaps even with the sheik's caravan—he'd heard they were on the way into the desert, where a man could disappear. And everyone needed grooms.

"It is from Iras, the Egyptian. Her father, Balthasar, is spending the next few days at the palace of Idernee. She would like to see you there, around midday tomorrow. She wants to congratulate you in person."

The spy was amused to see Ben-Hur blush while he answered, "Thank you. Does she need an answer?"

"No. It seems she expects you to comply." He could have said more, of course, but this young man, such a hero in the chariot, seemed delighted by the summons of the Egyptian woman. Who was reputed to be a strumpet or maybe a witch, and certainly trouble for a naive young Jew. The spy shrugged. That was done. So he turned away and vanished into the shadows.

＊　＊　＊

The streets of Antioch were as lively as Ben-Hur had expected, the noise as loud, the torches as bright. With a light cloak to cover his bloodied tunic, he walked alone and quietly on the straight Roman roads as the crowds thinned, then into the narrower streets as he neared the waterfront.

What could Iras want? To congratulate him. And then? In the last week he'd thought about nothing but the race and the horses: speed, equipment, the competitors, the possible outcomes. Iras had not entered his mind.

He didn't even know what was possible with her. What was usual. Between a Jew and an Egyptian—between a rich Romanized Jew and the daughter of an Egyptian wise man? He'd spent his life among men in the last years. Women had their place, but Iras did not fit into any niche that he knew of. Mother, wife, daughter . . . concubine, servant . . . What else was there? Well, he would wait and see, he told himself. But as he walked, he kept remembering how she had looked by the lake, with damp linen clinging to her legs.

It came as something of a shock, then, when Esther opened the door to her father's house. Esther the daughter. Esther the house-keeper. With the level gaze and the low, musical voice.

"I was listening for you," she said quietly. "My father was tired by the race, and I didn't want the bell to waken him." She closed the massive door. "Come up to his workroom. It's cool there, and I have some food for you. I thought you might be hungry."

"I am," he answered, surprised to realize it. "Is your father all right?"

"Oh yes!" she answered from the step above him. "He was so delighted! I have never seen him seem so . . . so *well*. It was as if your victory made him forget his pain. Truly forget, I mean." She paused for a moment, and he noticed how the lamp on the wall shone on her smooth hair. "It was tremendous. I don't even know what to say. Except to congratulate you." She continued up the stairs. "And you? Are you happy?"

Happy. Was he happy? He had won the race and wounded Messala. Did that make him happy? No, he thought. Whatever he felt at this moment, it was not happiness. Closer to disgust.

They reached the landing and she opened the door. In the center of the room was a table, set with platters of meat and fruit, a pitcher of water and one of wine.

Esther pulled back the single chair. "I will serve you. The servants are all asleep."

As he passed beneath a hanging lamp, she drew in her breath. "But wait a moment. Sit down and let me look at your face." She took his arm firmly and urged him into the chair, then put a hand beneath his jaw and turned his face so that the light shone into his eyes. "Stay like that," she commanded in her soft voice. "But close your eyes. You're lucky. He could have blinded you." He heard quiet movements, then felt a stinging sensation that made him flinch. "Just to get the dirt out," she explained. "It will never heal cleanly otherwise. I suppose you took care of the horses and did not think to see to yourself."

"You're right. But the horses worked harder than I did."

"Oh, I don't think so." Her hands went on pressing and dabbing. "All they had to do was run." The damp cloth paused for a minute. He opened his eyes and saw her wringing it out into a plate. When she faced him, she was frowning.

"Is it always so violent?" she asked.

He drew a deep breath. "Yes. No. Not like that."

She took hold of his jaw again and tilted his head back. Her fingers were cool. "Not too much more. I have some ointment that will help. You'll have a terrible bruise tomorrow."

There was silence. "And I am the lucky one," he finally said.

"Yes." The hands paused. "Did you mean to do that?"

"Damage Messala's chariot?"

She didn't answer but moved the cloth closer to his eye.

"I don't know. I have been wondering. Sometimes in a race, things happen . . . It's all so fast. Your intention is carried out even before you've made it clear to yourself. I am not proud of it, if that is what you are asking."

"He had whipped you. And the horses."

"This much I know, Esther: I did ask Malluch to find out the height of his wheels. I knew that the axle of my chariot had been reinforced with iron. And that it could cut through those gaudy elephant tusks like a knife through cheese."

"And that, if the chariot broke down, he could be trampled by the next team along. As he was," she said firmly, but her voice wobbled slightly. His eyes opened and he saw hers, close to him. Full of tears. She pulled back and turned away. "It was awful to watch."

He sat up straight. "I know."

"No," she said firmly. "You can't. You're used to it. How many men have you seen die?" He didn't answer. "You see? You don't even realize. For us women, it's different. We hear about what you do, armies and swords and so on. But to see it like that, one minute a man and the next a . . . a piece of meat! And you do that to each other! As a game, for a prize!" She was on her feet now, twisting the damp cloth in her hands. She moved over to the balcony and stepped outside.

Slowly he rose and crossed the room to follow her. A humid breeze from the river skimmed the raw spot on his face. He stood next to her, hands on the balustrade, facing the harbor.

"Never mind," she said quietly. "It was just a shock."

"I know." There was silence between them as the water below lapped against the wharf. "I can tell you this, though: I believe I am safer now, with Messala out of action."

"You mean he would have tried to kill you?" Her voice rose, and she pulled her shawl around her as if the breeze from the river had suddenly blown cold.

"Kill, injure, kidnap—who knows? He is powerful. He is Roman. He hates me. He wanted to get rid of me. It's easily done. Maybe he wanted to do it today, publicly and permanently. Maybe he hoped the Sons of the Wind would run away with me and smash the chariot into a wall. Maybe he tried to make that happen. We had guards on the chariot and they found a man with some tools sneaking around the stable. Was he Messala's man? Possibly."

"But did you set out to kill him?"

"Does it matter? You know what our Scripture says. An eye for an eye, a tooth for a tooth. He destroyed my family. My mother and sister are gone because of him. Should I not have my revenge, ugly though it was?" As he heard his words, Ben-Hur realized how much he wanted an answer to his question.

"I don't know," Esther answered with a sigh. She turned and went back inside. "Come, you need to eat."

"Will you sit with me?" he asked as he sat in the chair she held for him.

"I?"

"Why not?"

"Because I am a woman. Do women eat with men in Rome?"

"We are in Antioch," he answered. "And we are alone in this room." He stood and held the chair for her. "Sit down. I refuse to eat until you do."

She blushed but sat while he pulled a stool toward the table. "And I am your slave," she added. "It isn't right."

He poured a cup of wine and slid it across the table to her. "Who will know?"

"Malluch. He always knows everything."

"Your father is lucky to have Malluch."

She nodded. "As he said when you were discussing the King who will come, he has been very lucky, in some ways. Once his misfortune ended." She watched as he cut some lamb and tore off a piece of bread. "Will you do it?"

"Lead their army?" He took a few bites, thinking. "I still don't know."

"Why would you?"

"For the reasons they named: liberation from Rome, support of the King. To free Judea—that would be worth anything, don't you think?"

"Then why have you not made up your mind?"

He spat the pit of a date into his hand and laid it on the side of his plate.

"Selfish reluctance, perhaps." He looked at her and offered her a date. She took it with a little smile. "When I went to Rome, Arrius told me I could do anything, be anything. If I'd wanted to be a poet or a politician, he would have seen that I was trained, had what I needed, knew the right people.

"But I was angry. Rome might have rescued me, but before that she had held me prisoner for three years. I wanted nothing but to become a soldier. That was all I could think of to do with myself. I was so full of rage that I could barely breathe, and the training was what I wanted. In the palaestra, where you learn how to strengthen your body and fight man-to-man, I turned myself into a weapon. The next step was going to be training with the army, to learn to lead. And then Arrius died."

"And you were free."

He nodded. "Free to find your father. And any trace of my family."

"Instead Messala found you."

"Yes. And now, if I do not join with your father and Sheik Ilderim . . . what shall I do with myself? But if I do . . . do I really want the life I had planned?" He stood and stretched his arms over his head. "I will have to cut myself off from everything. I'll be an outlaw. Beyond the laws of Rome, which extend almost everywhere. It's a terrible step."

Esther rose as well. "Do you not believe in this King, then? Isn't he supposed to topple Rome from power? 'Born king of the Jews . . .' What else could that mean?"

"Yes, of course. But it won't happen at once. It could take years."

"And you are hesitating before years as an outcast," Esther said. "No one could blame you. The problem with being a weapon is that weapons are not human. It's a harsh choice to make for a lifetime."

"Yes, I'm beginning to understand that," he said somberly.

CHAPTER 31

SURPRISE

Ben-Hur didn't want to ask Esther how to find the palace of Idernee. That would have meant explanations. So he simply left the house above the wharf the next day with a vague excuse, trusting that someone would be able to direct him. Heading toward the big palace across the river seemed like a good start.

A small boy with a donkey pointed him in the right direction. He glanced at the sky. He had been summoned for midday. Was the sun high enough in the sky? What if he arrived too early? Would Iras think he was foolish? But he didn't want to be late. His hand, for the twentieth time, went up to the wound on his cheek. Esther's ointment had helped, he thought, but it was still puffy. He could barely see past the swelling when he looked at his feet, buckled into his best sandals. He wished he had brought better clothes to Simonides's house, even one of his Roman tunics.

Well, she had asked for him. And here he was, bruised and plainly dressed. He turned into the outer vestibule of the palace that he assumed was his destination. It certainly looked Egyptian, with its massive dark stone and a fountain in the shape of an ibis. Twin stairways were guarded by sculptures of winged lions, but no human presence betrayed itself.

He climbed the stairs, wondering. At the top, a narrow hall led him forward to a tall closed door. He waited for a moment, looking for a bell or a knocker, but found nothing, so he pushed the door open.

And there inside was the atrium of a Roman villa. Ben-Hur smiled. It was a clever idea, to hide this splendor behind the stern Egyptian facade. He stepped into the rectangle of sunlight at the center, where the ceiling opened to the sky. From there, the interior seemed shadowy. He stood listening. Strange, not to have been met. And strange that the house should be so quiet. Where were the servants? Someone should have come to welcome him, wash his feet, offer him a goblet.

Well, Iras was not a housekeeper like Esther. He tried to imagine Iras cleaning his wound. No—impossible. But his mind drifted to what she might say. Congratulations, of course. Admiration? Would she tell him how brave he was? Probably not. There was always something slightly challenging about her.

He left the sunlight and moved back into the shady portion of the atrium. It was vast, stretching deep into the house, and extremely luxurious. Tables and chairs were inlaid with patterns and the cushions woven to match. Elaborate gilded chandeliers hung from chains, and the columns supporting the ceiling were all hewn from colored marble, here green, there red, there white streaked with gray.

Whose palace was this? Why were Iras and her father staying here, anyway? He knew they weren't going to the desert with Ilderim. He thought Iras had probably insisted on a spell of comfort. He sat down to test the cushion of a divan. Soft enough even for Iras, he thought.

His eye fell on the mosaic next to him. The entire floor was covered with thousands of tiny tesserae, placed into designs and scenes and polished so that the furniture seemed to float on a mirror. Only when you stood near them could you make out the scenes.

At Ben-Hur's feet a beautiful woman with golden hair lay back, half-covered by an enormous swan. Of course—Leda, welcoming Zeus in the guise of the bird. She looked . . . He bent down. She looked quite delighted.

Was that a sound? He rose from the divan and stood tense. No. Nothing. He crossed the room, looking at the floor. Hercules, with his leopard-skin cloak, embracing . . . What was the nymph's name? Omphale? Another blonde nude lying back beneath a shower of gold. Ben-Hur looked away. It was very detailed.

Could he have made a mistake? No. The message from the little man had been clear: meet Iras at the palace of Idernee. She was just late. She had often been late for meals at the Orchard of the Palms. She was getting ready to see him. Putting something on, taking something off. A bracelet, a veil. Rouge from an alabaster pot.

But it might be worth asking someone where she was, if he could find a servant of some kind. He crossed the atrium back to the door where he had entered, hearing his sandals slap against the mosaic. *Slap*, he stepped on the tail of a mermaid. *Slap*, Apollo's chariot underfoot. *Slap*, the ornamental border by the door . . . which did not open. Push, pull. No.

He took a breath and tried again deliberately. Pushed the door with his shoulder, but it stood as solid as the wall. Pulled the elaborate handle, which did not move. He had entered through this door and now, plainly, it was locked.

Before he even thought about it, his fingers were unbuckling his sandals. Whatever else happened, he wanted to be silent. His body had decided that, and his mind belatedly agreed. That was what military training did for you.

He left the sandals by the door and prowled around the outside edge of the atrium. In most grand Roman houses these would be rooms for sleeping, for eating, maybe hallways to kitchens. But all of the doors were locked. He tried calling out once, but his voice echoed strangely.

Strange indeed. His mind had worked slowly at first but now reached one conclusion after another.

This was a trap.

No one knew where he was.

Whatever happened, there would be no witnesses.

And if he were to be attacked, he would have no help.

There were weapons everywhere, if he was given time to use them. The furniture could be thrown, the candelabra swung. The doors might even be broken down.

One conclusion he could not reach: was Iras involved?

No way to tell.

He resumed his pacing, stepping silently from one column to another. They were fortunately thick. A man could hide behind them. And the silence might be on his side. When they came, he would be ready. He could surprise them.

Whoever *they* were.

Time passed. The sun moved, and with it the shadows. New scenes on the floor slid out of the shade: Apollo chasing Daphne; Diana surprised while bathing. The columns laid bars of shadow across the myths on the floor. Ben-Hur thought there might be something useful there. Pull an opponent from the shade into the glare, or vice versa, take advantage of the confusion to his eyes . . .

But maybe not. Maybe there was no opponent. He sat down on a divan and put his legs up. Maybe the doors had been closed on him by mistake. Maybe he should have stayed in the vestibule. Maybe he had misunderstood the message.

He had not misunderstood the message, though. He repeated it again in his mind: Iras, midday, the palace of Idernee. But . . . tomorrow, perhaps? Did he have the day wrong?

No. He heard a footstep. He leapt to his feet and put the length of the room between himself and the door he had entered. There were two sets of steps now. Two men coming in where he had. Talking.

It was not a language he knew. Harsh and guttural, it came from the back of the throat. And the sandals, he could tell by their sound, were heavy things. He slid around his column to take a look at the men.

They stood by a chair, pointing at the carved wood. One sat in it and laughed with pleasure. The other gestured at the floor, where both crouched to run hands over an image, amazed by the smoothness of the tile. Then they stood, and Ben-Hur understood everything.

They were assassins, come to kill him. The taller was the Saxon with straw-blond hair who had won at wrestling the day before. The other was dark-haired, a bit shorter but equally muscular. As they turned away from him to look at a statue of a woman with a jug of water, the dark man caressed her smooth white marble haunches as if she were a live woman. The blond giant laughed and Ben-Hur identified him further.

Thord, who had taught him wrestling in Rome! He had seen the man the day before in the victory parade, his features half-hidden by the laurel wreath. Something about him had looked familiar, but Ben-Hur had not recognized him.

And now the situation was clear. Like him, the assassins were strangers to the house. Like him, they had been given their instructions and sent to follow them. For him, the bait had been Iras. For them, he supposed, money. But who could so badly want him dead? Surely not Messala, not in his current state.

They were in no hurry. They ambled around, examining, touching, admiring. Thord lay on a divan and pretended to snore. Ben-Hur watched and tried to think.

Two of them. One of him. No escape.

That was as far as he got in his thinking. Two of them, one of him.

If he was going to live, he would have to attack. Two of them; one would have to die.

How?

He crept backward away from them, considering his options. They had come in through the door, which he had thought locked. So either they had keys or they had help. He wondered if they had seen his sandals, but he thought not. They acted like men who thought they were alone.

He watched them for a moment as they examined one of the heaviest candelabra, a massive bronze column, branched at the top, resting on a set of rollers. Naturally they had to test its movement. Did it roll easily? Could one man move it alone? How quickly could it be made to move?

Not fast enough to be a weapon, Ben-Hur decided.

He considered his clothes, his sandals. Could he reach the door, throw a sandal, distract them, attack one man, disable him . . . ? No. Not with fighters of this caliber. He would have to separate them, then. Kill one and then the other. He began to look around the space again. Could he climb up a column, leap onto one man's back . . . ?

Thord said something to the dark-haired man, who wiped his hands on his tunic and nodded. They separated and started looking for him.

Ben-Hur decided to take the initiative himself. He stepped away from his column, into the bright square of sunlight.

"Who are you?" he asked in Latin.

They turned around and approached him. "Foreigners," Thord answered. He grimaced, though it might have been a smile. As he drew closer to Ben-Hur, his bruises from the previous day's competition were more visible. One of his eyes was dark and swollen while a tuft of his straw-like hair had been torn from his scalp.

"I know you," Ben-Hur said. "I saw you yesterday at the games."

"And I saw you," Thord replied. "But your horses are not here now."

His friend snickered.

"But I recognized you from before. You taught wrestling back in Rome. You taught me, in fact."

"No," Thord said, laughing. "I never taught a Jew."

"I passed as a Roman in those days."

Thord laughed louder. "Can't be done. I don't believe it."

"I'll tell you something else," Ben-Hur went on. "You were sent here to kill me."

"That much is true." Thord nodded. "And we won't get paid until we do it, so maybe we should start."

"Let me ask you—did you win much money yesterday?"

"Oh yes, some," Thord answered.

"Enough to make a bet with me?"

"About what?"

"I bet I can prove to you that I was your student in Rome. Three thousand sestertii."

Thord's face lit up. "Done! How will you prove it?"

Ben-Hur stepped out of the sunlight and began to take off his robe. "Your companion there—is he a friend of yours?"

Thord looked at the dark-haired man and spoke to him in their guttural language. "No."

Ben-Hur uncovered his head and laid his clothes on a chair. "Then I will show you, by fighting him."

"Oh, good!" Thord said. He spoke again to the dark-haired man and the two of them pushed a divan out of the way, clearing a broad space on the floor. "Wait until I tell you to start." He lay down on the divan. "This is funny! You two look so much alike! You could be brothers fighting!"

The two men, now stripped down to undertunics and bare feet, surveyed each other. It was true.

"All right, begin," commanded Thord.

The opponent raised his hands. Ben-Hur stepped in close. He feinted with his right hand. The opponent raised his left arm to fend off the blow. Ben-Hur caught that arm at the wrist. He shoved the arm forward across the man's throat, pressing into the windpipe. At the same time, he spun the opponent's body around, exposing his left side. With the side of his free left hand, Ben-Hur struck the man just under the left ear, breaking his neck. Done.

As the man slumped to the tiled floor, Ben-Hur stepped back. He noticed, beneath his victim's knee, the snaky severed head of Medusa. Thord leapt to his feet. "But I couldn't have done it better! I invented that move!"

"And I learned it from you," Ben-Hur said, looking down at the man he had just killed.

Thord knelt and gently wiggled the dead man's head. "Snap! Did you hear it? Clean as could be." He looked up at Ben-Hur. "But I swear I never taught a Jew."

"I was known as Arrius in those days," Ben-Hur said. He wished Thord would leave the corpse alone. "Who sent you here?"

"Messala," Thord answered as he closed the corpse's eyes.

"But . . . he could speak?" Somehow Ben-Hur had not envisioned this. He thought he had neutralized his enemy. Instead, it seemed, Messala and his hatred endured.

"Groans, mostly." Thord stood. "He truly hates you. He is going to pay me six thousand sestertii to kill you." His face fell. "But I haven't . . ." He turned to Ben-Hur with his hands raised as if to attack.

That was what Messala could do—keep menacing him. As Simonides demonstrated, a man could achieve a great deal from a chair. If Messala lived, Ben-Hur knew he would never be safe. A knife blade in the back, poison in a cup, an ambush in an alley . . . Forever. His eye fell on the nameless corpse. Dark hair, tall, strong build. An idea began to form.

Before Thord could step closer, he said, "Yes, here I am, still alive. And you owe me three thousand sestertii, since I proved I was your pupil."

Thord's hands dropped as he tried to work this out. Ben-Hur waited.

"I will just kill you and get the money from Messala," Thord finally announced, nodding to himself.

"Or make more money."

"How would I do that?"

"Very easily. You said this man and I looked like brothers. I want to trick Messala into thinking I am dead. If you help me do that, I will pay you."

"Oh, that is a good trick! How will we do it?"

"Easily. I will change clothes with him and leave the palace with you. Whoever let you in saw two of you—someone will see you leave with the same man. Only it will be me."

"How much will you pay me?"

"Messala pays you six thousand. . . . What would you do with ten thousand sestertii?"

"With ten, I would open a wineshop," Thord answered promptly. "Right by the Great Circus in Rome. It would be the best wineshop in the city. But where would the four thousand come from?"

"From me."

"How will I get it?"

"Tonight a messenger will bring it. But if word ever emerges that this man is not me, I will know that you betrayed me. And I will hunt you down. I will come to your wineshop in Rome and break every barrel in it and set it on fire."

"Oh, that will never happen. But maybe one day you will visit it and offer to throw me as you did this man, and I will pour you a cup of the best wine in the city," Thord answered. "This has been a good day for me!"

Ben-Hur looked down at the man on the floor. "Not for him, though," Thord added.

It was not pleasant to undress the body. The skin was cooling and the undertunic was far from clean. Ben-Hur was surprised by his distaste. Yet a bigger shock came when he and Thord had maneuvered the corpse into Ben-Hur's own clothes and arranged it on the floor. In Ben-Hur's own belted robe, with a skullcap lying next to it, the body looked weirdly familiar.

"It could be you," Thord said with satisfaction. He crouched down to move the skullcap closer to the body.

"It could *have* been me," Ben-Hur said quietly.

CHAPTER 32

DOUBT

The image stayed with Ben-Hur all day. Or maybe it was the idea. Himself, dead. Or—a version of himself? Could a man become different men in a lifetime?

Of course. Ben-Hur himself had already done that, he realized. He had been a prince's son and a galley slave and a Roman aristocrat.

Had he thought that simply by putting on a Jewish robe and resuming his name, he would once again become a new person?

It seemed so. He had been imagining, perhaps, a kind of outline he could step into. He had imagined himself as a respectable, prosperous Jew. The kind of man his father had been. Going to Jerusalem to ask questions of highly placed people and discovering . . . what? In his heart of hearts, had he believed that his mother and Tirzah would still be there, waiting for him?

Maybe that idea had lingered somewhere. Despite everything that had happened to him. Hidden behind what he thought were his plans and his reasons.

But now it was time to abandon the vision of a happy reunited family.

Anyway, he wasn't that man anymore. All those years in Rome learning violence—he couldn't just erase them. The violence was there, part of him. As that dead man in the palace of Idernee proved. And Messala, crippled for life. Unbidden, the image of a body floating in the burning sea came into his mind: the first man he had killed. The count, it seemed, was mounting.

This was something he would have to get used to. Striking first. Coldly. Carnage for a purpose. When he had killed before, it had been in self-defense. Even injuring Messala had been an act of vengeance. Killing that unknown man—his double—had been an act of ruthless aggression.

But the corpse would now bear his name, allowing him to vanish.

It was strangely disturbing. Oh, he understood how useful this was. Simonides would search for him publicly and insist that the new consul, Maxentius, investigate his disappearance. Word would reach Messala quickly that his nemesis Ben-Hur was dead. Eventually the procurator in Jerusalem would hear. No one would look for him. He would be free.

Free, but no one.

And if you are no one, how do you become someone?

He parted from Thord in the seething bustle of the omphalos, the very center of Antioch. No one would notice, amid the throngs, two men in ordinary clothes who were together, then were not. Even so, Ben-Hur was not ready to return to Simonides's house. What if someone sent by Messala was watching it? Or watching him?

Once again, as on his first day in Antioch, he found himself following the crowd. Return to the Grove of Daphne? Why not?

Of course, everything looked different than it had on his first visit. Ben-Hur realized that, in the short time he'd spent in Antioch, he'd become used to its lushness and its variety. He wasn't surprised by the exotic array of visitors or the abandoned gaiety of the temple servants. He sat under a tree, wandered by a stream, decided not to visit the stadium.

But he was not entirely surprised to find himself on the path to the Fountain of Castalia, where he had first seen Messala—and Iras, too. He had been going to get a fortune on that first day, with Malluch, but hadn't had the chance. Why not see what the oracle said, after all?

The fountain was just as crowded as the day he had visited it before, and he had to press through the crowd to get to the priest. He had a queasy moment when he realized he must use the dead man's money to pay for the fortune and would have given up but for a woman pressing against him and telling him to hurry. So he thrust his hand into the dead man's purse and pulled out a few coins.

The priest dipped the papyrus leaf and handed it to him, glancing at the leaf as he did so. He frowned and submerged it again. "Sometimes this happens," he explained in a low murmur. But no writing appeared. So he selected a new leaf and dipped it in the water swirling around his calves.

It too came up without writing.

The priest signaled to Ben-Hur to step aside and submerged the leaf of the eager woman. Ben-Hur saw the letters appear, though she whisked it away before he could read them.

"One more time," suggested the priest.

He dipped a third leaf and handed it to Ben-Hur with a piercing glance. "From time to time this happens," he said.

"I have no fortune? No future?"

The priest shrugged. "I only read them. I don't know what they mean. I always think, when no writing appears, that the gods themselves do not know what will become of someone."

Ben-Hur let the leaf drop as he walked away. No help there, then.

Eventually night fell and he felt it would be safe to return to Simonides's house. He had hoped to enter quietly, wash and change his clothes before seeing Esther or her father, but Esther met him on the ground floor as he came in.

She looked at the coarse robe and sandals with surprise. Then she looked at his face, her eyes narrowed. Finally she said, as if aware she'd been rude, "Peace be with you. We are glad you have returned."

"And also with you," he answered. It was hard to know what to add. *"I killed a man today? I no longer exist? Who am I? What am I to be?"* He tried a smile instead.

Esther reached out and touched the robe, then shook her head. "Come with me to the kitchen," she said. "I will clean your face again."

He followed her toward the big room at the back of the house, where she lit several oil lamps and set them high on a cupboard to create a cloud of brightness.

"Sit down," she instructed him, filling a bowl with water.

He sat on a low stool and let her dab at his face. It had stopped hurting much earlier. He knew it was on the way to healing. But the room was shadowy and quiet. And he liked the sense of Esther's concern.

"These are not your clothes," she stated.

"No."

"May I burn them?"

"Once I've taken them off, yes," he answered.

"Wait here." She left the room and he heard her giving instructions to a servant.

"Dinah will bring you a clean robe." Esther leaned against a table and looked at him. "What happened today?"

He didn't answer but stared down at his hands.

She moved away from the table and emptied the bowl of water into a cistern, wringing out the cloth afterward.

"Nothing good, it would seem," she said when she came back to him. "I have never met a champion of the Roman games, but I don't think you spent the day celebrating your victory."

"No." He looked up at her. Steady green eyes held his.

"My father was concerned," she said neutrally.

"I had . . . something to do. That didn't turn out the way I thought."

"For good or for ill?" she asked. Her tone was softer.

"I don't know." He shrugged. "More violence. I killed a man." She didn't react. "He was going to kill me. Messala had sent him."

"Messala! He had the strength?"

"And the hatred, it seems."

"But you can't . . ." She frowned as the implications became clear. "He could find you . . . Is that why you stayed away all day?"

Ben-Hur nodded. "Partly. It is known that I am staying here. His power, it seems, is still extensive." As he stood and stretched, his shadow leapt up the wall of the room. He walked over to the door and looked outside, then came back in.

He kept moving around the kitchen as he spoke, picking up a beaker as if he had never seen one and replacing it gently on the shelf. "But now Ben-Hur is dead." He glanced at Esther as he said it. "The man sent to kill me could have been my twin, so I took his clothes and dressed him in mine. I will ask your father to search for me publicly. Maybe the body will be found. There will be a commotion, in any event. The consul will have to take notice because of the chariot race. Word will reach Rome, and Messala will believe I am dead."

"Well, that is surely a good thing," Esther suggested.

"More than that—necessary." He returned to the stool and sat, looking up at her again. "I am now free to go to Jerusalem to look for my family. It would have been dangerous to do that while the son of Hur lived. Truthfully, I do not expect to find them. But I need to know that I made the effort. And I find I want to see Jerusalem again."

"And after that? Will you fall in with Sheik Ilderim's and my father's plan?"

He lifted his hands from his lap. "I think I must. Circumstances drive me to it. As Judah Ben-Hur, I no longer exist. But I must do something, and that is something I can do. I think."

"From what you said before, you have the training," Esther reminded him.

"Yes."

"Do you believe that the King is really coming?"

"I am not sure I do," he confessed. "But I don't think it matters, for me. I made myself into a warrior to wreak vengeance on Rome. The Jewish people do not have an army, and I may have the means to help build one. How can I turn aside from that?"

"It sounds very lonely," Esther said. "If you had the comfort of belief, it might be easier to bear." She stood and shook out her robe. "Dinah will be back in a moment with your clothes. I will tell my father you have returned, but I will leave the rest for you to tell him." She paused. "I know it's not my place to say this. I am young and a woman and your slave. But you seem sad. So it might be helpful to hear what my father told me once, after the second time the Romans beat him. I asked him why he continued to manage your family's businesses, and he told me that sometimes the best course of action is simply the one that presents itself. That may be true for you, too."

CHAPTER 33

RETURN

B en-Hur let Simonides make his travel arrangements. There was a ship going to Joppa, full of spices from the East. Ben-Hur was assigned a tiny cabin that smelled richly of cloves. From Joppa he rode a handsome mule, declining the offer of a camel. The mule's long ears were constantly disconcerting after the short arc-shaped ears of the Arabians, but she was an affable creature. He was sorry to part with her at the Joppa Gate outside Jerusalem. She had been company for him on the journey.

He found himself hesitating outside the tall, imposing gate. The tawny stone of the city wall rose above him, meeting the sky in regular notches while the gate itself was surrounded by a familiar tumult. A pair of scrawny dogs fought over a bone, a fishmonger sharpened his knife, two veiled women with market baskets argued over a pair of pomegranates. The sun beat down, hot and dry, but the shadows were lengthening. What was he waiting for? He caught sight of a lanky boy kicking up dust with his feet while he gnawed on a strip of dried meat. Dark hair, a tunic that had begun the day white, hands too big for the arms they ended—Ben-Hur shook his head. He had looked like that, he knew. He watched the boy, who watched everything: eyes roving over crowds, catching on details, overhearing snatches of speech.

He followed the boy through the gate and into his past. The streets, just wide enough to be comfortable but—unlike those straight Roman-built boulevards in Antioch or Rome—never meant for display. Everything hung in the narrow channels of air between the golden walls. The noise! Voices raised in argument, compliment, insult, greeting, dispute, complaint, every single word of which Ben-Hur understood without even thinking of them as words. The smells! Dust, animals, a resinous tang from the hills, a charcoal brazier, the bite of citrus as a vendor sliced an orange . . . Ben-Hur found himself smiling. Home.

He jostled a carpenter and apologized, understood and forgiven with a quick smile. He helped settle a jug on a woman's shoulder. She blessed him. A pair of rabbis pushed past him, deep in argument, their steps synchronized as they headed toward the Temple without even glancing at their route. A pigeon seller coaxed a pure white bird back into its wicker cage, pocketed some coins, and handed it to a customer. Home!

Suddenly he had to see it all, so as the sun on the hills grew ever redder, he walked from end to end of his city, down alleys he had never seen and through the palace gardens where he'd met Messala years earlier. He entered the courts of the Temple but left quickly, drawn away by his restlessness. Finally, at the end of the afternoon, he found himself seated on a boulder halfway up the Mount of Olives. His feet were sore and the hem of his robe was dusty. His mind buzzed with the things he'd seen and heard—one word overall:

Shalom. Peace. The conventional greeting in Judea. "Peace be with you." The polite answer was "And also with you."

Peace. What did that mean for Jews? For him? Was peace even possible? Messala had talked about the Pax Romana, the peace that the Roman Empire brought to the lands it occupied. Was that truly peace? And if so, peace for whom?

Could it really be broken? Sitting here in the glowing afternoon, looking down at the city of his birth, Judah wondered. Simonides and Sheik Ilderim were so persuasive, but were they right? Had the time come to shake off the Roman yoke?

He leaned back and placed his hands on the dusty hillside behind the rock he sat on. Above, the sky had lost its brilliance and was fading to a silvery pink. He closed his eyes and felt the stony ground beneath his palms. Each pebble took on separate significance. He let his head fall back and lost his sense of where his body was. Feet, hands, buttocks—close to the earth. Rooted. He rolled off the boulder and lay facedown on the hillside, cheek pressing against the sandy soil that still held some of the day's warmth. He felt as if he were embracing the earth. Judea—home.

And yet it could not be his home because Judah Ben-Hur was an outlaw. By now, his story was probably told everywhere. The son of Arrius and the Jewish boy flung to the galleys and the winner of the chariot race were known to be one and the same. It was clear that he had powerful friends and a grudge against Rome. The dead body on the floor of the palace in Antioch would confuse matters, but Ben-Hur knew he would never be safe under his own name.

Unless the Romans could be driven out.

And who better than he to do that?

He sat up, then stood and brushed off his robe before beginning to clamber down the hill. The trail was narrow and night was coming. In front of him the skyline of Jerusalem lost its details to the setting sun, and the Antonia Tower stood up proudly, a sharply cut black rectangle. The enforcer of the Pax Romana. Prison, it was said, to hundreds of Jews. Malluch had asked questions, from Antioch, about his mother and Tirzah. But he had not gone to the tower himself. That was Ben-Hur's task for the next day. In the meantime, he would do the more difficult thing. He would visit the Hur palace, his family's home within his people's home. He could put it off no longer.

CHAPTER 34

UNCLEAN

S ome deeds are best done in the darkness. Others, by the light of day.

When Pontius Pilate succeeded Valerius Gratus as procurator of Jerusalem, he did without the military parade. Instead, his garrison replaced the outgoing soldiers during the night, discreetly. No parade, no outcry, no unrest. It seemed wise.

Then Pilate thought further about Gratus's administration and how his own could be considered different. "The prisons," whispered a counselor. "You may find you can free some of those who have been detained. Always a popular move."

A daylight move. Gates creaked open; thin, cowed creatures crept outside, sometimes met by sobbing family members who'd long believed them dead. The blame fell on previous administrations. Pilate was the new broom, sweeping everything clean.

Including the Tower of Antonia in Jerusalem itself. A map of the cells was found. The list of prisoners was checked against it. The cells were visited. It took days. Many individuals were released. The cells went deeper and deeper below the walls than even the prison warden knew. The notch of worry between his eyebrows grew more marked as the days went past and there were still more stairs to descend. When he tried to imagine his report to the tribune—who would report directly to Pilate—he felt sick. There were no records at all for what he was finding.

It was perpetual night in those cells. Somehow the prisoners had been supplied with food and water. Another breakdown in the organization; how could that have gone unnoticed? But a breakdown to be glad of. Several times already cell doors had opened onto nothing but skeletons clothed in leathery scraps of skin. Disgraceful! Rome was stern, the warden thought, but she was not supposed to be vicious.

Valerius Gratus, though, had not been a model Roman. On the lowest level of the dungeon the warden and his appalled subordinates found prisoners whose tongues had been cut out. Or who had been blinded. Or both. The warden was already wondering how to restore these pathetic men to their families—which had been Pilate's promise. He was halfway up the stairs, carrying his own torch, when one of the jailers called him back. "He won't leave," the jailer said, pointing to what looked like an animated skeleton. There were noises coming from him—somewhere behind the hair and beard matted over his face. He pointed back into his cell, beckoning. "He wants us to come in. Must want to show us something."

"Does he understand?" asked the warden. "He understands we're freeing him?"

"Yes. But he keeps dragging us back. It must be important."

"I'm afraid I agree with you," said the warden.

* * *

It was the wrong time for the noises. To the extent that they could tell time, anyway. It was always hard and getting harder. But surely the plate had been pushed through the slot just a few hours earlier?

As if hours meant anything.

Still, it was a change. To hear noise from the hatch.

Then came the strangest thing. Even afterward, Tirzah always remembered the deep shock.

Light. A golden—where had that word come from?—glow. On the floor. Through the hatch.

"Mother!" she hissed.

Her mother had not spoken in a while, but Tirzah had heard her moving. Gently, with the utmost care. Just brushing the back of a hand along the floor. Because the fingers . . .

She heard a rustle. Then a whisper from nearby. Close to the floor. "What is it?"

The glow withdrew. "Hello?" a voice replaced it. A voice! The voice of a man! A healthy, robust man! "Is anyone in there?"

Tirzah felt herself pushed. Her mother, urging her forward. She crept close to the hatch. "Yes," she said. Or tried to. It was a croak. "Yes!" she repeated. "Two of us."

"Who are you?"

"Women of Israel. Who are you?"

"Roman officials. Here to release you."

"Praise be to God," Tirzah heard her mother breathe. "Water?"

"Water?" Tirzah whispered.

"Yes, of course," the male voice answered. "Right away. Just . . ."

"The light?" she asked. "Leave it?"

"Yes. Yes." The glow returned.

She backed away from it. Light! It . . . it showed things! A semicircle on the floor by the hatch, polished as smooth as marble. By them, she supposed. By her mother and her in all the time they had been here. The plate. Wooden. Plain. She looked away. Her eyes were already tired. The rest of the cell looked darker now. She could not see her mother.

"Where are you?" she whispered.

"Here." Outside the glow, a flicker of movement.

"Mother . . ." She crept over. "Mother! Is this . . . ? It is real, isn't it?"

The glow vanished. "Water," said the voice. "Coming through. And food, too. But where is the door?"

The familiar sound: a pan of water coming through the hatch. Followed by a plate.

Naomi pulled herself over to the hatch. "Thank you," she whispered.

"What was that? I didn't hear you."

"Thank you," she repeated as loudly as she could. "There is no door."

"Ye gods," the voice said, withdrawing from the slot. The light came back, showing the water. And on the plate . . .

"Grapes! Mother, grapes!"

"Gently," warned Naomi. "One. It's been so long . . ."

"I know."

They each ate a grape, slowly. Drank some water. Outside, tapping. Hammers, perhaps.

"Another one?" Tirzah asked.

"I think so." They each ate another grape.

A pebble fell at the back of the cell. Where they slept. Long ago they had called it the bedroom, in an effort to keep up their spirits. A little shower of rubble followed it.

Tirzah lay down, suddenly exhausted. She closed her eyes and laid her hands over them to keep out the light. Then took them off, rolling her head toward the hatch. To make sure the light was still there.

✳ ✳ ✳

It took hours. There had originally been a door, but it had been filled with stones and mortar. Hurriedly, the workmen told the warden. A number of years ago—but not fifty. Less than ten. There were prisoners in there? Women? Have to go slowly, then. What if they were buried in a shower of rubble?

The warden stayed. He didn't feel he could leave them, somehow. Though he had a feeling the shower of rubble might be the easiest solution. Whatever story these women had to tell, it was not going to look good for Rome.

They were very quiet. He kept thinking about the one who had thanked him. *Thanked him!* For a pan of water and some grapes.

✳ ✳ ✳

Finally a hole was pierced at the top of the doorway. "Look!" Tirzah whispered, but her mother didn't answer. Could she be sleeping? More light seeped in through the hole. The room was taller than Tirzah had thought.

After that it went faster. The workmen found the shape of an opening. The stones and mortar were swept outward, into the corridor. Light began drifting downward into the cell.

At last the warden had to speak to them again. He took the torch from the slot. "Stay away from the wall. Stones are still falling. We should be through soon, though. Would you like more water?"

"No," Tirzah answered. "But . . . blankets? Our clothes . . . We have no clothes." She heard the rustle as he withdrew and orders given to someone outside.

✳ ✳ ✳

"Blankets. Or cloaks—what you can find," he said to the jailers. "They'll be weak."

"What are we going to do with them?" the senior jailer asked.

"I won't know until I see them," the warden answered. "Find them a clean cell, up the stairs, with a window and a big bucket. The smell . . . We can't just send them outside like this. They'll need to be cleaned up. Probably fed. Maybe for a few days. Send physicians to them. Find out why they were here. And only then, try to find their family."

"A woman of Israel, she called herself," said the jailer. "Sounded educated. When they are released, it's going to be trouble."

"For Valerius Gratus, not for Pilate. Pilate will get the credit for releasing them."

"Ho, we're through!" shouted one of the workmen. "You need to . . ." Then with a clatter, he dropped his tools. In the flickering torchlight the warden saw him stumble backward across the pile of rubble. Eyes wide, he turned to the warden. "They're lepers!" he cried out and raced for the stairs.

"Unclean," came the thread of a voice through the doorway. "Unclean, unclean!"

In spite of himself, the warden stepped over to look and was instantly sorry he had. He knew he would remember the sight forever.

He had never seen lepers up close. Well, one didn't. A touch was enough to spread the disease—and what a horrible one. The skin seemed to devour itself, people said. Fingers dropped off, and noses. Eyelids shrank or split or disappeared. Some lepers were blind. Most had strange, high, scratchy voices—like the women in the cell. Eventually their inner organs would harden and cease to function. It was a slow, living death. And the women in the cell were more than halfway to being corpses.

The blessing was the hair. Theirs had grown and grown. Coarse and crinkled and a strange yellow-white but long enough to hide . . . a lot. They had turned their backs but still, their feet were barely human. One of them reached around to pull her hair closer, but it was almost a claw that he saw. Not by any means a hand.

"Unclean," one of them said again. "Touch nothing in the cell. Not the floor or the wall. And make sure anything we have touched is burned."

The warden stepped away from the cell. "I am beyond reach," he said. "But I must know who you are and why you are here. If you are strong enough to tell me."

The hoarser one spoke up. He wished it had been the other—she was easier to understand. But this one, evidently, was the elder. "I am the widow of Prince Ithamar of the house of Hur, of this city. He was a man of business, friendly with the Romans here and even with Caesar. This is my daughter. We do not know why we are here. Why not ask Valerius Gratus? It was on the day of his arrival that we were taken from our home."

"We do not know how long we have been here," added the daughter.

"Gratus is no longer procurator," said the warden. "It is his successor, Pontius Pilate, who chose to look into the prisons of Judea."

"Then blessings be on his name," said the young one.

"I will have clothes and water brought to you. Water to wash, as well. But I can do nothing else. We will have you taken to the gate of the tower and set free tonight. Could you eat some more?"

"Yes, perhaps. But may I ask one question, since you seem to be a kind man? Have you heard anything in Jerusalem about my son? On the same day, he was taken off by a cohort of soldiers. Is there a chance that he might be in one of the cells? Perhaps you have even freed him today?"

He could barely hear her last words, they were so quiet. It was a moment before he could formulate an answer. "I am sorry," he said. "I have not come across a prisoner—you say the name is Hur?" The white-haired head nodded. "I have seen all of the lists. That name was not on them."

The news seemed to hit her like a blow, for she crumpled against her daughter. There was something grotesque about the gesture of affection and tenderness with which the daughter gently guided her mother to the floor. "Thank you," said the daughter. "It's hard news. But I'm sure it's better to know than to wonder."

The warden did as he had promised—lavishly, in fact. Gowns, veils, sandals—could they even wear sandals on those feet? he wondered—were found and bundled up for the women, two sets of everything for each. A basket was filled with bread and dried fruit along with a flask of water. How would they live? From one day to the next, he supposed, until death came to claim them.

CHAPTER 35

FREE

The massive gate of the Antonia Tower creaked to a close behind them with a final echoing bang. They stood in the shadow of the walls, clutching each other's hands. Tirzah felt she should carry the basket, but the fingers of her right hand were mere stubs, so Naomi held it.

Everything was strange. The robe felt rough against her skin, the sandals against her feet. Her hair was noisy, hissing and crackling around her ears. The very air swooped around like a live thing, bringing scents and sounds she couldn't identify.

She did not dare look at her mother. It was bad enough to see, in the cold moonlight, the skin of her own wrists, covered with either thick silvery scales or, worse, oozing red welts. Her feet were the same, except that the welts bled in places. She knew that was not the worst, though. She would never again look into a pool of water to admire herself; she was sure of that. Whatever she looked like, it provoked horror. Everyone who had seen her in the hours since their release had flinched and gasped. She knew there was something wrong with her eyes; they didn't seem to close completely. And her mouth. She could have lifted her good fingers to touch it, but they had little feeling and she didn't think she wanted to know. She was afraid her lips might be gone.

They stood there trembling for several long minutes, waiting to feel strong enough to move. At last Naomi said, "We cannot stay here."

"No," Tirzah answered in a whisper.

"We must be gone from the city by daybreak."

"I know." Tirzah paused. "I am not very strong."

"No. Nor I. So we will go now. And stay in the shadows. Pull up your veil."

They set out. It was a quiet night—the guard had intentionally kept them indoors until after midnight, when the city watch had changed. They were so frail that he could not imagine them reaching their destination. And once there, how would they live? Would they have to beg, just to get food? Trail around the streets of Jerusalem, holding out a basket for small coins? Who would come close enough to give them anything? They would starve.

Or die of their disease. They would die, anyway.

It was slow progress for the two women. They crept along walls, leaning against them often; their ruined feet robbed them of balance. The streets were empty, though lights shone high in the Antonia Tower. Tirzah thought about commenting on this. She drew breath, but it was just too much effort.

"Do you know where we are?" Naomi whispered.

Tirzah didn't know. As a girl she had rarely left her home and certainly never alone. She had never learned the streets of the city.

"Look." Her mother pointed around a corner. There was a long wall with a tile roof. A palm tree indicated a courtyard. A smaller structure stood above the wall. . . .

Tirzah gasped. "Home?"

"It was our home," Naomi answered. "We must pass it on our way."

Tirzah stood still, gazing upward at the summerhouse. "Are we on the street where it happened?"

No need to explain what she meant. "Yes," her mother said. "We will walk past the very spot."

"Then let us do that," Tirzah said. "I will take the basket for a while."

It took them long minutes to stumble even the short distance to the corner of the old Hur palace. Once there, Naomi looked upward. The full moon spread silver on every surface. The shadows, by contrast, were deep. The palm tree's fronds whispered, but nothing else moved besides the two white-gowned, white-haired women.

"The walls," Tirzah whispered. "What is that?" She pointed at a fissure in the plaster with one of her shortened fingers.

"It has been neglected," Naomi answered. "I suppose nobody lives here. Nothing has been repaired." She nudged a pile of tile shards with her sandal. "See, the tiles are coming off the roof."

They inched along the wall to the gate. "And what is that?" Tirzah asked. She set down the basket and stepped forward. "It looks like a seal. Have they sealed our house?"

"To keep out thieves, perhaps. But look, Tirzah. Oh, look at the sign!" A foot above their heads hung a wooden placard. It had once been sturdy. The paint had been fresh, some eight years earlier, when someone had written, *This is the property of the emperor.* Now the paint was faded, but the message remained.

"'The property of the emperor'?" Tirzah asked. She should understand, she knew. What did it mean, that the emperor now owned their house?

"They have taken everything," Naomi breathed. She turned her back to the massive gate and slid down until she was sitting. "There is nothing left for Judah!"

Tirzah took five tentative steps away and surveyed what she could see of the vast facade. Then she hobbled back and sat down next to her mother. "I had not remembered . . . It is so big. So grand. I didn't know. We lived in splendor, didn't we?"

Naomi nodded. "At the time, it just seemed like comfort. And of course, we housed all of those servants. And we had tenants." She buried her head in her hands. "I never thought . . ." The thread of her voice rose. "Nothing for Judah!"

"Mother," Tirzah hissed, suddenly angry. "Judah is dead! He must be dead, or he would have found us!"

Naomi sighed. "What do you remember of that day?" she asked.

Tirzah sighed. "So little. More at first, but it has faded. I kept going over it, wondering if I could have changed anything. Maybe if I hadn't told Judah about the soldiers, he wouldn't have leaned over to see them? I remember I woke him with a song. And I remember our porter Shadrach, how they just . . . The blood." She shook her head. "I had never seen death. And the red cloaks everywhere. And those breastplates. All that glitter and those hard edges. And the shouting."

"Nothing they said?"

"No," Tirzah said. "It was so confusing. Did they say anything?"

"Did you remember it was Messala who named Judah?" Naomi asked.

Tirzah turned to look at her and was shocked, once again, to see her mother's ruined face. But what she had said was just as shocking. "Messala betrayed Judah? His *friend*?"

Naomi nodded. "And ordered them to take him to the galleys. Do you know what that is?"

"Ships?"

"Yes. Rowed by slaves. Judah was taken away to row in a Roman ship."

"And that's why you think he is alive?"

There was a pause. "No," Naomi finally admitted. "Galley

slaves . . ." She paused. "I cannot." Her voice rose, louder than she had spoken yet. "I cannot think of my son that way. All this time, I have not done it and I will not. I won't!" she cried. It would have been a howl in a healthy woman.

"If he is alive, he is a galley slave, Mother," said Tirzah. "Is that right? You become a galley slave for life?"

"For life," Naomi agreed, leaning her head back against the gate. "They are never freed."

"Then what does it matter? He is pulling an oar in a Roman ship somewhere. He can't help us. He doesn't need this house. He is as much dead as we are!"

"No, Tirzah," said her mother. Gently she placed her two twisted hands on either side of her daughter's appalling face. "We are not dead. While we live, we must hope."

Tirzah twisted her head away. "Hope!" she whispered. "Hope for what? All I hope for is death, and the sooner it comes, the better! Have you *thought*, Mother? You know so much more than I do. You know where lepers live. You know what they can do or not do. All I know is what I see in you—and what I feel in myself. Mother, we will not survive! Where will we get food? Who will give us water? You've said, to every person we've met, that we're unclean. Must we say that to everyone? Must we announce it where we go?"

"Yes," Naomi whispered.

"Can we go to the Temple, to seek blessing or comfort or wisdom?"

"No."

"Why not?"

Naomi's sigh was just a faint breath, stirring a few of her long silver hairs. "Because we are not clean. We carry disease and corruption everywhere. And we dare not carry it there, where the people of God gather in his presence." She paused. "We are considered the living dead."

"The living dead," Tirzah groaned. "The living dead! Then why not just finish life? Why be living at all? Why not be truly dead?" She banged her head against the gate as if to smash her skull, but she was too weak to make the gesture count.

"God numbers our days," Naomi answered. She looked up at the night sky. "It is not for us to interfere."

Slowly and clumsily, Tirzah clambered to her feet. "What is it you hope for?" she asked, looking down at her mother. "For things to go back to the way they were?"

Naomi pushed herself off the dust of the street and stood. "I don't expect to foresee God's goodness to me," she said. "I don't expect to understand him any more than Job did, or Abraham. Maybe his mercy to us will be death. Or something we could never possibly expect. I will wait for him."

Tirzah bent down to lift the basket. "All right. And where will we do this waiting? What is the place called?"

"We must leave the city by the Water Gate. We will follow the wall of our house to the opposite side, then take the narrow road downhill. I know the way."

"Good. And where is it we are going?"

"I have never been there. I have only heard of it. There is a well, and around it are caves in the hillside. We will live in a cave." She could not bring herself to tell Tirzah that the caves had once been tombs, and that the place was known as the Valley of the Dead.

CHAPTER 36

HOME

I t took them longer than they would have believed possible simply
to reach the other side of the palace. Even Naomi, who thought
she had known every inch of the building when it was the family
home and center of business, was astounded at its sheer size.

She was also horrified by its state of disrepair. The stucco on the
outer wall peeled down to the brick in places. Multiple rows of tiles
were missing from the roof, and birds' nests thrust out their spiky
twigs. Below, the walls were streaked with guano. The sight of the tall
palm tree in the central court accompanied their slow voyage around
the wall, and as the moonlight grew more slanted, Naomi saw that its
fronds were dry and shaggy. She even thought she could smell decay,
wafting over the walls, but she knew that could not be true. She was
quite sure that most of her nose was gone. Surely that would make
smelling impossible.

They stayed in the shadows. When they reached the corner of
the palace, she and Tirzah crossed the street into another patch

of shadows, because the south wall was so brightly lit—except for the gate, set deeply into the wall. Naomi looked across to see if it bore the same sign as the gate on the north side. Her eye was caught by a huddled shape. A vagrant, she thought, curled up at the gate. That was what the house had come to: shelter for the city's lost ones. Not that she was anything different.

But the figure in the doorway stirred and flung out an arm. Naomi thought she heard the man speak. For it was a man; she was sure of that. She drifted closer. Something . . . something drew her on. His shape? How could she have known? Her steps sped up. It couldn't . . .

It couldn't be. But it was. She knew it was. He lay in shadow, but she knew him. She felt Tirzah hover behind her.

"What is it, Mother?" Tirzah pressed close, looking over her shoulder. She felt her daughter's breath in her ear. "Mother, it's Judah!"

Naomi turned and buried her face in Tirzah's shoulder. She would have wept, but her eyes had long ago stopped providing her with tears. Instead she clutched Tirzah to her heart. "It is Judah!" she mouthed into her daughter's veil and robe. "It is Judah! He lives!"

"What is he doing here? Do you think he came to find us? Why didn't he go inside?" Tirzah pulled away from her mother, steadying her with a hand on each arm. She knelt, reaching out to Ben-Hur's shoulder.

"*No!*" Naomi croaked. "You must not! Unclean! We must not touch him!"

Tirzah recoiled and looked up at her mother in horror. "Not . . . Ohh!" It would have been a wail, but she could not sustain the breath. She sat back on her heels, clutching her elbows. "We can't touch him!" she echoed her mother.

"Not only that," Naomi whispered, kneeling next to Tirzah, "we must leave him. He can't know we are alive."

Tirzah stared at her, aghast, then understood. "No. Of course. If he knows . . ."

"He will find us," Naomi said softly, gazing down at her son. "He would find us and try to save us . . ."

"And he would get our disease. He would not be careful." Somehow, it was a warming thought.

"He would sacrifice himself," Naomi went on, agreeing. "To stay with us."

Why was it such a comfort? That vision of something that would not even come to pass brought solace. The two women stayed on their knees side by side, watching the man sleep. The moon moved, kindly sliding the shadow away from his face so they could both see him clearly. The son and brother, the hero they needed and did not waken. He lay on his back with an arm above his head, more handsome than they ever could have hoped, and they feasted their eyes. Their hands crept together and held tight. He was there. He was alive. He was beautiful. He would save them—if they would let him.

They would not let him. That much they could do. That much they could give him. It made them feel strong.

After a while, he stirred and muttered. Naomi glanced up at the sky and flinched. "Look, we must go; the stars are fading! We must be gone from the city before sunrise or we will be stoned!"

"Stoned?" Tirzah asked.

"It is what happens. People throw stones at lepers to keep them away."

Tirzah rose to her feet and held out a hand to her mother. "So cruel!"

Naomi did not answer. She bent down and kissed the sole of her son's sandal, then laid her cheek against it for a long moment. The unclean shoe, always shed at the threshold of a house, understood to have been in dirt and filth—this was as close as the mother could come to her child, since she herself was unclean. Tirzah thought she would see the image in her head forever and felt a moment's wonder. Then Naomi turned toward her and Tirzah helped her to her feet.

Tirzah picked up the basket and they crept across the street, back into the shadows.

Yet they could not leave—yet. Not while Judah lay so near! They leaned against the wall and stared.

"He looks well," Tirzah whispered. "Not . . . I would have thought, as a slave . . ."

"I know. He is healthy, God be praised." Naomi sank her face into what was left of her hands. "This makes such a difference! To know that he lives! To have seen him!"

"But . . . never again," Tirzah suggested.

"No." Her mother's answer was little more than an exhalation.

"He will grieve for us." Naomi only nodded. Tirzah went on, working it out as she spoke. "But if he found us, he would join us. And become like us." Finally she added, "We must be dead to him so that he can live."

"Yes, my dear," confirmed her mother.

Minutes passed. The moon moved. The palm fronds rustled. "Should we go?" Tirzah asked finally. "Is it far?"

"Yes," said Naomi. But she didn't move.

"I thought he was dead," Tirzah said. "All that time in the prison. But you thought he was alive?"

"I thought I would know if he was dead," Naomi answered. "Somehow."

There was another long silence. Then Tirzah asked, "Why didn't you tell me about Messala? Why did we never talk about that day?"

"I don't know," Naomi replied. "At first you didn't speak at all. Do you remember that?"

Tirzah just shook her head.

"I held you. I couldn't find any wounds. But whatever I said or asked, you didn't utter a word. I even put my fingers in your mouth, to see if you still had your tongue, in case the Romans had cut it out when I wasn't looking, though I thought I had watched you every moment. Then finally when you did speak, I was afraid."

"What did I say?"

"'Judah.' You asked for your brother. And I had to tell you I didn't know where he was. And you didn't speak again for many days."

Silence fell again. Across the street, the huddled figure stirred. Ben-Hur rolled onto his side and put his hands beneath his head.

"Would it hurt terribly to be stoned?" Tirzah asked.

"I think so."

"Couldn't we just wait a little longer?"

"Yes. But we must be gone before he wakes. He must never see us."

"He would not know us, Mother."

"No. But I am sure he is a good man. He would try to help us. I . . . To see him and hear him speak, and not answer . . . I am not sure I am strong enough."

"I understand," Tirzah said. She smoothed her mother's hair. "We will go soon, then."

"When the shadow of the palm tree reaches us," Naomi said. The dark slash of the trunk's shadow lay across the dusty street a few inches away.

"All right," whispered Tirzah. But a moment later she felt her mother stiffen beside her. Naomi raised a twisted hand in warning.

Tirzah strained her ears. There it was: a soft, regular crunching. Footsteps. Coming along the side of the palace. One set of steps, one person.

Naomi pulled Tirzah back, closer to the wall they stood against. Their block of shadow had moved so that they were almost exposed. Tirzah lifted the basket and carefully set it down next to the wall. The two women barely breathed.

The footsteps were light and close together. Not a big person, then. And not a furtive one either. Finally the figure turned the corner and they saw a small woman, veiled, carrying a basket of her own.

She was halfway along the wall toward the door when she caught sight of the sleeping figure, and she leapt back, hand to her chest.

She stepped into the street, closer to Naomi and Tirzah, to skirt the sleeper. "Mother!" Tirzah breathed. "Could that be . . . ?" She felt her mother's hand on her mouth.

"Not a sound!" Naomi hissed in her ear. "Be still; she must not see us!"

But as they watched, the figure stopped, then turned her back on them. She tiptoed closer to the gate, and the basket fell from her hand. An orange rolled in the dust unnoticed as she knelt, and the two women heard a smothered cry.

"It is Amrah!" Tirzah whispered, unable to contain herself.

Her mother just shook her head. Both women stared across the street.

The sleeper stirred. His head rolled; then his legs bent. Afterward they agreed that they both knew exactly when he woke. He went still and lay for a moment, then raised his hands to his face.

"Judah!" came the cry, and he sat up.

The little woman dropped to the ground and threw her arms around him. "Judah!" she repeated, in her thin voice. "Judah, you are alive!"

"Amrah?" he asked. Naomi and Tirzah clutched each other. To hear his voice! "Amrah, it is you!" His long arms wrapped around her. "Oh, Amrah! After so long! I have been searching! I never thought I would find anyone!" He held her away from him and gently pulled her veil back. "You are older."

"And you are a man, Judah," she answered, in the same tone of wonder. "The image of your father. But you are alive!"

"And my mother? Tirzah? I have come to try to find them. Do you know anything?"

Amrah shook her head. "I do not, Judah. I have been here ever since that day. I thought, if they were spared, they might come back."

"But how? Didn't the Romans take it over?"

"They don't know the house the way I do. I hid. They used to come to search. I would watch them searching. I hoped someone would speak of your family, but they never did. And nobody has bothered me for a while."

"So no one knows where my mother and Tirzah are?"

"The Romans might. I am just a servant. Nobody would tell me."

Ben-Hur stretched his arms above his head and groaned. "I have just returned to Jerusalem this very day. I was so happy to be back that I walked all over. How silly to fall asleep here! I thought I was just sitting down to rest."

"Now you will rest inside," Amrah said firmly. She scrambled to her feet and plucked the orange out of the dust. "I have kept your bedroom clean, more or less. You can sleep in your own bed tonight. Are you hungry?" She eyed him as he stood. "You don't look hungry. Someone has been taking care of you, at least." She put the basket down and hugged him, her arms around his waist and her head barely reaching his chest. "Oh, Judah, you have survived! This is a wonderful day!"

He patted her shoulder and picked up the basket. "The only thing that would make it better would be news of my mother and Tirzah," he said. "But we will hope for that tomorrow. Now show me your secret way into the house."

The two turned and walked into the shadow. Across the street, Tirzah and Naomi clutched each other. They would have cried, if they could. As it was, their shoulders shook and their mouths turned down and their breath came in jolting gasps. After a few minutes they regained control, and without speaking, they turned down the narrow street away from the Hur palace.

CHAPTER 37

STONES

They did not walk fast enough to reach the city gate before dawn. Long before that, they began to encounter people as Jerusalem awoke. They took turns calling out, "Unclean, unclean!"

Most people left them alone. Lepers, after all, were common, and anyone out before dawn had work to do or a load to carry or somewhere to be. They were too busy to bother with two leprous crones. Only at a market, a fruit seller setting up a table in the near darkness placed a handful of bruised persimmons in the road before them, then backed away.

But that was the single kindness they met. Once the sun rose, the streets filled. There was some sense to the leprosy laws, even beyond the Scriptures—walking in Jerusalem involved physical contact. If brushing against a leper meant being infected, lepers must be exiled.

Naomi and Tirzah kept trudging along. They rested briefly when they were alone. Naomi tried to choose streets she remembered as quiet, but the eight years they had spent in the Antonia Tower had dulled her memory. Dogs followed them, growling and barking. The sun got hotter. People threw things. Twigs, just as a gesture, to accompany a warning shout: "Get away!" They heard that often. Rotten fruit. Something rotten splashed to the dirt in front of Tirzah, and she was so startled that she almost fell, but she knew she must keep moving.

The stones did hurt. Even a well-aimed pebble. Boys were pitiless. They ran around in packs, daring each other to cruelty. The older and stronger ones were also meaner. By the time the Water Gate was in view, Tirzah despaired.

But Naomi dragged her onward. No words were said between them. It was simply Naomi's will that kept Tirzah upright and shuffling forward.

By then they had attracted a following. It was as if every bored and malicious urchin in Jerusalem had somehow heard of the sport they provided. A jeering ring surrounded them, moving with them, taunting and launching stones. Finally there were so many boys yelling that the guard at the gate intervened.

"You're blocking the street; move along!" he shouted, brandishing his spear. Apparently a tall, helmeted Roman was less entertaining than two miserable leper women. The boys dispersed, vanishing into alleys in search of new entertainment.

The guard walked alongside Naomi and Tirzah the rest of the way to the gate. Naomi had given the warning: "Unclean!" and he nodded as if he understood. He kept his distance, but he escorted them safely out of the city.

And then they still had to walk. It was hot. They were thirsty. They ate the persimmons. They drank from the flask in the basket but did not dare finish the water. There was no telling when or how they would get more.

Outside the city walls, the country began. Hills folded on hills, some bare and some covered with vines. Narrow footpaths climbed up and down them.

Naomi was not quite sure which way to go, but keeping her distance, she asked everyone they met. A laborer with a scythe set them on the route, and a shepherd carrying a single sheep confirmed it. When the sun was at its peak, they were lucky enough to be passing an untended orchard. The trees, Naomi said, were too old to give fruit. They sat and dozed in the dappled shade for a while, but it was still hot when they resumed walking.

"Not too much longer," Naomi finally said. They were on a hillside, looking down into a valley. "There is a well down there, called En-rogel. That is where we are going."

Tirzah nodded. The hem of her robe was spattered with blood from her feet, but her mother might believe that was from the rotten fruit earlier in the day. Earlier. In the world's longest day.

She had dreamed about this, about being free. At first she had thought about it constantly, when they were new to the prison. She had complained without ceasing, she realized now. Whined. She knew she had cried. Her mother had been patient. If Naomi had cried, she had done it in secret. Maybe while Tirzah slept.

When they were freed, Tirzah had been happy. She had thought only about the easy things: light and food and seeing the world outside.

She had forgotten she was a leper. And when she'd thought about freedom, she had remembered her old life.

How could she have imagined this? Even if she had been told, what would that have meant? *You will be outcasts. You will be infirm. You will be hated and feared, and people will pelt you with stones. And you will be hideous; every movement will cause you pain.*

Who could imagine such a thing?

And who could bear it?

For how long?

She looked down the hill to the well and saw a dry, rocky valley. There was a structure of sorts in the middle. Some kind of stone house, falling apart.

No movement, though. No shade. No future.

Just sun and rocks and the further decay of her body. Then death.

Maybe it would be fast. That was all she had to hope for.

She took a step, and another, and kept on walking. There was no other choice. When they finally reached the valley, shade had begun to creep down one of the hillsides. There was no sign of other people. Naomi said the hills were full of caves and that people would come out before dawn and after sunset. In the meantime, they would try to find an empty cave. That would be their home.

It was the worst part of the day. They would trudge up to a cave entrance and call out: "Greetings" or "Peace be with you." Naomi thought that if no one answered, they could hope that a cave was uninhabited. Several times cracked voices answered, "Peace be with you. This is our dwelling." Once there was no answer, but when they stepped beyond the mouth of the cave, they saw a . . . creature. A voiceless creature of no visible gender, lying on the ground, making a senseless gesture. They fled. The worst was the next cave they entered, thinking it empty. They had actually sat down, put the basket on the ground, when a shrieking woman entered and furiously hissed at them. Or maybe it was a man whose voice had gone high with the disease. The person had been tall. And frightening.

They ended up in a shallow cave near the valley floor. "It will be convenient to the well," said Naomi. Tirzah thought it must have some terrible flaw, or it would not be empty. But she was so exhausted she didn't speak, simply lay near the back of the space and fell asleep.

CHAPTER 38

CAVES

J udah refused to spend the night at the Hur palace. Malluch was on his way to Jerusalem to launch an inquiry into the fate of the Hur women, and it seemed foolhardy to risk being seen and possibly recognized by the Romans at a time when attention was drawn to the family. Instead, Ben-Hur promised to visit Amrah each day after dark. He would stay at a khan in the modest outlying neighborhood of Bezetha, north of the Temple.

But Amrah slept little on the first nights after his return; her joy kept her awake. Finally she rose from her narrow cot and wandered around the house, seeing its dilapidation as Judah might see it and regretting that he had forbidden her to so much as sweep. "You have been very clever to keep the house looking shabby," he had said. "When we start questioning the Romans about my family, they may return here. They must see a house that has been empty for years."

"And haunted, too," she added. "I hear about it sometimes in the market. There are stories about ghosts. Perhaps because of what happened that day. The emperor was to sell the house, I think. But there were no buyers. It was certainly thought to be cursed."

"That could not be better," Ben-Hur told her. "In time I may be able to buy it, secretly, and then, Amrah, you may clean and polish to your heart's content. But for now, leave your broom alone."

He hadn't told her not to cook for him, though. He had even left her money for food and a new robe and veil, more money than she had seen in the previous eight years. So she set out to the market that she knew would be open at dawn. They had the best honey. Judah had always loved sweets.

It was not a market she used often. It lay too close to the house, not far from the Antonia Tower. It was a small neighborhood affair with just a few vendors, the kind of place where people keep track of each other. Amrah had not wanted to be known.

On this morning, there was an unusual bustle. She felt the excitement and almost kept on walking, but the honey vendor looked up from his jars as she passed. "Have you heard?" he asked.

"Heard what?" she asked, pausing.

"The latest Roman horror! Right here in our quarter! Shocking!"

"And what is that?" Amrah asked. It might be something Judah would want to know.

"Well, you know, this new procurator, Pilate—he's been cleaning out the prisons," the honey seller said. "Turns out there were prisoners in there nobody knew about." He thrust his thumb behind him to where the tower loomed. "Dozens of them! So they've been releasing them. After dark, of course. Some were tortured."

Amrah stood still, all attention now.

"But wait, did you want some honey? I'm sorry. I am so angry I cannot think."

"I . . . Yes, please. A small jar. From your own bees?"

"Yes, of course. They're all from my bees." His hand hovered over a small jar, but he looked at Amrah and chose a larger one instead. "Here. For the same price. I feel the need to do something kind this morning, after what I have heard."

She nodded and thanked him. "Was . . . was that all? Were any of the prisoners women?"

He put the jar gently in the bottom of her basket. "Yes. That's the worst part. Do you know the Hur palace just around the corner? There were two women from that family! Princesses, no less, imprisoned by the Romans for eight years!"

Amrah felt her heart pounding. "And they . . . Were they tortured?"

"No," he answered heavily. "Worse than that. They are lepers. They had been placed in an infected cell and the door was covered over. The evil of it!"

The basket suddenly felt very heavy and Amrah put it on the ground, then found herself sitting next to it. Lepers! Her mistress and her lovely baby Tirzah!

The honey seller was at her side. "Are you all right? Forgive me; that was a shock. Perhaps you knew them?"

"No, no," she murmured. "But the idea. Those poor women! What has become of them?"

He helped her to her feet. "They were released in the middle of the night. There is only one place for people like that, you know. They will have gone to the Valley of the Dead, where the lepers all live together."

She scrabbled in her basket for the coins to pay him, but he put up his hand. "I'm sorry, good woman. I didn't mean to shock you. Take the honey. May it bring some sweetness to you."

She returned to the palace by a roundabout route, glad that the sun was not yet above the hills. Shadow was Amrah's friend. She slipped into the postern door and took her basket up the stairs to the tiny room she had claimed as her own. Once there, in her safe little burrow, she sat on the floor, nestled into a corner.

Was this terrible story true?

Why wouldn't it be? Grim accounts of Roman misdeeds constantly circulated in Jerusalem. Rabbis beaten, children killed, virtuous women assaulted—the same tales again and again. This, though, was a new one. And it had names attached to it. And a time span: eight years. Of course it was true.

Amrah let her head drop back into the angle between the walls and shut her eyes. She felt she might fly apart under the pressure of emotion. She was still trying to understand Judah's return, and now this horror had come upon her . . . and upon Judah.

If it was true. She took a deep breath and got to her feet. There was only one way to know, and sooner would be better than later.

As she prepared herself, she tried not to think ahead. There was some bread in the house and a small bit of meat. A jar for water—where people lived there must be a well. She put on a heavier veil and took up her basket again. The morning was bright when she pushed open the postern door, but the streets were still quiet.

She paid attention to her route out of the city. She tried not to imagine what she might find at the end of it. She tried not to remember Tirzah, her beloved and beautiful charge, or Naomi, the kindest of mistresses. Instead she carefully looked from side to side to keep track of where she was, noticing where the streets branched and marking the distances. It would be easier to get home that way. With whatever she had learned.

Unwittingly, she followed Naomi and Tirzah's footsteps. There was a different Roman on guard at the gate, and no one thought to bother a respectable-looking servant. She found the right paths and reached the well of En-rogel just as the sun pulled loose from the hilltop and spilled golden light into the valley.

There was a man at the well, not a leper but a drawer of water. Amrah approached him.

"May I fill a jar for you, mistress?" he asked.

"Not yet, thank you," she answered. "But perhaps you might tell me about this place."

"It is the Valley of the Dead," he said. "Those who dwell here are lepers. Did you not know?"

"Yes," she answered calmly. "Are there any who have just arrived?"

He shrugged. "By night, perhaps. Or in the middle of the day. They only come out when the sun is low in the sky, so I am here at dawn and sunset."

"And where do they live?"

"In the caves, of course," he answered as if it were obvious.

She looked at the hillsides and saw that their rocky surfaces were marked with dark gashes. One of them, not far away, opened to the east. It must be hot, she thought, by midday.

She shaded her eyes and looked closer. There were two white figures emerging from it.

Behind her, she heard a splash as the man dipped a jar into the well. She turned and saw a ghostly figure several steps beyond him. Man? Woman? Tall, so possibly a man. The figure was shrouded in layers of ragged garments, as if he had put on one worn robe after another in the effort to cover his body. A kerchief covered his head, but long, coarse white hair swung forward beneath it. He bowed his head and uttered something. The well man seemed to understand.

A jar stood on the ground between them. The well man used his own jar to fill it, then stepped back to the well. The leper nodded, walked forward, and picked up his jar. Amrah thought he might fall over with the strain, but he managed to grasp it in his arms. His sleeve fell back and she saw the mass of bulbous blisters covering his arm before he turned away.

Then she heard a shout behind her and a light clatter. The two figures from the cave had approached the well with a jar of their own. "Stay back! Unclean!" shouted the well man. A handful of pebbles dropped from his hand to the ground. "You must not come so close!"

Amrah watched the two figures. They could not have been in the valley for long—their robes were new, and they did not seem to understand the customs. She stiffened. No, it wasn't possible. They were old, ancient! Each of the women had white hair down to her knees! They moved slowly, hesitating as if each step pained them and the uneven ground might trip them. They could not be . . .

But then she heard a threadlike voice saying, "Is it . . . Amrah? Is that you?"

She approached them, ignoring the well man's muttering.

"Unclean!" one woman shrilled. "Come no closer, Amrah!"

But she still could not recognize them. They knew her. Reason said this must be her mistress and Tirzah. But where were those women? There was no trace of them in this pair of crones.

"My mistress?" she asked, faltering.

"I am here, Amrah," said the one on the left. "It is I, Naomi, princess of Hur. As you see me."

"But then—Tirzah?" Amrah looked at the other woman. The face was little but a mask, a distorted, thickened skin-like cover for a skull. The eyes stared out of the sockets and yellowed teeth thrust forth from the jaw.

But this apparition was nodding. And a voice came from it, saying, "Yes, Amrah. I am Tirzah."

They could not cry, but she could. In that stony place beneath the hammering sun, she felt her tears sheeting down her face, trickling beneath her chin and along her neck. All the grief she had been holding back for years, the tension and the anguish, the fear and the guilt, welled up in a storm of emotion. But within moments, Naomi's voice recalled her to herself.

"Amrah, are you come to help us?" She nodded, still gulping. "Then bring us some water," Naomi said. "Do you have any money?"

"Enough, I think," she said. "How much?" she asked the well

man, holding out some coins. He took the smallest of them and filled Amrah's jug.

"And did you bring food?" Tirzah asked.

"Of course I did," Amrah answered. "Not much. I did not know I would find you."

"Can you come every day, Amrah? Can you come without letting Judah know?"

She almost dropped the jar. "You know?"

"We saw you two nights ago," Tirzah explained as they began to work their way back up the hill. Naomi took the basket. Amrah, walking several yards behind, followed with the jug. "They had just released us. We saw Judah asleep."

"But we did not touch him, Amrah," Naomi added. "And you must not tell him you have seen us."

At that, Amrah's legs failed her and she almost dropped the precious jug as she stumbled. "But, mistress!" she protested. "He is looking for you!"

"I am glad to know it," Naomi said. "I am glad he has not forgotten his family. But he must not find us."

"Mistress, he is in agony," Amrah said firmly. "Your son longs for you!"

"Don't you think I long for him?" Naomi retorted. "But think of it, Amrah. What would happen if he came here?"

"He would want to embrace you, of course," Amrah answered slowly.

"Amrah," Tirzah said, "imagine how we felt that night. In our state, unclean. And seeing Judah asleep, knowing for the first time that he was alive . . . not being able to touch him. Mother just kissed his sandal. The sole of it. He must not become like us. Surely you see that!"

Their voices had been so changed by the disease that Amrah could not have known them. But somehow their grief and desperation could be heard.

"Yes," she said slowly. "I do. But I tell you again, he will be in agony."

"In agony, but healthy," said Naomi. "Isn't that better than being exiled to the living dead?"

"Of course, mistress," Amrah said, drooping over the jug. "Oh, mistress, my heart is breaking!"

Naomi paused and looked at her old servant. She shook her head. "So is mine. But this will be my consolation: I will sit on that rock outside our cave. And I will look over the hill, toward our old house. When Judah is in Jerusalem, you will tell me, and I will imagine his days. Yes?"

"Yes, mistress. I will come every day. The man at the well says he draws water at dawn and at sunset. I will be here, with my jug and your food. You will tell me what you need, and I will bring it."

"And you will tell us about Judah," Tirzah added. "Where he has been and what he is doing."

"Of course," Amrah agreed. "I will tell you now that he is about to begin a great search for you. He has a man who is going to the Romans. There will be a scandal, about the house and your imprisonment. I heard about you in the marketplace—there is ill feeling against the Romans on your account."

"Will he come here to look for us?" Tirzah asked.

"Not he himself, I think," Amrah answered. "I believe he will send men. They will not discover you if you choose not to be discovered."

"Because we are no longer ourselves," Tirzah added, and though her voice was not expressive, the words themselves were bitter.

CHAPTER 39

THE LIVING DEAD

Homecoming is so rarely what one expects. In all his years of exile, Ben-Hur had maintained a fixed idea of the Hur palace as it was on the day he left it. And so little had changed in Jerusalem! There was so much that he recognized in its streets, its light, its clamor, its smells, that he imagined his old dwelling would be the same. It was not until he followed Amrah inside that he really understood—the home of his childhood was gone. Only the spaces were unchanged: the same number of steps from a door to a window, the same length of a hallway or height of a ceiling. The silence and the mustiness and the grit on the floors insisted on the truth, though. The Hur palace was nothing but a shell for memories.

Worse, it was dangerous. The new procurator might not know about the episode with Gratus, but some of the staff in the Antonia Tower would. Ben-Hur could not safely stay so near to the Roman headquarters. Rome had spies everywhere. That was what he told

Amrah. It was also true that he could not comfortably stay in a place that made him so sad.

Yet even the sadness would have to be borne, and one might not perceive it shading off into anger. Anger, after all, was harsh. It prompted action. A man could use his anger as a source of strength, especially when it was allied with years of discipline. A galley slave does not get to do as he chooses. And a mysterious Jew fished out of a burning sea, and presented as an adopted son in Rome, has to earn his way as well.

So when Malluch arrived from Antioch with messages from Simonides, Ben-Hur already had a plan. He continued to visit Amrah after nightfall, largely out of kindness. She could have nothing to tell him about his family, he knew. But he would arrange to have Malluch keep her provisioned and provide her with a small income, and she could continue as the palace's caretaker.

Soon it would be time to take to the desert to build an army for the King who would come. Ben-Hur knew that would be an all-absorbing task. It would also be hazardous. It would be easier to face the danger if he knew he had no responsibility for anyone besides himself. And in his heart, he had little hope of finding his mother and Tirzah.

Malluch had refused to name a meeting point. He had simply assured Ben-Hur that he would find him. Ben-Hur was skeptical—how could Malluch, a stranger, find one man in such a big city? But the third morning he woke in the khan, he walked out into the courtyard and saw Malluch sitting at a table with a plate of pita, holding his face up to the sun. He opened his eyes as Ben-Hur approached, and smiled. "Peace be with you," he said, moving down the rough bench.

"And with you also," Ben-Hur answered. "How did you find me?"

"Luck, mostly," Malluch answered. "I arrived yesterday. I thought you would want to be near the edge of town. And there are not so many khans where numerous strangers come and go. You would have to be in one of those, out of caution. And then I asked for a tall stranger without a beard." His words were affable, but he was tearing nervously at the pita.

Ben-Hur put his hand to his chin and laughed. "I just realized today that I would have to stop shaving if I wanted to look like a native."

"And there isn't much you can do about your height," Malluch added. He looked down and saw the pile of crumbs on the plate and reached to cover it, but Ben-Hur sat down and grasped his wrist. Malluch tried to free his hand, but the grip closed. Like a fetter.

"You know something about my family," Ben-Hur said. Malluch shook his head slightly. Ben-Hur tugged on his wrist. "Tell me. *Tell me.*"

Malluch hissed, "Not here."

Ben-Hur leapt to his feet, dragging Malluch up with him. The dozen men moving around the courtyard—eating, chatting, loading a donkey—froze. It was the kind of place where fights broke out, but usually not so early in the day. The little fellow was going to get the worst of it; that was certain.

But the tall one glanced around and caught a few furtive eyes. He let the little one go. They sat down again. No one was close enough to see that the big man's body was rigid and that his hands, lying clasped on the rough table, were quivering.

"Tell me," he whispered to Malluch. *"Now."*

* * *

Malluch laid his own hand over Ben-Hur's. Looking directly at the younger man, he said simply and quietly, "They are lepers. They were released from the Antonia Tower several nights ago." He bowed his head and brought his other hand to cover Ben-Hur's clasp. There could be no comfort to accompany news like this. But one had to try.

"Lepers?" Judah repeated softly. His eyes sought Malluch's. "Lepers?" His voice was just a thread. "That can't be true." He shook his head. "No. There is a mistake."

"There is no mistake. The new procurator, Pilate, cleared out the prison and found secret cells. Your mother and sister were—"

"No," Judah insisted. "Not my mother and sister. It's not possible."

"It is, Judah," Malluch insisted. "The Hur princesses. Walled up for eight years. There was no record; these were secret dungeons." He kept his voice even. The words were bad enough.

Ben-Hur stood up again. "I can't sit here. I need . . ." He looked around at the modest, dusty enclosure, the shabby travelers, the plate of bread crumbs, but Malluch knew he saw none of it.

"Come, we'll walk." He took Judah's elbow and steered the big man gently around the table. "We'll go outside and walk. I will tell you what I have found out."

Judah Ben-Hur, the lean and graceful athlete, seemed barely able to control his limbs. He stumbled over a bench on the way out and brushed the gate of the khan so that his robe caught on the splintered wood and Malluch had to free it while Judah stood patiently like a child. "They were in the Antonia Tower," he said, restating the information. "They were released in the middle of the night. Given robes and some food and sent away. The warden did not want it known that they had been there."

"That they had been there," Judah repeated. "For how long?" He met Malluch's glance.

"Eight years," Malluch answered.

"Eight." Judah nodded. "Eight. Three while I was in the galleys. Five while I was in Rome."

There was no answer to that.

They were out in the street now, if you could call it a street. Really it was a wide path with houses here and there. Rocky hills rose before them. A goat was tethered near a long wall, and it watched them with its yellow eyes. Ben-Hur pulled his elbow from Malluch's hand. He was walking more steadily.

"They are *lepers*!" he shouted to the sky. "My family are lepers!" There was no one around to hear and the goat was unmoved. "How can this be?" He turned to Malluch. "Where are they now? Do you know? Can we go and find them?"

This was the hard part. Malluch trudged onward, trying to be calm and to set a steady pace. As if that would help. "They must be in the Valley of the Dead. That is where the lepers live."

"Must be. So you are not certain?"

"They could be nowhere else. They would be stoned," Malluch reminded him.

"All right. Then we will go. Now."

Malluch looked at the sky. "We could. But . . . why?"

"Why? Have you no heart? To see them! To rescue them!"

"No. There is no rescue. You know that. You might see them, just to look at them, but you can't touch them, Judah. You cannot. Or you will die yourself. Do you want that?"

"Yes! At this moment, yes, I do! Why should I live, strong and rich, when those women I love are . . . ?" He shook his head. "You know, I can't even imagine them. Whenever I see a leper begging, I turn away. I don't know what they are suffering."

"And they did not know what you suffered," Malluch replied. "It's just as well, don't you think?"

Silence as their footsteps crunched over the stony roadway. It was beginning to get hot.

"Yes," Ben-Hur finally said. "I am glad my mother and sister could never see the galley. But I am ashamed that I lived for five years in Rome while they . . ." He leaned down and picked up a stone, then hurled it against a wall. "While they rotted underground!"

"It's not your fault."

"No." Ben-Hur kicked at a stick. "I know. It's Rome. Again."

He straightened up. "Again. That heavy hand of Roman justice. Crushing us."

Malluch had no response to that.

They kept walking. They headed southward through the city. Past the Antonia Tower. Past the Hur palace. Ben-Hur pointed it out to Malluch. In the harsh morning light its shabbiness made him ashamed. Past the Temple, looming on its platform. Down into the Lower City. The streets grew more crowded and sometimes the men were separated. Not far from the Pool of Siloam, they stopped. "Do you know the way?" Ben-Hur asked.

Malluch nodded. "But I must ask: what do you think you can do?"

Ben-Hur gazed out over the hillsides with an unfocused look. "Nothing." He looked back at Malluch. "That's right, isn't it? I can't do anything for them."

"Very little. If we could find them, maybe ensure they have food and water."

"You don't think we will?"

Malluch shrugged. "The disease . . . Their faces may not be . . ."

Judah clenched his fists. "All right."

"You still want to go and see?"

"I need to." They walked onward. A while later, as if trying to finish his thought, Ben-Hur said, "If I am going to build this army . . ." There was another long gap as they strode down the hill.

Finally he added, "This army for the King who is to come . . . this army to defeat Rome . . . I must know that I made every effort to find my family."

* * *

The Water Gate was quiet during those hours of heat. The Roman guard strolled up and down, his sandals scuffing the dust. Everyone else—vendors, beggars, camel drivers, camels—sat or lay in what shade there was, moving as little as possible. For a few yards beyond the gate the two men walked abreast, but soon the path narrowed so that Malluch had to lead. Over the hills, past the orchards, on toward the valley they trudged. Ben-Hur pulled his kerchief lower over his brow, but that was little protection from the heat and glare. When they paused briefly to drink from Malluch's flask, the only noises were the rattling of twigs in a little breeze and the buzzing of thousands of insects. Their own footsteps, when they resumed walking, sounded very loud.

Eventually the path began to wind down into the valley. The air shimmered with heat in the distance, but most of the details were clear: the solid stone structure surrounding the well, the layers of rock and vegetation, the darker clefts that might be cave entrances, the tough little shrubs and trees that managed to cling to the steep hillside without providing shade or greenery.

They didn't speak until they arrived at the well, but then Ben-Hur turned to Malluch and said very quietly, "Where should we start?"

"There, I think," Malluch answered, pointing to the left. "And go from cave to cave, uphill and down. That way we will see them all."

Ben-Hur nodded and began pacing in the direction Malluch had indicated.

The first cave they came to was uninhabited. Or if there were inhabitants, they were concealed so far back in the depths of the cave that they could not be seen. At the second cave, a pile of rags by the wall turned out to be two separate people of indiscernible gender who just shook their heads at Malluch's questions. At the third cave a man without a nose told them to get out of his house. "Because it is my house, you know," he added, following them to the opening. "It is all I have left. You may want news of these women very badly, but you can't just go into the caves. For one thing, you risk getting sick yourselves. And for another thing, it's rude."

"But have you seen them?" Malluch asked.

"There may have been a pair of new women over on that side."

He pointed across the valley. Ben-Hur could not take his eyes off the hand, scaly like a chicken's leg and missing three of its fingers. "In the cave at the bottom. They may not be able to speak, though," he added.

"Why not?" Ben-Hur asked, startled.

The man put his horrible hand to his neck. "The disease sometimes takes your voice." He took his hand away. "Eventually it takes everything, of course. It's just a matter of time." He turned away from them and back into his cave.

They stepped away from the cave, and Malluch took a few steps toward the other side of the valley, but Ben-Hur stopped him. "Not yet," he said. "Your plan is good, going from cave to cave. I can never come back here. Our being here, our asking these questions, will attract attention. I need to know that I have seen them all." So they continued searching.

They stood at each cave mouth and called out. Sometimes the occupants came out to see them, standing always at a safe distance. "The days must seem endless for them," Malluch whispered after they turned away from one of these. It was a woman who had kept them standing there for long minutes while she wondered out loud about the various occupants of the various caves. Just as often, though, no one replied to their greetings.

"When we have finished, I still won't know if they were here," Ben-Hur said in frustration as they clambered down a steep rock. "They might be asleep. They might be hiding. They might not have come out at a time when anyone saw them."

"The well man will know more," Malluch answered.

"We should have asked him first."

"Perhaps. But we are here now. And we cannot come back."

"Then what good is it to have come?" Ben-Hur snapped. "I am wasting my time. And yours."

Malluch said quietly, "You will have done your best. If you will forgive my saying so, I think you are a man who does not shirk a task he has taken on, no matter how hopeless. Surely your mother, if she were aware of it, would be happy at that."

* * *

Which she was. Naomi and Tirzah had been watching Ben-Hur's progress ever since the men arrived at the well. "He is here!" Tirzah had said, on an indrawn breath, words her mother could not hear. She scrambled to where her mother lay at the back of the cave. "Mother, he is here! Judah has come!"

Naomi sat up. "Judah? Here?"

"We knew he would come, Mother! Or we hoped so." Tirzah took a few steps and shaded her eyes at the front of the cave. "He has gone into another cave. He is with another man. Oh, wait, they are coming out again. Come and watch."

Naomi joined her, then pulled on her shoulder. "Not so close to the front," she murmured. "They should not see us."

Tirzah turned and met her mother's eyes. Then she looked, really looked at her mother's ruined face; the long, coarse, yellow-white hair that flowed over her shoulders like a cape; the hunched shoulders and bowed spine. "I know," said Naomi, who understood her daughter's gaze. "He would not recognize us. But we must pretend we know nothing. He must not come close; he must have no suspicion at all."

Tirzah put her arms gently around her mother. "And he won't. We will do what is right, Mother. But isn't it some consolation to know that he followed us this far?" She felt her mother's head nod against her shoulder. "Thank God we have each other," she whispered. And her mother nodded again.

* * *

In his years as Simonides's proxy, Malluch had been to many countries and seen many kinds of people. He had seen the mighty and the miserable. The Valley of the Dead, though, horrified him. He kept having to remind himself, as they went from cave to cave, that these were *people*. They looked like mobile refuse. Certainly they had been discarded by Jerusalem. Some were barely alive, of course, but others, like the man with no nose, were alert. Had ideas. No doubt feelings, as well. And here they all lived, if you could call it that, simply awaiting death.

He glanced sideways at Ben-Hur, whose face had grown stony. No sign there that he hoped to find his family. He was simply carrying out his intention. And, Malluch thought, finding it far more painful than he had expected.

It was hard to tell the men from the women because their features were so distorted and because many of them had long, unruly hair. In a few caves, horribly, they saw what must be children, though they could only be identified by their size. The two men worked their way methodically up and down the hill until they reached the wide, shallow cave near the well, where two women had recently taken up residence. Or so the man with no nose had told them.

They stood at the mouth and Ben-Hur called out, "Peace be with you," and waited.

A cracked voice answered, "And with you also. We are unclean. Come no further." Then came a scratching sound as the two figures against the back wall stood. The cave was quite shallow and nestled into a pale-colored stone, so it was surprisingly bright. And hot. It was difficult to make out the outlines of the lepers. Their robes were white—or had been. And so was their hair. They melted into the pale background like figures drawn with a piece of chalk.

※ ※ ※

For Tirzah and Naomi, Judah stood silhouetted, his face dark in the shadows cast by the afternoon sun. They stood close together, hands clasped tight. Tirzah's heart fluttered in her chest, and she wondered what her mother could possibly feel at this moment.

"Forgive us for intruding," Judah said in his deep voice. Tirzah wished she could grasp and hold it, the sound echoing forever in her head. "We are seeking two women of Israel who have come recently to this place. Do you know anything about them?"

Tirzah waited for her mother to answer. But Naomi did not. She drew breath. She made a little sound in her throat. Tirzah looked at her. This was her mother's privilege—to send her son away, forever, to safety. To life. Naomi shook her head and looked away. She lifted her hand to her mouth and shook her head again. Her voice had failed her.

The women's eyes locked. Naomi nodded to her daughter.

"We . . . ," Tirzah began. Her own voice sounded shrill. She began again. "We do not. I'm sorry." That should have been enough. The other man, whose face she never saw clearly, had already begun to turn away. Judah, however, did not move. She wanted to cry, *"We are the ones you seek! Don't you know us? We are the same inside, your loving mother and sister!"* Instead, she said, "This is a place where we leave each other alone."

Judah looked around the cave. He hesitated. *One more word,* thought Tirzah. *Let him leave us with one more word!* She could feel her mother quivering next to her. She knew Naomi was holding herself back. The urge to claim her son must be nearly overwhelming.

"Forgive me," Judah said then and left them.

CHAPTER 40

SWORD AND SHIELD

The sun was still bright when they left the last cave, and they didn't wait for the man who drew the water. Ben-Hur was silent as they retraced their steps and reentered the city. He and Malluch were separated from time to time by the crowds as they continued northward toward the khan in Bezetha. Without discussing it, they skirted the Hur palace by a wide margin. Malluch noticed that Ben-Hur never glanced once in the direction of the Antonia Tower, which dominated the sky.

Ben-Hur had still not spoken when they reached Bezetha. But there was a tumult approaching, a low hum that resolved into loud voices as a group of men came around a corner arguing. Malluch knew, at a glance, many of the types of men within the Roman Empire, but he could not identify this group. They were burly, rugged country people, heavily bearded and dressed in coarse robes.

Some carried staffs; some were barefoot. All were angry. They muttered and shouted, but they were all headed the same way, with a common goal.

Ben-Hur stepped into the edge of the group. "Is there news?" he asked mildly.

"I should think so!" a red-haired man answered. "You haven't heard?"

Several others of the group gathered around. "It's Pilate, the new procurator," one said. "He's going to build an aqueduct. To bring water into the city, he says."

"Not that that will help us," a wiry older man added.

"We have our own water," someone else added. "We don't need Rome to provide it."

"Where are you from?" Ben-Hur asked. He loomed above them, taller by a head, but Malluch thought there was something else that made him seem like their leader. Composure, perhaps?

"We are men of Galilee," the red-bearded man stated. "Who are you?"

"A son of Jerusalem," Ben-Hur told them. "Newly returned from abroad. Is there something wrong with this aqueduct?"

"He's stealing from the Temple!" came a voice.

Others chimed in: "Using Temple funds!" "Sacred funds!" "Stealing!" "Robbing us!" The voices grew louder, and several of the staffs pounded the earth.

"Where are you going now, and why?" asked Ben-Hur.

"We are going to Herod's Palace to protest," answered the redhead, who seemed to be the leader. "The rabbis are there already. We must let this Pilate know that the Jewish people will not permit such thievery! And we won't stand here talking anymore!" He raised his staff in the air and turned away from Ben-Hur. "To the praetorium, where we will see Pilate!" he shouted.

"May I come with you?" Ben-Hur asked, keeping up with his long stride.

"If you want to see how men of Galilee defend what is right!" another man responded. And the whole band moved forward, full of righteous outrage.

Malluch had heard about Galileans. They were independent, outspoken, unruly. They lived north of Jerusalem in hilly country dotted with tiny villages. Some farmed, many raised sheep, others fished in the huge lake, but few ever bothered with Jerusalem.

Still, someone in this crowd was familiar enough with the city to lead the group unerringly toward the praetorium. Malluch stayed toward the rear, but Ben-Hur was visible in the center. He did not join the shouting, but Malluch could tell he was listening closely to the Galileans' complaints.

Soon there were other clusters of men clogging the narrow streets, all streaming in the same direction. Most of them were more urban than the Galileans: paler, more slender, less noisy, but every bit as concerned about Pilate's misuse of Temple funds.

Information, whether accurate or not, circulated as they hurried along. The rabbis and elders of the Temple were already at Herod's Palace. Pilate had come out to speak with them. No, he had *refused* to come out. The Romans had doubled the guard at the palace. They were not letting anyone in. No, the court was full of angry Jews. Waiting to see Pilate and present their case.

The courtyard, when they got there, was only partly full, but certainly the men there were angry. The guard at the gate had indeed been doubled, and the soldiers stood rigid, elbow to elbow, with their helmets and breastplates flashing in the afternoon sun. Malluch saw that sweat ran down many a Roman cheek.

When Herod had built the palace, he had broken a Jewish law by planting rows of trees in the space by the gate. Malluch thought the leafy shade, with seats placed here and there, looked appealing, but on this day no one would set foot beneath the trees. The protesters all thronged together, facing the gleaming marble facade of the palace. It stood on a raised platform, where the rabbis from the Temple clustered next to a closed door. A second message had just been sent to Pilate, demanding that he speak to the Temple leaders.

Long minutes passed. The palace door remained closed. More Jews crowded into the court as word traveled throughout the city. The Roman guard stood still. The sun beat down. The Galileans milled around, restless and angry.

Ben-Hur turned to their redheaded leader. "Why did you come here?" he asked quietly.

"To fight, of course."

"And you will lead the fighting?"

"No, it is every man for himself," explained the Galilean.

"Whom do you expect to fight against?"

"There is always somebody," the Galilean answered.

"That, my friend, is certainly true. But have you thought that you might be more effective if you stayed together? And fought as a unit?"

"You don't know Galileans if you expect them to do anything together!"

"I don't know Galileans," Ben-Hur said, "but I do know Romans. And I know how they fight. Would your men follow me?"

"Ask them," said the Galilean.

So as the crowd stood there, waiting for Pilate, Ben-Hur went from man to man. Malluch couldn't hear what he said, but he followed the exchanges through gestures and expressions: Ben-Hur introducing himself, explaining his idea, listening to objections. Sometimes many objections. Yet each conversation ended cordially, with a nod.

The afternoon wore on. The heat did not abate. The rabbis sent in a third messenger. Ben-Hur appeared at Malluch's side.

"Something will happen soon," he said. "You may want to leave."

"I am a Jew," Malluch answered. "Pilate's robbery from the Temple concerns me, too. I will take my chance that the Romans will overlook me. Are you sure it is wise to offer to lead these men? What will happen if you injure a Roman and are taken into custody?"

"I don't care," Ben-Hur said with a kind of vicious emphasis, and Malluch suddenly understood.

Of course he did not care. Ben-Hur, though he hid it well, was alight with rage. He was spoiling for a fight, and the fight had delivered itself into his hands. The Galileans were to be his tool to punish the Romans for what they had done to his family.

"Aren't you risking other men's lives?" Malluch asked, but a low growling sound came from the center of the courtyard, where the men were packed most tightly.

"They will be safer with me than they would have been without me," Ben-Hur answered. "And I think lives are already at stake."

Malluch didn't understand what he meant, but a moment later Ben-Hur had boosted one of the Galileans onto his shoulders to get a better view. "There are men fighting," the Galilean called out. "I see clubs—oh! They have knocked down an old man! A rabbi! They are beating him!"

"Who?" the redheaded leader asked. "Who is doing the beating?"

"I can't tell. Men with clubs . . . No! They are Romans, disguised as Jews!"

No sooner had Ben-Hur heard that than he lifted the man off his shoulders. Looking around, he called out with a loud voice, "Men of Galilee! Follow me! We need not let the Romans injure our leaders and disrespect the people of Judea! They seem to think there is no one here to resist them. We will surprise them with our force."

Malluch was not a man of conflict, and his instinct was to melt into the crowd, work his way to the gate, and leave the Palace of Herod before the blood started flowing in earnest. But he *was* a man of curiosity, and he wanted to know what would happen next.

To his surprise, Ben-Hur led the group away from the front of the palace, back toward the gate. The crowd had grown much thicker since they'd arrived, and at the center of the court was a heaving, pushing, noisy mass. "Not yet!" Ben-Hur called as several men tried to turn aside to join the struggling throng. "The Romans are armed with clubs, and we are unarmed. We will come back with arms and surprise them!"

Had he managed to hide a cache of daggers somewhere? Did he plan on disarming the guards at the gate? Malluch was puzzled until Ben-Hur led the group to the trees and reached up to a sturdy branch. "These will be our clubs," he shouted to the group. "Pull one off and strip away the small branches and leaves. Then we will show the Romans who we are!"

The Galileans set to work. Some of them had orchards and knew how to exert leverage to break off the sturdy limbs; one had a small knife that he used to strip branch after branch. Ben-Hur went from man to man, issuing instructions. "We will set on them from behind. They will be completely surprised. Aim for the head. Hit hard. Knock them out if you can and take their clubs. Stay together. But leave room for your brothers to swing their branches!"

In minutes they had re-formed as a compact mass, brandishing their improvised weapons. With Ben-Hur in the lead, they forced their way through the mob of people. The crowd had begun to shift, many of them fleeing from the Romans' clubs, but the Galileans pushed and squeezed, cheek to shoulder.

"You aren't armed, my friend," said a grizzled man next to Malluch.

"I had not intended to fight," Malluch answered.

"Nor I. But the tall one is a good commander, isn't he? He seems to burn with righteous anger. And he had a good idea. So I am following. Here, you take my branch. I will pick up a club from the ground."

So Malluch found himself tossed by the throng, brandishing a

tree branch and thinking about righteous anger. Rome had imprisoned Ben-Hur's family and turned them into lepers. His shock and
grief after visiting the Valley of the Dead had inflamed his need to
strike back. Here was his chance.

The Romans disguised as Jews had cleared a space in the center of
the courtyard, as bystanders shoved their way out of danger. Bodies
lay on the elegantly tiled ground, their blood smeared over the geo-
metric patterns in the smooth marble. Some of the attackers stood
panting, their kerchiefs pushed back and their clean-shaven faces
gleaming with sweat when the Galileans cut through the crowd and
fell on them, howling with rage.

Ben-Hur swung first, felling a tall man with a blow that split open
his scalp. Malluch thought afterward that he would always see that
sight in his memory: the rough bark of the tree branch meeting the
Roman's forehead and the instant spatter of blood in the air. Malluch
flinched at the sight and wondered what he was doing in this volatile
mob, clutching the branch of a tree. But in the next instant he felt a
club swing near his ear, and he did the only thing possible. He spun
around and met it with his tree branch, which splintered on impact.
The blow traveled through Malluch's hands and up to his shoulders,
but he barely noticed. The Roman had stepped back and prepared for
another blow. Malluch thrust his branch into the man's face. There
were a few twigs and leaves left on the end. He kept jabbing, lunging
forward each time, blinding his opponent and scratching his face.
The man screamed and dropped his club behind him. It rolled on
the ground and he stepped on it, falling backward. His elbow met the
marble and must have shattered because Malluch saw him instantly
clutch it with his other hand. But the real damage had already been
done. One of his eyes was a red mess in its socket.

Malluch froze. Had he done that? He looked around. Had anyone
seen him do that? He dropped the branch. But another Roman was
coming toward him with a club raised over his head. Malluch ducked

and grasped the club rolling on the ground. As the Roman took one last step to close the gap, Malluch flailed upward with the club, hoping to tangle the Roman's legs. The man fell forward, on top of his compatriot, and Malluch dropped the club.

He wiped his forehead with his arm and glanced around. The crowd of men on their feet had thinned, but the bodies were thick on the ground. Many groaned and writhed while some lay still. Dead, or near it.

"Men of Galilee!" Ben-Hur shouted. "The guard is coming. We must go."

"No, no, we should stay and fight!" came the objections.

But Ben-Hur overrode them. "The Romans have blades and we have only branches. We have done what we intended. Let us retreat so that we can fight another day. Come! Follow me!"

And they did. Malluch watched as they dropped their branches with mingled expressions of regret and satisfaction. A few kicked Roman bodies as they hurried toward the gate. The Roman guard moved quickly toward them, hip to hip with spears at the ready.

"Now we run!" Ben-Hur shouted, and the Galileans took off. Their sandals slapped on the marble and their long hair flew behind them. They were all panting as they reached the gate, safely ahead of the Roman guard.

The centurion leading them shouted, "That's it—run away like the Jewish dogs you are!"

Ben-Hur whirled around and shouted back, in his fluent Latin, "We may be dogs, but you are jackals, preying on the weak and wounded!"

"Wait!" the centurion called as the group fled through the gate. "Are you Roman? Consorting with this scum of Galilee?"

"I am a son of Judah, and proud of it!" Ben-Hur answered.

"If you are so proud to be a Jew, prove your prowess. Fight me!"

The Galileans, lingering in the gateway, cheered. They were still full of the fury of battle and eager to prolong the excitement.

So, evidently, was Ben-Hur. "Fight you single-handed?"

"Yes," the centurion answered, stepping closer. "Just you and I. For the honor of our nations."

Ben-Hur looked around. The hills surrounding Herod's Palace were covered with people who had come out to watch the confrontation about the Temple funds. Likewise every neighboring roof was packed with its spectators. The Galileans were cheering. The Roman guard stood behind their centurion, at ease, with eager smiles on their faces. Malluch, who stood close to Ben-Hur, saw him decide.

"Certainly," he said. "I will fight you. For the honor of Israel, with much of it looking on." He gestured to the natural amphitheater around the palace courtyard. "But I have no sword or shield."

"Use mine," offered the centurion. "I will borrow from the guard. That way we will each be using unfamiliar arms."

A space had been cleared for them just before the gate. The Galileans had all filed back inside to watch, while the Roman guard formed a human cordon, holding back the crowd that remained from the protest.

The centurion and Ben-Hur stood in the center. Ben-Hur's tunic was torn at the shoulder and stained with sweat and tree sap. A broad, rusty stripe marked the garment's back, but he didn't move as if he were hurt. He took the short sword from the centurion and hefted it. "This will do," he said.

"Do you want a breastplate? Or a helmet?"

"No," Ben-Hur said. "We will fight without them, if you agree." And he smiled fiercely. Malluch realized, with a shock, that Ben-Hur was looking forward to the fight.

"Oh, certainly, Jew, I agree," said the Roman. He accepted a sword and shield from one of his men. "The shield suits you?"

Ben-Hur turned it over to look at the design on its face, then slid his arm through the inner straps. "Yes," he said, taking his position, foot-to-foot with his opponent. "What I did not tell you before is

that I have often fought as a Roman. I am a Jew and I believe in the
one God, but I am no stranger to your war god, Mars, whom I see
on this shield. And now you are *going to die*!"

The fight took only a moment. The short swords flashed once,
twice. The Roman aimed at Ben-Hur's face, then pulled back, but
Ben-Hur stepped aside. He feinted at the Roman's head and ducked
below the counterblow. Then he lifted his shield. The edge caught the
Roman's right arm. Using his enormous strength, Ben-Hur pushed
upward, sliding the shield's edge down the underside of the arm in a
bloody strip. He shifted to the left and thrust upward, letting go of
the sword as the man fell forward onto the patterned marble. A pool
of brilliant blood flooded out beneath him, and the crowd on the
roofs and hills burst into cheers. Ben-Hur put his foot on the body
and raised his shield over his head, like a gladiator in Rome, meeting
the gaze of the guard at the gate.

He leaned down to pluck the sword from beneath the centurion's
body, then stood up to address the officer who approached him in
the stillness. "It was a fair fight, you'll agree?"

"Yes. Fair enough."

"I will keep the sword and shield," Ben-Hur informed him.
"A memento of Rome."

"That is your right," the soldier answered.

So Ben-Hur turned toward the Galileans at the gate. The sword
dripped bright blood on the marble. "Come," he said, "we must be
gone. We are safe for now, but not much longer." He found the redheaded leader. "I have a proposal for you all or for any of you who
want to fight for Israel. Meet me at the khan in Bethany tonight.
Bring the sword and shield so that I recognize you. We prevailed
today. We showed the Romans our strength. Fighting together, we
can do much more!" He handed over the weapons to the Galilean
leader. And then he melted into the crowd.

Malluch, making his way back to the khan through the narrow, crowded streets, heard passersby telling and retelling the tale of the Jews' triumph over the Romans at Herod's Palace. Ben-Hur's role was emphasized, even magnified—he became the hero of the episode. But Malluch was disturbed. The death of the Roman centurion had just been a piece of bloody showmanship. What kind of man killed so casually? What kind of leader would Ben-Hur actually be?

PART 5

CHAPTER 41
THE DESERT

There were many times over the next six months when Ben-Hur regretted that flamboyant, impulsive demonstration of force in the courtyard at Herod's Palace. At the time, he had told himself that he needed to show the audience on the rooftops and hillsides how to resist Rome. Ben-Hur knew that being a leader meant being seen and acting publicly. But had he killed out of fury after seeing the leper colony? A leader who acted emotionally was a danger to everyone. Rage had no place in the project before him.

Certainly building a coherent mass of fighting men required patience and self-control. Setting up the camp in the desert had been the easy part; Sheik Ilderim's men had chosen a well-hidden spot with access to water. There were wide spaces for drilling groups of men into infantry formations and steep hillsides for simulating ambushes. Between them Simonides and Ilderim kept the camp amply provisioned, and Ben-Hur was grateful daily that he did not have to concern himself with foodstuffs, arms, or the details of housing.

The Galileans presented challenge enough. They came; they went. They argued. They brought their flocks with them. The fishermen moped, surrounded as they were by desert. No sooner would Ben-Hur choose and train a cohort and appoint officers than a third of them would decide to leave because they needed to harvest grapes or catch a stray ram or replace the roof of a cottage. Ben-Hur always wondered how this news got through to their supposedly secret camp, but when he mentioned this to the Galileans, they swore they had told no one where they were.

What Ben-Hur found most frustrating was that they were wonderful fighters. What they lacked in discipline and finesse they made up for in strength and verve. Gradually Ben-Hur found that they responded best to simulated battle situations. Teach them a few rudiments of weapon handling, let them choose their own leaders, and send them out into the hills to attack each other: they would come back sometimes bloodied but always exhilarated. And it was then that Ben-Hur could form them into Roman-style cohorts, march them up and down with precision, teach them to handle Roman weapons and obey Roman orders.

So gradually, he built a force. Over the course of the winter, he identified reliable officers. These were men who were respected by their fellows but who also understood the value of discipline and even obedience. Bit by bit, Ben-Hur put more power into their hands. When the chill of winter began to recede, some of them traveled back to Galilee to recruit more men. Soon there would be three full legions. Word began to come back that in some Galilean villages, the men had adopted military training as a pastime.

When spring came, he took a group of officers east, to the harsh, forbidding black lava beds of Trachonitis, where the landscape itself was an enemy. Here, for long days, he trained with his best offi-cers in the use of the javelin and the short Roman sword that was always gripped in the fist and thrust at close quarters. For the first time since he had left Jerusalem, he began to feel that perhaps it would be possible to provide the coming King with a force worthy of him—a fighting force that was capable of defeating Rome and establishing a renewed Jewish state. For the first time, he thought he might be ready.

So it was with curiosity and a sense of anticipation that one morn-ing just after sunrise he saw a messenger on horseback picking his way across the stony hillocks of the old lava flow. The air was so clear and dry that Ben-Hur could identify the horse as one of Ilderim's, so he went forward to meet him.

"Have you come a long way?" he asked, breaking open the seal of the packet he was handed.

"From Jerusalem," said the messenger. He gazed around him with wide eyes. "I've always heard about this place. Not very welcoming, is it?"

"You don't always get to choose where you're going to fight," Ben-Hur answered with a shrug. Then he turned to the letter, which had Malluch's name at the foot.

A prophet has appeared, it said. *He has been in the wilderness for years, but now he is preaching widely on the east bank of the Jordan. He says there is another man coming, greater than he. I have gone to the Jordan to hear him, and I believe he is speaking of the King you await. Jerusalem is all abuzz, and the banks of the Jordan are thronged with her people. You should come—as soon as may be possible.*

It was the summons Ben-Hur had been waiting for. By the end of the day he had handed over his command and chosen a guide to ride with him through the desert. They saw no one, traveling fast by night and resting at hidden oases during the sunlit hours. But two days later, the sharp-eyed guide paused at the top of a ridge and squinted into the distance. Ben-Hur saw nothing. In minutes, though, a speck materialized, and within an hour he was watching, with amazement, an enormous white camel with a green howdah, led by a tall Nubian slave.

It had to be Balthasar! Who else had such a camel and such a howdah? And if it was Balthasar . . . Ben-Hur ran a hand over his jaw, feeling the grit embedded in his beard. Surely not, though; Balthasar would not have exposed his daughter to the rigors of desert travel!

Yet when the two parties had met, Iras preceded her father out of the howdah, setting foot on the carpet the slave spread below her as if she were entering a palace.

"Greetings, son of Hur," she said calmly. "We are happy to see you. My father was certain no harm would come to us since he carries a seal of Sheik Ilderim, but I did not quite share his confidence. I was glad to make out your features. Though I did recognize the horse first."

"Peace be with you," Ben-Hur answered. "What are you doing out here alone? Sheik Ilderim's seal would mean nothing to some of the wilder desert creatures. Let alone to lack of water."

"Son of Hur!" came the thin voice from the howdah. "Come up! You are well met!"

Ben-Hur met Iras's eyes and she gestured toward the howdah. "He is frailer than when you saw him last," she whispered. "Go and speak to him."

It was hard to make out Balthasar's features in the shade of the howdah, but he did look smaller, and his turban seemed even more overwhelming. But he greeted Ben-Hur warmly and added, "I heard you ask why we are alone. We are traveling with a caravan to Jerusalem, but I am so impatient! And they are so slow! Darme there said he knew of a faster route that went near an oasis where we could rest. But he has not found it."

Ben-Hur looked down at the Nubian and his own Arab guide,

shoulder to shoulder facing eastward, both of them gesturing. "He and my guide seem to be in agreement. But what a risk to take! And why the hurry?"

A tiny clawlike hand emerged from Balthasar's robe to clasp Ben-Hur's wrist. "Oh, son of Hur, I have been having dreams! Dreams of such power and clarity, like the dreams I had so long ago. He is here—I know he is—the Savior I have been waiting for!"

A prickle of shock slid down Ben-Hur's spine. How could this be? "And you thought to find him in Jerusalem?"

"No," Balthasar said firmly. "Near the Jordan. Not in the city. I hear the voice saying, 'Haste, arise! Go to meet him!' and I see a crowd of people by a river."

Ben-Hur reached into his robe and pulled out Malluch's letter. The talk of visions both disturbed and excited him. Had the time for battle really come? He unrolled the papyrus and summarized its contents for Balthasar: "A prophet has appeared whom men say is Elias. He has been in the wilderness for years, and he says that someone follows him who is truly great. He is preaching and baptizing near the Jordan and says we must all repent."

He was watching Balthasar as he said the last words. The old man clasped his hands, and a tear slipped down his wrinkled cheek. "Thank you, God, for bringing me here. I pray that I may live long enough to worship the Savior again. Then your servant will be ready to go in peace." He spoke freely, easily, as if to a friend whom only he could see, and Ben-Hur felt a twinge of wistfulness.

"But only if we can find this prophet, Father," said Iras's light voice as she stepped into the howdah. "We are in luck. There is water nearby, according to our friend's guide."

"All is well, my daughter," Balthasar said. "The Lord provides for his own. I have never doubted. Shall we continue onward?"

As he and Iras changed places, Ben-Hur felt her hand run up his arm as she whispered into his ear, "If I were to pray, it would have been you I prayed to encounter, son of Hur. We will have much to say in the oasis." He nearly missed his step clambering down from the camel's back and, for a few minutes afterward, felt almost dizzy. The stuffy air of the howdah's interior, the chiming coins of Iras's necklace, and the story of Balthasar's dream all fought with the clean, harsh landscape before him. He kept looking back to be sure the camel was really there. And that hand? That mouth? Had she . . . had she kissed him? Or had he dreamed that butterfly touch, the way Balthasar had dreamed of his Savior?

CHAPTER 42

IRAS

By the time they reached the oasis, the sun was nearly overhead and the animals were flagging as they trudged over the wind-ridged dunes. The hills rose up sharp and uninviting before them, yet a dark line in the rock face widened as they neared it. Wide enough, it transpired, for the horses—even wide enough for the camel. And on the other side, a spring welled up, surrounded by date palms and ringed with grass.

"From here," said the guide as he and Ben-Hur unsaddled their horses, "it is only a few hours to the Jordan. We could even sleep here for the night and leave at dawn if that would suit you. I gather the camel's owner is in a hurry."

"He is," came Iras's voice behind them. "We will rest now. Perhaps we could discuss our plans once the sun has gone down? Accept our thanks for the guidance," she said to Ben-Hur, meeting his gaze. "My father makes little distinction these days between what might be and what is likely. For my part, I find your presence here quite miraculous. I have been thinking of you."

She had been thinking of him. While he had been sleeping in caves and shouting at Galileans, she had been thinking of him. Ben-Hur lay in a spot of shade, listening to the breeze rustle the palm leaves, and let that thought roll over him. The horses grazed nearby. The Nubian servant had produced an elegant silken tent from somewhere and lay in front of it while Balthasar and Iras rested. What could she possibly think about him? How often? In what way? He knew so little about women! If Iras had been a pious Jewish girl like his sister, Tirzah, or a respectable matron like the ones he had met in Rome, he would at least know what to expect from her. But she was no more like Tirzah than the camel was like a horse or a panther. They were entirely different creatures, with different purposes in life. But if Tirzah had been raised to be a home-loving woman who respected the commandments of her faith, what exactly was Iras meant for?

Ben-Hur had not thought he would sleep, but the hard night rides had worn him out, and the next thing he knew, an insect was lighting on his face. Half-awake, he brushed it away, but it landed again, on the tip of his nose and then on his mouth. He did not need to see her to know that Iras was there; her heavy perfume moved through the air.

He was not pleased to be surprised like that. "If I had been your enemy," she said, leaning over him, "I could have stabbed you. If, for instance, I was a Roman guard at the Temple in Jerusalem."

His eyes flew open. "Who . . . ? What?" He wanted to sit up, but her face loomed above his.

"The one you killed."

"How did you know?"

"I know things," she answered, retreating. She stood and brushed back her hair. "Many things."

He got to his feet and stretched, playing for time. "You and your father rested well?"

"To the extent that we can, in that tiny tent," she answered, waving a languid hand. "I won't be content until we get to Jerusalem. The desert is no place for a man as old as my father." She turned away from him and took a few steps toward the spring. "Do you remember the lake at the Orchard of the Palms? I wish we were there again. I miss the water."

He was determined to get an answer from her, though he was distracted by the memory of Iras emerging from the water in a dampened robe. "You know things? What else do you know?"

"I *don't* know how it is with the Jews," she said. "But I have heard a Roman saying: 'Fortune favors the bold.' You won the chariot race. You killed that Roman guard in front of the praetorium, in the sight of thousands of your people. I think you are due some good fortune, don't you?"

They were standing side by side now, close enough that Ben-Hur could feel a layer of her fine robes caressing his leg. "And how do you define good fortune?" he managed to ask.

"You are also going to see this prophet," she said, ignoring his question. "Or whatever he is. I have heard of a mysterious army being formed in the remote desert. An army to serve the King who will come to Judea. I have heard that Sheik Ilderim sanctioned the use of his lands for this project." She turned to face him. "Sheik Ilderim, of course, owes you a great deal. I have also heard that hundreds of talents are being spent to raise and equip this army." A tiny frown line appeared between her arched brows. "And I know that the son of Arrius inherited a Roman fortune. Where, I wonder, is that money now?"

He stood still. How *could* she know? Whom else had she told? What did it mean?

Her hand slid around his arm at the elbow, thumb stroking his bicep. "I see you are worried. No need. Let's walk a little bit. I get so cramped in the howdah."

Ben-Hur glanced back at the campsite, but no one was stirring. Even the camel had its eyes closed. "Of course," he answered. "Your father will not need you?"

"My father," she replied with an edge in her voice, "needs nothing from me these days. He lives to see this Savior he expects. Nothing more."

"And you?" Ben-Hur asked. "What do you expect?"

"I expect very little," she said. "But what I hope for is a King." She dropped his arm and clambered up to the top of a hillock. "It is time for the East to rise again," she said, looking down at him. "Rome has ruled long enough, and it *can be displaced*. Now. With the leader who is coming. With the army you have built." She held out her hand to him. "I know you feel as I do."

He took two long steps and was at her side. Even the slight elevation changed the view: more of the valley came into sight and the campsite looked smaller. "What do you see?" she whispered. "You have known Rome and its might. Couldn't a new empire be born here? Can you see the new armies, with yourself at the head? In a chariot, perhaps? In your own palace? With your own wife?" With one hand she lifted the sheer veil from her hair. It shone blue-black in the afternoon light, pouring across her shoulders. One long lock fell forward across her face, and Ben-Hur reached out to tuck it behind her ear. Once there, his hand would not move; it cupped her cheek with a gentleness he didn't know he possessed.

He leaned down to kiss her, drowning in the sensation of her skin against his. Heat, moisture, movement, softness . . . He felt his heart hammering. His arms went around her, and she nestled neatly against his shoulder, that river of silky hair against his neck. "You see," she said, "I have known you for a hero since the first time I saw you."

CHAPTER 43

JORDAN

They left before dawn the next day. In the night, Ben-Hur had heard voices from the little tent and Balthasar declaring, "Daughter, I must go. You could have stayed in Antioch. There was no need to come with me. My life is very near its end, but I believe I will live to see the Savior. The dreams are strong and beautiful. I cannot waste more time here. We will leave in the morning." Then the voices subsided into murmurs, and he went back to sleep.

It was not until they were riding out of the little valley that Ben-Hur thought about those words. If Iras was not traveling to Jerusalem to take care of her father—as she had told him—had she come to see the King? Or . . . to see him?

She and her father were dozing in the howdah, and he rode alone behind the guide. Aldebaran picked his way nimbly among stones in a dry streambed, and Ben-Hur let the reins lie on his neck. The steady rhythm of the horse's gait helped him think calmly.

They might be riding to greet a King. Balthasar, however, thought they would see a Savior, an entirely different idea. A King would rule as Herod had or as Caesar did. A Savior would not be concerned with earthly power. A Savior, in Balthasar's view, would redeem the faithful to eternal life, out of love. They might find neither—Malluch's letter had simply mentioned a prophet. Yet Ben-Hur had a sense that something important awaited them.

His dreams—unlike Balthasar's—had been confused. Where the old man heard clear statements, Ben-Hur had seen fragmentary images. Crowns. Glittering armies. Vast throne rooms, councils of powerful men—powerful like Arrius, but men of the East in glowing brocades and neat black beards. He himself was never present in these scenes. He did not command the troops or speak in the councils. And Iras, too, had appeared, though he could never hear what she said, no matter how hard he tried. Then Aldebaran tossed up his head and shied at a large lizard, and Ben-Hur's mind returned to his surroundings.

He had remembered Bethabara as an insignificant crossing of the Jordan, so he was surprised when the guide pointed to a dusty blur on the horizon and said, "Look! We are not the only travelers to visit this place!" Soon they began meeting men who were either heading in the same direction or coming away. Shortly the crowds became more numerous. Their pace slowed to a walk, and Iras's hand looped up the curtains of the howdah so that she and Balthasar could see out.

The excitement was palpable. Ben-Hur's eyes roved through the throng as he tried to identify the man they had all come to see, but there was simply a sea of dark heads and dusty garments. He handed his reins to the guide and slipped off Aldebaran's back.

Looking around in the crowd, he noticed a tall, bearded man coming toward him with a shepherd's crook. He stepped into the man's way and said, "Peace be with you. Have you just come from the river?"

The man's eyes lit up. "Yes! Are you here for the prophet? He is preaching at the riverbank. You will see him soon!"

"What is he saying?" Ben-Hur asked. "What has drawn such a following?"

"Amazing things!" the man answered, throwing his hands up. "He talks of repentance. He says we must be baptized. And that God— our God!—loves us, each one of us!"

Another man nearby asked, "Is he the Messiah?"

"He says not, though everyone asks. He just says that someone greater is coming. And . . . something else . . ." He frowned, trying to remember. "Oh, I know: it was 'I am the voice of one crying out in the wilderness, "Make straight the way of the Lord!"'"

"'Make straight the way of the Lord!'" another voice responded. "I heard him say that too!" The two men nodded at each other with satisfaction.

"What did they say? Is he still there?" came a threadlike voice to Ben-Hur. He looked up and saw Balthasar leaning down from the howdah.

"He is. He is preaching. We'll hear him soon," Ben-Hur replied and mounted his horse.

But within a few minutes, the crowds began to shift. Ben-Hur could see that the lone figure who had been standing on a sandbar in the river stopped speaking. The mass of people on the eastern side of the Jordan divided, leaving room for him to walk up the bank.

"What do you see?" Balthasar asked.

"He stopped preaching," Ben-Hur said. "He's coming this way. I think if we stay here, we will see him clearly."

And he was right. The multitudes, murmuring quietly, parted before the man, and in moments he was headed directly toward them. But what a shock!

"That man?" Iras whispered. "He looks like a wild animal!"

His hair was long and matted, falling halfway down his back and into his large dark eyes. He wore what looked like a beast's pelt, or perhaps several of them stitched together just to cover his scrawny body. A few yards in front of the camel, he came to a halt, planted his staff, and looked around, catching the eye of man after man. "Prepare!" he said, in a booming voice. "Prepare the way of the Lord!"

The crowd drew back. There was something fierce and determined about the prophet, as if he could bend men to his will.

Yet a man in the robes of a scribe stepped forward. "Are you the Messiah?" he asked.

"After me comes he who is mightier than I," said the prophet, "the strap of whose sandals I am not worthy to stoop down and untie."

"But you baptized, did you not?" persisted the scribe.

"I have baptized you with water," came the answer, "but he will baptize you with the Holy Spirit." Then he lifted his staff and moved forward. But a few steps later, he pointed to a man in the crowd. "Behold!" he shouted. "Behold the Lamb of God, who takes away the sin of the world!"

The masses did not press forward but fell away again, leaving a man alone in a circle of well-trodden ground. Ben-Hur saw him clearly. Everyone who was there that day would say the same thing in later years—that they had seen him, that they remembered. Yet not one could describe him with precision. He was a man; that was all. Dressed in white robes, like many of the men there. He didn't speak. There would be arguments about his expression: Did he smile? Did he meet anyone's eye? Did he gesture? Why was it, then, that every man who saw him that day felt blessed?

Especially Balthasar. The camel, as ever obeying some compulsion of its own, folded gently to its knees. Balthasar clambered down from the howdah and walked a few steps until he could clearly see the man in white. He, like the camel, knelt with a grace he had not possessed in years. And Ben-Hur saw on his face joy and gratitude— and recognition. There was a moment of hush; then the voice of the baptist said with utter clarity, "This is he. . . . This is the Son of God."

The Son of God. There was silence. Even the air seemed to stop moving. The sun still shone. Perhaps it gleamed more brightly on the head of the man in white. Perhaps there was a sound, a chord of unearthly voices. Or just a sense of grandeur, hope, warmth—belief. For an instant.

Then the moment was over. The robed man moved on. The baptist disappeared into the throng. Balthasar slumped to the dirt, and by the time he was carried back into the howdah, there was nothing more than a crowd milling around—but a crowd that had seen something remarkable. As they rode on to the river crossing, Ben-Hur leaned over to ask a stranger, "Who was that man in white?"

The man shrugged and answered, "Maybe he is the Son of God. But others say he is the son of a carpenter from Nazareth."

And then Ben-Hur remembered. The face had been familiar to him, and the feeling the face gave him. It was a feeling of peace and patience and strength. And the last time he had felt it was when a stranger gave him water in a little village, on his way to the galley.

CHAPTER 44

JERUSALEM

Balthasar did not die on the spot. In fact, his glimpse of the unassuming man from Nazareth renewed his vitality. He refused, however, to return to Alexandria. Instead he insisted on staying in Judea to be closer to the man he called the Savior.

Where Balthasar went, so did Iras. In the days after the encounter with the baptist, this became clear. It also became clear to Ben-Hur that the pair were now somehow his responsibility. Balthasar claimed he would happily live in a cave, and that was obviously true. But it was unthinkable to house Iras in a cave, or indeed in anything less than a palace.

Fortunately, there was a palace available. With his usual crafty efficiency, Simonides had managed to buy the Hur palace from the Roman government. But if it looked to outsiders as if the Egyptian wise man owned the palace, that illusion might be useful. So Balthasar and Iras moved in. Balthasar, content, spent his time in reading and prayer. Iras found that Jerusalem offered few opportunities for a woman of her independence and sophistication, so she turned her energies toward refurbishing Ben-Hur's house. Everything was to be splendid, worthy of a king.

Ben-Hur himself knew little of this. Jerusalem, he felt, was too dangerous for him, and his family's palace even more so. He returned to Galilee, recruiting more soldiers, instructing more officers, inventing new drills and training schemes so that the young men in every village could raise an armed cohort, complete with weapons and supplies for five days' marching, within an hour. When the King declared himself, they would be ready.

And yet the King was puzzling. A year went by, and another and a third. The King—or at least the son of the carpenter from Nazareth—roamed the region. If he *was* a king, his retinue was far from impressive. He made few claims for himself, but many claims for God. He was patient and gentle, but firm. And people were drawn to him, it was true. They sidled up to hear him speak a few words and never left. Sometimes after hearing this Jesus, a man would leave his plow in the middle of a furrow and walk away, never to return. Or drop his corner of a net of fish. Or round up his brothers and cousins to hear the Nazarene speak just one more time. Something about his message made you long to hear it again and again.

He made men—and women, too—feel strong and good. He made them believe there was a sense to the world. He got them to look at each other, really *see* each other with kindness and compassion. Crowds in Judea often meant fights, but not the crowds around Jesus. Food was shared. The children ran around his feet, and he laid gentle hands on their heads.

By the end of the third year, the army was ready. Ben-Hur knew he could do no more. He had been traveling intermittently with Jesus, hoping to get a sense of the man who would be the leader. Would he want cavalry? What strategy did he favor? Would he choose to attack the Romans in Jerusalem or launch his campaign elsewhere?

These all seemed like reasonable questions when he was out in the desert watching his troops or discussing tactics by a campfire. Simonides, whom he visited periodically, showed a surprising grasp of military affairs and a great zest for violence. Ilderim had a way of appearing at the camp in a whirl of Bedouin horsemen, arriving at a gallop with banners flapping and spears glittering for the sheer excitement of it. He would stay for a few days and then gallop away, leaving a few new mounts behind, taking a few back with him, and always bidding a fond farewell to Ben-Hur's bay, Aldebaran.

Then Ben-Hur would visit a Galilean village like Cana and hear of the wedding banquet where Jesus had turned water into wine. Truly! Everyone had seen it! Or he would find the followers encamped in a large crowd, peacefully listening to the Nazarene's preaching, which was so simple, yet sent chills down your spine. He often felt wistful in the presence of the followers. They seemed to understand something that was still a puzzle to him. It was much easier to be in the army camp, where the goals were familiar. Killing people was a skill as old as man.

✳ ✳ ✳

Esther heard about Ben-Hur from her father. She suspected that Simonides knew more than he told her. Ever since the day of the chariot race, when she had betrayed her feelings, her father had not been able to speak of Judah without self-consciousness. Sometimes Esther found this endearing, but more often she was simply irritated. She knew that Iras had enthralled Judah. She knew that her own appeal—whatever it might be—was eclipsed beside the Egyptian's. She was resigned to invisibility. But there seemed to be no way to convince her father of this.

So she was apprehensive when her father announced that they

were going to Jerusalem for the Passover feast. At least in Antioch her duties kept her busy and, on the whole, satisfied with her life. What would she do in Jerusalem? It even occurred to her that Iras might contrive to put her to work. She knew nothing of palaces except that they were large. She was a slave; slaves worked. Would Iras try to put a broom into her hand? She flushed with anger, just imagining that encounter.

Yet Judah would be there. She tried to control her imagination, tried not to invent scenes of Judah's warm welcome, honest appreciation, admiring glances. Those, she knew, would be for Iras. But practical as she was, she could not master her stubborn, unrealistic hopes.

The voyage was long and difficult. Simonides traveled in a litter suspended between two camels, and Esther knew he was in pain most of the time. Yet as they neared Jerusalem, he grew both calmer and more cheerful. One night, as the caravan rested near an oasis, he told Esther and Malluch that he had never expected to see Judea again. "I had forgotten," he said, "how clear the light is. That alone is worth all the trouble and discomfort." He looked fondly at Esther. "I know they fall heavily on you, and I have sometimes regretted my determination to come. But I hope that, once we arrive, you will see why I insisted."

"I'm sure I will," Esther answered. It was a lie, but what else could she say?

Yet as the sun crept lower in the sky a few days later, she stood on the rooftop of the Hur palace and understood her father's compulsion. All around, the folds of tawny hills embraced the walled city. In the dry air, the grand buildings of the Temple gleamed while the sky shone like a great blue dome overhead, shading to pink and coral in the west. The Temple! The Holy Place was so near! The city was beginning to fill with pilgrims for the holy feast of Passover, and even from the rooftop, Esther was aware of a sober joy filling the streets.

She turned away from the view when she heard a squawk and the rush of wings. Malluch's arrival had driven a flock of parrots up into the palm tree where they roosted, chattering and dropping seedpods. He brushed a blue feather from his shoulder as he saluted Esther, saying, "Peace be with you, daughter of my master. I've been sent to tell you that the son of Hur is on his way."

"Thank you," Esther said, hoping she was not blushing. "I'm sure my father will be glad to see him."

"So will we all," came Iras's voice, accompanied by the jingle of her necklaces as she stepped onto the rooftop. "Are you surveying the city, Esther? How does it seem to you?"

Esther hesitated a moment, then said, "Compact."

Iras laughed. "The holy city of your faith and you call it 'compact'! So practical! But I suppose that is your role in life."

"And what do you see as yours?" Esther asked politely.

"Oh, I think we will be hearing more about that soon," Iras said, gazing at the mosaic floor. "Malluch has told you that Judah is on his way?"

"Yes, thank you," Esther answered. "But I will go now to tell my father." She caught Malluch's eye, and he nodded slightly as if in approval. How did she sense that he found Iras as trying as she did?

✳ ✳ ✳

"Can't you do anything about those birds?" Iras said as Malluch watched Esther slip down the stairs.

"The birds?" he asked, turning back to the Egyptian. "We have tried, you may remember. There was the poison and the hawk and the nets. Perhaps you could ask the son of Hur, when he comes, what his family used to do to keep them away. I am at my wit's end."

"Oh, never mind," she said. "We will have more important things to discuss. They just make such a mess. It gets everywhere. And I want Judah to be happy with the way everything looks."

"I will send someone to clean up," he said.

"No, don't bother." Iras wandered over to the divan in the summerhouse. "I want to be alone. But when Judah arrives, you can send him up to me."

He just nodded, watching her arrange her skirts so that her ankles showed.

"That is all," she said, catching his eye. "Oh, you could send up something to drink as well. Maybe Esther could bring us a tray. I'm sure Judah will be happy to see her again."

He felt a pulse of anger and dropped his eyes as he imagined her stepping barefoot into a fresh patch of bird droppings.

But the next time he saw Iras, she was wearing a pair of golden slippers and a smug expression as she hung on Judah's arm. The young prince had asked for the household to assemble in the high-ceilinged central chamber of the palace. Malluch pushed Simonides in on his wheeled chair to find Balthasar propped with cushions on a divan. Esther slipped in behind them, finding a padded stool that she set down next to her father. When Ben-Hur caught sight of them, he removed himself from Iras's grasp and crossed the floor. "Peace be with you, Simonides!" he exclaimed. "And with you as well, sweet Esther. Blessings be on you both!" He smiled as Esther rose to greet him and shook his head. "Please, be seated. It makes me very happy to see you both in my father's house. I hope the voyage from Antioch was not too difficult."

"Not easy," Simonides replied, "but worth taking. I am glad to be back in our land. I have been away too long. And glad also that Esther should see the land of her fathers."

Ben-Hur turned to her, and Malluch, watching closely, thought she blushed.

"What do you think of it?" Ben-Hur asked.

She considered, then stated calmly, "It is very moving to be at the center of our faith, among so many other Jews."

"Have you been to the Temple?" he asked.

"Not yet. Perhaps when the crowds have diminished after the holy days, my father and I will go."

"I hope I will still be here," he replied. "I would like to go with you."

"And you should go to the praetorium as well, to show little Esther where you slew the Roman," Iras's voice cut in.

"No," Ben-Hur said shortly. "I would not trouble Esther with that incident."

"But tell us your news!" Balthasar piped up. "You have us all assembled here. Surely you have something to recount."

"Well, I do." Ben-Hur looked around the group, then up at the distant ceiling.

✳ ✳ ✳

Esther understood his hesitation. The vast space of the room was overwhelming. She stood and said, "Why don't you stand over there, by the hearth? Here, I will bring my father's chair." But before she could move Simonides two paces, Ben-Hur had displaced her, lifting her hands off the back of the wheeled chair. In moments they were all ranged in a circle with the firelight glowing on their faces. It caught the glitter of Iras's snake bracelet and the golden embroidery on Balthasar's turban. Esther sat slightly behind her father, with her hand in his on the arm of the chair.

Ben-Hur gazed at their faces and took a breath. Then he shook his head and said, "You know what I have taken as a task over the last three years. We all believe in the importance of this man I think of as the Nazarene." He looked directly at Balthasar. "We all believe that he is the future leader of Judea. Born, as you know, to be king of the Jews. He is on his way here now. He will be here tomorrow. Something will happen; we don't know what. He refers to the Temple as 'my Father's house.' I have the sense that this is the climax, the moment we have all been waiting for."

He spoke, Esther thought, with the confidence of a man who often needed to persuade others.

"I have spent most of the last three years on the task that you, Simonides, and Sheik Ilderim conceived of—to provide this future King with the force he will need to throw off Rome's dominion. But I have not focused entirely on troop formations and battle plans. I have also, I believe, come to know the Nazarene as he has traveled around the countryside, preaching and teaching. And I can tell you one thing with certainty: he is a man, as I am, as you are. He eats; he sleeps; he feels the heat and the cold."

"Can you summarize what he preaches, son of Hur?" Balthasar asked. "I have been longing, all this time, to know just what it is that he says."

"Yes, I will. But before I do that, I have to tell you also that while he is a man . . . he is also something more."

"Something more? What do you mean by that?" Iras's voice seemed sharp. But Ben-Hur did not answer her right away, for into the room ran Amrah, who had been at the market when he arrived. She seemed ready to throw her arms around him but instead knelt at his feet. Because he had avoided the Hur palace, she had not seen him since finding his mother and sister. The next day she would go to them and tell them how magnificent he was—but for the moment, emotion overwhelmed her.

"Amrah!" he said. "I am so happy to see you! It has been so long!" He put his hands below her shoulders and lifted her to standing. "You look well! But . . . what?"

For she had buried her head in his chest and burst into tears. Although Esther and Simonides were newly arrived at the house, Esther was already very fond of Amrah, and she rose quickly to put an arm around the old nurse. Amrah only wept the more, but she turned away from Ben-Hur and let Esther lead her out of the circle of light.

"Are you all right, Amrah?" Ben-Hur asked. "Esther, can you find out what is upsetting her?"

Esther nodded and drew Amrah down next to her on a low bench. The two whispering voices could be heard for a moment; then Iras said, "Go on, son of Hur. This King—who arrives in Jerusalem tomorrow, you say—is something more than a man? A great warrior, perhaps? A chief? A sage? A magus?"

"None of those," he answered after a brief thoughtful silence. "For instance—" he scanned their eager faces—"this may make him sound like a magician . . . but I heard that at a wedding, he turned water into wine."

Iras laughed. "What good would that be for a King who should rule?"

"If he can turn water into wine," Simonides said, disapproval of Iras clear in his voice, "then perhaps nothing in the world is fixed for him. He could turn a legion of Romans into . . . a flock of ducks!"

They all laughed briefly at the idea of Romans as ducks, but Ben-Hur went on to say, "In fact, Simonides is right. I wasn't with him when another incident happened but . . . This was far away, up in Gadara. The group encountered two men who were possessed. And the Nazarene exorcised the demons, which went into a herd of pigs. The pigs rushed down into the sea and the men walked away, restored."

"So he has unusual powers, you would say," Balthasar suggested. "But how does he use them? Surely that is even more important?"

"I agree with you. But the way he lives is unlike any ruler I've known of. For instance, he travels with a group of humble men. They walk along the roads, talking; when they come to a village, the Nazarene will speak to anyone. He is kind to the weak, to children, to women. He preaches of patience and humility and compassion. The rough men around him show great kindness to each other. Even in the largest gatherings, there is no anger, no pilfering. People share

their food, take care of each other. This, Balthasar, is wholly his influ-
ence. And . . ." He paused and shook his head. "He heals."

Esther, across the room, spoke up. "He heals? He is a healer?"

"Not in the usual sense," Ben-Hur answered. "Not with herbs or
potions. I saw him once . . . We were leaving Jericho and there were
two blind men begging by the side of the road. They called out to
him and he went over and touched their eyes. And they saw. Just
like that."

There was silence in the great room, so that the crackling of the
fire could be heard.

"And then he healed a man with the palsy. He said to the man,
'Rise, pick up your bed, and go home,' and the man, who had been
shaking and twitching and barely able to move . . . he stood straight
and walked away."

"But how does that help us?" Iras asked. "Of course the palsied
man is happy, but what does this do to defeat Rome?"

Ben-Hur just held up a hand. "He has even, repeatedly, cured
people of the worst scourge. I was with him when this happened: a
leper came to him in Galilee. We would all have driven him away,
but the Nazarene wouldn't let us. He walked toward the man. Have
you ever been close to a leper?" he asked the group. "What a curse!
As if your body were devouring itself! And he was dressed in filthy
rags, hobbling on a crutch; truly the kind of beggar we all pass by in
the road and pull our robes close so that we don't touch them. Which
indeed Scripture requires. But the leper said—and you could barely
hear his voice—'Lord, if you will, you can make me clean.' And the
Nazarene reached out. He touched the man with his hand and said,
'Be clean.' And . . . he was."

In the shadows, Esther felt Amrah's thin shoulders tense, and the
old servant sat up.

"That wasn't the only time he healed lepers," Ben-Hur went on.
"There was a group of ten who came to him. And he told them to go

to the priest in the Temple, for purification, and that they would be healed before they got there. And it happened. He has such power. These are miracles, aren't they?"

Amrah murmured something to Esther and left the room, but it seemed only Esther noticed.

"Yes," Balthasar answered with satisfaction. "Those are miracles."

"I agree," said Simonides. "But this power—what else can he do with it?"

Ben-Hur walked away from the fireplace to the end of the room. He smiled absently at Esther and returned to his first position. "I hesitate to tell you because this sounds so outlandish." He glanced at Iras quickly. "He can defeat death."

They all gasped, and Balthasar muttered quickly in a language none of them recognized, a prayer or a charm of some kind.

"I saw it. He raised a young man from his funeral bier, down near Nain. The man's mother had been weeping and the Nazarene touched the body and said, 'Arise!' And the corpse, the man, stood up."

"Only God is so good!" Balthasar exclaimed, raising his hands above his face. "Only God could do such things!"

Ben-Hur shook his head. "It may be. Balthasar may be right. We don't know yet. In Galilee a while ago, we tried to crown him. You know the Galileans; they are impatient. We had been working so hard; we were proud of our forces; we wanted to . . ."

"To conquer!" Iras put in.

He nodded at her. "Yes, to conquer. So we marched to the Sea of Galilee, where he was teaching, and surrounded him, calling and shouting and . . . he vanished. He wanted nothing to do with us and our weapons and our shouts. He did not want our crown."

Esther looked up, hearing the bafflement, even disappointment in Ben-Hur's voice.

"And he is on his way here?" Simonides asked.

"Yes. He will be here tomorrow. There will be some kind of procession; the group around him is quite large by now."

"And it will become clear, tomorrow, who he is and what he intends to do," Iras stated. "He will proclaim himself King. Surely that is why he has come to Jerusalem!"

"He is our Messiah," Simonides said confidently, "come to restore the Jews to the power they once knew. The prophets have foreseen it all!"

Balthasar waggled his head. "He is the Savior of souls," he insisted. "He can bring men back to life, but, Daughter, he will not be crowned. His dominion will not be the earthly world."

Ben-Hur shrugged. "I don't know. I have seen as much of him as most men, and I am still not sure. But soon the wait will be over."

After an instant of silence, Esther rose from her stool and slipped quietly from the room to prepare her father's bedchamber. The image she kept remembering was that of a gentle man, strolling with his friends and curing the ill. She could not imagine that man accepting a crown. Nor, she suspected, could Ben-Hur, despite all his talk of triumph.

CHAPTER 45

CLEAN

One thing Ben-Hur was sure of: the Nazarene's entry into Jerusalem would draw crowds. The city was already full to bursting with pilgrims visiting for Passover. Tents speckled the hillsides beyond the walls, and the streets, always congested, were barely passable.

Emotions ran high at such times. Fights flared up. Roman soldiers patrolled, ready and eager to knock heads together. The Nazarene would need protection, and Ben-Hur was determined to provide it. He spent the night at the khan in Bezetha, where he had left a cohort of his trained Galilean fighters. The Nazarene would enter Jerusalem from the east, with his followers. The band had grown steadily larger and now numbered in the hundreds. But at the same time, word had reached into Jerusalem that a great leader was coming. No doubt crowds would hasten beyond the city walls to meet him. Whether or not they believed, his coming would provide some excitement.

And to a military man like Judah Ben-Hur, large groups of excited civilians were a threat.

That morning the Galileans were dressed in the everyday tunic and robe of the city dweller. They had been instructed to blend into the crowd and never to let their short swords be visible. They were present only to keep order and to protect the Nazarene. Ben-Hur himself rode a short distance out from the city gates, up to the brow of a small hill. Behind him, coming out from Jerusalem, was a huge body of men, thousands strong. They were waving palms, and as the breeze shifted, Ben-Hur could hear hymns almost shouted by the crowd, accompanied by small drums and cymbals. Young men danced on the edges of the road, apparently drunk with joy.

And just over the hill, climbing the slope, came the Nazarene himself, surrounded by a similar throng. Ben-Hur caught sight of some of the faces: the two fisherman sons of Zebedee and Peter, who trudged behind the Nazarene, scanning the crowd with a deep frown. The man at the center of the commotion sat quietly on a donkey in his white robes, mind apparently elsewhere.

He doesn't look very happy, Ben-Hur found himself thinking. It was as if Iras had spoken inside his head. *He doesn't look like a leader. He certainly doesn't look like a King.*

Someone tossed a palm branch onto the road in front of the donkey and immediately others followed suit. The narrow, stony surface was soon covered with greens. Here and there an extravagant soul laid down his cloak as well. The donkey trudged onward on the new surface, as oblivious as its rider.

That's not how you do it, Ben-Hur's thoughts went on. He'd seen parades. The Romans knew how to stage a spectacle. That was part of governing: You showed your might. You sat up high, where people could see you. You waved!

Where were the flags and trumpets? Where were the glitter and fanfare, the evidence of power?

A hundred yards farther on, the Nazarene reached the multitude that had come out from Jerusalem and the shout echoed off the hills. Far away, flocks of birds rose from their trees and wheeled around in panic. Even Aldebaran shifted his weight, disliking the noise. Which was odd, given how calm he had been in the tumult of the chariot race. Ben-Hur looked around for the Arab groom who had accompanied him. He slipped off the saddle and led Aldebaran to the man, who stood in a patch of shade with his own mount. "Just hold him until I come back," he instructed.

The road ran in what had probably been a gully long ago. When it rained, water no doubt washed down the little hills on each side and formed a stream. Now it was a stream of people, moving cheerfully but very slowly in the morning sun.

Ben-Hur eyed the press of humanity in the roadbed and decided to pick his way along the rocky hillside to catch up to Jesus. He had no reason for concern, he told himself. But . . . he just wanted to see. Would the Nazarene speak? Would he . . . command?

Would he say, *"This is the moment, my people! Let us throw off the Roman yoke!"* Or *"Jerusalem will be free!"* Would he suddenly sit tall on the donkey, raise his arms, call for victory?

No. Ben-Hur swung around a stunted tree and caught sight of the Nazarene. The vast crowd shuffled onward, but the donkey and a few of the disciples stood by the road's edge where Jesus had dismounted. Ben-Hur wasn't close enough to hear over the noise of the crowd, but the scene was familiar to him. This was what the Nazarene did: people in pain came to him, and he lifted their burdens. And now, as he was making his triumphal entry into the central city of his faith, he had turned aside from the cheering throng to listen to another supplicant.

A few steps from the roadside, next to a gleaming white boulder, stood a small dark woman—a servant of some sort—and two lepers. Their age and gender were impossible to make out. One of them must have cried out to attract the Nazarene's attention. The Nazarene stood still, listening. He spoke, though Ben-Hur was too far away to hear what he said. One of the desperate creatures gestured with uplifted hands. Jesus nodded and spoke again. Then he lifted his hand and blessed the lepers. Just for that moment, he looked happy. Then he turned and remounted the donkey.

Lepers, Ben-Hur thought, and something like despair shot through him. *That is the kind of King he is—the kind who turns aside from a triumphal entry to cure a pair of lepers. How will this unseat Rome?*

But then the small dark servant fell to her knees, and he recognized her. She held her hands out to the lepers, as if she wanted to embrace them. He had often felt that clasp! But what was Amrah doing with a pair of lepers?

Before he could think, his feet were moving. He leapt over rocks and scrubby plants, never taking his eyes off the trio. The lepers had fallen to their knees, hands to their faces, while Amrah looked after the Nazarene, barely visible now in the slow-moving mass of men. They didn't hear Judah's footsteps.

He halted ten feet away, out of habit. One didn't get close to lepers. He called out, "Amrah?"

She turned and recognized him. "Master, master!" she cried and scrabbled across the rocks and shrubs that separated them. "Master!" she said once more and reached out to clasp his hands.

He stepped back automatically, frowning. "Amrah, what are you doing?" he asked. "I saw you with those lepers. You are unclean now!"

Then he heard his name, almost whispered. Despite the clamor of the procession, he heard it. It came from one of the lepers. Women, it seemed. Both of them women.

"Is it really you, Judah?" said the other one. Her voice was stronger, more audible.

He turned to Amrah. "But who are they?" he asked. "Why do they call me by my name?"

She looked at him, eyes streaming, unable to speak.

One of them had taken a step closer. She looked better somehow. She stood taller and her skin seemed to be mending itself then and there, as he watched. "Judah," she said. "I am your mother."

He looked at Amrah for confirmation, then back at the leper. Moment by moment she was changing. He reached out to the thorny branch of a tree next to him and grasped it. The ground suddenly felt unsteady.

"Mother?" he tried to say, but it was like trying to speak in a dream with a closed throat and a tongue that wouldn't move. "Tirzah?" he managed to croak. He looked at the other leper. Already her hair had lost the coarse, crinkled texture and regained some of its color. Her eyes looked into his and . . . she smiled. "Tirzah!" he cried.

And then they were all weeping. They stood in a circle, just gazing at each other because Amrah kept her head. "You must not touch each other yet," she said firmly. "The clothes may carry the disease. Judah, stand back."

"Oh, Amrah, must I?" he said. "If you knew how I longed to touch my mother and my sister!" He gazed hungrily at them, a mere arm's length away.

They seemed to glow. They looked at him with such joy that the air around them shimmered. Moment by moment, their bodies changed and now he could see them as he had known them, the women of his family, whom he had loved and now could love again.

Because of the Nazarene.

He had seen these cures before. He had been astounded. But now! Now that healing touch reached into his own life! He wanted more than anything to fall to his knees. He would have kissed the hem of Jesus' robe. He would have raised his hands to heaven, as Balthasar did. Glory? Had he thought conquest was glory? Surely this was the true splendor!

"Judah, who is he? Do you think he is the Messiah?" his mother asked. She took a step toward him, then another, and maternal instinct drove out her questions. "I think we will be safe at this distance, don't you?" she asked. "Though I do so long to touch you! You are so large, Judah!"

He smiled at her, a broad, humorous smile that felt unfamiliar. "I believe I am fully grown now," he said.

"And so handsome," added Amrah, not to be left out.

"If I look at all like Tirzah," he said happily, "I must be handsome indeed!"

"Yes," Naomi said, turning to put her arms around her daughter, "Tirzah is a beauty."

They were themselves again. Long, glossy hair, smooth skin, clear eyes. Naomi kept running one hand over the other, checking that the fingers were all there, including the nails. Tirzah bent down to examine her feet, slim and beautiful in her coarse sandals.

"But you haven't answered," Naomi said. "Who is this man? Amrah was not sure. She just said you had told tales of his wonderful cures."

"I will tell you on the way, shall I?" he answered. "I have a horse just yonder and a guide with another one. The three of you can ride them, and the guide and I will walk."

"Where will we go?" Tirzah asked.

"We will find you a tent," Ben-Hur said. "A comfortable one. And new clothes. You will need to be presented at the Temple and—I don't know—perhaps take the ritual bath. Because now you are clean!"

"Clean, Mother! We never have to say the other word again!"

"What word is that?" Ben-Hur asked.

"*Unclean,*" Tirzah told him. "Because we were lepers. You know how they are required to warn everyone." She ran her hands along her arms. "Clean!"

"But, Judah, the man on the donkey!" Naomi said. "Tell me about him."

So as they picked their way across the hillside toward the horses, Ben-Hur told them what he knew about the baptizer at the Jordan River, the followers, the miracles. It was easier, he thought, to leave out his army of Galileans. He did not want to speak to his mother about vengeance and violence, not on this day.

"So he is the Messiah," Naomi said with certitude.

"Some think so," Ben-Hur answered. "He chose to come to Jerusalem now, after three years in the country. Something is going to happen, but only he knows what it is."

"And how did you come to be one of his followers?" Naomi asked. "If you are one?"

"Oh, the horses!" Tirzah exclaimed as they turned a corner and saw the Arab guide with Aldebaran and a delicate gray mare. Aldebaran lifted his head and nickered when Ben-Hur's scent reached him on the dry air. "Will they let us ride them? They are so beautiful; are they yours?"

"I had forgotten that you love horses," Ben-Hur said.

"So had I," Tirzah answered, beaming at him. "Though in truth, everything looks so lovely today!"

"It does," Naomi added. "This is a blessed day for us all!"

CHAPTER 46

PASSOVER

It took only minutes to make the arrangements. Ben-Hur sent the groom off to Jerusalem with instructions for Malluch. He would meet them at a specified location in the Kidron Valley, with tents and food and servants and clean garments for Naomi and Tirzah.

"He will be there by the time we arrive," Ben-Hur assured the women. "Now, Mother, can you mount if I lead Aldebaran close to this rock?" His mother and sister clambered aboard the bay, who submitted gracefully to his unusual burden. Ben-Hur and Amrah—who'd refused to ride—walked on both sides of the horse, surrounded by the thinning crowd of Jesus' followers. They talked all the way, and when they reached the location Ben-Hur had specified, Malluch stood smiling before three tents, pitched on a small grassy patch beneath a pair of olive trees.

They spent four days together. The women grew stronger. They shared their stories. The valley grew more and more crowded as pilgrims from all over Judea arrived for Passover, and on that evening, the first day of the festival, Ben-Hur left his family to return to the city.

Jerusalem's gates were wide open. The strategist in Ben-Hur noted how vulnerable the city seemed: the citizens and the visitors heedlessly thronged the streets, moving from courtyard to courtyard singing and eating, for all of the ritually slaughtered lambs roasting on thousands of fires must be consumed completely that night. The door to every house was open and voices called out, "Come in and join us!" But Ben-Hur walked on, lifting a hand and smiling regretfully.

He had spent too long with his family, he thought with a twinge of apprehension. It had been so easy, with Naomi and Tirzah, to let the hours drift past while they rediscovered each other. So easy and so urgent, at the time. He had felt as if, at long last, he were drinking deep from a cool stream.

They had asked all the questions at first. It had seemed strange: no one, in the previous years, had wanted to know so many details of his past. It was such a relief to share it: the tile, the capture, the forced march to the galley. He hadn't told them everything about the galley. Some things they should never know. He dwelt instead on the years in Rome and Arrius's kindness.

Their story was shorter. "The boredom was the worst of it," Naomi declared, but Tirzah contradicted her.

"Not for me," she said. "It was the anger. I wanted to kill."

"You did?" Naomi was shocked. "Kill whom?"

"You, out of mercy. Myself, out of despair."

"But—our days are held by God," Naomi said, still in shock. "We must endure what he sends."

"I know," Tirzah said gently, clasping her mother's hand. "And all along I knew what you believed. You were an example to me. I will never forget your courage."

"Knowing you were alive made everything easier," Naomi told

Ben-Hur. She and Tirzah exchanged a glance. "I still see you, lying in the moonlight beside our palace gate that night. Once we knew you were well, we could accept our fate."

"You were always more accepting than I was," Tirzah countered.

"You were the one who talked to Judah when he came to the cave," Naomi pointed out. "And turned him away. You were brave too."

Ben-Hur had been humbled by the exchange. The kind of courage he knew prompted action, and he thought that might be easier than resignation. The image of Jesus, silent on his donkey, came into his mind. As he shouldered his way through the high-spirited Passover crowds in the city, he wondered about the test ahead. Courage would certainly be required. But courage of what nature?

The crisis in the Nazarene's story was approaching. A constant relay of messengers had reached Ben-Hur in the valley, keeping him aware of Jesus' movements since entering Jerusalem. A cohort of Galilean fighters, well disguised, had followed Jesus everywhere, with orders to protect him. But all he had done was go to the Temple, as he had promised. Yet this was the great night of the Jewish year. Surely any leader would take advantage of this moment to declare himself?

When he arrived at the Hur palace, he was told that Simonides and Balthasar had gone out into the streets to see the celebrations. Iras, however, was in the great chamber.

Iras! Alone! Ben-Hur paused for an instant. He had forgotten about her! Somehow the four days with the women of his family had altered her image in his mind. Was it the contrast between the Egyptian and his sister that made him hesitate? Iras's sultry charm, her ambition, the flicker of cruelty he'd perceived in her?

Cruelty? As he climbed the stairs, he tested the thought. Yes, he decided, Iras could be cruel, even malicious. She was dismissive of her father and of Esther as well. Could she be blamed? he wondered. She was a woman of great ambition, thwarted by loyalty to her aging father. What was there for her in Jerusalem, anyway?

Iras was also, Ben-Hur admitted to himself, a woman of intense allure. As he pushed aside the curtain hanging at the door of the tall room, his heart raced. A seven-branched lamp stood at the center of the room, and Iras sat on a divan at its feet with her back to the doorway. Her gossamer veil moved slightly in the current of air as the curtain fell back in place.

She did not turn to face him. There was nothing soft or receptive about the view of her spine. So Ben-Hur crossed the room and stood before her, saying, "Peace be to you, daughter of Balthasar."

"Peace?" she said flatly. "I didn't think that was what the hero Ben-Hur was seeking. Or . . . wait. Maybe you are not a hero."

The edge in her voice was new. "I don't believe I ever claimed to be one," he countered.

"No? You certainly never contradicted me when *I* called you heroic," she said. "After the chariot race, for instance."

Ben-Hur sighed. He looked around the room for a chair, but Iras stood instead. "You will not need to sit down. I am not going to remain in the same room as a coward. No. Perhaps I should call you a cheat!"

He stepped back, surprised.

"Yes, a cheat," she went on. "You deceived me! That man, the Nazarene . . . you had me believe he would be King! King of the Jews—isn't that what you said?"

She pushed past him, striding to the end of the room. "I thought you understood me. I love Rome even less than you. This man, you said, was born to be King. You were building an army for him!"

"I was. I have," Ben-Hur broke in.

"Not for *that* man!" she spat. "I saw him, you know. My father insisted, frail as he is. The procession was impressive, I suppose, if you admire country bumpkins waving branches and wailing. I looked for a cohort of Galileans led by a prince of Judea, but I saw nothing so grand."

"I was detained—"

She didn't let him continue but waved her hand. "In fact, there was *nothing* of grandeur! There were thousands of grubby Jews in dusty robes. Some were gray and some were brown and some may once have been white. And the King himself, trotting along on the back of a donkey! Looking mournful—at best! Oh, my heart sank," she went on. "There is no glory here! Where are the swords and breastplates? The drums? There wasn't even a flag, not a streamer, not a banner. And do you know what your man did when he got to the Temple?"

"No, I have not heard," Ben-Hur answered. "I am glad you can tell me."

"I was on the porch. The courts were all full of people. The priests, at least, in their vestments, brought some splendor to the scene, but your man, the Nazarene—he entered the Temple on foot. He gazed here and there, like any dazzled rustic. Then without saying a word, without lifting a hand, he merely trudged onward and left by the opposite gate. So what do you have to say to that?"

She flung herself down on the divan again with her back to him, and for a long moment Ben-Hur was silent.

She was right, of course. In one way. He could imagine the scene as she had described it: the Nazarene entering the courts of the Temple, glancing at the gathered crowds, the massive walls, the mosaics, the turrets, the solid presence of the established faith. He had called it "my Father's house." And the Nazarene had seen it and walked on. Walked on to something else. Something different. New.

But of course that was not what Iras had wanted. Ben-Hur looked at her again, feeling both foolish and relieved. Whatever it was that the Nazarene had in mind, Ben-Hur knew it was nothing Iras would value.

"I am waiting for your answer," she reminded him. "What kind of King have you been supporting all this time?"

"I still don't know," he said. "Your father believes that he is the Son of God and that he will rule over a world to come, an eternal realm for our souls. Simonides and Sheik Ilderim and I thought, like you, that he planned an overthrow of Rome. A rebellion, like those the world has known before."

"And what do you believe now, this minute?" She turned around, frank curiosity on her face. "The fable? A story concocted for the credulous, like my age-addled father? I thought you were wiser than that."

He responded honestly. "I am torn. But I have seen that the Nazarene is capable of marvels. He can bend the world to his will—if he chooses. Tonight is the night for him to declare his earthly sovereignty. But he may look forward to a different kind of rule."

"Oh, nonsense!" she exclaimed. "There is nothing besides the earthly world." She stood and shook out her robe. "Messala was right about you from the first," she said, watching him to see his reaction.

He felt his eyes widen and his heart clutch. "Messala? What does he have to do with this?"

"He is the real hero," she said. "We met in Alexandria. We became lovers. He was sent to Antioch later. Where he goes, I follow. My father is so old, so silly, that I can persuade him of anything. Like meeting Messala at the Fountain of Castalia." She laughed as Ben-Hur visibly made the connection.

"And the palace of Idernee?" she went on. "You never did figure out who hired those assassins, did you?"

Now Ben-Hur was feeling his skin crawl. "You? And Messala?"

She nodded calmly. "He will never walk again. It was your doing." She crossed the room toward him, closer and closer. He tried not to recoil but could not help leaning back. All the same she put a hand on his shoulder. Ran it up his neck to the back of his head. Stretched up and kissed him on the lips, long and deep. "You thought I might be yours," she said finally. "I never could. Know this, son of Hur:

Iras the Egyptian is a consort fit for a mighty leader. And that man is not you."

The draft from her departure made the lights in the chandelier flicker, and he stepped over toward the divan, knees collapsing.

Iras and Messala. All along. He thought back to each encounter with her and saw clearly Messala's shadow. All that time! At the Grove of Daphne, at the Orchard of the Palms, even here, in the palace of his family—Iras had been living in Jerusalem as Messala's eyes and ears! All her talk of overthrowing Rome—had that been meant as a trap? Would she have betrayed him to the Roman authorities once he moved with his army?

Would she now? A chill ran down his spine. Of course she would, if she could. Iras would not hesitate. Yet on this night of all nights, with Jerusalem at its peak of festivity, Ben-Hur felt himself safe from Rome's reach. Let her go, if she could. Let her try to elbow her way through the crowds to the Antonia Tower and find the captain of a legion and make a complaint that she knew of a traitor. She would be ignored. The empire's guards and soldiers would have other preoccupations.

He shook himself. Thank God he had not mentioned his family to her! He had imagined sharing the good news, his relief and his joy, but now to link them, even in thought, felt unseemly.

"Judah? You're here alone?" said a woman's voice, and he spun around.

"I'm sorry I startled you," Esther continued. "I thought I heard voices and I wondered if my father had returned. What are you doing here? I thought you would be out with the Nazarene."

"I am on my way," he answered. "But I have just come from . . ." He paused and looked at her. Such a contrast to Iras! he thought. Her skin was like milk and her brown hair had an auburn glow. It looked alive in the glow from the lamp. "Come, sit down," he said, moving toward the divan. "I have such news! My mother and sister have been found! Amrah knew where they were all along, but they insisted she keep the secret."

He held out his hands and clasped hers, drawing her to sit next to him. To his surprise, her eyes were full of tears.

"Oh, Judah!" she said. "I am so glad for you! But why would Amrah keep such a secret?"

"They were lepers," he said gently, not wanting to shock her. "But they were cured by the Nazarene."

She pulled her hands away from his in surprise. "That night, when you were telling us the story—Amrah was sitting by me. And she heard you talk about him!"

"Yes, of course. And then she left the room."

"Did she go and tell them?"

"Yes, and they met him coming into Jerusalem! My mother called out. And I saw it, Esther. I saw the disease leave their bodies. Minute by minute, they became themselves again."

She was silent for a long moment while she wiped away tears. Then she nodded. "What a blessing," she said.

"It is. They are in tents in the Kidron Valley. In a few more days, they will go to the priests in the Temple for purification, and then they will come here. I know they will love you, Esther," he said to his own surprise.

"And I will love them," she said, blushing deeply. Then she stood and looked away from him. "But surely you should be out tonight. The Nazarene may need you."

"Yes, I am just going." He rose and closed the distance between them.

"Then I will see you tomorrow." Her hand reached toward his. "God go with you tonight, Judah," she said.

He could not help himself. For the second time that evening, on the same spot, his lips met those of a woman. But this time, he thought, she was the right one.

CHAPTER 47

GETHSEMANE

I t was jarring to be out in the streets again. Ben-Hur's mind was buzzing with images: Iras, Messala, his mother, Esther, Tirzah. The Nazarene. He tried to focus. The Nazarene! He needed news: where was the man now?

While he was in the Hur palace, the Passover crowds had become noisy. Movement in the narrow street eddied and halted like the water in a blocked stream. Up ahead, an obstruction straddled an intersection. Ben-Hur craned his head. A procession? Yes, there were torches. And gleaming beside them . . . were those the tips of spears? He began to push, working his way through the crowd, ignoring the protests. Spears were all wrong—this was a purely Jewish festival and the Romans had no business bringing weapons into the streets.

Yet there they were. And with them, oddly, priests from the Temple. High-ranking, by their robes and beards. Strangest of all, most disturbing, they were heading *away* from the Temple, toward the city wall. On this holiest of nights, why?

He shoved his way forward, using his height and weight ruthlessly until he was near the front, where the clustered flames shed their orange glow on the somber, bearded faces—one of which was familiar. It was one of the Nazarene's followers, Judas Iscariot, walking between a chief priest and one of the Temple guards. Stumbling, really, with an expression of desperation in his glazed eyes.

Ben-Hur had paused in shock, and a big man with a heavy wooden staff nudged him. "This is not your business," he muttered. "Keep moving."

Keep moving! Ben-Hur took stock of the location. They were at the edge of the city walls, near the Sheep Gate. As the group straggled through the open gate, many of the men turned back to rejoin the holiday festivities. There would be no songs or roasted lamb out on the rocky hillsides to the east of town. The men who stayed with the makeshift march were of two kinds now: the rabble who had nothing better to do and the band from the Temple. Ben-Hur let his steps slow and drifted to the back of the group. Where were they headed? And why was Judas not with the Nazarene and the other disciples?

Beyond the city gates the moon seemed stronger, shedding a cool wash of pure white light that dimmed the yellow gleam from torches and lanterns. Ben-Hur could make out the dusty roadway, the scrubby hillside, the scattered olive trees. Ahead the silver thread of a stream ducked beneath a wooden bridge, and shuffling footsteps were almost drowned out by the clatter of dozens of staffs and spears. The group was well armed—but for what?

Two roads like bleached scars on the hillside met in front of them. A wall stood on the uphill side of the intersection, restraining the dark foliage of an olive orchard. There were figures standing at the gate. The procession came to a ragged halt and silence fell.

The Nazarene stepped out in front of his disciples. The moonlight gleamed especially strong around him, or maybe that was a trick of his white robes. Either way, Ben-Hur could make out no face besides that of Jesus. He looked sad. He stood perfectly still, hands hanging by his sides.

Was this the moment, then? Surely it was! At least this was a confrontation between Jesus and earthly authority. Wouldn't he declare himself now? *"I am he that was born king of the Jews."* Would he say it at last?

Ben-Hur edged closer. He should be ready. He should have made a plan! What if the Nazarene called now for troops? Ben-Hur glanced back, calculating: how fast could he reach Bezetha, notify his cohort, send messages to raise a legion?

But perhaps this was *not* the moment. Maybe the Nazarene had a different plan. Ben-Hur counted surreptitiously—a dozen, maybe two dozen men with weapons. He himself could account for several of those. And the disciples—surely they would use staffs and spears if commanded?

If commanded. By whom? How exactly would those words sound? Ben-Hur tried to fit them into Jesus' mouth: *"To arms, men!"* Or *"Bring me a legion!"* No, not that; of course not.

But possibly . . . Ben-Hur ransacked his mind for plausible commands. *"Charge the Antonia Tower, using fire!"* Or *"Surround the procurator's palace!"* No. That lonely man standing so still in the moonlight would never say those words or any remotely like them.

Still, it was not too late. Ben-Hur knew he could command the men. He knew military strategy; he could create a plan that would dislodge the red-cloaked soldiers from Jerusalem forever! But this aching moment could go on no longer. The priests were shifting their feet and whispering to each other. He saw a Roman's knuckles grow white on the shaft of his spear as the tension continued to mount.

A charm, then! A spell, a miracle, whatever it might be. The Nazarene had given health; he could take it away. He had restored life—could he not also end it? A bolt from the sky! Ben-Hur had seen that once on board a ship: a lightning bolt that flickered down a mast and killed a man standing. Now! This would be the time! Or a creeping miasma, some quiet, constant, rolling death that would mow down these men like wheat falling before a scythe! Something to end this silence!

"Whom do you seek?" came the voice. Steady, mild, not even curious. The Nazarene often sounded like that. It was a beautiful voice, thought Ben-Hur. A warm voice, full of comfort. Even now.

"Jesus of Nazareth," boomed the head priest.

"I am he."

The disciples stirred behind him, hands on each other's arms. Should he have said that? Should one of them have stepped forward instead?

But no. There was Judas Iscariot, emerging from the armed group. "Greetings, Rabbi," he said and kissed the Nazarene on the cheek.

"Oh, Judas," Jesus answered, his voice heavy with sorrow, "would you betray the Son of Man with a kiss?" He looked around at the priests and the guards. "If you seek me, let these men go." He gestured at the disciples.

The party from the Temple took several steps forward and finally the disciples moved, too late but with vigor. One of them somehow wrested a sword from one of the guards and brandished it wildly. There was a shout, a scuffle, blood splashed on several shoulders—a slave's ear had been cut off.

But Jesus did not run. Instead he stepped over and touched the man's ear. In an instant it was restored. And the next minute, the hand that had healed was roped behind his back, to his other hand. The Nazarene was a captive.

He spoke again, this time with a hint of sternness. "Put your sword into its sheath," he said to the disciples behind him. "Shall I not drink the cup that the Father has given me?" Then, without changing his tone, he addressed his captors. "Have you come out as against a robber, with swords and clubs? When I was with you day after day in the Temple, you did not lay hands on me. But this is your hour, and the power of darkness."

Darkness indeed. A few of the torches had gone out and several lanterns had been broken, sending oily smoke into the air. Or possibly the moon, still sailing high, had dimmed? Even Jesus' own robe seemed less white, though it could have been dirtied in the scuffle. Ben-Hur glanced into the orchard, but he could no longer see the disciples. Where had they gone?

Meanwhile a rough procession formed to head back into Jerusalem. The atmosphere of excitement had diminished. The slave with the restored ear walked alone at the back, his neck and shoulder still blotched with his own blood and a spooked expression in his eyes. Ben-Hur watched them go, then impulsively shrugged off his robe and left it, with his kerchief, on the wall of the orchard. Dressed only in his undertunic, hoping to pass unnoticed, he caught up to the group as they recrossed the little bridge.

A heavy bank of clouds drifted across the moon now, and the road was invisible. Ben-Hur could only tell where Jesus was by the cluster of flickering torches. He edged forward. He needed to see.

What had happened? How was it possible that the Nazarene could submit to captivity after casually restoring the slave's ear? If he would help the slave, why not help himself?

And what was that discussion of a cup? It was almost as if he had a plan.

But if there was a plan, thought Ben-Hur, it was nothing familiar.

He was closer now. Jesus walked in the center of the group with his head bowed. A few steps ahead of him the priests muttered urgently, but Jesus paid no attention. He stumbled and nearly fell, but a guard yanked the rope that tied his wrists.

Ben-Hur suddenly remembered how that felt. All those years ago, he had been the captive, numbed by disaster and tripping over his own feet among a hostile guard. The memory was clear in his mind: an agony of despair and pain. It was Jesus, back then, who had given him hope! He pressed forward a little more so that he was walking right beside the Nazarene.

Jesus' face was hidden by his hair and he did not look up when Ben-Hur hissed, "Master!"

They had reached the fork in the road and the group spread out for an instant. "Master," Ben-Hur repeated. "If I bring you men to rescue you . . . would you accept our help?"

No answer from Jesus. A voice said sharply, "Who is that man? Is he one of ours?"

Ben-Hur stepped back into the crowd, but he had been noticed.

"No! He's one of them!" another voice shouted. "Capture him; bring him with us!"

He flung off the hand on his arm and leapt over a foot stuck out to trip him. Someone clutched the skirt of his tunic, but he tore the garment open at the neckline, leaving the length of fabric behind as he ran naked across the open field.

"Catch him; follow him!" someone cried, but a deeper voice cut through the hubbub.

"We must get this man to Pilate," declared the high priest. "Close up the guard, let no one near him, and move along. Quickly now!"

So they went on. Ben-Hur returned to the little garden, picking his way through the darkness. He watched the group draw away from him and closer to the walls of Jerusalem. Soon he could see only the torches, sparks in the blackness, and the voices died away completely.

He found the orchard wall by touch and inched along it until he reached his robe, which he threw over his head. Then he stood still for a time where Jesus had stood. Crickets sounded in the trees behind him and creeping nocturnal creatures moved through the scrubby grass. The air was perfectly still.

He could no longer see the group around Jesus. They had probably entered the gate of Jerusalem. Not in triumph this time, he
thought.

Yet—had the triumph seemed quite real? Ben-Hur wondered.
Was it Jesus' triumph? Or a celebration that overlooked his real
nature? The Jesus on the donkey was not so very different from the
Jesus with his hands behind his back: melancholy but determined.

Was it possible that he had known all along what would happen?
Ben-Hur shook his head. What good did that do? What was the
point of coming to Jerusalem and visiting the Temple and rousing
masses of people to hope—only to end in captivity? The guards were
taking him to Pilate, and Jesus' story would end, once again, with
Rome in charge.

Almost by habit, Ben-Hur started calculating. There was a legion
of Galileans in and around Jerusalem; he could bring them into the
city and storm Herod's Palace . . . No, he would need more men; it
would be heavily defended. Maybe another legion would be required;
they could be mustered and reach Jerusalem in two days or so. . . .

And the Nazarene? Ben-Hur pushed off from the fence he'd been
leaning against. The Nazarene! He wanted no armies. He didn't want
help of any kind. There was something else going on.

The cloud bank had passed from the moon and now a light haze
surrounded it. The clear brightness of a few minutes earlier was
veiled, but Ben-Hur could make out the path back to the Sheep
Gate. He began to walk, and as he walked, he admitted to himself
that he had failed.

He had failed. Or perhaps they had all failed. Or misunderstood.
Jesus had never asked for an army.

He thought of the slave, nervously fingering the ear that had been
lopped off and just as swiftly restored.

Restored—like Lazarus at Bethany. What had Jesus said then? "I
am the resurrection and the life." What could it mean? Yet Ben-Hur

had been there when Lazarus staggered out of the tomb, shedding his foul grave wrappings, and the women wailed in fear as much as joy.

This was something like that, something strange. Even tonight, even in his dejection, Jesus had been resolute. His work, or whatever you wanted to call it—his teaching, his leading—was unfinished while he was still on the road, trudging toward Pilate's presence.

And Ben-Hur realized, as he walked along in the Nazarene's footsteps, that he could only wait. Stay ready. Possibly offer his help again. And again, he resolved. Until it was clear that the Nazarene needed it no more.

CHAPTER 48

GOLGOTHA

He spent what remained of the night with his mother and sister in their tents in the Kidron Valley. He had not been able to face the Hur palace after the confrontation at Gethsemane. How would he tell Simonides and Balthasar what had happened? How could he possibly endure Iras's scorn? Instead he slept outside the city and had just wakened when two of his Galilean officers cantered up on a pair of shaggy ponies.

"You must come!" one called out. "The Nazarene dies today if you do not save him!"

"Dies?" he answered. "What has happened?"

"They captured him last night and tried him. The priests found him guilty of blasphemy and took him to Pilate. Pilate tried not to give a judgment, but the priests and the people were so determined that Pilate condemned him. So the cross is being made ready!"

"Oh no!" Ben-Hur cried. He snapped his fingers to a servant.

"My sword belt, my shield. Saddle Aldebaran." He looked back at the messengers. "This must not happen. We will fight." It all seemed so clear now! Jesus must be rescued. There would be crowds at Golgotha. But on horseback, he and a picked group of men might be able to sweep in, cut Jesus' bonds, carry him off . . .

"No, sir," one of the Galileans broke into his fantasy. "We cannot fight."

Ben-Hur looked up from his belt buckle. "Why?"

The two Galileans exchanged glances, and the one who had not spoken yet said, "We are the only men left."

"What do you mean? There were hundreds!"

"The rest have sided with the priests. They have vanished." The man was blushing behind his beard. "I am ashamed to say it."

Ben-Hur's hands fell to his sides. "All of them?"

They nodded. "All."

Gone, he thought. All gone? The men he had recruited. He had tramped from village to village to find them. He had persuaded and cajoled. He had spoken of a new leader on the way, and they had believed him. They had trained together, and he thought he had made them into a strong and loyal force. Now they had scattered? Vanished into the seething crowds packed into Jerusalem?

And yet who could blame them? Theirs was the human reaction. The man who had preached to multitudes about meekness and mercy was condemned to execution. Of course his supporters disappeared; they would be seen as treasonous. The wise man among them would throw away his short Roman-style sword and deny any knowledge of the Nazarene. But these two standing before Ben-Hur were loyal.

"Thank you for letting me know," he said. "I will come back with you." So a few minutes later they were on the road to Jerusalem while half of the Kidron Valley was still in shadow.

They didn't speak. The air was chilly, so they set the horses to a fast trot. The sun gilded the city walls, growing ever closer, and

Ben-Hur thought about loyalty. He could not blame the Galileans for dispersing. But he himself would not hide. He felt called to witness Jesus' death. He had not told his mother and sister where he was going because he could not have explained his reasons.

Maybe he needed to be present to atone for his failure to help the Nazarene. Or perhaps he simply needed to understand what Jesus had intended all along. Because the closer he rode to Jerusalem on that sunny morning, the more certain Ben-Hur was that Jesus had known how his story would end. He might have power over life and death—he might be the Son of God himself—yet he would die. Today. On a cross.

* * *

The word was out in Jerusalem. An execution! Two robbers and that rabble-rouser from Nazareth. The crosses were already fashioned, they said. The criminals were on their way to Golgotha. *"Quick, quick, if you hurry, you can see them stumbling along and carrying the crossbars!"* Such joy in witnessing someone else's humiliation!

The streets soon clotted with people. Guards led the procession with staffs to clear the way. People brought things to throw. The cobblestones grew slippery and the smells grew vile, but even that was part of the fun. A priest set his heel on a rotten cabbage leaf and went down with a yelp—hilarious! Shared cruelty intoxicated the crowd.

Ben-Hur worked his way along the walls of the buildings, trying to catch up with the procession. What a horrible contrast! Not a week earlier, the Nazarene had ridden into the city to jubilation, and now he was staggering out of it to a chorus of jeering and insults. The movement of the procession stopped and a narrow rectangle of wood reared up above the heads of the multitude. The voices roared. He had stumbled! Fallen down, dropped his own cross! Lay under it, face on the road!

Ben-Hur pushed onward steadily.

A sturdy Jew stepped forward and shouldered the cross. The Nazarene pushed himself to his feet and staggered onward. Ben-Hur caught sight of him and felt hollow. Someone had crammed a wreath of thorns onto Jesus' head, pushed it down hard and left long scratches on his forehead so that the blood ran into his eyes. He'd been beaten. Fresh bruises mottled his skin. His hands and knees bled from the fall. The injuries were bad enough, but in addition insults rained down around him: personal, nasty, inventive, crude. He showed no sign of hearing them or even of feeling physical pain. It was his despair that Ben-Hur pitied.

He had seen men like that in the galleys. He had been like that himself, reduced to endurance. Life existed as nothing more than this step and the next step. The only possible relief would come with death.

Jesus would die. In that moment Ben-Hur took in the truth. The man he had admired and followed, who had raised such hopes in so many people, was stumbling his way to a shameful public death. He had demonstrated, time and again, that he had power over death— yet he would submit to it himself.

This was the cup he'd spoken of, the destiny his Father had given him.

Ben-Hur felt the wall at his back end suddenly and took two inadvertent steps backward. He looked around, disoriented; it was a small courtyard, shaded by a tall old house whose shutters were closed. He took a few more steps into the shadow and crouched down, face in his hands.

All his hopes were ruined. Everyone's hopes, in fact! Jesus was not the king of the Jews! He was a teacher who had earned the enmity of Rome—and even of the Jewish priests. He was about to die for his teaching and leadership. What would become of his followers? Surely they were in danger too! But no doubt they had vanished like the Galileans. They would have saved themselves.

Yet as part of Ben-Hur's mind considered the disciples, he could not dismiss the image of Jesus' face as he trudged painfully through the mob. Utter desolation. And resignation. Ben-Hur sighed deeply and stood. It would be prudent to leave. But he could not. He could not let Jesus die surrounded by enemies. Nothing had ever been so urgent to him. He must follow the Nazarene to the cross and bear witness. He stepped back out into the slow-moving throng.

Everything was so strange that it seemed natural to see Malluch before him in the crowd. Of course Malluch was there. Of course Simonides and Balthasar were being carried along in a makeshift litter. Of course Esther walked next to them, head covered, eyes reddened with tears. On this nightmare morning, what was more likely than finding them in a crowd of thousands?

He slipped into the throng beside Esther and tapped Malluch on the shoulder. Malluch turned back and nodded to him. No words were needed. Naturally Ben-Hur had found them. Naturally he was headed out to Golgotha. This was how the Nazarene's story would end, and they all felt compelled to be there.

On the litter, Simonides and Balthasar lay head to toe, shaded by a canopy and mute with misery. Ben-Hur stooped down to greet them, and Balthasar met his gaze. "This is a terrible day," he said, barely louder than a whisper. "We will all regret it. We are setting out to kill God's Son, you know."

Simonides lay with his eyes closed and grimaced as the litter was jostled. "What will become of us all?" he groaned.

There was no answer to that. They plodded forward at the slow pace of the crowd. The sun grew stronger. Ben-Hur felt sweat prickling down his spine, but sweat was nothing. Not compared to what the Nazarene was suffering.

The mood of the mob changed. The cocky jeering had died away. Faces were somber now. As the horde filed through the gate, silence fell. Mockery had seemed safe before, but now, with the uprights of the crosses visible, dread prevailed.

"Why are we here?" Simonides asked. Then he answered his own question. "Because we must be, I suppose."

"I was present just after his birth," Balthasar replied. Ben-Hur had to lean over to hear him. "I have always followed him, even from afar. I must be here when he dies."

"It is the least we can do for him," Esther said tentatively. "Don't you think?" She looked at Ben-Hur.

He shrugged. "I am not sure. But I agree with your father. We must be witnesses to what will happen now."

* * *

The little hill—shaped like, and named for, a skull—was thickly covered with humankind, but at the top a ring of Roman soldiers held the crowd back. The open space they encircled lay lower, as if a giant thumb had pressed it down to create a natural theater on the hilltop. The three condemned men stood by their crosses, each of which lay next to a deep hole.

Rome and Jerusalem worked together that day. The high priest of the Temple, glittering in his vestments, instructed the centurion whose men would carry out the death sentence. "Go ahead," he commanded in a voice pitched to reach the crowds. "They must be dead and buried by sunset. Start with the blasphemer. If he is the Son of God, he should be able to save himself."

A shudder ran through the crowd. The crosspieces were fitted onto the trees of the crosses. The men were placed roughly, arms out, feet crossed.

"Esther, come here," came Simonides's voice. "Don't watch."

She bent down and rested her head against his shoulder, where her tears soon blotched his robe. She never told him that at each blow of the hammer, she felt him flinch.

"Raise him first," instructed Caiaphas, the priest.

"Facing which way?" the soldier asked as if he were talking of a signpost.

"Toward the Temple," answered Caiaphas. "He says it is his Father's house. I want him to see that he has not harmed it with his ravings."

The cross and its burden were lifted, carried a few steps, dropped into the prepared hole with a thump. The hands tore around the nails, but Jesus only said, "Father, forgive them, for they know not what they do."

How could he? At that moment, how could he beg for forgiveness—for his killers?

Once the crowd had seen the cross rise, the silence broke. First a gasp, then a tentative cheer. Someone read out the placard nailed above Jesus' head: "'King of the Jews!'" and another repeated the words. A clamor followed. Maybe it was mockery trying to drive out foreboding.

The two other crosses were raised and planted, but no one cared about a pair of commonplace thieves. It was the man who made the grand claims who had to be brought down. He had almost persuaded them that life could be other than it was! Some of them had even listened, had considered a system of kindness and compassion and patience and forgiveness. What a narrow escape they had made! The world did not work like that! Strength and violence and vengeance ruled—of course they did! It was terrifying to know one had almost thought otherwise. The man who said so must be punished.

So there was alarm among the gathered people already. Some were afraid of what they had almost believed. Some were afraid of retribution—God's or Rome's, or both. Some—for there were followers of the Nazarene on that hillside—regretted their months as disciples. Who knew where that could lead? And yet, while it had lasted, the illusion of a new kind of life had seemed so compelling!

Then the darkness came. It crept gradually among them, shade by shade of reduced light. Faces faded. Outlines vanished. "Are you there?" Esther whispered to her father while she still touched him.

The multitude fell silent. All you could hear was the shifting of feet. One of the thieves moaned. It went on and on.

Maybe it diminished. Maybe their eyes adjusted. As one hour bled into another, they could see that the crowd was thinning, and despite Esther's reluctance, their little group moved closer to the crosses. Balthasar crept out of the litter and insisted on kneeling in the dirt, facing the Nazarene.

Gradually some of the crowd regained its confidence and resumed baiting Jesus. Even one of the thieves called out to him, "Are you not the Christ? Save yourself and us!"

But the third man protested. "This man has done nothing wrong." Then, addressing Jesus, he said, "Remember me when you come into your kingdom."

There was a murmur, and Simonides tensed. Then they all heard Jesus answer in that voice of comfort, "Today you will be with me in Paradise."

Balthasar made a sound and clasped his hands tighter. Ben-Hur leaned down and saw that the old Egyptian's eyes were closed, but tears poured down his face. He murmured in a language Ben-Hur did not know—yet he did not look unhappy.

Above their heads, Jesus groaned. The guards huddled nervously and one of them picked up Jesus' tunic from the ground to fling it far away. They had tossed the dice for it, but things had gone so strangely, nobody would want it now. Another gasp for breath rattled the air, and everyone below fell perfectly still. Even those farthest away could hear when he said, "My God, my God, why have you forsaken me?"

Esther sobbed aloud.

Ben-Hur spotted a bowl on the ground next to the cross. It was full of liquid, half wine and half water. A sponge lay in it, fastened to the end of a long stick. It was a strange, small measure of mercy, made available to the dying.

Jesus should know that he was not forsaken. He should know that there were some left who pitied him. Years before, he had given water to a ragged prisoner in Nazareth. Ben-Hur seized the stick and moistened the sponge. He could offer this, perhaps, a small final gesture of kindness.

But above his head, there was a terrible cry. Everyone heard the words: "It is finished!"

Ben-Hur looked up into the face of the dying man. Jesus raised his eyes, and for an instant he looked glad. "Father," he murmured, "into your hands I commit my spirit." And the head drooped.

Ben-Hur dropped the stick and the sponge. He backed away from the cross, unable to tear his eyes away. *"Father,"* he kept hearing. *"Father . . ."*

But Jesus was dead.

As if in protest, the earth itself began to tremble. Wave after wave made the ground move like water, and the two thieves cried out from their crosses. Throngs of spectators fled from the hill. The light had returned the moment Jesus died and they could all see his body, but no one could stand to be near it, except for a small group of mourners. The Nazarene's mother knelt at the foot of the cross along with one of the disciples. Ben-Hur and his group clustered around another body, for Balthasar had died at the same moment as the Nazarene. Eventually they returned his body to the litter and Simonides rode back to Jerusalem with it. "He was wiser than I," Simonides said. "And perhaps death was his reward."

When they got back to the Hur palace, Ben-Hur went to Iras's rooms. He felt obligated to notify her of her father's death himself. But the rooms were empty. The only trace of her that remained was a whiff of that perfume. He left the windows wide open.

EPILOGUE

Ben-Hur and Esther married, of course. They chose to leave their bitter memories behind in Jerusalem and to live in Arrius's elegant seaside villa at Misenum. There Naomi and Tirzah helped raise their children. The whole family continued to follow the Nazarene's teachings and did everything they could to nurture the growing faith. Like others, they began to call themselves "Christians."

Esther did not attempt to persuade Simonides to join them. She understood that her father's joy came from his business; it was impossible to imagine him flourishing in the open, breeze-swept marble rooms of the villa. Instead, she and Judah took turns braving the sea voyage to Antioch every few years. Little changed at the house above the wharves: the ships still came in with yellow flags at their masts to signal successful voyages. Simonides, made old before his time by

Roman torture, now seemed ageless. Only Malluch gradually showed the years, growing gray and stout.

But finally Simonides's sight began to fail, and he announced that he would sell his ships. He summoned both Esther and Judah to Antioch, and for days they served as his eyes and hands. There were sailors to pay off and livestock to sell, cargoes to dispatch and a constant flow of details that Esther handled with her usual calm competence. Ben-Hur ran into her one morning in the warehouse, sweeping with an old broom, and could not help laughing. "You look just the same as the first time I saw you!" he exclaimed, putting his arms around her.

She smiled at him. "I think this is the same broom, too. Malluch never did care about the floors."

"Are you sad?"

"Of course. But my father is not. So I'm trying to follow his example."

He rested his cheek against her hair. "He is a man of great courage." He felt her nod. Then she tapped his back with the broomstick.

"I'm sure he sent you on some errand," she said. "You should go."

He released her. "Yes. I have to go see a camel driver. I wish Malluch were around. I would send him instead."

"Malluch is deep in the hold of the ship out there," Esther told him. "You could always trade places."

"No," Judah answered with a shudder. "Given the choice, I prefer the camels."

✳ ✳ ✳

That was the last vessel to reach Simonides's wharf, and by the end of the day its cargo of Greek olive oil and Egyptian wheat had been transferred to the warehouse. As the sun dropped into a coral haze, Ben-Hur, Esther, and Simonides sat together in the workroom, watching the lone ship sway at its mooring. Every flat surface in the room was covered with scrolls or tablets, many weighted with odd fragments like a piece of sandalwood or a shard of alabaster or the scrolled hilt of a dagger to which a blade had never been fixed.

"Even I am surprised," Simonides commented, glancing around the room. "Esther, hand me that little package there, the one with the seal." As she looked for it on the nearest table, he went on, "I thought I had a clear reckoning in my head, but I am so much wealthier than I knew. And so are you, Judah," he added with a piercing glance. "I had forgotten this until now," he said as he accepted the package from his daughter. "An Arab brought it earlier today and I put it aside. Can you read the inscription?"

"It's for Judah," Esther said. "With Sheik Ilderim's seal." For a moment she studied the tiny image of a swiftly running horse. "I haven't seen this for years." She passed the package to her husband, who ran his forefinger gently over the glossy wax before breaking it. He swiftly read the letter and lifted out a yellowed strip of papyrus, so faded that he had to step toward the open window to make out the words. In the waning light reflected off the river, he read the short message, and his shoulders sagged.

"Bad news?" Esther asked, coming to his side.

He handed her the papyrus. "Yes. No—not bad. Sad. Sheik Ilderim, our sheik, is dead," he said. "In a battle."

"As he would have wished," Simonides commented.

"Yes," Ben-Hur agreed. "The Parthians assembled their tribes for an attack. Young Ilderim, our sheik's son, writes that he took back the territory his father had lost and recaptured the horses. There is still an Ilderim ruling the desert."

Simonides bowed his head. "I will miss the father. He was a good friend to me."

Ben-Hur returned to the stool by his father-in-law's side. "And to me." He reached over and took one of Simonides's twisted hands in his own. "He has left me the Orchard of the Palms. How does he put it, Esther?"

Esther read, "'The oasis near Antioch shall be given to the son of Hur, who brought us glory in the circus there. It shall belong to him and to his descendants forever.'"

Judah sighed deeply.

"You are not glad to have the oasis?" Simonides asked.

"What am I to do with it?" Judah answered. "I have no need of an oasis."

"Sell it back to young Ilderim," Simonides suggested. "That's what I would do."

"Sell what to Ilderim?" Malluch's voice came from the doorway.

"The Orchard of the Palms," Esther answered. "Left to Judah by Sheik Ilderim, who died in a Parthian raid."

"I'll bet he took a few Parthians with him," Malluch said. "You may want to read this before you decide anything," he told Ben-Hur, holding out a scroll. "I'm sorry it arrives so late. A box from the steward's cabin almost got left on board."

But Ben-Hur was already reading. Esther saw a frown etched between his brows, and when he handed the letter to her, the line did not go away.

"Just tell us what it says," she suggested.

He nodded and clasped his hands, then bowed his head almost as if he were praying. He often stood this way before worship, gathering his thoughts and, Esther thought, listening for the Lord.

"The letter brings bad news from Rome," he said. "Before we left Misenum, we heard talk of it. The community in Rome has grown, thanks be to God. There are many followers there living by our Lord's commandments. But . . ."

"Wait," Simonides broke in. "We know how this story goes. The Roman authorities have begun to hunt them down and forbid their gatherings. Perhaps even . . ."

There was a silence. Everyone in the room remembered the brutality visited on Simonides and Judah.

"Yes. There have been episodes . . ." He clarified, "There has been violence."

"Romans, violent," spat Simonides. "Will nothing ever change?"

Ben-Hur unrolled the scroll again, but his eyes did not see the writing. "Nero . . . he must perceive a serious threat," he said, "to prompt the kind of measures described here. Our brethren in the capital must indeed be thriving. And they must be very strong in faith, to persist in the face of . . . But they have to have places to gather and worship. Churches have been destroyed," he explained, twitching the scroll. "Worship services are interrupted and—"

"Say no more," commanded Simonides. "We understand."

Silence settled over the room as all four of them remembered Roman cruelty in one form or another.

Esther watched her husband anxiously. The Romans again! Would the danger never end? Would they ever be able to forget the menace posed by the empire? Judah still dreamed of the galleys from time to time. He would wake panting and shouting and thrashing, and for days after he would have to work to control his temper. It was his faith, she thought, that kept him fundamentally kindhearted, but he would always struggle to be peaceful. He had known too much violence too early in life.

He was tapping his fingers on the scroll as he thought. "These two pieces of news arriving together . . . ," he said. "What if they are connected? Simonides, the oasis would fetch a sizable sum?"

"Oh yes," Simonides said. "A magnificent water source, so sheltered and so close to Antioch? Sizable indeed." He peered at Ben-Hur through the darkening room. "And don't forget, Judah. My possessions will be yours soon too." He silenced Esther's protest. "I leave this life happy, and I go to meet your mother, my dear. I have much to look forward to." Esther crossed the room and stood behind his chair to kiss his cheek. His hands came up to cover the hands she rested lightly on his shoulders. "You will have more than any man needs, Judah. What will you do with it all?"

Ben-Hur stood and picked up the slip of papyrus from the table where Esther had left it. He held the scroll in one hand, the papyrus in the other. "The Lord gives. The Lord takes away. Maybe what the Lord gives me now is the answer to a prayer. Esther and I have worked to help Jesus' followers in Misenum. We give alms; we have built a house of worship. We have always intended and wished to do more—isn't that true?" He turned to Esther for confirmation. She nodded. "But the sums I have come to possess are too great to disperse that way."

He fell silent for so long that Simonides said, "Tell us, then! What are you thinking?"

Ben-Hur answered, "I am thinking about Rome. Standing on its hills, with its straight roads and marble buildings. Temples and shrines everywhere. And beneath the ground, catacombs, built with equal care." He looked around the room, catching everyone's eye one by one. "The Romans respect the dead. Their places of burial are sacred to them. Could they not also be sacred to the Roman followers of Jesus? Could Christians use the catacombs?"

"Malluch, we need some light," Simonides said. "No need for everyone to be as blind as me. What exactly are you saying, Judah?"

As Esther and Malluch lit lamps, Ben-Hur explained. "Christians need to gather safely. We need to baptize, to worship, to break the bread *together*. This money that has come to me—perhaps it could be used for that purpose, to create safe places for the faith. These sums could pay for shovels and laborers and guards and bricks, men to draw plans and men to build tunnels." He looked at Esther. "What do you think?"

She came to his side. "I think it is a wonderful plan."

"I like it too," said Simonides. "It gives me pleasure to think of my money and the price of Ilderim's oasis being put to such a use on Roman soil. Underground. Beneath their very feet," he added with a chuckle.

Judah stood still, in the center of the room. "Yes," he said, "it is worth pursuing. Sometimes it is so hard to know what is right." He took a deep breath and caught Esther's eye. "Did I ever tell you," he asked Simonides, "about the last time I saw Jesus?" Esther smiled warmly at him.

"We all saw him together," said Simonides. "We saw him die."

"Yes. But I saw him again, afterward."

"And never told me?" Simonides asked, startled.

"No. You remember how those days were. I only told Esther later. It was too strange, almost like a dream."

"So much was strange in those days, Judah!"

"That is certainly true," Judah began while Esther settled herself on the floor at his feet. "We had to bury Balthasar, and Iras had vanished, and everyone in Jerusalem was on edge."

Simonides was nodding. "No one felt safe," he said.

"All the Jews who had come for Passover scattered back to their homes," Ben-Hur went on. "The Romans doubled their patrols in the streets, and they were watching everyone. All the same, Jesus' disciples managed to gather. Did you ever hear the story?" he asked Simonides. "Jesus came to them in a locked room."

"I did hear that," Simonides said. "And there was something more, wasn't there? About a disciple who didn't believe it was him?"

"Thomas," Esther put in. "Jesus understood. He let Thomas put his hand in the wound in his side. We tell the story often in worship. It's such a comfort."

"For those who need help believing, I suppose," Malluch suggested. "Because of course it's impossible."

"Yes. We believe the impossible," Ben-Hur agreed. "That's a good way to put it. But it's a hard thing to do. After a few days in

Jerusalem, I wanted . . . well, I felt I needed to find the disciples. I didn't know why exactly. But you remember, I had spent all that time creating an army. And then it was so hard to grasp that we had all misunderstood."

"Not Balthasar," Esther spoke up.

"No," Simonides said. "But he had unusual gifts. The rest of us just saw the world as it had been, a world of power and violence, and we prepared for that. Balthasar knew from the start that it was something new."

"I was still thinking about weapons and military strategies," Ben-Hur said. "Even after Gethsemane, when Jesus let himself be captured. I couldn't help believing force might rescue him. But . . ." He sighed. "Rome had taught me to think in terms of vengeance. That was not Jesus' lesson, though. I was slower than most to understand."

"Most of us have to learn his lessons over and over again," Esther said.

Judah nodded. "Anyway, after a few days I went to Galilee. I wanted to see how the disciples were managing. I thought I could learn something from them. Or maybe hear some of the words that the Lord had said when he appeared to them. It was evening when I got there. I went to the shore of the lake, thinking they might be there. They were fishermen. I thought they might be drawn to the water, and sure enough, when I reached the beach, there was a boat just setting out. I could recognize some of them, Peter and James and John. They were fishing. I sat on the shore and watched.

"It was comforting. The night was beautiful. The stars were so bright! I could even see the boat, though it was out in deep water. I could tell they hadn't caught anything. They cast and cast and cast. Nobody seemed disappointed."

"Sometimes merely doing the familiar is a comfort," Simonides said.

"And then dawn came. They were heading back to shore. And

they saw someone! I could tell when they all spotted him, even though the sun hadn't risen. He called out, 'Any fish?'

"They answered, 'No, none!'

"He said, 'Cast the net on the right side of the boat, and you will find some,' and of course they did. The net filled right away and they could barely lift it into the boat. I ran over to help them when they came ashore and we struggled to manage it. They were the most beautiful fish," Judah added.

"The man was Jesus. We all recognized him at once. I knew the disciples felt the same way I did: we were reassured. He had come back! He loved us, all of us. Even me, though I was not one of them. And he would still lead us. Somehow."

There was silence in the room as they waited for him to continue. "A fire had been lit and bread was there, fresh and warm. The Lord said, 'Come and have breakfast,' so we did. We cut open the fish and grilled them. It was a magnificent morning, I will never forget that. The breeze died down and the surface of the lake mirrored the sky. It was as if we sat in a bowl of light, above and below. Jesus served us. He spoke; he touched us. The nail wounds were still there, but he didn't seem to be in pain. Everyone felt such comfort."

He took a deep breath. "And then Peter asked him the question. It's the question we ask over and over again: *What should we do now?* I tell you this story because I had the answer wrong for so much of my life. But now I try to do as Jesus said, to the best of my ability. He said to Peter, and to all of us, 'Feed my lambs. Tend my sheep. Follow me.'"

Afterword

April 6, 1862, was the worst day of Lew Wallace's long, eventful life.

It was a tragic day for thousands of American families: nearly twenty-four thousand Union and Confederate soldiers were injured or killed on a swampy battlefield in southwestern Tennessee, near a church called Shiloh.

And it was a disastrous day for the commanders of those soldiers, who discovered just how destructive this war was going to be. Previous Civil War battles had involved smaller bodies of armed men; at Shiloh two immense forces met, wrought death and destruction on a massive scale, and limped apart, with no clear advantage to either. More soldiers died there than in all previous American battles *combined*. Those who had believed the War between the States could be settled with one decisive confrontation had to change their minds after Shiloh.

Lew Wallace never lived that day down. When it dawned, he was the youngest major general in the Union Army, a dashing slim figure on a tall bay horse, commanding a reserve division of eight thousand men with verve and confidence. By nightfall, when his sodden troops finally joined the battered and diminished regiments that had fought all day, he knew that his commanding officer, Ulysses S. Grant, was angry. At 9 a.m. Grant had ordered Wallace to bring his division to reinforce the Union flank.

And Wallace . . . well, Wallace and his men didn't arrive until well after 6 p.m., leaving Grant's forces exposed, exhausted, and on the verge of retreat.

The battle lasted another day and the Union (barely) prevailed, but the casualties made headlines in North and South. How could the Union have bungled so badly?

Grant had an answer: It was Wallace's fault.

Wallace had a rebuttal: His orders hadn't been clear.

Those were the two men's positions after the battle, and neither one gave an inch until more than twenty years later, when new evidence turned up and Grant relented, allowing that perhaps Wallace had been right all along.

By then, in the mid-1880s, one might have thought Lew Wallace wouldn't care anymore. He was rich and famous beyond anything he could ever have hoped for. But he felt to his dying day that his honor had been smirched, and he was a man who cared very deeply about this old-fashioned concept.

In many ways, in fact, Lew was born a little bit too late, out of step with the age he lived in. Throughout his life he reached for the colorful, the exotic, the adventurous, in a period that saw American life grow ever more steady, predictable, and humdrum. In the end, Lew's yearning for deeds of glory made his fortune, in a way he could not have predicted. So did the Shiloh episode. And maybe strangest of all, so did a chance encounter on a train.

The last occurred in September of 1876, nearly fifteen years after Shiloh. The intervening years had been mixed for Lew. He'd been relieved of his command soon after Shiloh, and it was months before he would lead troops in battle again. And despite successes at Fort Donelson and Monocacy, he was not promoted further. (This was

actually good judgment on the part of the Union command: as a soldier, Lew was inclined to be insubordinate and hotheaded.) Since he
was a lawyer in civilian life, he had served on the military juries that
tried the Lincoln assassins and the commandant of Andersonville,
the notorious Confederate prison camp. Then there was a confusing
spell when Lew went to Mexico to try to raise and train an army to
rebel against the French who had occupied Mexico in a misbegotten
colonial effort. Lew returned speaking Spanish but deep in debt,
having been swindled over armaments and supplies for forces that
never materialized.

Finally the adventures ran out. Lew had to settle down in
Crawfordsville, Indiana, to a humdrum legal practice that must have
felt like failure. There he was—a man who'd run away from home at
the age of twelve to join an earlier Mexican war; a man who'd raised
six regiments of Indiana troops and persuaded them to drill and dress
like Algerian Zouaves, in short jackets and long, loose bloomers, all
in the name of military efficiency; the son of Indiana's sixth governor
and brother-in-law of the thirteenth—and he was pleading cases in
stuffy small-town courtrooms in an effort to pay off substantial debts
to his banker brother-in-law.

On the plus side, he had a clever and pretty wife with a tart sense
of humor, a thoughtful young son, and the best hobby ever for a man
who required escape from daily life. For Lew Wallace, in his time off,
wrote novels.

In this, as in his personality, Lew was out of step with the times.
The 1870s were the days of realism in American fiction. Fashionable
novels immersed readers in urban poverty, the plight of immi-
grants, characters and dialogue you might encounter in daily life.
Lew, meanwhile, had researched and written an epic about Hernán
Cortés's 1519 conquest of Mexico, complete with archaic-sounding
language. *The Fair God* was published in 1873 and well-received,
though not such a success that Lew could quit his law practice. Still,

he understood clearly that his fiction habit was a constructive one, allowing him to mentally escape from the legal drudgery that paid the Wallace family bills. He enjoyed the research as much as the writing itself, and in fact he followed *The Fair God* with a novella about the magi. He wasn't a religious man, but in 1870s America, everyone more or less absorbed the Gospels from the culture. Lew the voyager, the seeker of adventure, was fascinated by the three men of different faiths who set out from their far-flung homes to follow a star in search of the Redeemer of mankind. It was something he might almost have done himself.

Nevertheless, in 1876 Lew was almost fifty. Healthy, but definitely aging. What more could life hold? How much longer could he stand to face off in a dusty little county courtroom against a tobacco-chewing judge and a defendant with poor hygiene, pocketing his fee at the end of the day only to confront an uncomfortable trip back home and an endless string of similar days?

No wonder he had planned to go to the Boys in Blue reunion in Indianapolis in September of that year. There would be speeches and music, possibly some drinking, and a march through the handsome downtown streets. There would be political campaigning, which interested Lew, though his own congressional campaigns in 1868 and 1870 had come to naught. He was a supporter of Rutherford B. Hayes, the Republican candidate for president, and the reunion would feature a speech from America's most impressive orator of the era, Robert Ingersoll.

That sounds strange today, but Robert Ingersoll was a superstar in 1876. Before television, before radio, before recorded music, live performance was a staple form of entertainment, and Americans turned out in droves to hear, believe it or not, men making speeches. It must be said, reading some of Ingersoll's work today, that the man had a terrific way with words. But even more than that, he had a remarkable point of view, for Ingersoll was America's best-known agnostic.

He was also a natural-born provocateur. One of his favorite pas-times was to engage strangers in debate about the divinity of Christ, which he denied utterly. And as it happened, Ingersoll was on Lew Wallace's train to the Boys in Blue reunion on September 19, 1876. Ingersoll invited Lew into his private compartment, and as the train clattered along the rails toward Indianapolis, the two men started talking.

Basically, Ingersoll took Lew apart. Did Lew believe in Christ? Yes. Why? He didn't know. Had he read the Gospels? Um . . . some of them. Did he really believe in those miracles? Um . . . maybe. Why? Did Lew really believe Jesus had risen from the dead? All that non-sense about Lazarus, three days dead and half-decomposed—how could an educated man believe such a thing?

Lew didn't know. He didn't know much, he realized. And his talk with Ingersoll embarrassed him. Faith was a vital issue in those days, and though Lew was no churchgoer, he recognized Christianity as fundamentally important. How could he, an educated, inquiring man, have reached his age without ever giving serious thought to his faith?

And then, being Lew Wallace, he decided to look into the issue, which meant writing a book about it. In fact, as he walked through the quiet Indianapolis streets to his brother's house that night, he realized that he had already begun it. His novella about the voyage of the magi—what else was it but the beginning of a novel about Jesus? He'd already written the Nativity section, and it would obviously have to end with the Crucifixion. The material in between would bring to life the ancient world of Jesus' time—and Jesus himself. The challenge and the pleasure would come in inventing characters and incidents who would personify the conflicts of the ancient world. The power and grandeur of the Roman Empire at its peak would eventually be embodied in Messala, the privileged Roman youth, while the oppressed Jewish population of Judea took form in the young prince Judah Ben-Hur. The action of the novel would focus mostly on the years before and during Jesus' active ministry, ultimately bringing Ben-Hur into the Savior's presence.

One factor that made *Ben-Hur* popular was Lew's evident faith. He wrote about Jesus and his ministry with authentic reverence and brought his readers along with him into the imagined presence of the Lord. Another component was Lew's devotion to old-fashioned adventure novels. *Ben-Hur* would not be famous today without the chariot race and the sea battle. The all-out enmity between the old friends Messala and Judah Ben-Hur pulls the plot forward.

But there was one more element that gave emotional power to *Ben-Hur*. The pivotal moment in the story, when the hero, Judah Ben-Hur, is launched out of his comfortable Jerusalem boyhood, is an accident. Judah knocks a tile from the roof of the Hur family's palace and it injures a Roman official. The swift, violent reaction tears apart Judah's world, separates him from his family, and ultimately turns him into a slave. It's his longing for reunion that powers the rest of the book—along with his yearning for vengeance.

This is fiction, of course. Lew Wallace never got close to a Roman galley, and his much-loved wife and son, Henry, formed a happy, united family. But Lew understood grievance and injustice. Judah Ben-Hur's burning need to right the wrongs of his youth echoed Lew's lifelong quest to clear his name of a wrongful accusation—the disgrace of Shiloh. Through Judah, he imagined the vengeance he might wreak on his enemies, the spineless military bureaucrats who refused to clear his name. There's real violence in *Ben-Hur*, and our devoutly Jewish hero breaks the commandments several times by killing, with great energy. Surely it is Lew's shame and rage that power Judah Ben-Hur when he cuts recklessly close to Messala's chariot in the last moments of the famous race. Just as it is Lew's belief that brings Ben-Hur at the end of the book to reluctantly abandon his plans for violence and accept the way of a different kind of Savior.

Ben-Hur had to be researched and written in Lew Wallace's spare time. Amazingly enough, it only took him four years, which were eventful ones for him, as the encounter with Ingersoll had ushered in a new era of Lew's life. Following the fateful Boys in Blue reunion, Lew took time out from his Crawfordsville legal practice to campaign energetically for Rutherford B. Hayes, and eventually that politicking got him out of Indiana. It was standard practice in those days to reward campaign allies with governmental appointments. Lew evidently came pretty low on the list, because it wasn't until 1878 that Hayes finally offered him a post, and a pretty shabby one at that: he could, if he chose, become governor of the fractious and violent New Mexico Territory.

The salary was small and the job was dangerous: New Mexico was almost lawless in those days, with warring factions of criminals engaged in the Lincoln County War. Worse—for Susan Wallace, anyway—was the primitive nature of Santa Fe, the capital of the territory. But Lew needed an adventure, and Susan was braver than she let on, so the Wallaces occupied the broad, one-story Palacio Real, built in 1610 and not much improved since then. Lew made enemies right away. This was, after all, the gun-toting Wild West, and he was there to restore law and order. The most famous outlaw was Billy the Kid, who threatened to kill General Wallace. Susan was told by a friend that she and Lew should never leave the shutters open at night in rooms where lamps were lit—it was all too likely a disgruntled criminal would take a shot at them.

And when Lew wasn't putting Billy the Kid in jail or trying to placate warring factions of cattlemen, he was burning the midnight oil writing *Ben-Hur*. In fact, he finished the first draft and copied it all out by hand in purple ink. In March of 1880, he took a leave from his office to personally submit the manuscript to Harper & Brothers, the publishing firm, in New York City.

It was accepted, but with reservations. *The Fair God*'s modest success and Wallace's personal prominence tipped the scale, but the publisher was concerned about a novel in which Jesus Christ appeared as a character. No matter how reverent the portrayal, no matter that the author had only given Jesus dialogue that came direct from the Gospels, Harper & Brothers worried that *Ben-Hur: A Tale of the Christ* could be seen as blasphemous. Nevertheless, they took the risk, and the book came out on November 12, 1880, in time for Christmas.

Wallace's political instincts were sometimes wrong, especially when it came to the Battle of Shiloh, but he had the good sense to send copies of *Ben-Hur* to some of his friends who now occupied high office. One of them happened to be James Garfield, the president-elect, who promised to read it when he had time. Amazingly enough, he actually followed up, a few months later. The sitting president managed to zip through the 550-page novel in six days and, on the strength of Wallace's sensitive depiction of the Middle East, offered him a new diplomatic post, as United States minister to the Ottoman Empire. The salary would be three times what Lew was paid in New Mexico.

It was just as well because sales of *Ben-Hur* were disappointing— Wallace's royalties for the first seven months of sales were less than $300. Considering that years had gone into the composition of the novel, those were skimpy earnings. Not long afterward Lew would write to his son, Henry, speculating that combined royalties for *The Fair God* and *Ben-Hur* might reach a steady $1,000 per year, if he was lucky.

But in a way, he wrote his novels as a hobby. Lew's vivid imagination made his extensive research as lively to him as actual travel. He often said that his characters were living beings to him—they spoke, they acted, they had wills of their own, and while he loved some, others he despised.

Nowadays we might look at *Ben-Hur* in another way as well.

Knowing what we do about Lew Wallace's life, we can see how his deepest concerns were written into what turned out to be his master-piece. Not only his sense of shock and shame about the Battle of Shiloh, but his reverence for women, his idealization of the family, his everlasting worry about money—even his grappling with issues of vengeance and forgiveness. Lew's formative years were spent as a soldier. Violence was built into his definition of manhood, and he gave that attribute to his hero, Judah Ben-Hur.

These were the concerns of many other Americans of the era too, and they must have contributed to *Ben-Hur*'s gradual success. By 1880 the country was groping its way toward reconciliation between North and South, trying to leave behind the bitter legacy of the war, just as Judah Ben-Hur has to accept that Jesus' leadership will not be one of violence, but of peace and redemption. Also by 1880 the Industrial Age was well under way, and wealth was newly respect-able—even glamorous. Lew Wallace wrenched his hero from the comfort of a merchant prince's palace to the brutality of a Roman galley, then eventually endowed Judah with an unearned fortune—no, two. And in a country where slavery was a fresh memory for too many, a hero who had been a slave gave new—but safely vicarious—insight into horrible conditions.

As we can see now, *Ben-Hur: A Tale of the Christ* had everything: adventure for those seeking entertainment, sentiment for the ladies, a rags-to-riches tale, even romance. Its meticulously researched descrip-tions brought vibrant images of the Middle East to readers who had never seen a palm tree and never would.

What set *Ben-Hur* apart, though, was the quest at the heart of Lew Wallace's original idea: to come to grips with the divinity of Jesus. The four years of research and writing convinced Lew that agnostic Robert Ingersoll was wrong. Lew believed, and *Ben-Hur* shows it. The Nativity scene and the Crucifixion scene were the work of a convinced Christian. Writing them as part of a larger fiction was an enormous risk, and readers were at first prepared to be shocked. But Wallace's sincerity shone through. No offense to the pious was meant, and none could be taken.

That didn't mean that the critics liked the book, though. They mocked the stilted language and the old-fashioned plot. Some of the scathing reviews must have stung Lew, and as late as 1883, *Ben-Hur* had netted him a total of only $2,800 in royalties.

But by then he had enjoyed several years of a more comfortable income as US minister in Constantinople—and exposure to a more exotic life than the dreamy Indiana schoolboy could ever have imagined. He and Susan traveled widely in Europe and throughout the Middle East; Lew was even able to check the accuracy of his descriptions in *Ben-Hur* and happily boasted that he found them all accurate. He managed to foster a cordial relationship with Sultan Abdul Hamid II, ruler of the crumbling Ottoman Empire. It was a satisfying and stimulating interlude, and when the Wallaces returned to the United States, Lew looked forward to a peaceful retirement from the law and the freedom to concentrate on his next novel.

Instead, his greatest success awaited him, as *Ben-Hur* caught on. Despite the critics, despite its initially slow sales, the novel found its readers by word of mouth. Literary fashion might have turned toward gritty tales of contemporary society, but Lew's colorful descriptions of the ancient world beguiled fans—and more fans. More importantly, though, his biggest literary risk had paid off. Taking the bold step of portraying Jesus in a novel could have alienated the churchgoing audience, which was dominant in nineteenth-century America. But instead, those readers were won over. Lew started receiving heartfelt confessional letters from readers who had been touched and moved, whose faith had been renewed by his portrayal of Jesus. Pastors recommended *Ben-Hur* to their congregations. Many Americans had never read a novel before: fiction was considered not only a waste of time, but worse, a depiction of falsehood. That made most novels morally suspect, but *Ben-Hur*'s piety and adherence to Christian doctrine put it beyond reproach from a religious point of view.

✳ ✳ ✳

Lew Wallace returned from Constantinople in the fall of 1885. Six months later, his portrait was on the cover of the national magazine *Harper's Weekly*. For the rest of his life, he would be an American celebrity, one of the first superstar authors.

It was an amazing change of direction from his low point just ten years earlier. In 1876, when he met Robert Ingersoll on that train, Lew was facing what looked like a joyless future, characterized by the legal work he'd called "abominable" and financial worries he couldn't escape. Worse, for the ardent adventurer, it had looked as if life's excitements were over. Soldiers' reunions seemed likely to provide the thrills from that point on.

Instead, as the sales of *Ben-Hur* continued to grow every year, so did the opportunities. Magazines and book publishers would accept anything from Lew's pen, or his wife, Susan's, for that matter. He was commissioned to write future president Benjamin Harrison's campaign biography. Not only did royalties begin rolling in—debts from bad business deals in Mexico were repaid, and Lew could begin saving. He went on lecture tours, speaking to audiences in the thousands. His subjects were "Mexico and the Mexicans," "Turkey and the Turks, with Glimpses of the Harem," and of course *Ben-Hur*. He read the chariot race sequence in Syracuse, New York, to eight thousand people. His tour, which extended for nearly six months, earned him almost $12,000 (close to $300,000 today).

On tour, Lew met an endless stream of readers who wanted to tell him how much *Ben-Hur* had meant to them. Those who couldn't meet the author in person wrote to him: alcoholics who gave up drinking, young men who reconciled with their families, skeptics who returned to the churches of their youth. Some readers wanted to let him know that they had found the novel too exciting to put down—Lew's old nemesis President Grant devoured the book in thirty hours. The publisher Harper & Brothers went back to press again and again, and by 1886, *Ben-Hur* was a major bestseller. It was the book everyone was talking about. Families read it aloud to each other; it was recommended in Sunday schools; cultured ladies dressed up and performed skits or tableaux inspired by it.

Before long, *Ben-Hur* was more than a book. In the 1880s many bestsellers were adapted for the stage. Lew himself, with his taste for the theatrical, had written a play that he'd ended up self-publishing. (He never could get it produced.) Requests for permission to adapt *Ben-Hur* started to come in as early as 1882, but at first Lew refused them. He was concerned that the reverent tone of his novel might not be preserved—after all, the theater was by definition a more sensational medium than a book. Finally Lew produced a libretto for a production of tableaux that went on to be mounted successfully all over America. A series of painted backdrops were augmented with readings from the novel and brief musical interludes, including an exotic dance sequence.

But by 1899, stage technology caught up with the scope of *Ben-Hur*, and negotiations began for a full-blown production that could only be shown in the largest, most sophisticated theaters. Lew, who had managed his money so poorly when he had none, struck a hard bargain, holding out for creative control and the lion's share of the royalties. He had the upper hand in the negotiations: *Ben-Hur* was by that point the bestselling novel of the nineteenth century (easily outstripping in twenty years *Uncle Tom's Cabin*, which had appeared in 1852). Lew also insisted on an unusual provision: Jesus must never be played by a human. Instead, the Christ would be represented by a powerful beam of light.

The special effects of the $75,000 Broadway stage production were eye-popping. Scenery consisted of multiple layers of scrims and elaborate constructions. Wrecked ships from the sea battle dropped through traps in the stage floor, and the chariot race took place on a treadmill with real horses. The animals rehearsed for six weeks, and the first to learn how to manage the treadmill was a three-year-old Arabian named Monk, owned by Lew himself. When the production finally closed twenty years later, Monk was the only original cast member still in the show. Charles Frohman, an important transatlantic theatrical producer, sat through one of the final rehearsals and commented as he left that "the American public will never stand for Christ and a horse race in the same show."

Of course Frohman was wrong. In fact, he put his finger on exactly the point that made *Ben-Hur* such a success: the American public could not get enough of Christ and a horse race in the same show. Or, more precisely, Christ and a horse race, portrayed with utter sincerity on the stage as on the page. And while the Broadway production was a great success, it was the road shows that made *Ben-Hur* a household word. If novels had been considered morally suspect among the strictest religious groups, theater was even more scandalous. Acting—putting oneself on show for money—was thought of as dangerously close to prostitution. Yet because of the inspirational content and the reverent treatment of Christ, *Ben-Hur* was acceptable. In fact, as with the book, church leaders urged their congregants to see it. Special trains were organized to bring small-town theatergoers to cities where the play was running. By 1904, a production of *Ben-Hur* was featured at the St. Louis World's Fair while versions of the chariot race appeared in the Barnum & Bailey Circus and at the Pasadena Tournament of Roses. The theatrical version of Lew's novel ran for over twenty years in the United States and was seen by an estimated 20 million playgoers.

Naturally that exposure sold a lot of books. Playgoers—or people who'd simply heard about the play—were eager to read the story. By 1908 there were nearly a million hardcover copies of *Ben-Hur* in print, and the national retailer Sears, Roebuck and Co. placed an order with Harper & Brothers for an unprecedented million copies of a cheap edition, to cost only forty-eight cents. It was the biggest single-title book order to date.

Lew did not live to hear about it, nor yet to enjoy the longevity of the stage version of his novel. He died of stomach cancer in 1905, and the flags at the Indiana State Capitol flew at half-mast for a full month. Planning for the grand Statuary Hall in the US Capitol was under way, and each state was allowed to nominate two of its famous citizens to be immortalized in marble in the rotunda. Indiana chose Lew—the only author in the group. The marble figure shows him in Civil War uniform, and the sober granite base identifies him simply as "Soldier. Writer. Diplomat."

Lew and Susan's only child, Henry Lane Wallace, had long been managing the business of *Ben-Hur*, which was a full-time job. One constant concern was protecting the copyright. While in the 1880s the concerns had been tableaux or readings of excerpts accompanied by "lantern slides," by the time of Lew's death, copyright threats came from a new art form: moving pictures. A somewhat-primitive film released in 1908 featured a chariot race shot on a beach in New York City and interior scenes in which the actors wore costumes borrowed from the Metropolitan Opera. The movie business was so young that the producers hadn't felt obliged to purchase film rights for *Ben-Hur*. That was a huge error: Henry Wallace joined forces with Lew's long-time publisher and the producers of the stage version of *Ben-Hur*, and they sued the film production company.

It was an unprecedented situation: the film producers, the Kalem Company, claimed that the movie actually provided advertising for the book and play. After three years of appeals, the case reached the Supreme Court and the Wallace team won. Kalem had to pay $25,000 plus expenses, and the *Ben-Hur* case established that copyright protection extended to film adaptations.

Not that Kalem's idea was wrong—*Ben-Hur* was obviously ideal for filming. But Henry Wallace wanted to wait until film technology had matured before he sold the rights. Part of the appeal of his father's book was its potential for sheer spectacle; Henry needed to be sure that the eventual film would do the spectacle justice. Finally in 1919, after holding out for more than a decade, he sold the film rights for $600,000 (nearly $8.5 million today). One of Lew's original stipulations endured: Jesus could not be depicted by a human actor. Instead, his presence would be inferred from a hand or a foot or a footprint.

It took seven years and close to $4 million to actually make the movie, which was the most expensive silent film of the era. The studio, MGM, ended up losing $1 million on it, but the prestige of the project was so great that they were satisfied. Still, the life span of the silent movie was short, and by the 1930s, the black-and-white *Ben-Hur* (which starred Ramon Novarro in the title role) felt quaint and outdated. It was in the 1930s, too, that Lew's book finally toppled from American bestseller lists, replaced by another colorful historical saga, Margaret Mitchell's *Gone with the Wind*.

Yet *Ben-Hur* remained a household word in America, not only because of the millions of copies of the book on shelves across the country, but also because of the array of consumer products that had borrowed the name. They ranged from life insurance to flour, from cigars to bicycles, from perfume to fences. The Ben Hur moving company is still in business, while Ben-Hur spices can easily be bought on eBay. Lew's book had reached an enormous audience at the same time as the growth of consumer culture in America. Advertisers and marketers found it useful to link their products with *Ben-Hur* to create positive associations in the public's mind. Soaps and hair products might refer to the Egyptian femme fatale Iras (improbably portrayed in the silent movie as that height of glamour, a platinum blonde). Bicycles, cars, harnesses, sleds, and even oil and gasoline were clearly linked to the chariot race. The Ben-Hur tent company seems especially clever, though there's a big difference between a camping tent and the Bedouin encampment that features in the novel.

By the 1950s, film technology had made immense strides, but movie audiences were being wooed away to television. Naturally Hollywood responded with what TV couldn't yet offer: big, colorful epics. MGM turned again to *Ben-Hur*, and the resulting blockbuster starring Charlton Heston broke all kinds of records: for the cost of production, for advance ticket sales, for Oscar nominations. It took in nearly $40 million in the first year and was rereleased commercially in 1970. Since then, TV broadcasts have been frequent, despite the running time of 213 minutes.

And now, more than fifty years later, *Ben-Hur* comes to the screen again, taking advantage of innovations in film and returning to the original story of two young men from different backgrounds, making different choices. And a third young man, Jesus, whose role on earth is nothing like theirs but drives the choice ultimately made by that durable hero, Judah Ben-Hur.

About the Author

After graduating from Princeton University in 1977, Carol Wallace took a job in publishing in New York. A little over two years in the business convinced her that writers had more fun than editors, and she left to join their ranks. One of her first assignments was cowriting a little humor book called *The Official Preppy Handbook*.

This was followed by *To Marry an English Lord*, coauthored with Gail MacColl. First published in 1989, it returned to public notice in 2012, when Julian Fellowes cited it as an inspiration for *Downton Abbey*. In February 2013, *To Marry an English Lord* appeared on the *New York Times* bestseller list. Other publications include more than twenty books and dozens of magazine articles, focusing on humor, social history, parenting, and fiction. Her most recent title is a historical novel, *Leaving Van Gogh*, published in April 2011.

Carol is the great-great-granddaughter of Lew Wallace, author of *Ben-Hur: A Tale of the Christ*. Adapting the original novel for contemporary audiences was both an honor and a thrill for her.

"I want a study, a pleasure-house for my soul. . . ."

General Lew Wallace, author of *Ben-Hur*, desired to create a unique space near his home in Crawfordsville, Indiana, where he could pursue creative endeavors. Throughout his adult life, he considered Crawfordsville his home, though his career in the military and as an attorney took him around the world. Wallace served as an officer in the Mexican War, a general in the Civil War, an attorney, a military judge, governor of New Mexico, and the US minister to the Ottoman Empire.

In spite of all these accomplishments, he considered *Ben-Hur* his greatest achievement.

Since its completion in 1896, the Lew Wallace study has been a local landmark in Crawfordsville, and in 1976 it was recognized as a National Historic Landmark by the United States Department of the Interior. Constructed of an unusually hard red brick and Indiana limestone, this eclectic building reflects General Wallace's varied experiences and tastes. Wallace served as his own architect for this unique combination of Greek, Romanesque, and Byzantine stylistic influences. The interior has been fully restored to its appearance when General Wallace was in residence, including frescoes, stained glass, and elaborate lighting. It is fully furnished with Wallace's original possessions.

The General Lew Wallace Study and Museum is open for tours Tuesday through Saturday, 10 a.m. to 5 p.m., February through mid-December. For more information, call (765)362-5769 or go online to www.ben-hur.com.

CP1029